**Alexandra Bradley** was born in the West Midlands. As a child, it was her younger sister who always had her head in a good book, with Alex being the sibling to centre her hobbies around sport. Encouraged by her primary school English teacher to pick up a pen and have a stab at writing, at age six she was published in several young writer anthologies for poems created in her nan's spare room.

Alex studied Media and Communications at university, during which – whilst observing lifeguards in action on a holiday in Cornwall – the idea for her debut novel *Two Worlds Collide* first blossomed.

She works for a law firm in the city, residing in her family home in Sutton Coldfield, along with her sister, mum, dad and adopted Borador. Her dreams are to one day live in her very own cottage, writing full-time in the Cornish town of Padstow – the place where her heart truly belongs.

# TWO WORLDS
# COLLIDE

To Colleen,

Thanks for your support,
I hope you enjoy!  :)

*AB*

ALEXANDRA BRADLEY

ISBN, paperback:     978-1-80227-243-7
ISBN, ebook:         978-1-80227-244-4

This book is typeset in Book Antiqua

*For Mum - My first reader and the person who gave me the confidence to go for it.*

*I love you very much.*

*x*

*To cross paths with someone; to be, by chance,*
*in the same physical place at the same time,*
*as a result of two completely separate journeys.*

# PROLOGUE

It was that time again. That time in the unearthly hours of the morning. Too early for the sun to even consider rising, but far too late for any right-minded sixteen-year-old to be getting home. Except, he wasn't in his right mind. In fact, he was further from it than ever before.

His dark, shaggy, greasy hair flopped over his washed-out face as he stumbled up the ramp towards the grotty door of the tower block. He knew he should feel guilty, because once again he'd broken his promise. Yet, at that very moment, as he aimlessly searched for his key with shaking hands, all he could think about was downing the last drop of Jack he'd hidden under his mattress.

His long fingers poked through a hole in the pocket of his jeans where he thought he'd placed the small object only hours before. His hazy head lolled back and forth on his thin neck, and he didn't even notice his right arm rising as he made it to the entrance. He pushed the main door, which like usual, opened with ease, and with the help of the wall, he began staggering down the darkened corridor before reaching the bottom of the stairs leading to his flat. Throwing his head back, he sighed. Maybe she'd be sober enough to let him in.

He hadn't intended to stay out that late. He hadn't intended to go out at all. But when she'd returned home, barely able to stand with a random man on her arm, something inside of him had snapped. He'd grabbed his phone and brought up Liam's number whilst storming down the stairs of the high-rise building.

'Shoreditch Park. Fifteen minutes. Bring the stuff,' he'd spoken coldly before hanging up.

He'd pulled the hood of his black sweatshirt over his head and picked up his pace. He had been in no mood to explain himself and he knew Liam wouldn't ask questions.

The result of this, as he stood peering up at what seemed like an infinite stairwell, meant he hated himself.

Gripping the chipped handrail, he sluggishly hauled himself up. His vision blurred, his heart beating at an abnormally fast pace to be deemed safe, and the cold sweat forming on his body, inevitably made him feel like he was climbing a mountain rather than a small flight of stairs. The only confirmation he received that he was nearing the top was the familiar stench of cigar smoke emerging from Mr Sheppard's flat. The old man was nearing his eighties and struggled with his hip, which was one of the reasons he smoked insistently night and day.

Eventually, placing a foot on the landing floor, he gave one final push and stumbled forward. Relief flooded him. Resting his shoulder against the wall to steady himself, he placed both hands on his knees as his heavy head slumped, and closing his eyes, took several long breaths. That was the part he dreaded; the come down. Alcohol was fine at numbing the pain, but coke was on another level, it meant he could forget completely. The aftermath, though, he wasn't so keen on.

Opening his eyes, he set his unclear sights on the flat door. With a deep exhale he propelled himself forward, using the wall once again as his guide. Gradually, with one foot – more or less – in front of the other, he reached Number 12. Their flat.

Attempting to stable his trembling body, his barely operational brain was only just able to register his clenched fist lifting. But as he'd mustered up enough strength to knock, he was halted. His heavy breaths hitched in his throat as he stared through his blurred vision at the shabby door, because he could've sworn he was looking at a small gap between the door frame and the wall.

His eyes narrowed.

It was, *open*? It was never open.

No matter how drunk she got she always locked the door.

Not trusting his drugged-up mind, he placed his palm on the wood and pushed, slowly, with a little pressure, and sure enough, it opened.

His mouth dried. He didn't know if it was a side effect to the serious amounts of cocaine consumed that night or the apprehension he felt for what may be before him. His fingers fiddled anxiously with the sleeves of his hoodie. The room was black.

He stepped inside and winced as the floorboards creaked under his scuffed shoes. He tried to adjust his vision to the darkened room, but it was futile. He could hardly see as it was.

Just as he was about to search the wall for the light switch, his attention was snapped straight ahead to the sound of shuffling coming from the bedroom. Her bedroom. His clumsy feet couldn't have moved faster if they had tried. Practically bumping into everything in his path, he quickly reached her room. Shoving the door open, his shaking hands searched the wall until he found the switch.

He was hit with a blinding light.

But it wasn't the sudden brightness which made his whole body shudder. It wasn't the intense glare which rendered him completely helpless. And it wasn't the fierce beam which left him utterly broken. Because what he saw in front of him had snuffed any light from the room and left only emptiness and despair in its place.

He couldn't move.

He couldn't think.

He couldn't breathe.

His entire world had been shattered in a matter of seconds. He'd battled the darkness for so long, but at that moment, as he stood frozen staring at the scene in front of him, he knew it had finally consumed him.

# *ONE*

## Six Years Later

Monday rush hour. The bane of modern-day life.

Standing with my back squashed into the far corner of the carriage, an unfortunately positioned handrail is digging into my hip and a tall man's armpit resides gracelessly in my face. And even though this particular armpit is allowing me to bask in the pleasant scent of a well-groomed man, it is one face full of armpit too many on this almost insufferable humid morning.

Men in suits and backpacks, and women with infinite handbags and ready-to-go trainers, squeeze through the crowded coach, mumbling their apologies as they unintentionally scrape arms and other undignified body parts in a hurried struggle to clamber off before the doors close on them. With every one person escaping, it seems two more scramble on, vehemently cramming into the already packed carriage and confining me to the corner of this stuffy Tube.

My mood isn't helped by the fact that in my frazzled urgency this morning, I'd neglected to remember my earphones. At least they would have provided me with a little distraction from the awkward silent atmosphere surrounding the huddled mass of Londoners, whilst the screaming of the train, as it whooshes through the underground tunnels, reverberates inside the brimful coaches. Instead of immersing myself in the smooth vocals of a Lewis Capaldi song, I'm having to find other ways to keep occupied.

It's funny the things you notice when you pause and take in your surroundings. Everyone has their heads down, completely entranced in whatever's on their phone screens, oblivious to the outside world. With the number of people in one area the silence is strange, but no one's aware of this; they never are. And I can't deny that I would be doing the exact same thing if my arm wasn't securely trapped at my side.

The undignified a.m. crush always reliably keen to cheer on my aversion to this claggy city.

The familiar bell dings as the comforting smell of warm freshly made bread fans my nose. My stomach growls immediately, reminding me it hasn't been fed.

'Nice of you to show up.'

I'm not even halfway through the door when my attention is directed towards the lacklustre voice behind the counter. 'Good morning to you too.'

'You made good time. I wasn't expecting you for another hour.' Hannah's back is turned away from the door as she wrestles with the worse for wear napkin holder she dropped about two weeks ago.

'Neither was I. The Tube was a bloody nightmare.'

She grunts at my remark, but I think it's more likely caused by her annoyance at the dented metal dispenser in her hands.

Having worked incessantly last week, I *was* looking forward to a well-deserved day of rest, but being uncouthly woken at half seven by a frantic Albert stressing like an old lady who forgot to put her bins out, meant my planned Monday lie-in had been cancelled. Cathy called in sick, which apparently appointed me the chosen one. The chosen one who had to haul herself out of bed and rush around like a headless chicken to get into work for 9 a.m..

Not that I'm complaining. The more money I can save, the better. It's merely the suffocating journey which churns my mood. I'd checked my phone the minute I'd fought myself through the rush of Waterloo Underground and was pleasantly surprised to be only ten minutes late.

Passing the counter and rounding the corner, I hang my bag on the coat hook next to the office. Albert's silhouette is obscurely visible behind the patterned glass window, his head down as he types on his old computer. Taking the cleanest apron from the hook opposite, I return to the front of the shop, tying the straps into a bow behind me and snapping on some clear disposable gloves.

'I would've snagged another half an hour in bed purely for the inconvenience.' Hannah's still trying her best to force more napkins into the crooked hole.

'And give Albert a coronary?' I quip, before grabbing an empty tray from behind the glass screen display. The fresh batch of bread rolls from the side are transferred onto the parchment paper.

'I don't know why he stresses so darn much. The shop doesn't get busy till gone twelve, and I am a pro at multi-tasking, as you know.' A cocky hand is placed on her hip when she faces me, puffing at a stray piece of hair on her cheek.

As a small bakery in the middle of London, *For Goodness Bakes* does tremendously well.

It's therefore still a wonder why Albert puts up with that ancient computer in his office, but as a sixty-year-old who's soon to retire, I guess he's simply a stickler for the old ways.

'Hmm.' My stare briefly meets hers as my fingers continue to meticulously position the rolls, before it wanders to the dented holder in her grip. 'I can see why he was so worried,' I tease.

Her lips purse as she too flickers her attention to the contraption. 'On most days I am a fantastic go-getter with plenty of enthusiasm to make every customer's day, but it just so happens that on *this* particular day,' she waves the dispenser in my face, 'I was nursing an extreme hangover.'

I scoff as she places it on top of the counter, shuffling it around until she finds the exact spot she's happy with. 'Are you sure it didn't have anything to do with a certain regular?'

Her shoulders stiffen. She knows exactly which regular I'm referring to. 'No,' she answers sheepishly. 'It has nothing to do with *him* and everything to do with the fact your friends ordered us all twenty shots each the night before.' Her hand returns to her hip, the blush which tinted her cheeks fading as her accusatory eyes zone in on me.

Han was already a supervisor when I first started working at *For Goodness Bakes* two years ago. Our friendship was instant and over the years her friends have become mine and vice versa, however, we've since established our groups are at completely different life stages. Whilst mine are kickstarting their partying fresher ways, hers are deep in job and relationship mode, and even though both enjoy a good party, we've discovered the freshers like to go that little bit harder. Still, I didn't hear her complaining when they brought the drinks to the table.

'Whatever you say.' My smile causes her eyes to roll, because we both know it wasn't the hangover which made her drop that napkin dispenser.

'You'll miss me when you go off to university next month.'

'Don't pretend like you won't be heartbroken to see me go,' I reply, grinning at her quirked eyebrows.

A merry head peers around the corner, cutting off our conversation. Albert definitely looks cheerier than he sounded on the phone this morning.

*Cheerier now he's dragged me out of bed.*

'I thought I heard voices. Good morning, Emily!'

My smile copies his, but his twinkling friendly blues are a step too far to match.

'I really appreciate you coming in,' he chirps as he slides his rectangle spectacles onto his receding silver hair.

'Not to worry, Albert,' I respond, trying my best to sound enthusiastic, even though simply opening my mouth is proving to be a strenuous task this early in the morning.

After a little small talk between the three of us, the chatter soon turns to sales and numbers, but with it being 9.15 and my brain not having the capability to function properly before at least ten, it's blocked out. So with my tray now full, I slot it back onto the shelf next to the other delicious smelling cakes and pastries on display.

'We'll need another round of cupcakes baking as well.' My hearing returns just in time to catch Albert's words.

'Already measured and weighed. I thought Emily could mix and bake,' Hannah's transformed eager tone replies, and before I have a chance to protest, our boss is already agreeing.

'Great idea! I'll leave you girls to it. Be in my office if you need me.'

A quick wave is given before he disappears from sight, leaving us in charge of his bakery.

My scowl is fired in her direction, met with a wide sarcastic smile. Her status as supervisor means she can make me do whatever task she pleases, and she knows I hate fiddling with cupcakes.

'You are right though; I will be heartbroken. You're my favourite person to boss around,' she laughs, resuming our chat. 'You better not forget to visit!' She glides the cupcake mixture across the tabletop and over to my side.

'Don't be silly, of course I won't.' As I place the cases into the baking trays, I begin to muse over our change in topic. 'It's William I'm concerned about, who will do his washing? I'm pretty sure he doesn't know how to turn the machine on.'

'How is the cradle snatcher?'

'Hannah!'

'What? He is older than you,' she replies innocently.

'Only by five years, that's under the ten-year rule which you yourself made up and fail to stick by, and considerably less than some of the Granddads you've been with, thank you very much,' I fire back. After pulling forward the big mixing bowl, Hannah's pre-weighed butter, eggs and all my other ingredients are thrown in, the electric mixer jumping into vigorous rotations.

'One: they're not Granddads,' she yells over the machine's grinding.

'Questionable,' I mutter.

'And two: times are hard, and they like to splash their cash. Anyway, we've conveniently steered off topic.'

Turning the giant mixer off, I use a spatula to scrape around the sides of the bowl. My head lolls to the side as my brain ticks, conjuring up my answer. 'He's fine,' I lie.

'Speaking of, how's he feeling about the uni sitch?'

'Alright, I think.' Another lie.

'Yeah? He's okay with you moving all the way to Sunderland?'

I avoid looking at her, swirling the cake mix unnecessarily.

'Em?' she pushes.

Out the corner of my eye I notice her hand is back on her hip, her stare burning a hole in the side of my head. The anxiety in my tummy is drawn out through little nibbles of my lip before a breath is drawn. 'I kind of haven't told him yet.'

'You are joking?' she exclaims. 'You're leaving next month! Are you just not going to say anything and wait till he sees your bags packed by the door?'

'No, I am going to tell him.' I risk gazing at her. At birth, Hannah was gifted a deadly frown which has the ability to make you feel like you've done something wrong, even when you haven't. It's terrifying! And right now, that frown is pointed directly at me.

'I wish you luck when you do, because I don't know what he's got stuck up his arse lately,' she breathes on a shake of her head.

'He's had a lot on with work,' I defend – even if it is through gritted teeth.

'Emily, he works for your father, the man who owns a billion-pound law firm.'

'Yes, I'm aware.' I'm well aware of that man.

'If I was earning his wages, I'd be skipping around like a fairy on drugs.'

I sigh, showing my disapproval on the outside, but inside agreeing entirely, because she's right, things between William and I haven't been good these past few months, but the reasons why are justifiable – despite the frustrations.

'It's not all butterflies and rainbows when you work for my father, Han. No matter what the salary.'

She frowns at my excuses.

'I'll tell him today.'

'You better.'

'I will!' Maybe. Possibly. Depending on what mood he's in later.

'It'll be beneficial in the long run, trust me,' she says, flapping a rag out in her hands before reaching for Mr Muscle in the cupboard.

'How do you mean?'

'Well, the sooner you tell him you're leaving, the sooner you'll know if he truly is a decent person and is willing to make it work long distance, or if he is what I've always thought him to be.'

'What?'

'A complete arse.'

My hand dismisses her and mixing is resumed. I'm aware of her feelings towards my boyfriend, it's been obvious for a while now. William is a busy man, which means our plans have to schedule themselves around his life, and I understand that. Most of the time I appreciate he's older and career driven and hardworking, so I let it go, however I'm not perfect, and there are times when it becomes more difficult. It's those moments of infuriation which generate a torrent of rant-filled bakery shift confessions. Hannah hears my side of the arguments, not his, and in being my best friend, her opinions are biasedly formed.

She moves to the big window with her cloth and a few grunts escape as she attempts to reach the far corners. Seeing my mixture is now smooth, I turn the machine off and pick up two tablespoons.

'Remain calm,' Hannah puffs. 'Our regular is approaching in the near distance.'

I crane my neck and peer out the window to see the man in question striding up to the bakery door. 'He's gone with the navy suit today,' I notice.

She waggles her eyebrows at me. 'My favourite.'

My lips curl up as I concentrate on scooping the mix into each cupcake case. 'Just be cool, I know that's almost impossible for you, but try not to scare him off. We don't need another dented serviette dispenser,' I warn, bending down to open the oven door and slide the first batch inside. She brushes me off with a wave of her hand, but her sudden nerves seem to be swirling in the air, and with every inhale I'm breathing them in, my body bracing itself for the inevitable gauche encounter.

Following the sound of the bell, a throat is being cleared. I don't bother getting up, I don't need to. I'm hidden from his view and Hannah's already leaning against the counter. I do, however, discreetly peek over my shoulder, purely for my own amusement. Her fingers are twirling her long blonde locks at the end of her pony, a coy smile forming on her lips.

Being seven years older than me, naturally anyone would assume she's gathered enough experience to fathom out how to talk to a nice guy successfully. They would do well to think again. While there have been a number of Hannah-to-male encounters, most of them are not worth drawing upon and are best forgotten.

'You're looking rather cheerful this morning, Han,' Shawn expresses, resting his palms on the glass counter.

'Am I? Well, I'm certainly happier for seeing you.'

Here we go.

'Usual?' she asks, still twirling the same piece of hair like a candy floss machine.

'You know I love my apple turnover.' Shawn nods. 'Especially from this place.' The complimentary remark meets his warm brown eyes, they're glistening as he watches her prepare his routine morning order of coffee and turnover.

'Lucky for you, I made some fresh earlier.' Hannah dances around, first adding the shot of coffee to the machine, then steaming the milk before filling and setting the takeaway cup in front of Shawn. She drops nothing and hardly spills a thing.

'Lovely.' He rubs his hands together.

Next, she snatches a paper bag and prises a pair of tongs, choosing the biggest turnover from behind the display, knowing full well he's watching.

But that's when I realise she hasn't said anything for a while. Whether she doesn't know what to say or she's worried a whole load of nonsense will gush out of her mouth if she dares to open it, I can't tell. Either way, a dreaded silence has now fallen upon the room. I should be a good friend and step in, but before my legs can prop, it's too late. Her mouth is opening and I'm sinking back down on a grimace.

'You know, my granddad's most favourite pastry was an apple turnover.'

'Really?' he asks, genuinely interested in her words, his eyes following her movements closely. I, on the other hand, can't bear to look.

'He swore by them,' she continues, nodding as she passes him the bag, swapping it for a ten-pound note.

'Your granddad had good taste.'

'Yeah, dead now though,' she utters, her eyes drifting off to the side. 'It was terrible really… a horrid head injury. There was an accident in our local supermarket.'

His face drops, sympathy taking over as he believes her desolate state. 'Jesus, that's awful.'

'Mmm, slipping on a pork pie whilst picking up a box of turnovers is the worst way to go.

But that was Granddad, ironic as ever.'

The whirring air con in the corner of the room is the only sound to be heard.

It doesn't matter what farcical tale Hannah tells – which are very much untrue, because dead her granddad may be, but not from a rogue pork pie, more so of lung failure from all the smoking – they never fail to leave me in hysterics. However, today is different, as it's not the tale I'm laughing at. It's the flustered storyteller.

The awkwardness of Shawn not quite knowing what to do or say only lasts a few seconds before Hannah begins giggling to herself. 'Your face!' The giggling soon develops into a cackle – a cackle which could only be described as a raucous guinea pig.

I'm gnawing my bottom lip, trying to stifle the laugh that so desperately wants to escape.

And just when it couldn't get any worse for her, or me for that matter, she snorts. Like a fully-grown pig. I'm tipped over the edge and my arm is clamped to my mouth.

Sparing a quick glance to see Shawn's reaction, I notice he's laughing too, but not at her like I am. He's laughing *with* her. Marvelling at her craziness.

Hannah must hear me spluttering because she turns – appearing rather rosy – and fires me her infamous frown, supplemented with an inconspicuous kick to the leg. Not expecting the blow, my balance is lost and I'm gasping in shock.

'Emily? Is that you down there?'

I draw in a breath to contain my amusement.

'Shawn! I was just checking on the cupcakes.' I clear my throat and swallow down the giggles, the countertop being used as my hoisting mechanism. 'Nice to see you again,' I offer, brushing my hands on my apron in a subconscious attempt to distract myself from the grin which is painfully being held back. Hannah's avoiding any sort of eye contact with the man who appears very entertained.

'I didn't think you worked Mondays,' Shawn says, his perfectly squared jaw clenching as he flashes me a curious look.

'I don't usually,' I reply quickly, pursing my lips.

Silence again.

His gaze shifts from me to Hannah and back to me again. On a shake of his head and a chuckle, his coffee is grasped. 'Well, thank you, ladies, always a pleasure. Keep the change.' He grins, amused but confused – as those always seem to be when they come into contact with Han. 'You have a good day, same time tomorrow?'

'Yep, yeah, definitely. See you then,' she stutters.

Winking in Hannah's direction, he skilfully balances both items in one hand and pulls on the handle.

We stand still. Not uttering a word. Right until the door closes.

Everything I'd forcefully trapped inside comes racing out, my laughs filling the small room. 'Every time, Hannah! If it's not dropping dispensers, it's spurting ludicrous tripe. What happened to playing it cool?'

Her hands rise to cup both her glowing cheeks as she gawps at the place where Shawn stood not five seconds ago. 'He's so hot! And he winked, did you see? That's it, we're getting married and having Shawn and Hannah babies.'

'You don't even know his second name.'

'That's a minor detail,' she dismisses. 'The point is I haven't scared him off yet, that's a step in the right direction, isn't it?'

I shake my head, grinning from ear to ear. 'Why don't you ask him out?'

'What? Did you not see me? I turn to jelly. My brain doesn't process sensible, normal words. I tell stupid stories about pork pies. How am I meant to form the sentence, 'Do you want to go out sometime?' It's impossible,' she blurts, waving her hands manically.

'Just take a deep breath and let it spew. The worst that can happen is he says no,' I attempt to reason, taking on the role of mother to a twenty-five-year-old.

'Then I have to see him every morning. The word *tit* will be written across my face.' She stiffly mimes an invisible line across her forehead.

'Like it already isn't.'

'Em...' she pleads.

'Look, would you rather walk around wondering *what if?*' I offer more seriously. She needs to take that leap of faith. I'd love for her to find someone worthy, and Shawn seems like a frankly decent guy. The fact he has never once pulled a face at how flustered and weird she can be, is all the evidence she needs. He's dropping by tomorrow morning, like he has done every morning for the past two years. Because he likes her too.

She pauses, contemplating my words. 'I hate it when you're right.'

'I know.' I beam, patting her on the back and returning to the second batch of cupcake mix on the side. 'Where do your ridiculous stories even come from?'

'I get my madness from my dad, Em. His head's full of crazy yarns, my mum's the only sane one in our family,' she answers, returning to her window cleaning. 'The irony being, Granddad did genuinely once slip over on a pork pie... it was at a birthday party...'

Her voice carries around the room but it's like white noise to me. My smile falters, because I can't remember the last time Dad and I had a proper conversation, let alone shared silly tales with each other.

The cruel reality of having a father who cares more about his career than his own daughter. A father who is managing to suck my boyfriend into the same godforsaken belief that work is everything, even if it means overlooking the people they are supposedly meant to hold dear.

# *TWO*

The red man flickers to green and the bleeping sound of the pedestrian crossing resonates in my ears. Along with the horde of strangers, I follow the path towards Shelton Street.

William texted after my shift asking to go for a coffee as he was in the centre concluding a meeting, to which I agreed. Any time spent together is precious, even if my stomach is knotted with apprehension.

Hannah's voice has been in my head all day. He needs to know I'm moving away, but the uneasiness in my gut is forming because even if I don't want to admit it, I know our situation will only worsen when I move into university halls. We're hardly spending any proper quality time together as it is and being up in Sunderland means it's only going to dwindle further. And even though I'm excited to go, announcing it to him is acknowledging that it's happening, which is incredibly daunting. I don't know how William's going to react, and above all, I'm fearful of what this means for us. So I've held off. I've kept the cat zipped tight in the bag. But Hannah's right, I'm leaving next month. It's time for the kitten to be let loose.

The Coffee House sign in the distance grows closer and he's below it, leaning against the window of the café. One ankle is crossed in front of the other, the newest iPhone to his ear as his free hand flutters about, being used as a useless emphasizing mechanism to whoever's on the other end and can't see him.

If I didn't know him, I would think he was a lot older than twenty-three. Not only does his lofty height, chiselled jawline and groomed stubble add to the mature look, but the expensive suits he wears and the way he handles himself so professionally, add at least five years to his appearance. He is extremely handsome, there's no denying that fact. He's the type you could imagine in all the gossip magazines, walking arm in arm with a glowing Victoria's Secret model. I do sometimes catch myself thinking if Dad hadn't introduced us…

The silly musings are shaken from my head when he gestures me over, dismissing the person on the phone. 'Hey, babe,' he greets warmly. His hand meets my waist when he leans down. The feel of familiar soft lips seems to relax my taut muscles, giving me a brief break from my prudent thoughts.

'How has today been?' I ask on a smile as we pull away.

'Stressful, as per.' He doesn't elaborate, instead reaching behind me to open the door. 'Shall we?' His palm is placed on my lower back to guide me inside.

The café is packed, with chatter and the clinking of crockery ricocheting off the walls. A barista finishes clearing a table in the corner, so I take my chance. Settling into the seat, my eyes complete a full circle of the room;

most sit laughing with their friends, as others chill on their own tapping away on their phones and laptops. They eventually land on William at the till. Taking out his wallet from the side pocket of his blazer, my attention is drawn to the cashier, running her eyes hungrily over his frame as he searches for the right card.

My own narrow, observing closely.

A few moments later she places a tall glass and a mug onto a circular black tray and he flashes her a cheeky wink before idling over. The disappointment is clear on her face as he rests my hot chocolate with all the trimmings down in front me.

'What a day,' he breathes, collapsing into his chair and running his hand through his perfectly quaffed hair.

His gaze holds mine for a moment. 'You must have a pheromone magnet which attracts every female towards you.'

'What?' he questions, taking a sip of his Americano. He's acting oblivious, but I know he's very much aware.

'That barista, she was gawping at you.' I motion slightly with my head to the girl steaming water on one of the machines. 'Practically ripped your clothes off with her eyes.'

'Huh, which one?' His eyes roam the room casually. 'The fitty in the glasses or the posh bird with the *exceptionally* tight skirt?' He grins playfully.

'Glasses.' I play along. 'I could give her your number, if you want?'

'Would you? You're such a darling, I've always had a thing for blondes.' He waggles his eyebrows at me and I hate myself for not being able to hold back my coy smile. We get it everywhere we go. If he had a flute, he'd be the Pied Piper, attracting women across the globe. He wraps his hand over mine which is resting on top of the table and presents me with the signature William Garcia wink.

'So, what happened today that was so taxing?' I pose the question whilst sweeping some whipped cream onto my finger, even though I know he won't go into detail. He never tells me about his work. Dad employed him when he graduated at twenty-one with the aid of his father – who also happens to be in the same industry – and William's salary is safely inside the six-figure mark, however I'm not one hundred percent certain what he actually does. I know he's as an associate, but I don't know the specifics of his daily tasks, only that they're so incredibly stressful – as he's keen to regularly express. Whenever I ask, the only answer I receive is, 'You wouldn't want to know, it's boring stuff,' and then he's back tip-tapping away on his phone… just like he's doing now.

'Am I keeping you?'

'Hmm?' His head lifts a little, but his eyes remain fixed on the screen. 'Oh, nothing, just something your dad's having me sort out. Absolute nightmare,' he sighs, a frown painted on his face. The usual.

Slurping at my hot chocolate, which I'm finding should be renamed to lukewarm chocolate, I figure he won't ask me about my day, so I begin prattling to keep myself entertained. 'My day was great. I made a load of cupcakes, sold a few buns and I think Hannah might ask out this guy called Shawn, I've told you about him, but you probably weren't listening...' I watch him pay no attention to me. Hannah's scowl works its way into my mind. Shuffling in my seat, my lips part as I take a breath, figuring this will earn me his attention. 'William, I've been meaning to talk to you about something...' He's still engrossed in his phone. My throat is cleared. 'You know I finished my A-levels this year, well I don't get my results until Thursday, but the University of Sunderland have already given me an unconditional offer, which is amazing and it's a course I think I'm really going to love, so I've made the decision to accept and move away.' I wait through gritted teeth. But he doesn't look up, he doesn't even flinch. 'William?'

Nothing.

'William...' I press.

Still nothing.

I reach across the table in annoyance and snatch the phone straight from his hand.

'Emily, what–'

'Did you hear what I said?'

'Of course!'

I purse my lips and raise my brow, daring him to lie again.

'Okay, I didn't. Sorry, go ahead.' He leans forward and motions for me to continue. I choose to ignore the quick glances he's throwing to his phone in my palm.

'Right, so I've been thinking a lot about my life, and you know how I–

The phone buzzes repeatedly in my hand before I can finish, or even begin. We stare at it with entirely dissimilar expressions; mine infuriation, his anticipation. My frustrated gaze then meets his pleading eyes.

I know he won't fully relax and absorb what I have to say, so I give in. Letting out an exasperated sigh, I unwillingly toss it back.

'Sorry,' he mouths, tearing his eyes from mine and answering the call.

My chin is slapped into my palm as I peer around the café again, bored and irritated. Can't we have five minutes without being interrupted, is that so much to ask? I notice the barista with the glasses watching us, so I avert my gaze.

'Okay. I'll see you in a short while. Bye, mate.'

*A short while?* I thought he'd finished for the day?

My face holds a questioning glint as his chair screeches along the floor.

'Don't hate me, babe…'

*Count to ten, Emily.*

'Emergency meeting at work, something to do with a client's case.'

'You have to go straight away?' I'm staring up at him now, my eyes tightening at his not so guilty expression.

'Yeah, I'm sorry. We can talk about that thing you wanted to tell me tomorrow. Don't wait up for me, you know how long these meetings go on for.'

I fold my arms as my chest expands. I'm fully mindful of what *these meetings* consist of; him drinking himself into oblivion with his colleagues afterwards and stumbling in at two in the morning.

'Here.' He reaches into his new designer blazer, pulling out his wallet. 'Take this and order whatever you fancy.' Tugging out one of his many cards, he holds it between his middle and index fingers.

'I have my own money, William.'

'I know.' He waves it about in front of my face.

I sniff in deliberation, but swipe it from his fingertips nonetheless, tucking it safely in the pocket of my jeans. He treads around the table and kisses my cheek tenderly, but I don't return the affection, simply staring ahead in displeasure. 'See you at home,' he says as his attention is yet again drawn to his ringing phone. He holds it to his ear and talks down the line, giving me a final brief wave as I watch him through the glass windows, disappearing into the crowd on the pathway.

I drum the glass in my hand and slump in my seat. Alone. Once again. Shooting back a couple more gulps, my mouth contorts at the now cold liquid running down my throat. So, deciding I've had enough, I haul my bag from the chair before weaving between the tables, throwing a smile to the wandering eyed barista as I make my way out.

My relatively good mood from this morning has rapidly taken a sour turn.


I'm hungry.

That seems to be my thought process 24/7, but right now I'm so famished it hurts. Even in my determined haste, the empty driveway seems everlasting with the fridge so close yet so far away.

My key meets the lock in a short and forceful exchange and I'm immediately greeted by giant paws knocking me off balance. 'Hey, Bud,' I murmur, attempting to stroke, as well as shuffle around him to close the front door.

I kick off my shoes and drop to my knees, petting and fussing my excitable Collie. 'Just me and you, Buddy. I'm thinking extra-large pizza!' After smothering me in enough kisses to make up for our time apart, he follows me into the kitchen as I slide in front of the double-door fridge. Grimacing at all the health-conscious foods William insists we buy, I opt instead for a bag of giant chocolate buttons before grabbing a handful of dog treats from the cupboard beside it.

I jerk out the nearest stool from underneath the breakfast bar, place Buddy's treats on the tiled floor – of which he devours straight away– and sigh in satisfaction, my mouth being stuffed with chocolaty goodness.

The explosion of delight only lasts for a tock of the kitchen clock as I'm soon focusing on the air. Soundless air. The silence becomes more and more palpable by the second, and it's something I'm very familiar with. I've grown accustomed to the thoughts that haunt my mind when living in the stillness which lurks in houses like these. Everything about this place is incredibly modish and luxurious; clear marble top counters and tiles so new they sparkle when the sun light beams in through the windows, all around lavish furniture and ornaments decorate huge rooms. It's a house some would kill for, yet the silence it bears is something I know all too well, and more often than not, like in this moment, it can be deafening.

It's William's parents' home really, passed on to him when his nanna became ill. They, along with his fifteen-year-old brother, moved out last year to be closer to her and freely left it to their beloved eldest son. Mr and Mrs Garcia. Kind people who wouldn't dream of looking down on anyone, yet are somehow oblivious to the fact that buying fresh silk bed linen once a fortnight is generally not a normal thing to do.

It would seem to most he's had the perfect upbringing, growing up in a shielded bubble of fine dining and deluxe five-star holidays in Monaco; a life of financial security. But his father is a hardworking man, he's earned this life, and he's taught William that nothing good is ever earned by doing nothing. An intense work ethic has been drilled into his brain since he was in nappies, and that's commendable, it's ensuring a child doesn't grow up entitled. For a family as wealthy as the Garcia's, it's right. Only sometimes I wish it wasn't.

My lungs relax as I let out the breath I wasn't aware I was holding and bring up an app to order my food. I choose my pizza, tap the payment option, and pull out William's card.

*I suppose he's good for something.*

My tired head shakes. I shouldn't think that. At least I have him! That's what I have to go back to whenever my head strays into murky territory – usually when alone. Because without him, I would still be living with Dad.

At least here with William, I'm not entirely invisible.

# *THREE*

*Thump! Clang! Bang!*

My body stirs as my eyes flutter open.

*Thud!*

I sit up straight. Quiet, holding my breath, listening.

Silence now.

I swivel my head to gage the time on my alarm clock. 11.43.

*Bang!*

Buddy growls from his bed next to the door. I shift the covers off me and fumble my way through the dark, throwing on William's hoodie from the bottom of the bed as I go. Buddy sits up, growling once again as another thud echoes from downstairs. I know he's probably smashed, but is he not capable of being even just a little bit quiet?

The landing and staircase is ill-lit and as Buddy thunders down to the hall, I have to use the banister to blindly feel my way to the bottom. Downstairs isn't any better; it's pitch black. My brow furrows. Where is he? A shuffling of footsteps causes a low grumble from Buddy beside me.

'William?' I call as my feet carry me into the kitchen. A draft tickles my body, sending a shiver down my spine.

I flick the light switch, but instantly wish I hadn't. My gasps fill the room, my pulse doubling.

Eyes wide, body frozen in shock, the figure dressed in black stands tall on the other side of the room, their back to me. He holds a glass in his hand filled to the brim with water, and that's when I see the back door behind the hand; it's wide open, the cold air filling the kitchen.

'You should really get a check on your security, Miss Lambert. Anyone could walk in.' His hoarse voice is low and murky. He observes the glass before lifting it to his lips and gulping down its contents.

I scorn my dazed mind. I had been so tired, I'd forgotten to lock the back door after letting Buddy out before we went up to bed. My scolding only lasts for seconds before fear is overriding any other feeling. The man pivots on the spot allowing me to see him more clearly. His black hair is slicked back and his eyes are dark and heavy, but what catches my attention the most is his Northern accent.

Our eyes lock: mine wide with horror, his calm but dangerously menacing.

He spoke my name! How does he know my name?

'W–ho…' I try, but it comes out broken and unsteady, the words trapping themselves in my dry throat.

His sudden sickening laugh reaches my ear drums, causing my heart to pound out of my chest. 'They said it would be difficult, but you made it so easy.' He sniggers, flicking his focus to the glass in his hand. It slips from his grip, tumbling in slow motion through the air before crashing onto the tiles. Fragments shatter and fly, scattering themselves as the water pools the floor making me wince. He inches towards me, the broken shards crunching under his worn black boots and I instantly try to shift my heavy limbs to re-create the space lost.

'I...' I choke on my words, tears beginning to blur my vision.

'I expected the daughter of *the* Francis Lambert to be a little more perceptive, but evidently she's as dumb as her mother.'

My breath hitches in my throat as I stagger backwards. *Mother*? How does he know Mum and Dad? I will my legs to run, but they've turned to jelly. His face twists into a wicked sneer as my back smacks into something solid with his sluggish pace eating up the space between us, as though he's enjoying it; feeding off my panic.

'I do apologise, gorgeous girly, but you have your father to blame for this.' The gap is swallowed and his towering body presses against mine. My head swings to the side, every part of me tensing when the back of his gloved hand strokes my cheek. I writhe, mustering all the strength I have to try and get away, but it's no use. His warm, nauseating breath fans my ear when he chuckles and it's then I notice him reaching to his hip. My eyes widen at the sight with bile rising in my throat. 'Tell your mum I said, *hey*.'

A black object is drawn and it's as though my mind

catches up with itself, suddenly releasing the rest of my body. In a state of terror, I thrust my knee up and connect with his groin. His grunts fill the air as he doubles over, giving me a brief second to escape and I take it, stumbling over myself as I make a dash for the front door. But I never reach it.

I stumble, my body falling through the air. It crashes down and I'm left gasping as my knees throb from the blow, as I notice Buddy's tennis ball rolling away down the darkened hall. But the pain is quickly pushed to the side, because the door is five feet away, and his voice sounds closer.

'You're going to regret that, little girl!'

Every fraction of myself is like lead as I try to stand, battling against the skiddy floor and my feeble limbs. I don't dare look behind. He's going to reach me any second.

'Arrrgggghhhh!'

I stop breathing, my body rigid as the harrowing scream bouncing off every wall in the house momentarily paralyses me. Over my shoulder I can just about make out the face of my attacker. It's scrunched up in agony, his body on the floor, legs flailing in the kitchen doorway.

I then see it, or rather, *him*.

Buddy.

His mouth, clamped around the man's leg, tugging with force. 'Fucking mutt!' he yells as he struggles to shake him off. Buddy doesn't release. My chest heaves in shock as I stare openmouthed at the sight.

Panic sets in when I notice the man desperately clawing out, blindly feeling for something in front of him. I follow his outstretched arm and notice the object he'd pulled from his hip now laying on the floor.

His gun.

Without thinking, I crawl as fast as I can, kicking his hand away when he attempts to grab my leg. Swiping the surprisingly weighty weapon into my palm, I claw at any scrap of strength in my legs and manage to scramble to my feet, peering behind. The man's crazed dark eyes are glaring back at me.

'You little bit–' he strains to spit, but Buddy digs his teeth in deeper causing another earth shattering wail.

I make a dash for the stairs this time, my breathing frantic and my body screaming under the pressure to keep going as I haul myself up the never-ending case. Sprinting across the landing, I make it to my bedroom, the pounding of my heart in my head throwing me off balance. With nothing but the thought of 'Call the police!' in my mind, I wobble to my dressing table and snatch my phone. Except everything seems to be working against me as I bounce nervously, waiting for the device to turn on and the screen to light up.

'Come on, come ooooon,' I quiver.

Mercifully, I'm finally illuminated by the bright light, but before I can act, I'm jumping as a loud bang rumbles around the house. My head shoots up and my mouth screams for air when more clatters reverberate, with what sounds like thumping footsteps storming across the landing.

My phone is dropped, the gun being pointed towards the door. I have no idea how to use this thing, but I don't know what else to do. There's no time to hide.

The door bursts open. I hold my breath.

I'm hit with a wave of confusion. The now lit landing illuminates the figure stood in the doorway. His arms fall to his side and I quickly notice that this isn't the man from downstairs, this one is bulkier – and balder.

'Miss Lambert, it's okay.' He holds a hand out, his face showing concern.

'Who– who are…'

'It's okay,' he repeats more slowly. 'I'm not going to hurt you. My name's Guy, I work for your father. Are you alright?' he asks evenly, fumbling in his pocket.

I don't answer, still suspicious. Still in entire disbelief. An ID badge is thrust into the air, landing at my feet. Somehow a rational part of my brain fights its way through, slowing it down enough to take in the words on the card. *LAMBERT LAW SECURITY.*

My arms fall limp, my chest rising and sinking drastically. 'Jesus… Christ,' I rasp between pants.

'Are you alright, Miss Lambert?' he presses. I stare at him. I don't know the answer. Physically, yes. Emotionally and mentally, not so much.

I nod slowly. 'Where is he? That man… whe–

The sentence is left unfinished as the lump in my dry throat cuts into me when I swallow.

'He ran out the back when he heard us come in. Norman has gone after him. I had to make sure you were safe.'

'What do you mean he ran? Bud…' My veins burn in realisation. 'Oh no!' I race past Guy and practically fly down the stairs. A relieved sigh leaves my lungs when I see my Border Collie at the bottom. He limps forward, holding his front leg up as if too painful to apply pressure.

Once I reach the final step, I collapse onto the floor and throw my arms around him in a giant hug – the gun still in my hand. 'You are an incredible dog,' I whisper into his fur; his familiar scent filling me with a comfort my body is desperate to soak up. He nestles into my neck and I pull back, gently taking his paw into my palm. He whines. 'I'm sorry,' I coo softly. 'Oh, what did he do to you?'

My body jumps when a breathless, proportionately cumbersome man with a buzz cut and an untucked white dress shirt races through the front door, which I can now see is virtually hanging off its hinges. He searches around frantically, a bead of sweat noticeable on his crinkled forehead, before locking eyes with me. Guy marches down the stairs, arching his eyebrows at the flustered man who shakes his head in response.

'The bastard got away, took off in a bloody Corsa. I got the plate though.'

Guy nods. He turns to me, his eyes watching my quivering form closely. 'We need to take you to your father.'

I let out several short pants, attempting to calm down. Dad is the last person I want to see, but that psycho mentioned Mum. I need to know what the hell is going on, and I'm suddenly very keen to get out of this house. 'Okay,' I agree. 'But Buddy needs help, he can hardly walk and I'm not leaving him here.'

The two men catch a glance. 'Fine. I'll notify your father. He can arrange a vet transfer to the firm,' Guy replies.

Norman is given his instructions, leaving to fetch their car around to the front as Guy escapes to the kitchen with Dad on the line.

I'm left alone.

Buddy's head is resting in my lap as I sit, leaning against the wall next to the staircase, feebly trying to gather my thoughts. It's all hazy. My pulse is slowing, but a sickly feeling is now settling in my stomach as the adrenaline fades away. My body and mind are completely disorientated. I should be breaking down, hysterically crying into Buddy's fur.

I was nearly *killed*!

But all I'm able to do is stare vacantly at nothing in particular. Completely emotionless. Completely numb.

Battling against the impenetrable bubble forming in my throat, I peer down to see the intimidatingly angry looking gun still in my grasp. It feels heavy, as though I'm holding a giant rock.

Checking around me, I carefully place it in the big pocket of William's hoodie and make a mental note to hide it in my bag when I eventually muster the strength to stand. But for the moment I remain.

My fingers subconsciously cling to my pyjama bottoms. The material bunches in my fist, mirroring my tightly knotted stomach.

# FOUR

Lambert Law. One of the grandest office towers in London. Fourteen stories, complete with state-of-the-art boardrooms, office quarters, panoramic windows and marble tile flooring. Luxurious as hell, and all owned by Mr Francis Lambert – dear old Dad.

'This is a total shit storm!' Dad runs his hands over his face vigorously as he stares out of the giant window overlooking the brightly lit city, his back to us.

It's nearing one in the morning. I'm sat with a dazed William to my right and a serious looking Guy towering over me on my left. I was wide awake in the car with thoughts and questions running amok in my mind, but the events of tonight are catching up with me and my body is exhausted. I had to scramble to grab my phone, wrap the gun in one of my jumpers and hide it in my backpack before Guy and Norman ushered me into the car.

When we pulled up outside in the blacked-out Mercedes Benz, I'd watched as an unimpressed Norman had carried Buddy into the building first to meet the vet. Guy told me to leave my bag in the car, which I was hesitant to do, but did so after he said we probably wouldn't be staying long. Walking through reception, I saw it was completely abandoned, apart from one man sat behind a large lavish desk and a couple of security men who gave nodding gestures to Guy as we passed through the airport-style x-ray machines. I was thankful Guy told me not to bring my bag, because they would've seen the gun and thought I was here to assassinate Dad!

When we'd reached the twelfth floor in the mirrored lift – which reflected a dismal and scraggy looking girl – I'd trailed behind the bulky security man to the end of the corridor, slowing my pace right down. I was in no rush to see *him*.

William was already inside when I'd reluctantly passed Guy who stepped aside to allow me through. Sat in the chair opposite Dad's desk, he'd been chewing anxiously on his thumb whilst his leg bounced up and down, his usually seamless hair unruly and his blazer absent, revealing his tailored white shirt. Dad must have called him and told him what had happened, because when his eyes met mine, he'd sprung from the chair and suffocated me with his arms. His hand never left my back as he'd steered me over and sat me down in the chair like I was going to break at any given moment. Which I'd felt as though I might.

Dad had been glued to his spot at the window, showing not a hint of concern. Typical. The tops of his hair seem significantly greyer since I saw him last, his brown eyes darker, and his usually healthy figure cuts a much slimmer fit under his tieless white dress shirt with his carelessly rolled up sleeves. He looks worn out.

I fiddle with my fingers in my lap as he swings around. 'I thought you had it under control!' He throws a stern finger towards Guy, who doesn't flinch under Dad's angered scowl. It's almost comical watching my much less brawny father yelling at a man as muscular and strong as Guy – a man twice his size. Dad doesn't need muscles to show power though, his intense glower and harsh tone enough to put even the toughest of men to shame. I learnt that as a little girl, watching him more often than not scream down the phone at the poor recipient.

'I'm sorry, sir, we reached the property, but he entered through the back before we had chance to check out the area. There was no reason to suspect anything was wrong, until we heard the yelling.' His body remains fixed, he seems so composed and unfazed. Dad eyes him before flopping down in his office chair behind the large glass desk on a lingering sigh.

'And where the bloody hell were you?' Dad barks, training his glower to a zoned-out William whose arms are folded, his fingers playing with his lips as his attention is brought back to the room.

'Don't put this on me! I was trying to sort your crap out,' he snipes back.

'Visiting a client doesn't take all night, son.'

I'm growing more confused and annoyed by the second.

'Will someone please tell me what is going on!' I finally snap. The room falls silent. 'Since when has our home been under surveillance?' William's visibly tense form is angled away from me, so I point my hardened stare towards the man who seems to know so much. 'Who was that man, Dad?'

'No one you need to concern yourself with,' he brushes off, leaning back further into his chair and fiddling with an elastic band in his hands.

I stare at him in disbelief. He can't be serious. 'No one I need to concern myself with? He tried to kill me!'

'Yes. Which is why I'm sending you away for a little while,' he replies, and I have to double take. The room is soundless once again. Everyone staring at the man who suddenly appears to be so interested in the rubber band he's twisting around his fingertips.

'I'm sorry?'

He stops fiddling, placing the band on the table before his chest expands and he exhales, glancing in turn at the three people opposite him. 'Give us a minute,' he directs at Guy who obeys and swiftly turns on his heel, exiting the room without another word. Dad then focuses his daggering eyes on William. 'You can leave too.'

I look to my boyfriend, mentally pleading him not to go. William appears troubled, glaring back at Dad, his mouth parted as if to speak up, but it's as though he talks himself out of it knowing there's little point. His shoulders drop and he places a hand on my shoulder, squeezing it lightly. And before I have a chance to object, he's across the room and slamming the door shut. Leaving me all alone with the person who is still managing to ruin my life.

'Emily, I'm going to need you to listen to me carefully.'

Fuck him. 'You do realise I'm meant to be starting university in a month,' I fire, folding my arms across my chest. Along with Hannah and my friends, he knows about my plans, but unlike Hannah and my friends, his reaction to my news was as cheerful as a dying fish. *Sending me away.* I'm not in the mood for his crap, I've put up with it all my life and he's kidding himself if he thinks he's ordering me around now.

'I know, and I will make it my duty to ensure this mess is cleared up by then. You'll be free to come back and do what you wish.' He's leaning forward now, his hands intertwined on his glass desk.

'Where am I going?' As soon as the question passes my lips, I dread the answer.

'I'm sending you to your aunt's cottage in Cornwall. I rang her as soon as I heard about what happened tonight and she's setting up the spare bedroom for you. You're aware she lives in Rockstone now? A little place called Marshlyn Bay. It's the safest area I know. A small town away from the city, it's just until this blows over. No one will know you're there apart from William and a few of my trusted staff.'

'And I get no say in this?'

His stony eyes say it all.

'What has Aunty said about this inconvenience?' I ask, settling back into the cushiony chair. A subtle dig. Aunt Maggie isn't exactly a fan of Dads and he knows it, she cut him off completely when we lost Mum. Mum was her younger sister and her death hit Maggie hard, I used to see her nearly every weekend, but after Mum died, we drifted. I get the odd phone call here and there, a card through the post on my birthday, but that's about it.

He dismisses the sarcasm in my voice. 'She actually agreed that it will do you some good. She said she's looking forward to spending some time with you.'

I can't tell if he's being truthful or not; an advantage he has as a lawyer, but a disadvantage to whoever is on the receiving end, and right now that's me.

'What did you tell her? That her niece is a prime target for some maniac who holds a grudge against her father and consequently wants her dead, or does she think it's a lovely spontaneous catch-up?' I mockingly smile.

'She knows there has been a little trouble and that I want you to spend some time away from London while I clear it up. I've told her not to ask any questions.'

'A little trouble,' I mock under my breath. If that was a minor inconvenience, then I certainly wouldn't want to be involved in a major one.

Dad flickers his eyes down to his large interlaced hands, his index finger tapping his knuckle, if I'm not mistaken, in a rather nervous manner. I frown at him, my own question running around in my head.

'What did you do that was so bad?'

He's quick off the mark. 'It doesn't matter, Emily. It's not your problem.'

'Well, quite clearly it is.' He's somehow managed to drag me into this and now he's not telling me a thing.

He lets out an irritated sigh. His head lifts again, focusing on me. 'There are some people out there, bad people, who aren't my biggest supporters at the moment. That's all you need to know.'

'There's more than one?' Oh, fabulous. A thought then prompts its way into my mind. I remember what that psycho said earlier.

They *said it would be difficult.*

I fidget with my sleeves anxiously. 'What's their issue with me?' I question, determined to dig the answers out of him.

'Emily...' he warns.

'No, Dad! If I'm having to move away because of these people, I want to know why!'

He stares at me blankly, his face straight and unreadable. And then a breath is drawn. 'Always so persistent, just like your mother.'

I swallow, stunned. This must be the first time he's mentioned her since she died. His eyes seem to relax marginally, his crow's feet evening out as he exhales. Tilting his head back as if gathering himself, he straightens from his chair and paces around the table to stand directly in front of me, resting his lower half on the desk.

'*He* mentioned Mum,' I say dejectedly. Dad's eyes are fixed on me. 'He spoke as if he knew her.' I search his face as if it will give me any clue as to what he's thinking, but it's to no avail.

'He's deranged,' he retorts loosely. 'He would've said anything to get to you,' he adds, clearly uncomfortable as he rushes his words.

'He said your name too, he said I had you to blame.' I gulp. 'Dad, how does he even know she's–'

'Enough, Emily Rose! I'm dealing with it.'

Anger fills me, because he's treating me like a child.

'Guy will accompany you. He'll take you straight to your aunt's and you are to get in the car without argument. Do you understand?' The moment of abnormal gentleness seems to be over, the typical, obstinate man I've come to know all too well returning.

'I'm not a little girl anymore, you can't order me around and expect me to bow down when I don't even know what's going on. I'm eighteen, legally allowed to do what I want,' I say, making my point of not being his puppet. He will not control me.

'Sweetheart, listen to me.' His tired eyes plead with me, and for the first time in my life, I see weakness behind them. The thick-skinned, emotionless man I've grown up with is beginning to show signs of cracking. As much as I hate to admit, I feel a pang of remorse for him. Dad can usually handle anything. It must be bad.

I look down at my lap. 'What about my stuff?' I bet he hasn't thought about that.

'I've had someone go to the house to pack some things. William spoke to them so you should have what you need. If they've done what I told them, it'll be there when you arrive.'

My mouth falls open as my head shoots up – that assassination idea doesn't sound so immoral now. 'So not only are you sending me away against my will, you've had someone go through my wardrobe? My personal stuff!' The thought of a stranger looking through my underwear makes me cringe. I shake my head, pulling my eyes away from his. I can't look at him.

'I'm doing this for you, Emily,' he says, being almost credibly compassionate. To anyone else it might seem believable, but I know him. The actual truth is by doing this I'll be one less problem to deal with, this is his way of getting rid of me. 'There's something else...' he hesitates.

My lips straighten into a firm line as my eyes tighten. Of course, there is.

'Your phone. You'll have to delete every social media account: Facebook, Twitter, Instagram, it all has to go. For the time being, at least.'

'You're joking?'

He shakes his head slowly. 'You have to keep this to yourself. Tell your friends you're having a detox, spending some time away.'

I'm probably the only teenager in the world who doesn't have their phone constantly glued to their hand, anxiously editing photos in order to boost likes. It's never been me, so deleting them won't be a problem. But that's beside the point. For someone who basically wanted nothing to do with me growing up, he's now suddenly in control of my whole life and I'm not happy about it. I've reached the end of my tether.

'Are you going to tell me what's really going on, or are we done here?'

'We're done.'

'Right. Thanks for nothing.' I've had enough of this. I'm so drained, I don't have it in me to fight him anymore. I stand abruptly and stride across the room.

'You may not see it now, but all I want is what's best for you.' His gentle tone stops me in my tracks. 'I'm your dad, Emily. Believe it or not, I do care about you.'

I scoff at his statement, my fists clenching into tight balls as I take a glance over my shoulder. He's motionless, his eyes fixed on my tense figure.

'You've never been a *Dad* to me,' I snap before walking away, not giving him a second look.

'Can't you come with me?'

'I've got to stay and take care of a few things here,' William tries to reason.

I'm still in my Pyjamas outside the giant revolving doors of Lambert Law. The chilly nighttime breeze blows wisps of hair from my bun and onto my face as I pull the sleeves of William's hoodie over my hands.

'Just think of it as a holiday,' he encourages, stroking the stray strands from my face. The faint smell of alcohol on his breath brushes my nose as he talks.

'A holiday where I'm watched like a hawk.' My head motions in the direction of my newly appointed bodyguard, his stance rigid next to the Mercedes with his hands clasped behind him and stern expression focusing directly past us.

William chuckles softly but offers me a sympathetic smile. 'He's there to keep you safe.'

'Safe from that man? That man who I've never seen or met before yet somehow knows everything about me and wants me dead?'

The word *safe* puts me on edge, as do the many questions swirling around in my head. Am I really safe? What if he finds me again? How did he even know where I lived in the first place? And just how many of these *bad people* has Dad pushed over the edge? After all, he's made it abundantly clear, he's the type of man to anger a lot of people.

William scratches his head. 'Yeah, from him.' His eyes dance around the area, gazing at everything except me.

I study him closely, he's being weird. He's been acting strange ever since I stepped into Dad's office. I thought it was because he'd simply been relieved to see me, and maybe it was partly relief, but this is something else…

It makes sense. He's virtually Dad's double. He probably knows the ins and outs of everything.

'You know who he is, don't you?'

His face looks pained, as if he's battling with himself. He physically deflates on a sigh, finally fixing his brown eyes on me. 'Listen, baby, I know we keep saying it, but you really don't need to be worrying. You're safe now.'

There's that word again!

'Guy's only with you as a precaution.'

I draw in a breath, parting my mouth before closing it promptly. It's useless, I'm getting nowhere.

'You'll be back in a few weeks or so, and I'll come and see you if I can get away from work.'

'Promise?'

'Promise.' He nods. 'I'll text you later.' He brushes my hair behind my ear before leaning down. His soft lips connect with mine, but it's not the longing kiss I was expecting. It's not a kiss you would expect to be given if there was a possibility you wouldn't be seeing your boyfriend for a whole month. I throw my arms around his neck in an attempt to deepen it but he pulls back. My nose scrunches.

'I'm sorry.' He shrugs. 'Just tired.'

I search his face. Something's wrong.

Guy clears his throat, indicating time to go. Entertaining his wordless instruction, I unwrap my arms but keep a hold of William's slightly unbuttoned shirt which is giving me a view of his smooth chest, not willing to leave just yet. I glimpse to the backseat of the Benz and see Buddy's nose peeping through the tiny opened crevice of the window as he waits for me – at least I have him with me, I suppose. My focus drops to the ground.

'It'll fly by,' William says as our eyes lock. 'I'll see you soon.'

My lips remain in a straight line as I bob my head sluggishly and reluctantly let go. He smiles encouragingly which does little to reassure me, before I solemnly drag my feet over to the car door Guy is holding open. I slide into the back and watch William gradually become a small indistinct blob of nothing as we drive away.

If I didn't think my life made any sense before, it sure as hell doesn't now.

It's an utter mess.

# FIVE

'Miss Lambert?'

I'm drawing in a lungful of air as my mind rouses. Scrunching my dry eyes together to clear away the drowsiness, I forget where I am before catching Guy's tired brown gaze in the rear-view mirror.

We've stopped.

I scan the area outside my window. We're parked on a sloped road overlooking the ocean, separated by a hilltop and a cluster of trees – the sun is in the midst of emerging in the sky, glistening on the calm water. It looks pretty. Tranquil. My neck cranes to see what Buddy's side has to offer. It's hard to capture every detail, but it's easy to recognise that in front of me stands a cottage.

We're here.

'What time is it?' I ask on a yawn, my voice weak and scratchy.

'Almost half six, Miss Lambert. Shall we get you inside?'

Aware of its developing drum, I bob my head gently and open my door. Might as well get the initial awkward greeting over and done with. It's when I step out of the car that I see the cottage in its entirety and the first thing I note is that instead of brick, the front is made entirely of cobblestone.

My bag – which I'm conscious possesses the gun – is grasped as Guy strides around to the other side to help Buddy hop out of the Mercedes. The vet said there wasn't anything majorly wrong with his leg and the discomfort would eventually subside, so she wrapped it up and gave him some pain relief. I'm not sure how I would have coped if anything more serious had been the outcome.

Making my way around the front of the car, I notice Guy's parked in a small lay-by right outside. The road, I now grasp, is a single-track lane with a few other cottages dotted along and facing out to sea. A parking space to the left is occupied by an old, but well–polished, red Golf.

I meet Guy and Buddy by a wooden gate attached to a white picket fence which runs around the front of the cottage. Before I have the chance to move first, Guy is already unlatching the gate and stepping aside, letting me pass as he hands over Buddy's lead. My tri-coloured Collie walks through on a limp and I follow suit.

I'm stood on a cobbled path leading up to an oak front door. On either side there is a freshly mown grassy lawn with several groupings of colourful flowers, all planted systematically to follow the edge of the fence and meeting each end of the cottage. There's a swing bench on the left side of the lawn, placed at a slight angle in front of a window; I imagine, positioned to catch the best possible view of the ocean beyond the hilltop. It's the sign next to the swing bench which catches my eye next. '*Maple Cottage*' is written in white on a grey-coloured slate plaque which occupies a space on the wall adjacent to the front door, and two baskets hang evenly on either side with white and pink flowers assembled creatively in both. My lips curl up into a smile, it's all so perfectly maintained and beautiful. It's all so Aunt Maggie.

I've barely taken two steps and Guy's only just re-latched the gate when the oak door swings open. A bright pink dressing gown is the first to catch my fatigued attention, it's being wrapped tightly around a petite body as similarly bright pink fluffy slippers shuffle along the floor, down the porch step and across the cobblestone path. Despite it being over thirteen years since I last saw her in person, Aunt Maggie shows little difference in the way of looks as to how my vague memory recalls – with the exception of a haircut and a couple more wrinkles here and there. Her silver hair is short, choppy and a little messy. It used to hang below her shoulders, now it doesn't even reach past her ears in the boy-cut she has, but it suits her; a kind, pretty face. Just like Mum.

As she approaches, her thin lips stretch into a smile which reaches her sparkling grey eyes. 'Oh, Pidge, you're here!'

I beam at the familiar nickname carrying through the air.

'And this must be Buddy.' She pauses in front of us, placing her hands on her knees and hunching over. Buddy wags his tail, nestling into her leg as she strokes his head. She was the first person I told when we had him. That was seven years ago. All she's seen up till now, are photos.

Aunt Maggie makes a move to hug me, but stops suddenly, surprising me as she takes hold of my arms instead. Her eyes rake my entire body, taking in my appearance – my dishevelled appearance. 'My goodness, you're so tall,' she says, seemingly staggered that my body has done something so conventional as grow. 'Look at these long locks,' she continues, twirling my blonde hair around her fingers – which is now loose as it scruffily falls down past my shoulders. 'But you do look like you've been in the wars, dear,' she remarks, appearing rather concerned as I flash her a sleepy smile.

With a bare and pale face, complimented with exceedingly tired eyes and flat hair, I probably look like death warmed up. 'It's good to see you, Aunty,' I greet as she rubs a comforting hand up and down my arm. It's funny, whether it's because I'm tired and not as fully alert as I generally would be, but the air around us doesn't hold the awkwardness I feared. It feels somewhat normal.

Her eyes drift over my shoulder.

'Oh, I didn't realise we had another guest.' She hugs her dressing gown closer to her body in a bid to cover up. She's studying Guy. Very closely. My eyes flicker between them as she continues to stare as if taking everything about him in, Guy not uttering a word.

'Dad didn't mention it?' I ask, now beginning to wonder exactly how much she knows about what's happened.

She breaks her stare and turns to me. 'No, but after all these years, I've come to learn your father isn't one for great communication, if any at all.'

I glance to the floor. I know all about that. If there's one thing I know about Dad it's that his words are very much focused in and around his workspace, which means whatever spare lexicon he can gather is left for family – and that's a sparse range.

'Will you be staying also?' Aunt Maggie asks. 'I'm afraid I don't have another room to offer, but there is a sofa, it's relatively comfortable... *relatively*, being the operative word. There is a TV, and I can offer a nice brew?'

He chuckles. Guy chuckles. The iceman, whose face I haven't seen shift from a straight line in the several hours I've been with him, is raising a smile. I must be dreaming. That's what it is. I'm overly tired, groggy and hallucinating.

'Thank you, that's very kind, but there's really no need. I'll be staying at the hotel down the road,' he replies formally.

I can't tell if the picture on Aunt Maggie's face is depicting relief or disappointment, but judging by the way she's been eyeing him, I'd say it was more so the latter. 'Oh... really? I don't mind it's no both–'

'I'm perfectly fine, honestly. I couldn't possibly intrude,' he cuts in and this time there's no denying the small smile. 'I'm only here to make sure Emily is okay.'

He's met with a blank stare from Aunt Maggie. 'Her father worries,' he affirms.

'Of course he does.' The sarcasm radiates off her and I feed off it, because I of all people know those words are anything but the truth.

When Mum died, I was four years old, and that's when it all began. His distancing. I don't know why. You'd think when a family goes through something as horrific as that, you would be brought closer together. Not in our case. It had been slight at the start; I'd noticed the signs. First, it was not tucking me in at night like he used to, then it was sending someone else to pick me up from school – a nanny, who I spent more time with than him – and when I reached my teens, I was lucky if I saw him more than twice a week. I lived in that house with him, but to me he was a stranger, coming in and going out. That's why I took it upon myself to find a part time job whilst I was still at school, not only did it give me an excuse to spend as much time away from home as possible, but it also gave me a starting chance towards my independence. I refused to accept money from that man. I was, and still am, determined to make my own way in this life, to be the best person I can, to make Mum proud and to show Dad that no amount of power and fake concern can buy back the time he lost for us.

'Right. Come on in, Emily, you must be exhausted,' Aunt Maggie says as she begins back down the path, her fluffy slippers scraping along the floor with every shuffle. Buddy follows when she collects his lead, surprisingly quickly for a dog with a limp, but it probably has something to do with the biscuit Aunty is not so discreetly pulling out from the pocket of her dressing gown.

I turn to Guy, solemn. He's only here because of me and although I know this isn't my fault, I can't help but feel terrible that he's stuck here alone. He probably begrudges us all.

He reaches into the breast pocket of his blazer. 'Take this.' The piece of paper is small with the edges teared, on it a scribbled number. 'Put it in your phone and if you need anything give me a text or a call. I won't be going anywhere, I'll be staying with you until we hear anything more from your father, so you don't need to worry about being on your own.'

'Thank you,' I reply on an appreciative smile, whether it meets my eyes I'm not entirely sure, but I try my best to appear as grateful as I can. It seems to work as his lips curl upwards. The fact he's here is providing me with a lot of comfort, nevertheless, that doesn't discourage my guilt. He nods curtly, turning on his heel before pausing and glancing over his shoulder.

'Oh, and the content of your bag,' he says, his eyes motioning to my backpack as mine widen, 'keep it hidden and safe.' Those are his only words before he's returning to the car. I'm both shocked and relieved. No wonder he told me to leave my bag in the car outside Lambert Law. He knew I kept the gun. Relief is quick to overshadow the shock, because that man is still out there, and even though I have no idea how to use it, it's giving me a little peace of mind. And I think Guy knows that.

I teeter around on the spot as my eyes wander over the little cottage and I draw in a deep breath. This is all extremely strange, but there's no use trying to get my head around it now because it's currently pounding and I'm struggling to keep my eyes open. I need uninterrupted sleep.

Idling into the unfamiliar home, I step into a narrow corridor. The first thing I notice is how immaculate it is. Cream walls adorned with several painted canvasses and oak flooring make up the hall, and the very end reveals part of a kitchen. There is a slightly agape door to my left which I presume leads to the living room, whilst Aunt Maggie leans against a banister attached to a staircase beside me.

'Someone left your case outside the door, so I put it in your room.' She's very happy for someone who has been woken up so early. I'm far from surprised though, because she's always been a bubbly person; never one to let her emotions show, especially on our brief phone calls. Never about her, always how I'm doing. 'I've laid a few blankets out for Buddy in the kitchen, your dad didn't give me much notice so I'm not really prepared, but we can go and pick out a dog bed for him later on today.'

'Thank you. I'm sorry for getting you up so early and for all this trouble,' I say, apologising on Dad's behalf, knowing it wouldn't have even crossed his mind to do so.

'Oh, nonsense! It's no trouble at all, I'm just glad I get to see my beautiful niece.' She sighs contentedly, a beaming smile never falling from her face as she studies mine. 'It's so good to see you, Em.' She jerks me into a giant hug, which, being in desperate need of one, I happily return as I breathe in her soothing lavender scent. Holding me tight, she gives a final squeeze before pulling away and placing her hands on my rosy cheeks. 'I have missed you,' she whispers.

'I've missed you too.'

I have missed her. A lot. I know I should have made more of an effort to talk to her and even see her over the years, because I'm standing here now, peering into her glassy eyes, feeling incredibly guilty for not doing so.

We stay like this for a few more seconds before Buddy totters off into the kitchen and Aunt Maggie starts up the stairs. I follow her to a door at the end of the landing and she pulls out a long silver key, unlocking it with ease.

'Now, I'm sorry it's nothing extravagant, but I like to think of it as cosy.' She idles ahead to switch the bedside lamp on before placing the key onto the table. A single made bed is against the back wall with a double casement window above and grey curtains drawn, blocking out the rising sun. It's unquestionably much smaller – and with the wooden beams overhead, much darker – than the room William and I share back home, but I really like the homey feel. In fact, I much rather prefer it… less empty space where silence can reside.

I take a few steps in, seeing my suitcase lying down

in the middle of the room. Still very conscious of the gun wrapped up inside, I place the bag on my shoulder down carefully next to the case, Guy's words playing on my mind. I need to find a hiding place as soon as I can.

'It's perfect.' I smile sincerely as I take in the room. I'm trying my best to appear upbeat and grateful, but it's not working as I'd hoped, and I know she can sense it because she's watching me diligently.

'Good,' she replies with relief in her tone, yet still her eyes carry an unwavering concern which I'm trying not to meet. 'Well, I'll leave you be.' She rubs my arm as she shuffles past and towards the door, gripping its handle. 'Get some sleep, Pidge. You look like you need it.' Her eyes flash me a warning look; like a grandmother scorning her grandchild for not eating. I know she doesn't mean it maliciously, but I can't help the grimace which appears on my face before the door clicks shut. I'm very aware of how awful I must appear, though hearing it from someone else is undeniably a kick in the teeth.

Unpacking doesn't even cross my mind. Flicking my shoes straight off, I follow Aunty's orders and jump straight into bed. A plus which has come out of all this, I'm already dressed for sleep. The duvet is pulled up to my chin as I stare at the ceiling and let out a deep sigh, mentally praying no unwanted visions plague my dreams.

A futile wish, I feel.

# *SIX*

It feels like minutes have passed when my eyes blink open and focus on the dark wooden beamed ceiling. The cawing and pitter patter of gulls on the roof echoes around the near empty room. I shift under my sheets, scanning the foreign setting, before eventually remembering where I am and drawing in a lungful of air. It wasn't a dream.

Rubbing my hands over my face, I push my head up and rest on my forearms as I try to blink the sleepiness away. It takes me mere seconds to come to the conclusion I am in no mood and collapse back into the springy mattress on a low groan. I woke a few times from my restless sleep; my heart had thumped in my chest and sweat had dampened my skin. I feel like his cold evil face is now forever etched in my brain, there to haunt every dream, turning them into bleak unconscious worlds.

Not ready to face the day yet, I will my body to roll over, but I'm instantly reminded that this is not my normal king-sized bed. It's too late to stop myself and before I have the chance to grab hold of anything, I drop onto the floor, landing with a colossal thud.

'*Ugh!*' My face screws up and I grit my teeth, kneading the dull ache in my arm. This is not a good start.

Once the worst of the pain is worked away, my bearings are gathered, and I crawl around the bed.

Reaching my backpack, I unzip and blindly fiddle around for my phone before turning it on. My fingers drum the floor impatiently as the lock screen finally glows, but my hope sinks.

No message from William.

I tell myself not to be disappointed, because he's more than likely busy at work. He'll text me later like he said. In a bid to distract my mind, I pull Guy's number from the pocket of William's hoodie and save it to my phone.

The bright light has allowed my eyes to adjust, so I take in the time – *1.20* – and snatch the charger from the side pocket, searching the compact room for a socket. I plug it in below the bedside table and scoop up my backpack, setting it on the bed.

My mind works hard to prepare my senses for what I'm about to see as I carefully pull out my black hoodie. The weight is held in my hands for a moment as I will myself to shake the image of that psychotic face away, but it's no use. I figure he's not going to disappear anytime soon, especially with his weapon now in my grasp.

I unravel the material steadily, noticing how my palms are shimmering with sweat as I swallow the lump in my throat, my vision fixated on the gun. Last night could have ended so differently because of this deadly device. It almost doesn't seem real. Like the whole event was a dream. A nightmare.

The sight of it becomes too unnerving so I wrap it up and cautiously put it back in the bag – zipping it closed.

My eyes dart around the room, the space is mostly empty apart from a small wardrobe against the wall and there's a risk Aunt Maggie might go in there, so I settle on hiding it under the bed instead, praying it's the safest option.

Forcing myself to forget about it, I decide a freshen up might be the ticket to easing my tense body and mind, so make my way towards the door. It protests under my touch, creaking open and allowing me a peep through the small gap. The door next to mine is closed, as is the door straight ahead, however something catches my eye. I squint, seeing a yellow post-it note stuck to the whitewash door ahead. Curiosity carries me across the landing.

> *I've placed some fresh towels and bubble bath*
> *on the washing basket.*
> *Have a soak and relax.*
> *P.S. The hot tap's a little stiff.*
> *M x*

My heart warms. The smile on my face genuine and unthinking. Pushing the door ajar, I see just what she described: a wicker washing basket with two fresh white towels folded on the lid, and an unopened bottle of bubble bath lying on top. I don't wait a second longer.

Aunt Maggie was in no way joking. I had to use both hands with a firm footing to get the tap to budge. But it was worth it; this feels like heaven. I feel like I'm cleansing away all the stress the past fifteen hours has thrown at me.

It's easy to see that Aunt Maggie must love it here, because as I relax further into the tub and swirl the mounds of bubbles around my hands, I start to take in the highly decorated, coastal themed bathroom. The walls are light blue and the cabinets white; every accessory is colour schemed to perfection. Opposite the bath, a long marble sink top displays a couple of pretty features: a shell jar occupies one corner whilst a candle in a rustic lantern is placed in the other. A large mirror is above and different sized faux starfish rest on top of its frame. My eyes roam over the three mini shelves beside it; miniature scrolls concealed in light blue glass bottles and white coloured coral adorn each one. The whole room is distinct and different, there's a relaxing yet quirky feel to it and I'm totally in love. I don't really remember Aunt Maggie's old house with Uncle Jerry, but I just know it was as finely decorated and well-kept as Maple Cottage.

The serenity of the room is allowing me to reflect though, and right now that's not what I want to be doing. I make different shapes with the floating bubbles as my mind races. I was so angry at Dad for sending me away. I still am. It's not that I didn't want to see Aunty, of course I did. I do. It's the principle of why I'm here. I don't see Dad for months, then suddenly there's a strange man breaking into my boyfriend's house trying to kill me because of something *he's* done. And instead of an explanation, I'm banished to another part of the country. I'm confused, I'm annoyed, and I'm filled with hate. All because of him.

Despite everything, I'm trying desperately to claw at the positives, because if I don't there's a possibility I might implode. Maybe me staying here will be a good thing. I get to spend some time with Maggie and enjoy a different scenery; I know Buddy will appreciate the beach – and the ice creams. I may not have the faintest idea of the situation back in London with Dad and William, but I'm in Cornwall. I'm with my aunt and my dog. I'm going to make the most of it. Screw Dad and his shitty secrets. Like William said, think of it as a holiday.

After talking myself into parting from the warm tub, I check the coast is clear before dashing across the landing in my towel and shutting the bedroom door. Diving straight for my suitcase, I unfasten, dreading what state I'll find my clothes in. Dad mentioned William had some input, so I'm hoping he guided them well.

My concerns are put at ease when I toss open the lid and see a neatly folded case. Not everything I would have chosen is in here, but what I have is decent and the worry of not having enough underwear is washed away. Even though the thought of someone rummaging through my drawers still sickens me, I dismiss it, happy with the contents.

Throwing on my denim jeans and a grey T-shirt, I tie my hair into a messy bun and decide against hanging my clothes in the wardrobe, opting to live out of my case. Dad said I would be here a month, but plans change, and if they catch that man, I might be out of here sooner than expected. That's what I'm willing for. After all, university packing isn't going to sort itself out.

I grasp the towel from the floor and fold it neatly, reaching halfway across the landing as the clattering of pots and pans bustles up the staircase. A high-pitched brassy whistling follows, and I imagine Aunt Maggie tinkering around in the kitchen with a skip in her step. The fear of the awkwardness between us is still present, yet not as heightened as it was on the drive down here, and it's much more to do with me rather than her. Thirteen years of brief phone calls and no face-to-face contact is a long time. She would never admit it to me, but I hope she doesn't hate me for not making more of an effort. I don't think the guilt I'm currently feeling will ever disappear.

Draping the towel over the bath to dry, I slowly make my way down the stairs; the whistling has stopped with the front door wide open.

My eyes widen at the sight as I surreptitiously peer around the corner. Aunt Maggie is holding a tray with a mug resting on top, and if I'm not mistaken, a stack of Digestives piled high. Her fluffy pink slippers are on her feet and one leg is up in the air as she leans deep inside the passenger window of the Benz, before handing over the mug and biscuits to Guy sat inside.

I smile, entertained as I watch her struggle to push herself out. She eventually succeeds, shaking her head as if swishing her hair around – if it were long enough to swish – whilst strutting back up the path, empty tray in hand. Taking a seat on the stairs, I wait for my not-so-subtle aunt to appear. Oblivious to my presence, she closes the door on a contented sigh.

'What were you doing?' I chorus. My eyebrows raise, an accusing look spreading across my face.

She jumps on a gasp, facing me as her hand flies to her chest. 'Oh, Emily!' She whacks my leg with the tray. 'Don't do that! You scared me to death.' Her lips eventually curl into a smile. I shoot her a knowing glance, smirking. 'Stop it,' she warns, very much aware of exactly what my face is implying. 'I only made the man a cup of tea.'

'Wearing that?' I nod to her low-cut top revealing a noticeable cleavage. I'm not someone who claims to be an expert in the area of flirtatious behaviour, but I know a seducing outfit when I see one. Yanking up the front, she brushes me off and throws her thumb towards the door.

'I really don't know why he's sat in that car, he's more than welcome to come in.' She ponders in thought. 'Unless I've scared him away.'

I laugh, but my thoughts are now drifting to the cynical part of my brain. She's acting as though this is normal, as though nothing's wrong. I don't know how much she's aware of and I don't know how far to push it, but surely she must be wondering what exactly happened. I'm also very curious to know what story Dad actually fed her. My face falls, and Aunt Maggie notices.

'What's on your mind, Pidge?'

I take a breath as my gaze meets her reassuring one. I know Dad told her not to ask questions, but he said nothing about her answering them. 'What has Dad told you?'

She seems to freeze momentarily, before smiling sadly. 'I wasn't going to dwell on it because it makes my blood boil, but seeing as you asked.' She pauses, spinning the circular tray slowly in her hands. 'Your father told me there was a break-in whilst you were home alone.' She shakes her head and I notice that her fingers clenching the tray tighten. 'These yobs,' she tuts, 'I'm telling you, this day and age no one is safe. Not even in our own homes.'

As suspected, he's fed her a lie. She's as clueless as me and I'm no closer to finding out what's going on. 'You think it was a yob?'

'Who else is it going to be? Scum of the earth, that's what they are. I hope the police find whoever it was and put them where they belong. No one is getting away with hurting my niece.' Her tone is stern, her forehead creasing as her glare hardens with every threatening word.

'He didn't say anything else?' I push, not expecting him to have given away any information, but if there's a chance then I have to try.

'I tend not to query your father. I've learnt over the years that it typically ends with a side stepping of the truth and more questions. Trust me, asking him anything is more trouble than it's worth.' After a beat of silence, her face softens. 'As long as you're okay, that's all I care about.'

I fiddle with my hands in my lap. I understand her words of reason, because asking Dad what the hell happened last night only led to more questions. I don't think he's given me a straight answer for anything my entire life, and I seriously doubt I'll ever understand what goes on inside that head of his.

The mood has shifted and Aunty is very much aware, because after a clearing of her throat she's straight into doing what Aunt Maggie does best, cheering people up. 'I'll make us something to eat, you must be starving.' And on a turn of her heel, she strolls away into the kitchen.

I feel disheartened. There's a sensation which has settled inside and it's hard to depict, but it's a feeling I know will not be waning anytime soon, and it's heavy; exhausting. On a sigh, I heave myself up and follow down the hall, knowing it's something I'm simply going to have to get used to until this is all over.

She scuttles across the kitchen, moving the stovetop kettle off the hob to refill. I take a seat at the little wooden table in the middle of the room.

Just like the rest of the cottage, the kitchen is small and orderly. As the gas clicks into flames, I spot the harbour style mural painted on the tiles behind. Hanging around the room, I notice an anchor, a couple of ceramic sailboats, as well as a sign reading *Rockstone* above the door. I smile, embracing her love of the local nautical culture.

'Did you sleep okay?' she asks as she searches the fridge and pulls out a few bits and bobs to make a sandwich. Her perkiness has returned with no sign of our brief solemn conversation ever happening. It doesn't matter whether her aim is to take my mind off it or she's completely oblivious that her current character is lightening the mood, because either way it's working, and I'm happy that it is.

'Really well actually,' I lie. There's no way I can tell her the truth. What's the point in worrying her? I only hope she can't read my face, because I've always been a terrible fibber and it's difficult to ignore the shudder creeping down my spine as the guilt of doing what I hate the most taunts me. My elbow rests on the table with my chin in my palm as I gaze out of the sash window above the sink, where my eyes avoid contact and find interest in three plant pots resting in a row on its ledge.

'I'm glad,' she replies, scampering around the room, opening drawers and cupboards seemingly unfazed. I feel a nudge on my leg before Buddy's furry head appears from under the table and he knocks my hand, encouraging me to stroke him. 'I popped out this morning whilst you were sleeping and bought Buddy a dog bed and some treats. Oh! And a snazzy new lead. I hope you don't mind.' The kettle whistles as it boils and she plonks two teabags in mugs. 'Sugar?' she asks. I tell her one before she pours in the hot water and a dash of milk, placing it in front of me and collapsing into the chair opposite. The big fleecy dog bed in the corner catches my eye, next to it a water and food bowl.

'You didn't have to do that,' I say as Buddy leaves my side to sit closer to Aunt Maggie who is buttering bread. Traitor.

'Don't worry, dear, I wanted to.' Assembling the salad and dressing on top of the ham, she slices the sandwich into two big triangles and hands it to me on a speckled plate, which I thank her for. 'You haven't turned into a vegetarian, have you? I should have asked.'

'No, definitely not,' I reply, shovelling in a bite. I tried giving up meat during one of my teenage phases; never again.

'Eat that and then I thought we could go and visit my shop.'

I'm halfway into a bite when I pause and glance up. 'You have a shop?' I mumble through a mouthful of food.

'I have to make a living some way, Emily. It's a little surf shop down by the beach, you must have driven past it on the way,' she says whilst cutting the crusts off her own sandwich and digging in.

'Oh, I fell asleep.' I can't eat my food quick enough. I didn't realise how hungry I was.

'I'll introduce you to the girls, it will be nice for you to meet some people your own age around here.'

'You're all the company I need, Aunty.' I swallow down my food on a giggle. 'Mind you, if I'm going to be competing with Guy, maybe I should find some other people to talk to.'

I'm met with a deadpan expression.

'So that's his name. Mystery man has a name.' Her eyebrow quirks in thought. 'Interesting.'

I study her. Aunt Maggie has really taken a liking to this man. She only met him briefly this morning and she's already besotted, which in my eyes, might not be the best thing to be. 'I wouldn't become too emotionally attached. I don't think he's the settling down in a nice cottage type.'

'Come on now, I only made the man tea.' She winks, repeating her statement from earlier. 'Now, are you going to make me ask?' Her accusing eyes are locked onto me as she takes a bite of her sandwich.

'Ask what?' I question innocently, but I already have a feeling I know the answer just by the look on her expectant face.

'About your man.'

I was correct.

'I hope he's treating you well.'

My eyes instinctively flicker down as I focus my attention on the crusts in my hands. 'Yeah, he's great,' I retort, not so believably.

'Last time we spoke you were planning on moving in.'

My lips purse as I realise the last time was over a year ago. I truly am a terrible person. 'I moved. It's nice. He's nice.'

'You don't sound too convinced, dear.'

She watches me closely, but my eyes are diverted away from her scrutinising greys. Distracting myself, I feed Buddy the crusts in my fingertips. I wish I was better at acting. In fact, no, I wish William would be more present so I wouldn't feel the need to act.

'Oooh!' My attention is drawn up as her fist thumps the table. 'I must get you a spare key cut.'

'Don't you have a spare?' I ask, glad of the topic change.

'I did, but I gave it to someone else. It's no bother, I can do it tomorrow seeing as you'll be here for the foreseeable future.'

I offer her a small smile, disguising the heavy, indescribable sensation in my gut which I've just been reminded of.

We finish our food and slurp down the tea. We talk a little and giggle a lot. It feels good to be able to do this with her, after all these years. Actually, it feels good to be doing this full stop. Christ knows, it's a rarity back home.

Dusting off her hands, she rises from her seat. 'Right, go and get your shoes on! We'll leave in a couple of minutes.'

My chair scrapes along the floor as I pass her my plate and stand. I make towards the kitchen door, though before I leave, I can't help but grin as I catch Aunt Maggie feeding Buddy her cut-offs by the sink.

I think he may have found his new best friend.

# SEVEN

The beach on my left grows clearer as we stroll down the lane and the trees disperse. Marshlyn Bay is – according to my biased Aunty – one of the best beaches in Cornwall, so I'm eager to see it in its entirety.

The sun is high in the sky, beating down on the masses of holidaymakers occupying their spots on the sand. A slight breeze is making for a pleasant atmosphere – not unbearably hot and perfect for tanning.

'It's certainly busy today,' Aunt Maggie expresses as we wander over a small humped bridge. She gestures towards the hundreds of cars parked on the hill in the distance, all of which are giving off a shimmering heat haze, but my attention is soon drifting when we're emerged in a sea of people lined up to buy ice cream. I spot a little shop on the corner. Hanging up outside are a selection of postcards, beside them, different sized wetsuits and two big crates each filled with beach balls and toys. 'Maggie's Surf Shack' reads on a pinned surfboard above the entrance.

'Here we are.' She moseys over to the doors as I come to a stop, bubbling with anticipation. 'Come and see your aunt's pride and joy!'

The smell of lavender strikes me before anything else as I find my vision adjusting itself from the brightness of outside. Managing to blink away the blurry specks, I turn 360 degrees, admiring the spacious interior which looks like it shouldn't belong inside the outer structure.

'Sooo, what do you think?' Aunt Maggie asks, watching me study the space.

There are two rooms, and we're stood in the bigger room. Rows of shelves with T-shirts, shorts, flip-flops and other varieties of beach style clothing fill most of it, the rest is made up with bodyboards, buckets and spades and random seaside objects. The second room is much smaller, and I can see through the opened-up walkway that it's occupied solely by wetsuits and surfboards. Old beams run overhead holding promotional multi-coloured surfboards, which I hope are strapped up securely. The wooden flooring groans underneath our feet as we amble further into the shop.

'It's huge,' I breathe, brushing my hand across a selection of sail jackets hanging on a metal rack.

'Well, why do things by halves?'

I nod in agreement, my eyes circling the room. Just as I expected, the shop is full of seaside visitors. I'm drawn to one particular little girl out the corner of my eye. Begging her dad for a bat and ball set, he eventually gives in and bends down to pick her up before taking the set from the shelf. He whispers something into her ear which makes her giggle and then hands it to her. She's quick to take hold of it and begins waving it in the air, letting out a tiny squeal of delight. But it's not the girl who makes my heart sink, it's her dad, and the way his eyes are completely focused on her; how his face is beaming with pride at her happiness. To anyone else, it probably wouldn't seem like anything important. They most likely wouldn't even notice the trivial moment occurring between a daughter and her father. But I do. And it's a moment which causes a small pang in my chest. Because it's a moment I can't remember ever having.

'Emily?'

My head tilts to the side. I swallow, shaking away the dejecting thoughts. 'Yeah?' I reply, playing off my brief daydream and providing Aunt Maggie with my full attention. She's resting against a counter where two cashiers stand behind nattering.

'Are you alright?' she asks, concern written on her face.

My hands clasp behind my back as my lips press together. 'Fine,' I reassure, rather unconvincingly.

Aunt Maggie observes me for a moment. I try my best to look believably happy, hoping she doesn't push it further. Her eyes narrow, but thankfully she's quick to move on. 'Come and meet my girls.'

I comply, eager to distract my thoughts, and edge toward the counter.

'Girls, this is my niece, Emily.'

I notice straight away that the two girls are in fact very pretty. One is tall, tanned, and blonde, the other slightly shorter with fiery red wavy hair, but both equally as beautiful. So much so they're rather intimidating.

'Oh my God! I thought you looked similar,' the redhead shrieks. She skips around to the front of the counter and wraps her arms around me. My body stiffens, but before I have the chance to return the hug, she's pulling away and studying my face. 'Mmhmm, yep. I was right, you have the same button nose.'

Aunt Maggie chuckles and I smile awkwardly at how the girl, whom I still don't know the name of, is showing no signs of moving out of my bubble.

'I'm Lily, by the way.' She finally takes a step back. 'And this is Vicki.' She jerks her head in the direction of the blonde girl as she returns to her original position behind the counter.

'Hello.' I wave.

'Don't mind her, she's a little crazy,' Vicki says on a grin. 'But we love her.' She nudges Lily's shoulder, rolling her eyes.

'I didn't know you had a niece, Maggie,' Lily muses, elbowing Vicki back teasingly in her ribs.

I'm pulled into Aunty's side, her arm reaching behind to rest on my hip. She places her free hand on my arm and grips it, giving it a gentle squeeze – an affectionate squeeze.

'My little secret has come to visit me.'

I pretend like this action doesn't affect me, because

it does. Her face is radiating genuine joy. Her eyes are sparkling. She looks so content and happy, and her reluctance to loosen the grip she has on my arm and waist tells me why. But this gesture is only adding to the guilt I'm already feeling for not coming to see her before now, because although this is technically a *visit*, it isn't one, I'm ashamed to say, of my own choosing.

'I wanted Emily to meet people her own age. Although I am incredibly fun to be around, I don't think you'd appreciate being stuck in that cottage when the local ladies gardening club come round for our weekly social.'

'You're in a gardening club?' I ask. No wonder her garden is so well maintained.

I hear a reply, but Aunt Maggie's lips aren't moving. '*Ugh!* Don't get her started. My mum's a part of it and all she talks about is how quickly her begonias are growing,' Vicki groans. 'Trust me, I know the pain. If I hear another conversation about plants, I might end it all.' She leans forward on the counter. 'Don't worry, Emily, you'll be safe with us. We have strict no boring agricultural talk rules,' she declares, and I laugh. I like these girls already.

'I'll pretend I didn't hear that,' Aunt Maggie says on unamused puckered lips.

Vicki's sniggering at her own comments and Lily's quite clearly tickled, but Aunty looks far from it with the daggers she's shooting them both.

'Right, I'm off.' Vicki claps her hands together,

recovering from her giggles. 'James is taking me to dinner and I need to doll myself up.' She reaches behind her. 'I'm going to demolish the biggest burger you've ever seen in your whole entire life.' She replicates Lily's actions and bounces around to the front, bag in hand, wrenching me into a hug. 'It was nice to meet you, Emily. I'm sure I'll be seeing you around.'

'Yes, definitely!' I reply, keen to make a good impression for Aunt Maggie, even though I'd much rather be snuggled in my duvet hiding from the world.

Vicki pulls back, her face bright and excitable as she backs away. Seeing her strut to the exit lures my eyes to her long, bronzed legs. I really should soak up some rays and exercise while I'm down here, because these sad, pale excuses for legs simply won't do if I'm going to be around such heaven-like limbs.

The slapping sound of Vicki's disappearing flip-flops is momentarily overshadowed by laughter approaching from outside.

'Looking good, Vick!' a cheery male voice exclaims, but it's out of my eyeline.

'Still trying your luck, Dex?' Vicki's carefree tone replies.

'Someday you'll cave.'

'You keep dreaming, surf boy!'

Her fading voice is surpassed by Aunt Maggie as she leans against the counter. 'Sounds like it's break time,' she announces. I keep my attention to the door, curious about the person in which the voice belongs.

'Small warning, Emily, Dex can be a bit of a handful. Just ignore him, that's what I do,' Lily advises as I turn back to her. A hint of a smile plays on her lips. I'm about to ask her who he is, but my question is answered without needing to be spoken.

'Mags!'

My head spins. The loud guy throws his hands in the air.

'How's my number one lady?'

I'm presuming this is Dex, because he's definitely exuding the confidence which might entertain being, as Lily put it, 'a bit of a handful'. The guy beside him, though, appears the total opposite. A smirk resides on his face, but he's quiet as they stride through the doors.

Both are sporting red shorts with *'lifeguard'* written down the side in yellow. While Dex is wearing a plain white T-shirt, the shaggy-haired male to his left has on a red and blue sail jacket, just like the ones on Aunty's rack across the shop. But the view which is drawing my attention the most is his *extremely* toned torso on full show through the opened jacket.

'Hello, boys,' Aunt Maggie says as Dex strolls up to her, his arms wide open. He warmly embraces her, rubbing her back before pulling away and pointing both hands in Lily's direction.

'Don't think you're being left out, my number two.' He makes a move to hug her over the counter, but Lily is quick to throw her arm out.

'Number two?' She tilts her head, questioning him. 'That makes a change from last week, wasn't I number five or six after those surf school girls?'

'Think you were seven actually, Lil,' the shaggy haired guy laughs. He joins us, standing beside me. He doesn't flash me a look, instead keeping his eyeline focused forward on Dex and Lily. He's tall, *very* tall, and I'm at the perfect angle to watch his tremendously sharp jawline clench and unclench as he talks – I can't seem to tear my eyes away from it.

'Is this some kind of conspiracy?' Dex asks, bumping the man next to me out the way to slot himself closer to Aunt Maggie, but in doing so he creates a domino effect, and the tall guy knocks into me. We catch each other's gaze and for the first time he notices my presence, and I notice his eyes: they're green, or rather, more emerald in colour– a bright emerald green. They widen a little as he realises he's bumped into a complete stranger. Offering a small apologetic smile, he scratches his head awkwardly, turning back to Dex. Unlike Dex's short and spiky hair, Emerald Eyes has floppy, dark and more dishevelled locks. Shorter curls shape the sides, with the top longer, brushed back off his face with sunglasses sitting atop.

'You've always been my number two,' Dex continues, drawing me away from my curiously detailed observations of Emerald Eyes. 'After this sexy senorita.'

He slings his arm around Aunty and puckers his lips, planting several fleeting kisses on her cheek.

'Oh, stop it!' Aunt Maggie slaps him playfully and Dex pulls back on a grin, maintaining hold of her.

I laugh quietly at Aunt Maggie's expression which attracts his notice. 'Who's this lovely lady?' Dex asks, his eyes seeming to enliven.

'This *lovely lady* is my niece, Emily,' she answers for me.

'Ah, I can see it now,' he retorts, brushing his finger up and down the middle of his face. 'The button nose.'

I flash Lily a look. My lips part, baffled as to how they both picked the same feature to compare us. Her eyebrows raise as if to say, 'I told you so.'

'She's come all the way from London,' Aunt Maggie continues.

'Another one from London? Any more and we'll be taken over by the Cockneys,' he laughs, nudging Emerald Eyes' side. 'Dex.' He slithers his arm from Aunt Maggie and holds his hand out for me to shake, which I do.

'Nice to meet you.'

He smiles back with a cheeky glint. I briefly glance up at Emerald Eyes, expecting his own introduction, but instead a slight husky chuckle rises up his throat, his head shaking as his stare lands on his flip-flops.

'You'd flirt with a brick wall if it talked back, Dex.'

My eyes narrow, as do Dex's. Was that an insult? Whether it was intentional or not it's struck a nerve, and I can't control the irrepressible words which spill from my mouth. 'Better to be a harmless flirt than a condescending jerk though, right?'

All eyes land on me. I don't know where that came from, but it's in the air now, and I'm trying my best not to shrink under the taken aback intense green eyes glaring down at me.

'Exactly,' Dex agrees resolutely. 'Oh, I like you, Emily,' he says on a smirk.

'Thanks, got a touch of the old Maggie morality,' I retort, my mood suddenly improving as I see a grin form on Aunt Maggie's lips.

'Excuse me, madam, who are you calling old?'

We all laugh, except one. I keep my focus on Aunty, not wanting to meet the hard stare of the stranger I just indirectly insulted. He thumps the back of his hand against Dex's chest. 'Come on, we've only got five,' he says, seeming to brush away the conversation rather quickly.

He's awfully welcoming.

Striding his long legs over to the fridge behind Aunt Maggie, he picks out two bottles of water.

'Alright, alright.' Dex rolls his eyes.

'What's got your pickle in a twist?' Aunt Maggie asks, her orderly eyebrows furrowing.

That's exactly what I would like to know.

'He's pissed they've got him working on his day off tomorrow,' Dex replies. His hip now leaning on the counter.

'I'm not pissed...' Emerald Eyes tapers off as if thinking about his next words carefully. 'Just had plans, that's all.' He shrugs, sliding Lily some change and shoving one of the bottles into Dex's chest.

'With *O*-livia?' Dex croons.

Lily appears amused at his remark, but quickly wipes it from her face when Dex winks in her direction. I risk a peep up at the sour-faced lifeguard, his eyes are narrowing at Dex's insinuation. Whoever Olivia is, she's struck a chord.

'Come on, Dexter,' he urges. 'See you later.' He strides away, giving a brief half-hearted wave.

Dex huffs. 'Guess break times over. Au revoir, my beauties.' He blows a kiss to the three of us before following Emerald Eyes out the door.

'What was his problem?' I ponder aloud, moving back to my original spot closer to Aunt Maggie.

'Who, Jackson?' Lily probes.

*Jackson.* More like Jackass.

'He's a lovely boy really,' Aunt Maggie answers. An automatic grimace finds my face. I find that hard to believe. 'He's just tired. They've all been working overtime recently, what with it being the busy summer season.'

Lily nods. 'Doesn't seem to tire Dex out, mind. No matter how much I wish it, that boy never runs out of energy.' Her tone makes it sound as if he's a burden to her, but I can't help notice the light blush on her cheeks as her words pass her lips. 'Have you got anything planned for the rest of summer, Emily? Apart from being here, of course,' she says, changing the subject and glancing to me.

'That's a good idea!' Aunt Maggie interjects, straightening suddenly as if someone has poked her from behind.

'What is?' I ask, my momentary relief of her interruption quickly overshadowed by confusion.

'A job. It'll keep you occupied. There's always a place here,' she tries to persuade. Her already big greys widen further, silently encouraging me to agree. Lily and Vicki seem nice, and Aunt Maggie's right, I don't particularly want to be stuck with her gardening social having nothing to do, which will in turn allow my head to wander and remember the events of last night. I guess a job will be a good way of getting to know everyone, and with any luck, it might take my mind off things back home.

*Home.*

I didn't get a chance to tell Albert about not returning to work at the bakery. I didn't even get a chance to say goodbye to Hannah.

'Okay, sure. Why not?' I settle with, trying not to ponder too much on the topic.

'Brilliant!' Aunt Maggie beams. 'You can start tomorrow. Lily can train you.'

'How exciting!' Lily cheers.

My mouth opens but all I manage is a smile as they continue in conversation. Not quite the holiday William had told me to embrace it as being, but maybe this is a good idea. After all, a holiday threatens too many quiet moments for the mind to reflect – this will keep it busy.

# EIGHT

I rustle through the kitchen drawer to pick out Buddy's collar and new lead.

He's sat with pricked ears and big eager brown eyes gawking up at me, his tail swishing across the tiles. It's hard to believe it's been seven years. He is *the* most adorable tri-coloured Border Collie to have graced this earth, so I will never understand how someone was ever capable of leaving him out on the cold streets all alone. I found him as a scruffy pup, left in a small cardboard box on the side of the road on my way home from school. After a lot of begging and a torrent of tears, Dad – whose cogent words stated that he would be *my* responsibility – reluctantly agreed to keep him. Following a day at the vets and finding out he wasn't chipped, we adopted him. He hasn't left my side since. And after what he did for me last night, he's proven just how much of a special and remarkable dog he is.

Clipping the lead to the collar now around his neck, I'm hauled to the front door, with his injury apparently forgotten. I have just about enough time to close the door before I'm being dragged down the path. We make it to the gate in a flash and he waits with quivering limbs as I reach down to work the latch.

'Good evening, Miss Lambert.'

Guy's voice directs me to his relaxed frame leaning against the Benz. He's facing the horizon, observing as if in deep thought. I push the gate open and Buddy tugs us through.

'Evening,' I say, leading my dog around the front of the car before pausing – much to his displeasure.

'Taking a stroll?' he asks, his arms and ankles crossed. His casual jeans are loosely fitted, and combined with his suede jacket, he is cutting a far more laid-back style to his professional black suit.

'Yeah,' I pause, 'you can come if you want. I don't really know what the rules are with this whole situation.' I fumble awkwardly with the lead in my hand.

'No rules, just make sure you're careful and keep your wits about you for anything you think is out the ordinary. I'm only here as a precaution.'

I want to say, 'Everything about this is out the ordinary', but I don't. 'Okay,' I reply instead, hesitating for a moment. 'You don't need to stay out here.' I don't know if I even believe what I'm telling him, nevertheless I go on. 'I know you're doing it to ease my nerves, but honestly, I'm fine.' Of course, it makes me feel better knowing he's out here, but how can I let him do that? It's not very fair. 'You should go for a walk or get some food… enjoy yourself.' I swallow, a part of me afraid he might agree.

'Father's orders, Miss Lambert,' he asserts.

I keep up my pretence. 'I won't tell if you don't.'

He shuffles, his head turning in my direction for the first time. 'I couldn't. Besides, Ms Taylor brought me out a three-course meal earlier, so I think I'm good for the week.' His smile reaches his eyes. 'I won't stay much longer,' he affirms, his face snapping back to its set, neutral appearance. 'I personally feel better in the knowledge that you know I'm right outside.'

My teeth gnaw on my bottom lip, not really knowing what to reply. I can't pretend I'm not a little relieved, but I still feel awful. 'Thank you, Guy, but really, I couldn't be more okay.' I try to make my smile seem as sincere as possible, hoping my eyes aren't giving me away. I spin, beginning the descent down the hill with Buddy tugging on the lead.

'I've been in this business a long time, Miss Lambert.'

I freeze.

'I can tell when someone isn't being entirely truthful.'

I reluctantly peer over my shoulder. He's facing me directly now, his arm resting on top of the Benz.

'I'm paid to make you feel as safe and relaxed as possible, so that's what I intend to do. And if you want me to stay outside overnight, I will, but you have my number if you need anything at all.' I must still have an unsure look on my face because he's quickly reassuring me again. 'Don't worry about me, miss.'

After a few seconds of debating whether I should comment again, I settle on a curt nod and allow myself to be dragged down the hill – not uttering another word and feeling the guilt swirl around my stomach.

Alexandra Bradley

We quickly reach the bottom of the lane and instead of walking all the way past the shop to get to the main walkway, I find a small hidden entrance carved out between the bridge and a thorn bush. I wouldn't have even noticed it if Buddy hadn't stopped to cock his leg. Jumping down a large step onto the soft sand, I notice the trees create an archway above us as we follow a short trail leading out onto the open beach. It's low tide, proving Aunt Maggie's opinion of Marshlyn Bay being the best beach around. It's massive, and absolutely beautiful.

I unhook Buddy's lead and let him bound off. He sniffs the cliff banks and climbs over the rocks with his big bushy tail wagging happily in the air. The sun is beginning to set as the night draws in, leaving a cooling breeze. A shiver rushes over my body, so I hug my jacket closer and glance out at the glow the colourful sky leaves on the calm ripples of the ocean.

After trudging along the uneven surface, I take a perch on the smoothest rock I can find, and watch Buddy splash through a rock pool in the distance. Whilst inwardly praising myself for remembering to take the wrap off his leg beforehand, I breathe in as much sea air as my lungs can hold and close my eyes, doing nothing but listening to the serene, soft sounds of the waves breaking on the shore. When they open, I see the beach is not completely deserted, but much quieter than earlier with a few groups packing away their tents and windbreakers with others cooking on disposable barbeques. There are still several cars in the overspill on the green hill, but it's getting emptier and emptier as the minutes pass.

I don't think I've been this at peace and composed since, well, ever. It's nice. It makes me want to shut my mind off entirely. I don't want to think about Dad and all the shit he's put me through. I don't want to think about the fact William hasn't called or text to ask if I'm okay. I don't want to think about how I'm missing Mum more than ever. I just want to be present. To soak up the sea air and watch my dog chase the seagulls up and down the sand, because I know as soon as I leave, those thoughts will come racing to the forefront of my mind again, like Usain Bolt sprinting for gold.

Buddy would stay out here all night, and if I had a tent and a sleeping bag, I would too. But I'm getting chillier by the second, and Aunt Maggie will most likely call a search party if I don't get back before dark. So, I unwillingly haul myself off the rock and call for Buddy to follow. I throw him a treat as he hurtles up to my side, clamping his mouth around the flying dog biscuit.

We reach the sheltered archway and I pull the lead from my jacket pocket. 'Sit,' I instruct, pointing to a spot on the ground close to my feet. Buddy complies, his tongue flopping out the side of his mouth as he pants heavily. Usually, he's well behaved and will do whatever I tell him, but irritatingly, when treats become noticeably apparent in the picture, the advantage of having complete control goes right out the window.

As I bend down, the Milk-Bone treats rattle around the box in my pocket. I wince as Buddy's ears prick instantly. I persevere, praying he'll sit still long enough for me to unearth the loop on his collar under the mass of fur. I fail. He's soon up on his feet, sniffing frantically around my groin. 'Buddy, stop. You can have one in a minute!' I'm patting his neck desperately now. 'Buddy, please,' I beg when his paws meet my chest, striking me off balance. I feel cold metal under my fingertips. *Aha!* I attempt to part the knotted fur from around the clip whilst getting knocked around. Almost there. Nearly got it. And… '*Oof!*'

My feet stumble backward.

'Ooh, shit!' I groan, helplessly watching the lead plummet to the sand and my dog sprint away after a seagull. 'Buddy!' I yell, swiping the sandy lead from the ground and darting after him. Thank God it's not a busy main road! 'Buddy! Come back!' I cry in vain. My feet hit the tarmac, and I race over the bridge as he races around the corner next to Maggie's Surf Shack, disappearing from sight.

As I approach, I notice a small track leading past the shack. I peer up it, Buddy and the gull nowhere to be seen. Shifting my feet again, I sprint toward the opening, still crying out his name even though all of my attempts thus far have been futile. Eventually, I make it to an open space with parked cars and apartment buildings in a square-like arrangement.

I slow, narrowing my eyes and scanning the entire carpark which is packed out with every car imaginable. Laughter, followed by a startled scream, pulls me forward. Old wooden tables and benches are positioned outside a pub facing the carpark. Children sitting on top of the wall play on their Tablets, whilst their parents drink beer, large glasses of wine, and smoke cigarettes. It happens at once. Every pair of eyes shift to my dog bounding around the tables with the seagull now perched on the roof of the pub. It throws its head back, producing a squawking cackle as if taunting Buddy who is voicing his frustration back at it.

Heat rushes to my cheeks as I start toward him. The seagull takes off again and my pace increases, ready to sprint after my four-legged pest, but this time, before Buddy has the chance to bound away, he's grabbed by his collar.

Instant relief strikes me, my muscles relaxing in knowing that my dog is safe and they haven't got to exert themselves any longer. 'Thank you so much,' I breathe, gratitude clear in my tone as my focus trains on Buddy who scratches to get to me, as if nothing has even happened. My fingers clip the lead onto his collar, with ease this time, as he nestles his head into my leg, and I ruffle his fur.

'Don't mention it.'

I tense. My eyes reluctantly lift to meet his sparkling emeralds. *Oh great.* Jackson's sporting a plaid flannel shirt with the sleeves rolled up to his elbows and black jeans, his sunglasses still sit in his rugged wavy hair. I know he recognises me, because he doesn't even try to hide the amused expression on his face.

'Some bark on him,' he says, motioning to Buddy who is flicking his gaze all around, no doubt in search of that damn gull.

I grit my teeth, his conceited appearance only irking me. 'He's a great guard dog. You ought to see his bite,' I taunt, knowing the full truth of that statement.

He chuckles, his casual stare fixed on me. 'I don't have to if it's anything like his owner's. Ruthless, I should imagine.'

My eyes narrow, but before I can wrack my brain for a comeback, he's being called over to a table. He flashes me a wink before idling over to a group of people. The irritation from his wry attitude is all I need to give a tug on the lead and march away.

Smug bastard.

I risk a turn of my head as I stride across the car park. Emerald Eyes has taken a seat on top of a table; his feet perched on the bench. A hand meets his arm which directs my line of vision to a bobbed raven-haired girl who strokes it up and down tentatively, before stopping on his bicep. His facial expression doesn't match her toothy grin though, whilst she's clearly not worried about expressing all the feelings she has towards him at this precise moment, he's not giving anything away, his face nonchalant. His mouth opens, but he's too far away to make out the words, nevertheless, it was clearly so *very* funny, because the girl throws her head back in hysterics, using his bicep to inch herself closer to him.

My head snaps forward, wanting to get back to the cottage. It's safe to say my planned relaxing evening has once again taken a turn for the worse. This is becoming far too regular for my liking. Note to self: must train Buddy on treat and seagull etiquette. We can't be having a repeat of this every time we go for a walk.

I hurry over the bridge, wanting to create as much distance from that pub and me as possible, but my strides inevitably slow when I begin the climb. My fitness levels are a major concern. If a fifty-something-year-old can do this without breaking a sweat, then an eighteen-year-old should be able to no problem. It's really quite embarrassing.

I'm about to pause for a moment to take my jacket off when I feel a buzzing on my left buttock. I'm a little surprised; firstly, at the fact I'm able to get a signal so close to the beach, and secondly, at the name illuminating my phone screen.

'William?'

'Hey,' his raspy voice answers.

I'm anticipating what this conversation will bring. He'll either reveal Dad has, by some miracle, fixed everything, and I can go home. Or he tells me nothing more, and I have to continue living in a world of constant worry and confusion, with the strain on our already crumbling relationship only growing stronger. But since the former is very much unlikely, and with the atmosphere I can sense through the phone, I'm already prepared for the latter.

'How are things going? Are you settled in yet?' he asks.

I take a breath, trying to keep my flustered state – which could and probably would cause an outburst – at bay. 'It's only been a day and I've been asleep for most of it, so I'd say not completely, but there are worse places to be.'

'That's good.' He sounds crackly, but with only one bar, I'm amazed I can hear him at all. A short gasp travels the line, as if he's about to say something else, but no words enter my ear.

'You're talkative.'

'Sorry,' he replies meekly. 'It's been a busy day at work, and what with the late night last night.'

My eyes narrow. 'Well, I apologise for the inconvenience.'

'I didn't mean it like that,' he sighs.

I can picture him running his hand over his perfectly structured face like he always does when he's stressed. We're both stressed and I'm channelling my frustration in his direction, which isn't fair. I know he feels guilty about leaving me on my own, it would be hard for anyone to deny if they had seen what state he was in in Dad's office last night.

'I know. I'm sorry,' I say regretfully, knowing we're both tired. I don't want to argue. 'So, what's happening back home? Has Dad said anything more?' I scrunch my face up, anxiously awaiting the reply which will determine whether the weight on my chest will be lifted.

A pause. 'Not really... I've had my own things to be getting on with, so I haven't spoken to him today.'

Wow. His girlfriend is being threatened and he's acting like he couldn't give a rat's arse. I wasn't expecting him to have any answers, but a little care in his tone I wouldn't have thought would be too much to ask. 'Hmm.'

'Are you in a mood with me for some reason?'

It's becoming progressively easier to hear him as I climb, but I'm quickly wishing our connection would cut off altogether.

'No. Not at all.'

'Sounds like you are.'

'I'm not! I just think if it was the other way around, I'd be doing as much as I could to help.' Which is the truth. I would. I can't understand how someone who appeared so concerned last night suddenly doesn't seem bothered.

'Emily, there's only so much I can do. I'm not Francis, I'm not the police, I can't call the shots.'

'But can't you see it from my point of view? I'm all the way down here not knowing what the hell is happening, and if I'm being honest, I'm scared. I'm scared to bloody death. And my boyfriend isn't doing anything to help, or even seem to remotely care.' I let the words spew from my mouth rather loudly, not caring if people in the nearby cottages can hear me. I just need *him* to hear me.

'Babe, I do. I do care. And if I could come down and be with you then I would. It's just–'

'You're really busy. I know.'

'Don't be like this.'

'I'm not being like anything.'

'I'll be in the office tomorrow, Em. I'll talk to your dad and let you know if there's been any developments.'

'Thank you.' That's all I wanted to hear.

'I know it's hard, but he's doing everything he can.'

I roll my eyes even though he can't see me.

'Listen,' he says on a sigh, 'I need to talk to you about something.' His pause is brief but the tension it brings is palpable. 'It's a little… delicate.'

'Is it to do with the break-in?' I ask rashly, my ears suddenly pricking.

'Not exactly,' he answers faintly, it's hard to tell if it's because of the poor signal or because he's speaking gingerly – I convince myself it's a combination both.

I don't hold in my groan. What could possibly be the matter now? I think back to yesterday when I wanted to talk to him about the move to university, and how he couldn't bear to be apart from his phone for one minute. He's my boyfriend, and I know he looks after me, but sometimes I think he cares more about his job than anything else. Me included.

Well, whatever it is, I don't want to hear it. At least, not tonight.

'Can't it wait?' I ask, simply wanting to get back to Maple Cottage and throw on my pyjamas.

'Not really.'

As much as I'm intrigued, I'm still exhausted from last night and I have to be up early in the morning. I don't want anything else to have to think or worry about – especially since I already know I'll be kept up by nightmares. So, I do something which could be seen as a little immature, but completely justified in my mind.

'Sorry…Will.. I…ca.. you…break…up.'

'Em, I can hear the seagulls perfectly in the background.'

Damn gulls!

'Emily?'

'I didn't get a word of that, sorry, William. I'll call you tomorrow, yeah?'

'Emily, I need to talk to you now, just listen for a second. Don't hang u–'

My finger ends the call with haste and Buddy turns his head, his big eyes holding accusation as he peers into my soul.

'Don't look at me like that. You're supposed to be on my side.' On a deep exhale and a rub of my forehead, I let Buddy tow me up the hill.

Please, let tomorrow be somewhat more bearable. For my own sanity.

# NINE

'Don't get uppity.'

'I'm not getting uppity. All I'm saying is, I don't get why I wasn't asked to train Emily. I've been working here a lot longer than you.'

'Yes, but you went off to stuff your face when Maggie appointed the position. Plus, you're hardly ever here anymore because of your lifeguard training.' Lily's hands are flailing as she makes her point next to me. 'Besides, I clearly work the hardest. It's a known fact.'

'Excuse me, who struggled to pick up and tidy away those surfboards earlier? *Twice*, may I add,' Vicki expresses, pointing toward the now perfectly stacked boards in the other room, pausing briefly from her task of aligning some multi-coloured T-shirts on a rack by the door.

'Only because *you* were the one who knocked them over, *twice*.'

Vicki's face contorts as she attempts to summon a comeback. 'Okay, I did do that,' she admits.

'Brilliant at riding them, terrible at stacking.' Lily laughs and I join her. I've had to listen to the back and forth teasing between them all morning and it's been quite entertaining. It's made the mundane job of learning the ropes somewhat more enjoyable.

'Can't argue with that,' Vicki says, smoothing down a couple of shirts.

I'd managed, although jaded, to make it through the door at nine on the dot. Lily had been waiting for my arrival, raring to go. As soon as I'd stepped a toe inside, she was skipping around the shop explaining what was what, as I'd endeavoured to take in the mass of information she was hurling at me. Aunt Maggie is such an intricate person, everything to the smallest item is positioned in some kind of order or pattern. Therefore, realising I was failing to get my head around every single detail, I took to making sure I grasped the most vital.

My most dreaded was till manning. The code to unlock it is *1234,* not very secure in my opinion, but thankfully easy to remember. It's a very old machine, so Lily said we have to calculate the change ourselves, which only made me more anxious, because numbers and maths have and will never be my specialty. Even at the bakery Hannah was always in control of the money, while I prepared the order – we had a very effective system. I like to compare my relationship with maths to the controversy that is pineapple on pizza; individually there's potential for great things, but together, it's a recipe for disaster.

'I'm going to the pub to get lunches, did you still want the chicken salad, Em?' Vicki asks from the doorway.

'That's me,' I reply, surprisingly eager to get a taste of my healthy food.

I decided last night that I'm going to start my fitness

forward goal today. The first step of which being a nutritious lunch, followed by a short and steady jog later on this evening. If I'm here for the duration then I might as well make most of the unpredictable terrain around here, and I'm hoping the exercise and fresh air will give me a break from thinking about everything racing around my mind. It's exactly what I need.

I'd stuffed a bag with some shorts and a baggy shirt so I could get changed here, then throw my stuff into the cottage and go. If I have to walk back to get ready, I know I'll end up sitting down and losing motivation, so I thought it best to prepare. I did quickly realise the shoes packed for me are not fit for running in, luckily, Aunt Maggie and I share the same tiny feet, so her size four trainers are a perfect match. She promised me a shopping trip this week, and I'm excited to get some brand spanking new ones. These hills will not know what's hit them.

'I am in dire need of a wee.' Lily's voice pulls me out of my head as Vicki leaves.

'What! Now? What if people come in?' I say, sudden panic striking me. I haven't served anyone yet, I've only watched Lily assist three customers. I can't do it alone.

'It is a shop, Em, that's what tends to happen.' Her flippant tone is not helping my mounting nerves.

'But what if–

'I'll only be gone two minutes and it's hardly busy. I've shown you what to do, you'll be fine. Trust yourself,' she assures, moving from her spot beside me, which was providing me with a lot of comfort.

'Just hurry back,' I plead.

'I'll tell my bladder to make it a quick one, don't worry.' She dances around the counter, disappearing out of my sight and SOS calling range.

My eyes immediately scan the area, preparing for how many customers I could potentially make a fool of myself in front of. There's an older-looking couple moseying around the postcards, easy to handle; a woman and her son looking at the buckets and spades, again, manageable; and then in the far corner, a girl who looks to be about my age shuffling through the tops on the shelf, simple. Three groups of people max – that's doable Relaxing a little, I begin to fiddle with a few of the odd bracelets and keyrings positioned at the front of the counter. As I align them neatly, I hear the old couple to my right shuffling toward the door. I flash them a kind smile, but as I watch them exit, my eyeline is drawn to someone placing a surfboard on the floor outside. He straightens and that's when my heartbeat escalates as I realise who it is.

My focus shoots down to the desk as I return to twiddling the bracelets. By keeping myself occupied, I keep myself calm.

Satisfied with their positions, I notice a pen and a pad of paper on top of the price list. Doodling. Doodling is a great distraction.

I click the nib down, but like the nincompoop I am, it slips through my fingertips. 'Crap,' I hiss, not being able to do anything but watch as it clatters to the floor. On a sigh, I bend and snatch it up, however as I rise, I recoil, met with his intense gaze.

'Just this, thanks,' he says when I don't move. He holds up a round block of surf wax and places it on the counter. His eyes drop from my tense figure as he concentrates on reaching behind him to grab his wallet from the back pocket of his lifeguard shorts, his white shirt tightening across his well-built frame as he twists. A wave falls onto his forehead and I notice his sunglasses aren't perched in his hair today – this time they're hooked on the front of his shirt. 'Is everything alright?' he asks as our eyes find each other again, and that's when I realise I haven't moved or said a word since my brief shock. His fingers find his hair, running them through. So effortless. So smooth…

'Yes!' I snap from my trance. My first customer. Of course, it had to be Mr Smug, but it's okay. I can do this. All I have to do is appear as though I know what I'm doing and somehow not make a fool of myself.

I go over everything Lily told me step by step in my head. Firstly, keying in the code to login – check. Then I find the price printed on the bottom of the wax's wrapping and begin to enter £4.99. So far so good.

It's next my problem occurs, as I punch the number nine down on the pad, it sticks. I press it again, thinking – and praying – the force will somehow free it, but it doesn't. It only makes it worse. Before I have the chance to blink, the number nine is zooming recurrently across my screen. I blindly hit random buttons to try and stop it, but what consequently arises is far worse. The most horrendous beeping sound blares from the crappy piece of technology, making me gasp.

My cheeks redden as I feel his stare on my flustered form. 'Sorry. Never actually done this before,' I admit, even though he's already well aware of that fact. I keep thumping random buttons, but the beeping remains.

*Shut up!*

'You're my first,' I continue to ramble not daring to look up. 'That's quite a special thing, isn't it?' I'm trying and failing to distract him from my stressed state. The silence from his side only putting me more on edge.

I don't know what I do, but my constant tapping somehow works. The nines seem to stand to attention before the till exerts its next act of trickery. The drawer flies into my stomach. My breath traps itself in my throat, but I do my best to keep my pain buried, focusing instead on the beeping which is still deafening, making my ears ring along with it. 'Just stop!' I cry in frustration this time, going back to punching every button on the pad.

A hand comes into view. I flinch as it whacks the top of the till twice and the side once. The noise stops. My eyes narrow.

'Magic hands.' He smirks, wiggling his fingers in the air.

My scoff is instant. 'You enjoyed that, didn't you?'

'What can I say? We condescending jerks have a thing for watching people struggle,' he says, casually leaning his side against the counter. He's really holding on to that grudge.

I stare back, my mouth agape as he slaps a ten-pound note in my open palm.

'How's your handsome dog?' he asks as I go about totalling his change.

The unexpected question brings my eyes to his. His face is neutral, unreadable, but his tone is the complete opposite.

'Buddy's fine.'

'You seem to have a habit of creating some form of commotion, don't you?' There's a slight twitch on his lips. He wants to smirk again. Is he purposely trying to shame me further because of my one-off remark yesterday?

'And you seem to have a habit of making unnecessary comments.' I will not encourage his brashness, and I will not allow myself to feel humiliated by, or in front of him, again. If I have a habit of making a commotion, then he has a habit of being an arrogant prick, and he's getting on my last nerve.

'They're not unnecessary, I'm simply making conversation,' he defends.

'Your annoying smirk says otherwise.'

'Oh, so you've been checking me out?'

'No.'

'Yet you noticed my smile.'

'Smirk. And it's hard not to focus on you when your massive head fills this entire room.'

'I was right about that bite of yours.'

'This is just a nibble. Do you want to push it further?' I test, eager to send him and his conceited arse out of Aunt Maggie's shop.

He tilts his head, his eyes seeming to enjoy my increasing irritation as they hold their sparkle. 'Maybe some other time.'

He really does think he's God's gift.

Out the corner of my eye, I notice something which miraculously creates a shift in my mood. Apparently, God has been listening, and he's on my side. I slam the till drawer shut. 'What's your take on karma?'

If he gets off on watching me suffer then I'll return the gesture.

'I'm sorry?' he asks, his face scrunching.

'Apology accepted,' I retort before continuing. 'And a little piece of advice, in future, I wouldn't leave your surfboard outside near an ice cream stand unattended.'

'Why's that?' His eyes narrow, and my own smugness grows with his confusion.

'Because a seagull's just crapped on it.' I smile wryly, nodding toward his board which is now painted beautifully in gull droppings.

His head shoots over his shoulder. 'Oh, bollo–

'Your change,' I interrupt, thrusting his coins across the counter on a toothy grin. 'Sorry, we're out of fives.' I'm not sorry one bit.

He frowns on a sigh, opening his hand and keeping those emeralds locked on my blues as I transfer the change from my fingertips into his palm. Self-satisfaction is planted contentedly on my face. Balance has been restored. I'm happy.

'I leave you alone for one minute. I heard that alarm all the way out the back.' Lily breaks our eyeballing as she idles her way to her place beside me.

'I did tell you not to go,' I defend, my attention now being pulled away from Emerald Eyes' displeased expression and focusing on Lily's cheery one.

'It happened to me the first couple of times, but you learn that you don't work the till, the till works you. I keep telling Maggie we need a new one.' She raps her knuckles against the drawer, and I flinch away, not wanting another surprise blow to my stomach.

'You didn't tell me there was an alarm, it scared me to death!'

'How did you get it to stop? I forgot to tell you about the special smack.' Yes. She did.

A small cough prevents me from scolding her about failing to warn me, which makes both of our heads turn. I realise I'm still holding his wax in my other hand.

'Sorry, Jackson,' Lily mumbles, providing him with her full attention. I hold out the wax.

'It's cool, we've all been new at one time or another.' He looks me dead in the eyes, his glistening with amusement. He's clearly back to his obnoxious self – my victory short lived.

'I'd de-crap before you wax,' I snipe back.

He lets out a low chuckle. 'What revolutionary advice.'

'There's plenty more where that came from.'

'I bet,' he replies, twiddling the surf wax in his hand. Out the corner of my eye I can vaguely make out Lily's confused expression. 'Thanks,' he eventually says. He turns to leave, but almost instantly clicks his fingers and snaps back around. 'Oh! Lily, Dex wanted me to ask if you were still coming tomorrow?'

She gapes at him, curiosity painted in her eyes. 'Did he? Well, you can tell Dexter I will be, as long as he remains at least ten feet away from me at all times.' She leans forward on the counter, convincingly showing her disapproval for the boy. But I reckon she's trying to reassure herself that she wants him to keep his distance more than anyone else, if the glow on her cheeks is anything to go by.

'Noted,' Jackson snickers, clearly thinking what I am too.

'What's tomorrow?' I ask Lily, not being able to help my curious nose.

'It's a lifeguard's birthday, we're having a get together on the beach.' My focus is back on Jackson as he answers for her.

'Oh, please. *Get together,*' Lily air quotes, 'more like a piss up.' The back of her hand meets my arm as she gasps. 'You should come, Emily!' Lily peers up at me with big, excitable eyes, making it almost impossible to decline.

A party with a bunch of people I don't know, not really my idea of fun. 'Wouldn't I be intruding?'

'Don't be silly, you can be my plus one. The more the merrier, right?' She throws a look over to Emerald Eyes, as if encouraging him to shadow her enthusiasm in the idea of me coming. Somehow, I don't think she's going to get that.

'Yeah, Leo's pretty easy going.' Jackson shrugs nonchalantly.

'Some would say *too* easy going,' Lily remarks, pursing her lips at him. He snubs her comment.

'It's on the beach anyway so it's hardly private property, and he's going to be too pissed to notice any gate crashers.' He concentrates on flipping the wax as he responds to my previous comment. He's entertaining Lily, but it's clear he seems indifferent as to whether I attend or not, and his mannerisms and tone couldn't be more dissimilar to Lily's excitable aura if he tried.

'C'mon, Emily, pleeeeaaaase,' she begs.

I contemplate for a moment, but one look at the girl clung to my arm forces me to make an impulsive decision. I can hardly say no when I have Lily's big puppy eyes gawping into my soul. Besides, I receive my A-level results tomorrow, and it'll be a good excuse to celebrate… or possibly forget if they're particularly awful. Obviously, I care about my final grades, it's what I've worked so hard for, but I'm glad I don't have to worry too much. 'Okay, sure.'

'Yes!' she cheers.

Jackson smiles at Lily's reaction, before reaching into his pocket to grab his phone and flicking his eyes to it briefly. 'Better go, my shift starts in five,' he says, sliding it back into his shorts. 'Thanks for the wax, newbie! See you at the party.' He seems genuine, and it shocks me.

'Sure,' I reply, taken aback.

'I would leave Buddy at home this time though, we wouldn't want to cause another scene now, would we?'

And there it is. The personal use of my dog's name from his lips takes me back a little, but it's quick to be countermanded by displeasure.

I roll my eyes as he takes his annoying grin out the door. He shakes his head at his crap-covered board before picking it up from the other end and marching away.

'What's he talking about?' Lily asks, her eyebrows furrowed as she watches him too.

'I have absolutely no idea,' I lie.

# *TEN*

The bag filled with my clothes is thrown into Aunt Maggie's hallway. Forcing my earphone jack into my phone – thankful my mysterious packer had tossed them into my suitcase – I stride back outside, down the path and out the gate. I notice that Guy's car is parked in the lay-by, but there's no sign of him. He must have taken himself off for a walk, unless Aunt Maggie is holding him hostage in the cottage.

Shuffling through my playlist, I scan over my songs, on the hunt for a good running beat to kickstart my endorphins. But before I get the chance to choose, my ringtone is echoing in my ears as Hannah's name flashes on the screen.

A deep sigh escapes me. Taking a moment, I debate whether it's a good idea to accept the call, because I know I'll be hit with a mass of questions – many of which I won't be able to answer. But by not responding, I'll only worry her further which will result in more questions when I inevitably end up speaking to her. I wish she knew, because the idea of venting all the thoughts and emotions I've been keeping trapped inside is too tempting. They've been building with each minute of every hour that passes, and it's all starting to overwhelm me. I'd give anything to confide in my best friend.

Biting the bullet, I accept. As expected, she's straight into her interrogation, denying me of a chance to respond.

'Em? Emily, Jesus where the fuck are you? Albert said you resigned. What's going on? Is everything okay?'

'Han, calm down. I'm fine.' I thrust my phone into the back pocket of my shorts and pick up my pace, turning my leisurely walk into a slow jog down the hill. I came to run and that's what I intend to do, the phone call might even distract me from the burn I'll no doubt feel very soon from my lack of physical activity I've partaken in since school.

'Okay, good. When you didn't turn up yesterday I got worried, no text, no phone call, nothing.' Her voice gains some composure but there's still question to her tone; she's confused. Her and me both.

For a moment I wonder how Albert knew I wasn't returning, and then mentally kick myself. Dad. As mad as I am at him, I'm thankful he took it upon himself – or whichever poor staff member he ordered to did – because I have no idea what I would've said to my boss.

'I know, I'm sorry,' I say. I don't know what else *to* say. I was going to ring her last night. Snuggled in the sheets, I was staring at her number on my phone, but I couldn't bring myself to hit the button, because I knew I'd have felt as I do right now: useless. I can't give my best friend the answers she wants. How could I burden her with concern? If I was to tell her I was attacked and the man is still out there living freely, possibly plotting to find me and finish what he couldn't the other night, and offer her no explanation why, she would most certainly flip. She doesn't need that weight on her shoulders. Besides, if I make her believe I'm perfectly fine, I don't need to worry about her worrying, and that's less weight on mine.

'How come you quit? You didn't tell me,' she says, hurt clear in her tone.

'Something came up. I had to get away for a bit,' I answer, not divulging the truth but also avoiding a big fat lie.

'What something?'

'Just something. I'm visiting my aunt in Cornwall.' I'm not sure Dad would be too happy with me revealing my whereabouts, but it's Han, and she'd only continue to push and push until she received a response which met her satisfaction.

'Your aunt? I thought you hardly spoke to her?'

I'm digging myself a massive hole.

'I don't really. I mean, I didn't. It's just a visit, a rekindling if you like. I'm getting away from the city for a little while.' I manage to stutter my way through. Again, not completely the truth, but not technically a lie.

'Have you and William had an argument or something? Oh! Christ, he hasn't kicked you out, has he?' I hear her gasp travel through my buds and deep into my ear drums.

'No, of course not!'

'Because you know you're always welcome at mine,' she says, being her usual kind and supportive self. It makes me feel a whole lot worse for not telling her the truth.

'Thanks, Han, but we're okay. Honest.' I can't work out if that's a fib or not. I don't really know where we stand at the minute, but the response leaves my mouth before I have the chance to trap it inside. I only hope I've said it convincingly enough for her to drop the subject.

Thankfully, she does.

'Why are you out of breath?'

It's now that I realise my breathing has indeed grown heavier, but I think that's more so from trying to keep up my pretence whilst answering the questions she's badgering me with, rather than the physical exercise itself.

'I'm on a run,' I reply as I reach the bottom of the hill before the bridge.

'Excuse me? What the hell is happening here? You never run!' She sounds as shocked as I feel. Emily Rose Lambert is really doing this

'Trust me, I'm feeling the effects of that right now,' I puff, slowing down as I spot a group of men in wetsuits carrying surfboards up ahead. Observing as they cross the road, my vision zones in on a particular face as I try to calm my heavy pants. He's at the back of the group chatting to another guy I don't recognise, his board secured under his arm, pressing against his bare torso.

The five pause when they reach the sand to fix their surfboard straps to their ankles. I find my feet slackening to a walk as I reach the middle of the bridge. My arms rest on top of the wall and I overlook the shore, watching as Emerald Eyes hoists the top part of his wetsuit on which had previously been suspended below his waist. His back is to me, and I study how the muscles contract and stretch as he slides his arms inside. I don't know why I'm staring. Maybe because it's an excuse to have a mini break. Or, maybe it's because I'm watching these guys laughing and smiling with each other, appearing as though they haven't a care or worry in the world. Maybe I'm staring, because I'm wishing that I had a happy place like they do, where every bad thing diminishes, and only happiness and positive thoughts remain.

'Em?'

My brief daydream evaporates as Jackson and his group race toward the sea and Hannah's words resound in my ears.

'Emily, you seem a little off. Are you sure everything's okay? Are *you* okay?'

I inhale deeply, giving Hannah my attention but still gazing around the sizeable beach. A refreshing breeze blows wisps of hair out of my ponytail and cools my warm body. 'Sorry, I'm here. I'm fine. Everything's fine,' I repeat, realising I'm not doing a great job of reassuring her. 'Will you do me a favour? If the others ask, tell them I'm spending some time with my aunt?'

'Of course, but how long are you going to be away for?'

'That, I'm not so sure on.' I make out Jackson in the distance reaching the water.

'You're still going to university though?'

He lies flat on his board and uses his arms to drive himself further in. 'Yes, I can assure you on that. University will be happening.' I sincerely hope it is. It's what I have my mind set on.

'Good. I want to see you before you go,' she continues as I watch Jackson catch his first wave. He propels himself forward before lifting into a stooped position as it forms, he gains his balance and sticks his arms out whilst straightening his legs with a slight bend in the knee. He twists and flicks the board, effortlessly riding the wave as his damp curls stick to his face. I hate myself for it, but I can't help but be in awe of him gliding through the sea, dominating the wave in his own little world. Eventually, losing his balance, he collapses backward with a huge splash, but as soon as I drop sight of him under the water, he's back up again, flinging himself onto his board.

'Me too,' I retort, dragging my feet over the bridge. I pull my eyeline to the hill ahead which I'm determined to jog up.

'Oh, before I forget! Guess who asked out Shawn Thomas!'

'What!' I exclaim astounded. She really did it.

'Uh huh.' I don't need to see her to get a sense of how smug she is right now.

'You found out his last name, then?' The grin is plastered on my face, just as I know it is on hers. I've been waiting for this moment for months on end.

'You bet I did, he's taking me out tomorrow night. Can you believe it? Me, on a date with a hot guy!' she shrieks, which only makes my cheesy grin grow.

'I'm sure he's got a lovely personality too, Han.'

'Oh, yeah, of course. I mean, I hardly know him and he's already making me so happy!'

A part of my heart sinks a little, and I have no idea why, because this is all I've wanted for her for so long. The endless late-night phone calls and all the conversations we've had in the bakery over this man, I thought I'd feel nothing but pure joy when it did eventually happen. So why, now that it has, do I feel a hint of sadness?

'That's amazing, Hannah.' I smile, but there's no denying the trace of melancholy in my tone, but I think – I hope – only I notice. 'Listen, I'm going to carry on with this run, if I don't, I'll only end up talking myself out of it and turning back,' I reason. It's an excuse to get off the phone. I truly am over the moon for her, but a sudden and surprising urge to run away has taken over my body, and I want to get going before it vanishes, leaving me with zero motivation.

'Okay, try not to kill yourself. Promise me we'll talk soon.'

'Promise,' I reply. I swear. 'Enjoy your date and remember to be yourself. If he doesn't like you for you, then he's an idiot and not worth it!'

'Thanks, Em. Oh, and good luck for tomorrow, even though I know you don't need it. Love you, pal!'

'Love you too!'

The call ends and I surprise myself as I sprint off with Jackson Browne's 'Running on Empty' blasting through my earphones. I persist up the road, which is far steeper than I first anticipated, but I'm spurred on by the feeling of running away my problems. I'm spurred on by the impulse of escaping everything and everyone, even if only for a little while. I'm spurred on, because the thought of never finding my own happy place hurts significantly more than the burning feeling coursing through my body as I continue to climb.

# ELEVEN

Last night's run has unearthed and worked muscles I never knew I had. I'm hobbling down the stairs, gripping the banister and rethinking my whole fitness plan.

The last stair mirrors my poor muscles and groans in discomfort. My legs breathe a sigh of relief as I tread over Buddy who is lying beneath it. His ears prick when I grab the spare key Aunt Maggie had made for me from the perfectly dusted window ledge, and after giving him a tickle behind his floppy ears, I wander out the door.

My exam results appeared in my inbox at nine o'clock on the dot. My heart had thumped as my finger hovered over the email, but the nerves were quickly replaced with relief and utter joy. Two A's and a B. My hard work paid off!

It seemed, however, the emotions of opening my results would in no way match the unease for what the rest of the day would entail. I've been stood in front of the bedroom mirror all afternoon, holding up and throwing down every outfit from my case. I thought I'd finally struck gold with my casual summer dress, but a FaceTime call from Lily immediately placed it on the 'no' pile – along with everything else I own. After explaining I'd packed light and didn't have a clue what I was supposed to wear to a beach party, and that I had no other options, she proceeded to express, 'Gok Wan has nothing on me,' then gave her orders to be ready and outside in ten minutes. She insisted she would be picking me up so I could explore what her wardrobe had to offer. Lily left no room to decline, so I settled with informing her I was putting all my trust in her, however nerve wracking that may be. Lily's style is vivacious, whereas mine is far less.

I track down the cobblestone path, and it takes me a second to process what's happening. Aunt Maggie is resting against the fence, her arms folded and her head nodding along to whatever Guy is telling her as he leans against the Mercedes. I shake my head on a smile, they haven't stopped talking since the moment we arrived. Which is a good thing, because if Aunt Maggie wasn't so involved, Guy would be bored to tears. And as I've recently discovered, too much Maggie is far better than no Maggie at all. At least she's keeping him entertained.

As I reach out to open the gate, my body freezes.

*Bang!*

My eyes widen and I feel the blood drain from my face. The drum of my heart ricochets in my head and everything inside me is screaming to get back inside, but I can't move. My head is angled towards where the sound emanated from, but it's like I've zoned everything out; my vision is a blur and my hearing is purely drumbeat.

A hand is placed on my shoulder and a face blocks my sight. Guy's mouth is moving, his face composed, but I can't hear what he's saying.

It's only when something red catches my eye that I begin to understand. Another bang explodes from the old

Beetle, followed by a cloud of thick black smoke escaping from the exhaust as it comes to a stop on the hill.

'Miss Lambert, you're okay.' Guy's deep voice pulls me out of my trance and draws my attention to his furrowed brow. I nod slowly, gathering my composure and mentally slapping myself at how silly I must've looked.

I turn to see Aunt Maggie at the window of the car, I can just about make out Lily in the driver's seat bobbing her head to Aunty's words.

'Ms Taylor said you were going to a party tonight. Do you need me to come with you?'

I relieve my strained lungs by drawing in a deep breath as my brain goes into time lapse mode, attempting to place together where I am and what I'm doing. *Party. Tonight. Lily's come to pick me up.*

I shake my head. 'No, I'll be okay. Besides, we're trying to avoid questions, and I think turning up with an older man no one has ever met before may spark a few comments.'

'Point taken.' He nods in understanding. 'Remember, I'm just a phone call away.'

'I know, Guy. Thank you.' I smile, even though he and I both know it's forced.

I hurry through the gate knowing his eyes are trained intensely on my back, and head over to Lily's Volkswagen. I feel like a fool. I knew Lily's car was old and made ridiculous noises because she'd warned me about it on the phone. I also knew she would be pulling up any minute, so why did I just panic?

I've been trying to convince myself that I am mentally stable, but the absolute truth is – and that momentary fright has just confirmed – I am well and truly spooked, and the idea of going to a large open area at night whilst unprotected is freaking the hell out of me.

'Here she is,' Aunt Maggie croons as I reach her. She pulls me into a hug, completely oblivious to my recent distress. The comforting smell of her clothes and perfume engulf my senses and ease my nerves as I close my eyes and squeeze her a little tighter.

'Get in, get in. We've only got an hour!' Lily waves frantically as she stretches to see through the rolled down passenger window. I throw a thumbs-up over Aunt Maggie's shoulder just as she pulls away.

'You girls be careful.' She points a stern finger as the door squeaks open and I slide in. She leans inside the window. 'Don't go drinking too much, madam.'

A brief moment of bewilderment passes through me, because I'm not used to having the genuine concern of an adult over me. Most people my age would roll their eyes, but for someone who has been deprived of it for most of her life, it's a long-awaited feeling of gratitude.

'Don't worry, Maggie, I'll look after us,' Lily insists, almost on top of me as she cranes her neck, one hand on the steering wheel ready to go.

'That's what I'm worried about,' Aunt Maggie replies and I raise my eyebrows in question at Lily who shrugs her shoulders. Seems like I'll be the one looking after us, I gather.

'I'll be fine.'

She nods, unaware that the comment was my attempt at trying to reassure myself more than her. 'Okay, off you go.' She steps back and with another loud bang, which makes me shudder and sink into my seat, Lily pulls away with a jerk and a screech. 'Have a great time!' I hear Aunt Maggie yell, before Lily turns the old car around and we reach the bottom of the hill.

'You excited?' she asks, her eyes trained on the road ahead, both hands wrapped firmly around the frayed steering wheel as she concentrates.

The thing is, I was, before the whole mini freak-out. The second I heard that bang every feeling I felt the other night came racing back, and now I am very much on edge. But if I appear tense then Lily will ask if I'm okay, and I can't be dealing with being questioned like that, so I do what I've done my whole life; put on a smile and pretend everything is peachy.

'Yeah,' I breathe, shooting a small smile in her direction as she glances back at me briefly, a grin on her face. 'I don't know what to expect though, I have no idea who anyone is,' I admit.

'I wouldn't worry. Everyone's super easy going, and you have me and Vick.'

I do feel better knowing I have them to stand next to, slash, hide behind if anything embarrassing happens, which, knowing me, probably will. Especially if Emerald Eyes is there. We haven't had a smooth interaction since we met, so I don't hold out much hope. I'll just have to do my best to avoid him at all costs, and with any luck I'll survive the night with my dignity intact.

'Do you know Maggie's friend well?' Lily asks, changing the subject entirely and catching me off guard.

'Maggie's friend?' I reply, acting the innocent. Obviously, she's referring to Guy, but I need to buy time to come up with a plausible answer. I should've thought this through sooner, because of course people will start asking questions when a man they've never seen before is all of a sudden hanging around the cottage.

'The bald man. I saw him talking to you before we left.'

'Oh, that's Guy. He's a friend of my dad's,' I say, not looking in her direction.

'Yeah, Maggie mentioned that he's an old friend. I've never seen him before.'

I nervously fiddle with my fingers in my lap. 'I told my dad I wanted to see Aunt Maggie before I leave for university next month, and Guy offered to drive me. They must've met through Dad a long time ago.' I shrug through my lie.

'I have to say, she could do a lot worse, he's rather hunky.'

My face scrunches up as I shoot an alarmed glare at her with a small shiver slinking its way down my spine. Cringe. I don't think I could stomach the idea of him and Aunt Maggie, *getting it on.* Also, not once have I looked at Guy and thought *hunky,* but that's maybe because I haven't had a chance to properly observe. I suppose, I can see where she's coming from, because Guy definitely radiates self-assured confidence, but I don't think I could ever see him as anyone but my temporary bodyguard and, quite frankly, Dad's lackey.

She notices my shock. 'I mean, obviously *I* wouldn't, but if I was in Maggie's position I sure as hell would jump on that muscle mach–

'Subtilty, nice,' I cut in before she goes too far. 'You're like the opposite of Mrs Robinson.'

'I'm just saying,' she defends. 'I've definitely seen worse older men.'

'You remind me of my friend back home.'

'Yeah? Is she totally amazing too?' she asks, a cheeky smile plastered on her plump lips.

'She's completely obsessed with men.'

She throws me a scowl and I meet it with arched eyebrows, but I can't keep it up and when my disbelief fades, we're both overcome with giggles.

We sit in a comfortable silence for a little while, and I use the quiet time to digest the beauty of the sunset illuminating the sky in swirls of bright reds and burning oranges. The fading sun gleams through the trees as we drive around the lanes, and I look to Lily as a question comes to mind.

'Have you lived here your whole life?' The sun's sparkle sheens her face, highlighting her features and making her side profile glow angelically, with her glossy red hair fierce in the light. She bites on her lip, nodding.

'Born and bred in Cornwall. Not a bad place to grow up, I suppose.' Her focus remains forward, her head particularly still as if she's scared to take her eyes off the road.

'It's certainly beautiful.' I peer out of my window again, absorbing the majesty and serenity of Marshlyn Bay. Noticing animals grazing on the fields with the ocean behind, and the luminously lit sky adding to the tranquillity, is making me hate myself more for not coming down before now, and I'm a tiny bit jealous of Lily for having this all at her fingertips.

'What about you?' Lily asks.

'Born and bred in London,' I mimic, and she smiles. 'Lived with my dad for most of my life, but I recently moved in with my boyfriend on the outskirts of the city.' I keep my eyes on the view, trying not to think of the fact I haven't spoken to him since our not so great phone call the other day.

'What's your boyfriend's name?'

'William,' I answer, keen to move on. 'So, come on, are there any boys on the scene?' I'm genuinely curious, a part of me is waiting for her to mention Dex after seeing their interaction. Or perhaps I've read it completely wrong, and Dex really is just a serial flirter and Lily truly does dislike him.

'Nope. Forever a single pringle. I'm eighteen, I don't have time for relationships, more trouble than they're worth if you ask me. I've been studying fashion at college, that's my true focus,' she declares, her eyes briefly waver to me, but as quickly as they do, they're flickering back to the road.

'What are your plans now?' I ask, not even surprised by her choice in career, her wild red hair and flamboyant gold studded trousers with matching bracelets enough to tell anyone she excels in the creative sector.

'I've been offered an apprentice job in London, funnily enough, but I don't know if I'll accept. London's so far away.'

'If you do, you can always call on me whenever I'm not at uni.'

'Ooo, that would be fun,' she says on a quirked brow. 'What are the clubs like?'

'Expensive.'

'Well, if you're not out for a good night then you might as well stay home.' She laughs and I shadow, thinking back to the start of summer which was full of drunken mishaps with my friends and Han back home... before all of this. My laughter dwindles as my mind ticks over, because those memories were so close to disappearing along with my life.

'What about Vicki?' I ask, keen to distract my bleak thoughts but also curious, remembering she mentioned a boy the first day we met.

'Her and James have been together for a solid year and a half. We call them Mum and Dad, purely because they're the most sensible out of all of us.'

My lips curl up as I think about their little group. I push further, eager to find out more about the people who call this their town. 'So, how old's Leo?' I ask, remembering that's the name Jackson used in the shop yesterday.

'This is his twenty second. Him and Jackson are both twenty-two, James and Vicki are twenty-one and Dex is twenty.'

'So we're the babies?'

'We're the babies,' she confirms on a grin.

The sun is vanishing rather quickly, and even though we've only been driving for a few minutes, the narrow lanes seem considerably darker than when we left the cottage. As I begin to wonder how far away her house is, she indicates right and pulls onto a driveway, parking next to a white Citroën.

Only a couple of other houses are around Lily's and they're relatively close together, the rest of the space is purely fields. Acres upon acres surround its perimeter and as I climb out, I see in the near distance Marshlyn Bay's enormous sandy beach. The sea is glistening, and it's only now I fully take in the vastness of its serene water. My eyes drift out into the distance until I can no longer distinguish ocean from sky as I tread backward. Imagine waking up to this every day of your life. Lily couldn't appear more unfazed by the view with her fingers tapping away on her phone as her other hand shuffles her keys around.

'Vicki said she and James will pick us up in fifty minutes,' she says as we march up the front porch steps. She unlocks the door and I follow her through, stepping into a hallway complete with impeccable cream carpet.

'Are your parents not home?' I ask, spotting a living room to my right and the kitchen up ahead but no signs of movement anywhere. I catch myself in a large full body mirror on the wall next to me and grimace at my messily scraped up wind-swept hair. I hope Lily is a miracle worker.

'No, they're out on some date night thing,' she retorts, placing her keys on a wooden cabinet. 'More importantly,' she claps her hands together, 'we need to get upstairs, girl.' She unzips her boots and shimmies out of her jacket.

I slip off my shoes, quite relieved I haven't trodden any dirt onto the carpet, and follow her hasty pace up the staircase. My mind goes into overdrive, imagining what I'll be looking like in fifty minutes time.

My neck twists over my shoulder, before repeating on the other side. I'm trying to get a feel of every angle, but they're all equally as shocking. I had to do a double take when I bent down to put my shoes on, because I did not recognise the girl staring back at me at all. I'm still trying to take in my transformation.

'Are you sure this is acceptable?' I ask, jerking the hem of Lily's petite red dress down. I know I'm a little taller than her, but this is riding up places it really shouldn't be.

'You look breathtakingly hot, Emily. Stop stressing.'

I do another once-over before accepting that even with my objections, Lily won't let me change back into my far less promiscuous jeans and T-Shirt. The plunging lace V neck is concerning me the most. It's showing more cleavage than I'm used to and, more importantly, comfortable with. I'm worried if I bend over one boob might just pop out to join the party. With that thought washing over me like ice cold water running down my back, I tug each side of my jacket over my chest to cover myself up.

A five-beat knock raps on the door and I peer at Lily through the spotless reflection. She's sat on the stairs sliding on her black ankle boots. She nods, giving me the signal. I toddle to the door, tugging at the hem of the dress before swinging the door open. I'm met with an elegantly poised blonde. Vicki's long and flowy maxi dress reaches her ankles where simple, yet gorgeous brown strappy sandals cover her feet, and her wavy hair cascades effortlessly past her shoulders. The whole look is modest yet hot, and as a matter of fact, the dress is very similar to the one I have in my case back at the cottage – the one which Lily completely dismissed. I immediately turn to the girl on the stairs who is still slipping on her boots, my mouth is agape, my eyebrows raised, and she knows why, because she also meets my stare.

'Emily, you can blend in or stand out in life.' She pushes herself up. Her gold, sparkly T-Shirt dress trickles down to the tops of her thighs as she fluffs her red curly hair which is half up and half down to show off her big hoop earrings. Evidently, she's not one to blend.

'Bloody hell, Lil,' Vicki scoffs next to me, her bemused nose wrinkling.

'What? Dress to impress!' Lily unhooks her leather jacket from the banister and swings it over her shoulder.

'Dress to pull, you mean. I don't know why I'm surprised.'

'Look good, feel good, my girls,' she says before ushering us out the door, paying no mind to our amused expressions. 'You never know who's watching.' She winks as she sashays down the driveway and towards the car at the bottom of the drive. It's dark now, the dazzling headlights our only source of light.

I automatically shoot a tickled grin over to Vicki who turns to me with a shake of her head. She holds up a hand, knowing full well what I'm about to remark.

'I've learnt to just go with it, it's the option which summons less of a headache.'

I laugh as Vicki follows Lily's movements and heads down the driveway. I, on the other hand, stand unmoving, contemplating my tremendously short dress. With all the outfits Lily threw at me, this was the most modest of an incredibly sexy bunch. A feeling of dread embeds itself in my stomach, because unlike Lily, I'm really hoping this skimpy outfit doesn't draw eyes in my direction. With any luck her extravagant attire will keep the attention on her.

As if reading my mind again, Vicki yells back, her trim figure disappearing into the fulgent headlights. 'You look amazing, honey. Let's go!'

Beckoning some confidence with a deep inhale of sea air, I follow suit.

I slide into the back with Lily, and a head of blond waves twizzles around from the driver's seat. The interior light above us remains on as Lily clips her seatbelt in place, which gives me a perfect view of James. He is stunningly attractive. Shoulder-length shaggy locks, trimmed stubble and piercing blue eyes. It must be a trend around here for the boys to have unruly surfer-dude hair. But contrasting to Jackson's intimidating emerald eyes, James's are kind, smiley, and far more welcoming.

'Hey.' He beams, the corners of his eyes crinkling. 'You must be the Emily everyone's been talking about. I'm James.' He twists in his seat and reaches his large hand out towards me. I take it, scoffing at his words.

'*The* Emily? I didn't realise I was famous.' I've never

had people care enough to truly acknowledge me, let alone talk about me behind my back. Even at school I wasn't noticed, not really. I had my group of friends but that was that, and I was completely fine with it. I've always been someone who prefers to be another person in the crowd, rather than the centre of attention – I'm more comfortable that way. I like to think I take after Mum in that respect, as opposed to Dad, who is unapologetically brazen. And with my current situation, it's very much an advantageous character trait.

'Damn right you are, you've become something of a celebrity around here. No one even knew Mags had a niece.'

'Well, here I am,' I say, because I can't think of anything else. Once again, I'm feeling that guilt which is now well established inside of me.

Just as Vicki leans forward to change the radio station, Lily coughs twice into her hand and we oblige with her wordless instructions to give her attention.

'Is that a glitter ball I see out the corner of my eye or is Lily out for a good night?' James jokes, peering at her through the hole in the back of his head rest.

Lily flashes him a scowl before flicking the interior light off. The sudden darkness only emphasizes the material she is dressed in. Her dress is sparkling, as James said, like a glitter ball.

'Hello to you too, James.' She sighs. 'Can we get going now, please? Us ladies are in desperate need of alcoholic beverages.' My eyes widen at my inclusion. I wasn't planning on drinking a lot in fear of making a fool of myself, however now that she's mentioned it, maybe a drink will help settle me – I think I'm going to need it with this outfit.

James chuckles, amused by her demands. He holds up his hands in surrender and spins back to his original spot. 'Your Highnesses,' he utters whilst backing off the drive.

'Good boy,' Vicki says, patting his shoulder. I may not be able to see her face, but I can tell she's stifling a laugh, just as I am.

The car rocks back and forth as James steers us across the potholed car park and pulls up to the beach bank.

'Party time!' he declares as we clamber out. Being so close to the sea means the air is slightly chillier, which I'm oddly thankful for. It means I can hug my jacket closer to my body and hide my cleavage without Lily badgering me to *embrace my sexiness.*

I stand at top of the bank, observing the party below where a large fire burns, highlighting many bodies dancing, drinking and laughing. Music blasts from God knows where, but I recognise the song, 'Ex's & Oh's' by Elle King, as everyone chants along to the words.

Two hands grab the back of my shoulders and Lily's head appears over my right side. 'Let's shine, baby,' she whispers into my ear. Without a moment's thought, she clasps hold of my hand and yanks me down the sandy bank, my feet working hard to prevent me from stumbling.

My heavy muscles are crying out when we reach the bottom, and I curse myself for being too tired to stretch after my run last night. James and Vicki join us as my eyes scan the area. I notice two big speakers on the back of a red truck parked next to an old, worn surf hut – which is apparently a storing place for beer, spirits and plastic cups tonight. Logs have been placed randomly around the blazing fire where a few people are sat chatting and snogging, and everyone else is up, dancing like they haven't got a care in the world.

'Leo knows a lot of people,' I say. Vicki nods.

'They're all his old school friends and some I know as lifeguards from other beaches around here,' she replies as my eyes drift across the crowd.

They land on the beaming face of Dex, then down to the beer bottle in his hand. An arm is draped around his waist, and after squinting a little to focus my vision from the dazzling flames, I notice it's the same raven-haired beauty from the beer garden the other evening.

Stood next to them is Emerald Eyes, and it's as though he catches wind that he's being watched, because his head turns in my direction.

# TWELVE

The tall neck of the beer bottle in Jackson's fingers is lifted to his lips. His eyes scan the crowd, but they luckily never find me.

'I'm going to join the boys,' James says, planting a peck on Vicki's lips and leaving our small group.

'Right, drinks?' Lily claps, rubbing her hands together eagerly. Before we can reply, Raven Hair calls after Lily and Vicki as she treads across the sand, balancing three plastic cups in her hands.

Lily spins and waves in her direction, but as she whirls back around, her eyes roll into her head. 'Here comes the wicked witch.'

'Play nicely,' Vicki murmurs to her friend who grimaces in reply, and I'm left curious as to who she is and why she's got Lily's back up so much.

'Girlies! Get these down your necks,' she chirpily instructs when she joins our circle. Her black leather skirt is as short as my dress, but I take it hers is intentionally skimpy as it's paired with a thin lacy bralette. Coast girls must have far warmer blood than others, because I feel like I'm in a completely different climate as I hug my jacket closer to my chilly body.

Lily accepts the drink, downing hers straight away. Vicki takes the second cup but hesitates. 'Need I remind you I have a training day tomorrow.'

'You'll be fine, you're practically a fully qualified lifeguard anyway,' Lily tempts, tipping the cup with her index finger up to Vicki's mouth.

'Exactly. One won't hurt, you've surfed on worse,' Raven Hair encourages, which seems to convince Vicki.

'You, ladies, will be my downfall.' She points her finger at both of them accusingly before gulping down the liquid.

'Didn't take much convincing,' Lily giggles in my ear and I chew on my bottom lip, suppressing a laugh. Raven Hair flicks her gaze.

'I don't think we've met?' The contrast of the dark night and the bright fire is making her brown eyes glisten as they bore into my stiffened figure.

'Emily,' I respond, offering a small smile.

'She's Maggie's niece,' Lily adds for me.

'Oh, I didn't know she had a niece. I'm Olivia.'

*Olivia.*

This is the girl Dex mentioned the other day in the shop – the girl Jackson had plans with. A rush of insecurity drifts from my stomach all the way down to the tips of my toes. She's gorgeous and she knows it. Maybe it's her confidence I'm finding intimidating, but something about the air around her is suppressing the want inside of me to get to know her. I'm all for feeling self-assured in your own body, however I'm starting to understand Lily's choice of words, because she's not giving me a good vibe. It's as if she believes she's above everyone on this beach as she flicks her silky hair and pushes her full chest out, making her presence very much known. Nonetheless, when her arm stretches out toward me, I take the red plastic cup without objection.

'Welcome to Marshlyn Bay.'

'Thank you, it's definitely different to what I'm used to,' I admit, taking a sip of whatever concoction is in my hand. It trickles down my throat, burning my insides.

'You're a city girl? Personally, I couldn't think of anything worse.'

'It's not so bad,' I defend. To everyone back home, it's well known that I've never been much of a fan of the hustle and bustle of the city, but right now I'm feeling protective over my roots.

'Buuut, no beach parties,' Olivia sings, swaying her hips to the music.

'No. No beach parties,' I echo, placing the cup to my lips again, feeling a sudden urge to be drunk.

'This town has the best, far better than any city nightclub. Come on, the others are by the fire.' She grabs Lily as Vicki presses her lips together and shakes her head dismissively, linking my arm as we trail behind them.

'She's perfected the art of making you see what she wants you to see,' Vicki says, watching them skip ahead. 'On the outside she's as sweet as pie but get on the wrong side and the inner dragon is unleashed. She once hurled a glass at Lily because she snogged a boy she fancied at a party.'

I swing wide eyes in her direction. 'Guess I'll avoid getting on the wrong side then.' I'm not very keen on the idea of glasses flying my way, so just like my intention is with Jackson, I'll probably be staying well out of her way.

'She always finds a way to make everything about her. Lily plays along to keep her sweet, and I've gotten so used to it now, it's just one of life's many chores. Grin and bear it, that's the only way.'

'Understood.' I nod.

She finishes the remainder of her drink and I copy. The strong liquid makes me shudder, but it's starting to warm me up and I'm thankful. Taking Vicki's empty cup, I set them both beside a vacant log before glancing ahead. Olivia dances her way straight to Jackson's side whilst Lily holds back as she waits for us to catch up.

He has his back turned, talking to James. Olivia, now beside them, rests her shoulder into his side and my stomach flips, my plan to avoid him crushed and thrown violently out the window. I'm trapped with no means of escape.

'Hey, it's the niece!' Dex calls out merrily.

This puts a stop to their conversation as Emerald Eyes glances over his shoulder, catching my gaze. Vicki's arm remains linked with mine which I'm grateful for; I feel far more confident having both her and Lily by my side.

'Don't call her, *the niece,* Dex,' Lily retorts over the loud music and crackling of the burning fire – which is providing a welcomed warmth to my goose pimpled legs.

'I do apologise. Emily, the *fabulous* niece.' Dex winks and I can't hide the smile on my lips at his lopsided grin.

Jackson lets out a scoff. His biceps are incredibly prominent in his black T-shirt and I watch as they swell when he takes a swig of his beer. The fire brings my attention to a small silver band ring on his pinky.

'You've met?' Olivia's voice pulls me away, her eyes narrowing curiously as she studies me, before they drift up to Jackson who also seems to have found an interest in my face.

'We have.' He bobs his head weakly as he answers instead of Dex. 'She gave exceptional customer service in the shop yesterday. Well, I say exceptional, we got there in the end.' His lips twitch and I immediately squeeze Vicki's arm, feeling embarrassment and consequently irritation building from his cocky expression.

'How did the de-crapping go?' I ask, glaring at his tall frame.

'Brilliantly, as good as new now.' The stony exterior of his eyes and the way they're focused solely on me is making me squirm on the inside, but I can't let them get the better of me, because he knows he bothers me and he's playing on that factor. I can tell he likes using his simple mannerisms to push my buttons, and I would love to know why he's so keen on making me feel uncomfortable. I was starting to think maybe it's simply the way he is and he's like it with everyone, but the more I come into contact with him, the more I'm realising it only seems to be me. Surely, he can't still be holding a grudge against what I said.

'I'm glad,' I reply dryly, trying desperately to ignore the fact our conversation has drawn every pair of eyes within the group to us both. I'm feeling hot now, and it's not because of the minimal amount of alcohol I've consumed or the thunderous flames.

'Okay...' Dex's waning voice breaks the silence, his curious eyes flickering between the two of us. 'Can we please take a moment to address the glittery goddess?' he motions to Lily, who lifts an eyebrow in reply, almost as if she's daring him to continue.

I feel instant relief when the eyes that were on me drift over to Lily and her effervescent dress. Taking my chance, I furtively slide my arms from my jacket, manoeuvring it to drape over my shoulders. The loosening of the material on my skin starts to cool my hot flush, but I'm still content that I'm safely covered up.

'I said she looks like a glitter ball,' James agrees, a big grin on his face to match Dex's bright eyes.

'You do realise it's a beach party, Lil,' Dex says, taking in the sight of her stood next to me; one hand on her hip, her finger tapping her hip bone. He's winding her up, pushing for a reaction. Sounds familiar. Even though Lily and I are extremely different characters, at this moment in time, I've never related to her more.

'Leave her alone, boys.' Vicki tuts but I notice how her lips twitch as she struggles to suppress her grin.

'Honey, *beach party*, is simply a name. Lily motions between myself and her. 'We dress to impress.' She grabs me by the wrist. Her harsh tug makes me stumble over my own feet with my jacket falling to the floor before I can stop it. Faltering into her side, Lily's teensy dress rides up my backside and I'm left exposed with every aspect of my skimpy outfit on full show.

I don't have to look around to know all eyes are now on me. Heat rises to my cheeks, my calm composure lost once again as shame takes over. Scurrying to swipe my denim jacket from the sand, I don't bother brushing it down, instead throwing it on immediately. My focus remains firmly on the ground, sensing one particular set of eyes more so – and they are especially overpowering. I'm willing the ground to swallow me up.

'And impress you have,' Dex's chipper voice speaks up. I can't bring myself to look anyone in the eye. If only I had the confidence Lily had, this wouldn't be an issue.

A throat clears and Olivia's sweet tone interrupts the brief silence. 'Leo said we're running out of cans, help me get them from your Jeep?'

My attention lifts to Jackson's towering frame. He's staring at me, but the smirk's disappeared. His lips are lightly pressed together, his bold eyes unreadable, and I bizarrely find myself wondering what's running through his mind. Olivia notices his attention is elsewhere so places her palm on his arm, her fingers give a light, prompting squeeze.

'My keys are in my hoodie in the speaker truck.' He snaps out of whatever the hell he was thinking about and strides away without another glance or word, Olivia latched to his side.

'Isn't that the dress you wore to Vicki's party last year?' Dex asks, evidently completely oblivious to everything and everyone around him apart from Lily and her dazzling outfit.

'I'd love to talk fashion sense with you, Dexter, but since you don't have any,' she rakes her eyes over his white T-shirt, orange shorts, and all the way down to his brown flip-flops before blinking in astonishment back up to his face, 'we have a date with Mr Cîroc, so if you don't mind.' She begins to push me and Vicki in the direction of the surf hut just as Dex takes a step forward.

'The keg was running low anyway, I'll come with you and change it,' he says, idling past her with a big cheesy grin.

'Oh, great,' Lily mumbles, rolling her eyes as he passes her.

I turn to Vicki, both of us tickled. She jerks her head in the direction of a free log and James and I back towards it.

'We'll save you a space, Lil,' Vicki teases.

'Come on, my glittery goddess,' Dex calls behind him as he strides across the beach. Lily clamps her eyes shut and sighs before throwing a sarcastic thumbs up in our direction. She spins dramatically on the spot and drags her feet away.

As I perch on the rough surface, a group of people I don't recognise wave James over. 'I'll see you ladies in a bit.'

Vicki nods, falling down beside me.

My dress has now ridden up so much I'm pretty sure my arse is hanging out, and the sharp splinters are scratching and digging into my skin. I stand abruptly and brush my bum. Without thinking, I rid of my jacket, placing it on the log before plonking myself on top – the new protective layer of smoothness very much appreciated. Vicki's eyes question my behaviour.

'It's either hide these babies and suffer, or get the girls out and be comfortable,' I explain, pointing to my breasts. 'There's no one looking, so I choose comfort.'

'Why are you so self-conscious? You're drop dead gorgeous, Emily.'

'I'm not used to getting my lady parts out and putting them on show. Plus, being in Lily's tiny dress, I feel like an adult in kids clothing,' I admit on a frown.

Vicki laughs as she happily observes the snapping and crackling of the fire, and I watch Lily's dress light the way in the distance.

'What's the deal with those two anyway?'

Vicki turns to me and I nod in the direction of the pair who have just reached the hut.

'Oh, they're in love, they just don't know it yet.'

I knew it! I knew I wasn't imagining it. My inner elation at this fact is quick to subside when a small group of people dance past us and around the fire. I hug my arms across my body, knowing they're not in the slightest bit interested in me, but not being able to stop my insecurity from taunting my mind.

Vicki, oblivious to my brief timidity, continues. 'I don't care what she says, Lily likes the banter, it keeps her on her toes. I just wish they'd stop tip-toeing around and get down to business,' she says as I observe them both. Lily rests her hands on her hips, standing over Dex who is bending down and fiddling with a beer barrel.

'Down to business?' I ask on a laugh, tickled by her choice of words.

'You heard how he remembered what she wore to my birthday party last year. What boy remembers a girls' outfit? They're perfect for each other, Emily!' she exclaims, keeping eye contact with me as she swings her arm in their direction to make a point. 'I just know it,' she breathes. Lily is now knelt down next to Dex, helping him with something. So much for her wanting to be ten feet apart from him.

My sight of the pair is suddenly blocked by two figures taking up a stance in front of them. They're both cradling several cans to their chests.

'Unlike two certain someone's.' Vicki scoffs, having noticed them too.

I keep my focus on the bodies by the hut for a few more seconds before sighing and turning my concentration back to the fire. 'You and James?' I joke.

'Watch it, newbie.' She laughs. 'I mean Marshlyn Bay's hotty and Miss Prim.'

'I'll take it you're referring to Jackson as *Miss Prim*, because that is spot on.' The unfamiliar name tests itself on my lips as I realise it's the first time I've spoken his name aloud. Vicki snorts, a grin on her face, and I ponder for a moment, before daring to ask the question which has been circling my mind for the past few days. 'What's his story?'

There's a brief pause between us. The pounding music and the many voices swimming around the air which had become a general background buzz during our chat, grows louder in my ears as I'm left anticipating her response.

'Do you like him?' she finally asks cautiously, as if she was debating whether to question me or not. She flashes me a look out the corner of her eye which I can only take as intrigue.

'I'd rather eat my own foot,' I state resolutely. 'No, I'm just curious.' I'm curious to learn about the guy who is everywhere I go and everywhere I turn, and who appears to be so very popular in this town. But mostly I'm curious to find out about the boy who seems to continuously ignite feelings within me, from resentment all the way to embarrassment, leading to something I can't quite determine... a feeling which draws my attention and keeps it there, even when he's driving me insane.

'Just as well you're not interested because no one else can get a look in.'

'Because of Olivia? Are they together?'

Her face contorts. 'Oh no, far from it.'

'Friends with benefits?'

'Definitely the benefits part.' She pauses, her lips puckering in thought. 'Jackson doesn't really do relationships. The closest thing to a girlfriend he's had is his surfboard,' she states, clearly proud of her little joke as her lips twitch upwards. 'He's a bit of a closed book that boy, I've only ever seen him with Olivia, but I know there's other girls. James told me he sleeps around when he's feeling low, a sort of, *pick-me-up*, I suppose.'

My eyes narrow. 'What makes him feel low?' He doesn't seem unhappy, a little moody and arrogant, yes, but I wouldn't pin him as sad. But then again, I know all about facades. Even when living in places as beautiful as this, in a kind of hideaway – a safe haven – bad thoughts don't care. They're persistent, festering no matter where you live or who you are.

'Like I said, closed book,' Vicki reiterates on a shrug.

'And Olivia's okay with that? Him sleeping around?' I continue to pry, shocking myself with the unexpected questioning. I've always loved gossip. But as I'm pushing these questions, and as Vicki is happily telling me all she knows, I find myself not only getting that usual buzz from knowing someone's business, I'm feeling something else as well: intrigue. And it's building with every second we spend talking about him. I'm finding myself wanting to dig deeper.

'Who knows what goes on inside that head of hers, Em. She's clearly blinded by his charm and good looks so I think she tries to overlook it. As long as he's paying her attention, then that's all that matters. If you ask me, she's giving that boy too much power over her.'

I'm about to change the subject to prevent myself from pressing too far, but I'm saved from searching my brain for a topic.

'Hey, pretty ladies!' a raspy, unfamiliar voice calls.

Our gazes shift over to James who has his arm slung over someone's shoulder. The guy in question appears to be tipsy to say the least as he staggers and trips on the sand.

'Happy Birthday, Leo. I would ask if you're having a good time, but I think the answer's pretty clear,' Vicki remarks on a chuckle.

So, this is Leo.

A few of his buttons on his white shirt are undone at the top, not enough to reveal his torso, but enough to give people a cheeky preview of what's underneath, and judging by the rest of him, I'd say it's probably in tip-top condition. They both pause as he extends his drink towards us, and with a wink and a stumble, the bottle is placed to his lips. He takes a long swig before gasping in pleasure, licking his lips. Oh yeah, he definitely likes to be looked at.

'*Who* is this?' he asks as James helps to guide him over to the log. He plonks himself beside me, looking me dead in the eye.

'Emily,' I say, offering my hand to shake.

'Emily,' he repeats, testing it on his lips. 'I like it.' He takes my hand but not to shake, instead he lifts it to his mouth and lightly presses his lips against my knuckles.

*Okay...* I shift awkwardly on the log as a sheepish smile forms on my face.

'Right, big man, I'm going to get you some water,' James mercifully interrupts.

Leo lets go of my hand and his drops to his side. 'Water is for wimps,' he declares, or rather, slurs.

'You won't be saying that in the morning,' James stresses, living up to Lily's association of being a responsible Dad-like figure. Leo grunts in reply before guzzling more of his beer.

'I don't know what's taking Lily so long, I'll go and see where our drinks are, Emily,' Vicki says, pushing herself up. I'm mentally crying out for her to stay, but the pleading look in my eyes must not be as noticeable as I'd hoped as she starts walking away.

'You don't mind staying with him, do you? I won't be a minute.' James doesn't give me much of an opportunity to decline.

'Well, act–

'Thanks, Em. If he says anything weird just ignore him.' Blanking my pleas, he chases after Vicki, wrapping an arm around her waist and pulling her close. I scowl at their backs, watching them disappear past the bonfire.

I sigh quietly to myself before turning back, staring at nothing in particular and trying desperately to avoid Leo's keen gaze.

'And where have you been hiding?' I can smell the alcohol on his breath, and my nose wrinkles as I keep my eyeline focused forward.

'London,' I reply plainly, trying my best to sound unfazed, even though I am without a doubt extremely uncomfortable. Not only do I have Leo sat too close for comfort, but my bum feels like it's been anesthetized by this horrendously rough log.

'You look familiar, are you sure we haven't met before?'

My eyes shoot down to my leg.

*Is that his hand on my knee?*

I make the mistake of turning my head in astonishment. He smirks, knowing he's now grasped my full attention. The fire is lighting his face to reveal every detail, from the bloodshot eyes, flecks of blond in his spiky hair, to his rugged beard and slightly crooked nose. He is irrefutably easy on the eye, and he knows it. His drunken personality, however, I don't feel quite measures up.

His cheesy pick-up line has most likely been used countless times before and is clearly a technique – along with the attempted drunken smoulder – to pull the ladies in. Although, the more I stare at him, the more I'm deducing. I have seen him before! Well, one thing's for certain, Jackson seems to have a similar pattern when it comes to friends, because everyone I've met so far has been extremely confident, some overly so.

That's it! He was one of the faces of the group Jackson was with outside the pub the night Buddy went rogue, and he was with the surf guys I saw the other day on my run. Leo begins drawing gentle circles around my knee and I realise I need to answer him.

'No, I don't think so, I never forget a face,' I lie. Give him what he wants until James comes back, and then run as far away from here as possible.

'Now why would someone like you be living in a place like London?' he asks, watching his own fingertips caress my knee before gazing back into my eyes.

'Someone like me?'

'Yeah, you don't strike me as a city girl. You look like you belong riding the waves.'

'Riding the waves?' I splutter in bewilderment. Does he turn into a hippy when he's drunk?

'You look like you should be free.'

I'd love to be free from this situation.

'So, come on, what's London got that old Cornwall hasn't? Certainly not me.'

'If you must know I live with my boyfriend there,' I say, hoping the boyfriend card might just make him back off. It doesn't. If anything, it seems to encourage him as he inches even closer.

'It's okay, when we get married you can move here permanently.'

I raise an eyebrow. 'And when are we getting married, Leo?'

'Whenever you want, baby. A beautiful girl from a faraway city visits a small town in Cornwall, falls madly in love with a blue-eyed, mysterious stranger with extraordinarily great hair, and it all begins on a log, next to a blazing bonfire.' His voice softens as his face dares to edge closer. 'It's very romantic,' he whispers, and that's when his fingertips leave my knee, taking the chance to tickle higher up my leg.

I push his hand away, standing abruptly. 'I think someone's had a little too much Dutch courage.' I was giving him the benefit of the doubt and allowing his drunken self a harmless hand on the knee to keep him here as James asked, but this is too much. I tug my jacket on. 'I'm just going to see where James has got to with that water.'

'Come on, it's my birthday. Stay and play,' he pleads, leaning a little too far backward before balancing himself and placing the beer bottle in between his lips again.

'I won't be long,' I say, pacing away.

'Your loss, blondie,' he cries over the music and chattering. I don't look back, already scanning the crowd for familiar faces.

'I very much doubt that it is,' I murmur.

I search in the direction of the beach hut where a small crowd is gathering around the drinks table, to see Lily stood with Dex and a couple of other people I've never met. I then find the person who was supposed to be getting his friend water. He's attacking Vicki's face with his lips against the side of the hut. I sigh, cold, uncomfortable and alone in a place where I know hardly anyone.

Isn't a party supposed to be enjoyable? Because I feel not much enjoyment has been had on my behalf. In fact, the idea of climbing into bed is becoming more and more appealing. My eyes flicker around the beach at all the fun-loving bodies who seem to be sucking the energy out of me and using it for themselves. Standing here alone, watching everybody simply be with their friends, makes me think of the one person I've been pigheadedly avoiding.

Enough of this.

I spin, un-wedge my phone from my jacket and saunter towards the steps leading to Maple Cottage.

His name appears at the top of my screen and I start typing:

*Can we talk, William? I'm sorry.*
*My head's been–*

'Where are you going?'

My fingers pause as several pairs of trainers appear in my vision and I'm forced to stop in my tracks. My head lifts and in front of me are three boys around my age ogling me, each with a plastic cup in their hands. I'm feeling impatient and irritated as it is, I can't be bothered to deal with insolent, drunken teenagers.

'Home. Excuse me.' I attempt to tread past them. The middle guy steps to the side, preventing me from getting any further. It's much darker and quieter than it was a few minutes ago, verifying how far away from the party I've sauntered.

'So early? Come on, there's still lots of celebrating to be had,' he says, a glint of eagerness flashing across his face.

'I don't feel like celebrating right now.'

'You just need to loosen up, let's get you a drink.' The guy to my right offers, but I step back, frustration bubbling inside me.

'I'm fine!' Seriously, go away! Why do men always think it's a funny game to harass?

'I can see that. You can't come out dressed in that pretty little number and not expect attention. Come on, gorgeous girl, let me give you the attention you deserve.' The middle boy steps into me and my frustration immediately shifts to panic.

I remember the sickening man addressing me in that way. Visions of the other night flood my mind; images of *his* body edging toward mine, feelings of jelly-like limbs mixed with sheer terror as I felt his hand on my cheek, along with the panic which swamped me from seeing his gun being drawn. It's all closing in on me. Anxiety is building, my breathing is deepening, and my vision is distorting.

'I said, I'm fine,' I repeat, losing strength. I grip my phone tighter as my hands begin to tremble, and fretfully peer around in search of anyone I know. It's to no avail, we're too far away from the bonfire.

I feel a grip on my arm and my head snaps to see the middle guy has a hold of it, but I don't give him a chance to move any closer as I shove it off.

'That wasn't very nice,' he says, grabbing my wrist once again. I fight it, but this time he doesn't loose.

'Just have a drink, darlin'.' another voice says.

I continue to fight, but it only seems to encourage them.

'Let me go!' I cry.

Before I can lift my leg to kick him where it hurts, the slimy hand is being ripped away as another is placed on his chest, forcing him back.

'Don't you know when to quit, Aaron?'

Aaron's hands fly out in surrender.

Overcoming the initial shock, I soon realise an arm is out to the side and positioned in front of me, blocking me from all three boys. I can't help but stare up and notice his strong jaw tensing.

'Whoa, mate, we were just having some fun, weren't we, darlin'?'

'Funs over,' Jackson declares. There's no hesitancy or wavering, and his tense body in front of mine is showing no sign of backing down. I can feel the warmth radiating from his back and it's as though I'm absorbing it, my skin heating involuntarily.

'Yeah? Says who?' Aaron asks, squaring up to Emerald Eyes whilst still maintaining some space as if wary of what he might do.

'Me. And I'm pretty sure none of us want a repeat of last time,' his deep tone warns. I'm very much unaware of the event in question, but clearly the sheer mention of it is enough to make Aaron pause. The gears churn behind his eyes as if debating whether it's a good idea to push it further or not.

'Okay.' He holds his hands up in surrender, motioning to the others to back away. 'You can have her anyway, too stiff for us. See you around, beautiful.' They leave, chugging their beers apathetically. Relief leaves me on a scoff of disgust.

What just happened?

I'm in shock, my face most likely looking like a deer in headlights. Jackson moves, shuffling around on the spot, watching them walk away with a look so fierce it frightens me.

'You alright?' he asks. His eyes immediately soften when they meet mine, but that doesn't seem to relinquish their intensity. My attention is solely held on him. What was he doing this far away from everyone? He couldn't have been following me, could he?

'Thank you,' I reply quietly as I try to locate my voice.

'Don't mention it... again,' Jackson remarks, and it shocks me when there's not a hint of sarcasm to his tone. His unfathomable emeralds mesmerize me as our eyes linger on each other for what feels like minutes, but must only be mere seconds, before someone yells his name. I'm too stunned to work out whose voice it is, but as soon as it's said, he's gone, leaving my side in a flash.

My vision remains fixed on the air where he stood, eventually lowering to the ground as I gather myself quickly and scurry off the beach.

Three thoughts consume my mind as I begin up the hill. The first: I am never wearing anything of Lily's ever again. The second: Jackson willingly stepped in to help me. But the third and most prevailing is an image. An image of those emerald eyes gazing right at me, and then disappearing, just like that.

# THIRTEEN

I shut the passenger door and meet Aunt Maggie by the boot to grab the shopping bags. The humming of the Mercedes' engine and the creeping of its tyres signals the arrival of Guy behind me.

Aunt Maggie drove us – with Guy in convoy – to St Iven, which is one of Cornwall's quaint places for retail shopping, and the quality time together was well spent. She'd insisted on buying me new trainers, so I obliged, there's never any point arguing with her determined mind. I also purchased some new clothes to make sure the whole red dress debacle *never* happens again. Aunt Maggie bought a few things too, she even picked up some items for Guy – mainly toiletries and things she insisted he would need, even though he's staying in a hotel.

I'd confided in him and asked if he would accompany us, explaining that the incident at the party last night had shaken me. I was deliberating whether to tell him, but as soon as he saw me this morning, he knew something wasn't right. I've quickly come to learn nothing gets past him. I didn't tell Aunty to protect her from having to worry, but even more so to protect those boys from being thrown off a cliff. If she found out, I wouldn't put anything past her. With any luck Jackson will keep quiet too. It's concerning me how I haven't been able to stop the scene replaying repeatedly in my head. I keep feeling his towering presence in front of me, those piercing eyes boring down into my own; intense, yet the concern behind them undeniable.

'If you grab those, I'll go and unlock,' Aunt Maggie says as she rummages in her handbag for the key. I nod, happily reaching in to take the rest. She pauses for a moment, gazing musingly at me. 'I had a really lovely day today, Pidge.'

'Me too.' I smile back before she sighs happily and shuffles through the side gate.

I reach up and slam the boot down, and as I do, my phone buzzes in my jacket pocket. Manoeuvring the bags into one hand, I wedge it out with the other and stride through the gate. My feet pull up with my throat constricting as the caller flashes on the screen.

Buddy's scratchy paws pound against the cobblestone path when Aunt Maggie unlocks the front door, his erratic pants fill the air as he races around, sniffing the plants on the lawn, but I'm only narrowly aware of this. My brain too focused on the name glaring up at me.

Feeling his towering presence, I peer up. Guy is standing three feet away, a remorseful look clear on his face. It's his eyes which I notice the most because they're sympathetic. He knows what's about to happen. This isn't going to be good news. He takes the bags from my grasp and flashes an encouraging smile before wandering inside.

I collapse back onto the swing bench and Buddy trots up, sliding down to lie at my feet. My eyes rake over the ocean through the trees, the serene setting in no way helping to simmer the dread. A groan rises in my throat as the phone is lifted to my ear.

'Dad?'

'Hello, sweetheart,' he says with a firm and stable voice.

I hate it when he calls me that, it's a term of endearment he uses only to try and sugarcoat sour news, he's used it all my life:

'*Sweetheart*, I can't come to your Nativity, I'm working…'

'Sorry, *sweetheart*, we can't have dinner together tonight, but Sandy your nanny will eat with you…'

By now I should be used to it, but it seems the years of overuse have only built-up abhorrence for the word.

'How's Cornwall treating you?' he asks, and I have to bite my tongue.

'Not bad. Aunt Maggie's been great,' I reply, my tone deadpan as I prepare for what's coming.

'Guy tells me she gave you a job, that's good. It'll keep you busy.' He's delaying the matter.

'Why are you calling me?' I push bluntly. It's very rare he calls to simply ask how I'm doing and given the situation, I wish he'd get to the point. 'Because, unless it's to tell me that man's been caught, I don't want to know.'

'What you have to understand, Emily, is that I'm doing all I can.'

'Which means?'

'I thought it best if it comes from the horse's mouth and that I tell you early.'

'Tell me what?'

There's a short beat of silence before he exhales, and I can feel his apprehension through the phone. 'The situation is proving harder to resolve than I first anticipated.'

I know what's coming.

'Emily, you may have to stay down there a while longer,' he says quickly and without compassion, in a way which tells me I have no choice.

'How much longer?'

'Indefinitely.'

'What do you mean, *indefinitely*?'

'You need to stay with your aunt until I say it's safe to return home.'

I pause for a moment, my chest tightening with every word spoken. Anger surges through me. I stand, treading over Buddy and pacing forward. 'Did you not hear me the other night when I told you? I'm supposed to be going to university next month. That's in just over three weeks' time!'

'I know,' he responds, but I can hardly hear him over the rage which is coursing through my veins and causing my pulse to drum in my ears.

'What am I supposed to do?'

'Hopefully it won't come to it, but you may have to entertain the idea of deferring for a year.'

It still doesn't sound like there's any remorse in his voice, and honestly, I'm not even surprised. Why is this happening to me? I've been planning this stage of my life since I can remember and now he might be ripping it from under me, just like he ripped away every ounce of normality after Mum died.

'You're kidding, right? Please tell me this is one big joke. Do you know how hard I've worked for this? Do you even understand how much I've been looking forward to doing something I enjoy? Something which will give me purpose. Because, God knows, I've had a life of nothing but grief and disappointment.' I gasp and close my eyes, pinching the bridge of my nose to attempt to calm myself. 'This was my chance to be happy,' I breathe on a quieter tone.

'I understand that, sweetheart. I'm not saying you can't still go. I'm simply preparing you for the worst possibility.'

He doesn't understand, a man like him never could. 'You really don't get it, do you?'

'I didn't want to worry you with the facts, Emily, but these people are incredibly dangerous and unpredictable.' His voice is growing sterner.

'Yeah, I found that out when I had a gun pointed at me.'

He dismisses my remark, not even acknowledging it. His ability to empathise really does overwhelm me sometimes.

'I have an excellent team working on this. I promise you I'm trying my best.'

'Try harder,' I fire back. I'm fed up with him and his empty promises because that's all they are. Empty. I'll be amazed if these monsters are ever dealt with. I'm not holding my breath, and I'm certainly not getting my hopes up on the idea of ever finding out what the hell is even going on. At this moment in time, I've never hated the man more. I don't care what he does or what he says, after all this is over – if it is ever over – I never want to see or speak to him again.

'I'm sorry, Emily.'

I sniff. 'Okay, Dad. I've heard that before.' I take a sharp intake of breath. 'Can you just answer me one question?' He doesn't reply so I take it as my cue to continue. 'These people you're talking about. Who are they?'

There's a pause. 'Stay safe and remember any problems, Guy is there.'

The line goes dead.

I keep the phone to my ear, gazing at the peaceful ocean, though unable to fully take in its beauty, feeling anything but. My eyes close and I feel a single tear escape. I'm trapped.

I vaguely hear the front door creaking open, and I don't have to look to know Aunt Maggie's head is peeping around its frame.

'Would you like a cup of tea, Pidge?'

The lump in my throat is gulped down, the damp streak on my face wiped before a smile is forced onto it. 'No, thanks. If you don't mind, I think I'll go for a walk.'

'Everything okay?'

'Perfectly peachy,' I respond, letting my smile drop as soon as my back is turned. I tug the gate closed behind me, hearing her chirpy voice as she calls Buddy inside. The last sound my ears pick up is his bark before everything is zoned out – one destination in mind.

Gusts of wind blow my hair across my face. It's a little before dusk now so the air is cooler, and more notably, the sun is setting, making for a beautiful red sky. Just what I need.

I'm trudging along the cliffs, a little out of breath, even though they're not as steep as I first anticipated. When James parked up last night, I'd spotted a path leading to the clifftops and knew instantly they would be an ideal place to think, escape, and simply be alone. Even the trek up here allowed me to reflect, and it all makes sense now; why William delayed calling me and why he seemed so off when he eventually did. He knew, and he couldn't tell me. That night when we were stood outside Lambert Law, he knew it would be longer than four weeks, that's why he was acting so strange. I guarantee Dad told him to keep quiet.

My irritation is rising again, but as though it heard the garish cries in my mind, a bench is mercifully revealed up ahead. It's perched near the edge, off the track and faced to overlook the horizon. More importantly, it's vacant. Perfect.

I collapse down and bring my legs up to my chest, wrapping my hands around my knees. My head falls back and my eyes close. It's partly relief of not feeling the heaviness from keeping them open any longer, but it's also the distant hissing and crashing of water against rock below which is aiding in calming me down. I hum to myself, absorbing the harmonious serenity that mother earth is providing.

'Look who it is.'

My lids fly open, my head remaining against the back of the bench, but my eyes flicking to face the voice.

What the hell is he doing here?

He settles on the other end, his eyes finding solace in the view, but mine not deviating from him. 'I hope you're not debating whether to jump, because I really don't feel like cliff diving tonight.'

Jackson's jaw slackens when his mouth parts to allow his tongue to run over his lips painfully slowly. The two drawstrings of his hoodie have been pulled tighter to shield his neck from the breeze, and his unruly soft curls are a flurry in the wind. With his arms folded across his chest, I catch sight of the rings on his fingers, however the one which stands out sits on his left pinky. The ring I'd spotted illumed by the bonfire flames last night. But what I'd missed are the indents on the band. They look alien, like symbols I've never seen before.

My head snaps from him to the ocean, not liking how he's drawn me into his particulars. 'Rude *and* condescending, do you know how well you're coming across?' I snap back. He may be frustratingly attractive, but he's certainly got the personality of an arse which has been sat on for hours – in my opinion at least, Olivia might beg to differ.

'I've heard that sarcasm is the lowest form of wit.' He flicks a glance in my direction but I don't give him the satisfaction of my attention.

'So is being a dick,' I respond, not even surprised at my language. I was already annoyed, and I'm not willing to put up with him as well as everything else. I've come here for some alone time and yet again he's somehow managed to find and irk me.

As he gazes back out at the everlasting ocean, he runs his fingers through his rugged hair. 'Touché,' he says, before his mouth finally closes. For the tiniest of seconds, I believe he might allow us to sit in silence, but of course, I'm wrong. 'You should be nicer to the guy who saved your life.'

*Strike one.*

'You didn't save my life. I was handling it,' I lie. I really wasn't handling the situation last night very well at all, and if he hadn't intervened, I'm not sure what I would've done. But there's no way I'm giving him the satisfaction of knowing that.

'Of course, you were,' he scoffs.

'What were you even doing that far away from the party?' I ask curiously.

'I could say the same about you.'

'I asked first.'

'Let's just say it's a good job I have a weak bladder.'

I roll my eyes as he shifts his body in my direction.

'Look, I wouldn't let it get to you, those guys are harmless. They're Leo's mates from football. They like to hang around and try to act the big bollocks, when everyone knows they're idiots.'

'You mean like you?' I mock, raising my eyebrows proudly.

'Someone has really grinded your gears, haven't they?' His elbow meets the back of the bench, giving me the impression he's not going to back down and leave anytime soon.

I sigh. 'Try several someone's.'

'Right, well this is usually my place to escape and be on my own, but because I'm nice–

'*Nice* is a loose term, I'm gathering.'

He ignores my remark. 'I'll allow you to sit there and be you with your, quite frankly, scarily evil frown, but

I'm staying put, so I'd appreciate a bit of hush.' He shifts away from me.

*Strike two.*

This guy doesn't have an off switch; his arrogance is relentless. Exasperated, I scoff and twist my whole body to face him. 'Excuse me, you're the one who-'

'Ah, ah, no talking.' He waggles his ringed index finger in the air, and I have to work hard to fight back a slap.

'Are you-'

'Shhh,' he interrupts again, tilting his head back and closing his eyes. I release a riled groan which causes his hand to fly out and his finger to flick in my direction. 'Okay, clearly you're not understanding the concept of quiet.'

*Strike three and I'm out.*

My raging hands slam onto the bench, forcing my body up. I stumble from the stiffness in my legs, but I'm quick to gather composure. 'Fine, you win! You can have your space to your obnoxious self. I'll find somewhere else to sit and reflect on the fuck up that is my life.' I storm past him, every fraction of me shaking. He sits up, watching me go.

'You're a very angry person, aren't you?'

His words move through the air, grab me by the arm and whirl me back around, a stern finger being lifted at his infuriatingly relaxed form. He's resting his forearms casually on his thighs, enveloping his fingers together whilst all the while maintaining the focus of those damned green eyes on my tensed-up body. 'You don't know anything about me. You might be happy in your own flippant world, Jackson, but that doesn't mean everyone else is, so fuck you!' And with that, I march away.

I'm considering giving up and heading back to the cottage, but then an idea stems. How I'm feeling right now, I'm going to need something significantly stronger than Aunt Maggie's tea. Something that's going to dampen these rampant emotions. Something Leo had right last night.

I'm going to need alcohol, and lots of it.

# FOURTEEN

I've lost count of the amount of shot glasses I've lifted to my lips. I ran out of cash about fifteen minutes ago, but luckily – or rather unluckily for my liver – after a chinwag, the barman told me he owed Aunt Maggie a favour for some business thingamajiggy, so whatever I wanted was on the house. I can't see how this is repaying Maggie, in fact it'll most likely make her mad more than anything, but hey, who am I to refuse this lovely man?

Seeing as it seems to be the local hangout, I took a risk coming to the pub at the back of Aunt Maggie's shop – which I now know, having not been distracted by Buddy and a seagull this time, as The Marshlyn. But thankfully, no one I recognise is in here, just holidaymakers and a few old men who I'm assuming are regulars – they look like regulars anyway, you can always tell a local from a tourist and I'm not sure why.

'Can I have two more please... Billy, was it?' I ask, waving the small empty glass in the air, whilst swivelling on my stool at the bar.

'It most certainly is, and you most certainly can,' he replies, shifting away from an older man – a local – he'd pulled a pint for at the other end.

'Thanks. They're actually not that bad,' I say, smacking my lips together to try and make out the exact flavour. 'Fruity.' I settle with the obvious, my mind not working properly. It's either something to do with the stream of nonsense problems floating around my head, or the seven or eight shots I've already consumed.

'Aye, that's the summer berries for you,' Billy confirms, lining up two more shot cups and pouring the contents into both, running the bottle across in one smooth motion. 'Our most popular vodka. It doesn't even taste like alcohol, that's probably why people end up leaving not knowing who they are. But at least they're having fun.' He chuckles as he slides them in front of me.

'Hmm.' I could do with forgetting who I am right now. 'I don't suppose you could leave the bottle?' I grimace with a pleading look in my eye.

'Sorry, no can do. It's our last one until tomorrow,' he says, placing it back under the counter.

'Oh.'

'Although…' He stands with his thin lips puckered, a thought running through his mind. 'No, I shouldn't really.' He shakes his head, but I can see he's debating with himself.

'Go on, Billy,' I push, raising my brow, a cheeky smile forming on my lips.

'We're testing a new flavour wine; it's meant to be an explosion of sweet berries mixed with the dryness of the white, want to try?' His eyebrows waggle temptingly, even though he and I both know my answer is already set.

'You read my mind.'

I watch with keen eyes as he slips off a wine glass from the rack above our heads and grabs an unopened bottle from the back shelf. He inspects the two before deciding to plonk them both to the side of me. 'I'll just leave that there,' he says, tapping the wine bottle. 'You look like you could use some cheering up.'

'Is it that obvious?' I breathe, throwing a shot back. My face doesn't contort, my throat now used to the burn.

'You know, it's said barmen and maids are the greatest therapists, we don't judge, we just provide the shoulder and the medicine.' He motions to all the rows of alcohol lined up on the back wall. 'You want to talk about it?' he asks, rolling his sleeves up and leaning his forearms on the counter. 'Boy trouble?'

'Something like that.' I sigh. More like one man and his little puppy trouble. 'No, it's okay. It's too much of a long story and I don't even know half of it myself.' I shrug, swirling around the contents in the tiny shot glass subconsciously. I wouldn't even know where to begin.

'Alright, petal, but don't keep it bottled up, you'll end up driving yourself crazy,' he says, straightening. 'I'll leave you to it, please don't overdo it or I'll have Mags knocking with one of her gardening shovels.' He grins cheekily, slinging a towel he'd been using to wipe the counter with over his shoulder.

'Thanks, Billy,' I offer on a lopsided smile.

'You're very welcome,' he replies as he idles back down the bar to serve another customer.

I swill around the last shot between my thumb and index finger before sighing and throwing it back, gasping as I swallow.

Another fifteen minutes and half a bottle of white later, with my jacket now splayed on top of the bar, my hazy head and blurry eyes are proving Billy right, because I'm slowly losing my inhibitions. Never mind forgetting who I am, with each guzzle more of me doesn't care.

A round of loud cheers brings me out of my daydream cloud of tipsiness as I glance behind me to the far side of the room. It shows how determined I was to consume alcohol when I stormed in here, because I failed to miss the birthday party going on. Balloons – with the number thirty boldly broadcasted in their centre – have been placed all down a long table. They sway to the beat of the music as the guests gradually stand and make their way to a small square – the dancefloor. A DJ is set up and confined to the corner, a couple of women with wine glasses in their hands loiter around his mixing desk. They hoot and holler when the volume is turned up, before shimmying to the middle of the floor.

My foot taps on the footrest as S Club 7 sounds out around the room. A few unimpressed – mixed with plenty of amused – looks are thrown towards the large group of laughing men, women and children from fellow restaurant goers who are finishing their meals.

It's like my body decides for me with my brain having no say whatsoever as I chug down the remainder of wine in my glass. I grab the half empty bottle from the bar and propel myself off the stool. My wobbly legs stumble, but my determination soon composes them, just in time for the chorus.

I throw both arms in the air and prance myself over to the now packed dance floor whilst singing the lyrics at the top of my lungs. A couple of the women cheer and applaud as I twirl myself into their group. Swigging from the bottle, I sway my hips and lose myself to the beat of the music. I feel a grip on my arm and turn to see an old man – probably the Granddad – as he takes one of my hands and twizzles me around, before taking me into a ballroom hold as we pivot on the spot. His face is all wrinkled and cute, and a big cheesy grin makes its way onto my face as he laughs in utter joy.

We break away and I skip around the dancefloor, watching children charge and skid on their knees. My body takes control when I climb onto a chair and step up onto the long empty table, pointing and singing to a couple of older women sat at the end who are bopping in their seats.

The lyrics tell me to put my hands in the air, so I do, performing to the audience sat in the restaurant. It's clear, I should've become a professional entertainer, because I'm busting out moves which are quite honestly to die for, and the whoops and whistles I'm receiving from the party group tells me I'm right.

However, as I take another gulp from the bottle, I make the mistake of gazing over to the bar, and that's when I see him. Jackson. He's ogling me with those fierce eyes of his, leaning his side on the counter and watching my every move with a smirk on his lips. I whip around so my back is to him and wave over a girl to join me on the table. I help her up and we dance together, flick our hair, sway, and sing with total abandon.

Drunk Emily has balls, I like her. I really should do this more often because I feel on top of the world. I'm elated and high on nothing more than summer berries and the notion of not being Emily Lambert for three and a half euphoric minutes.

It seems, nonetheless, I'll never be able to escape me entirely, because as I attempt another spin, my foot gets tangled around a balloon string. In a terrible attempt to unravel it, I misplace my other, which throws me off the surprisingly high table.

I'm falling through the air, my landing sealed with an immense crash.

There's no pain. However, knowing that won't be the case tomorrow doesn't perturb me. As I blink away the specks of dizziness, I notice I'm still clinging onto the wine bottle with a firm grip. My quiet giggles soon develop into complete fits of laughter as I hug the bottle to my chest, cradling it like a newborn. Before I can take another sip, it's snatched from my hands, and I'm being hurled into a standing position by my arms. My feet falter beneath me as I try to find my balance, but it seems I don't have to, because I'm held firmly in place by none other than Emerald Eyes. His strong arm is hooked around my waist and my wine bottle is in his other hand.

'Are you okay?' he asks, but I don't reply, my mouth being covered by the back of my hand to control the giggles. I really don't know what's so funny: the fact I fell off the table because of a balloon, the fact I was still clutching my wine with all my might, or the fact I'm currently being held upright by a man I've been thinking about none stop since I arrived. The fact none of those are funny seems to completely evade my tipsy mind. I reach for my wine, but he stretches his arm away which instantly halts my laughter. 'Let's get you sat down, party girl.' I meet his stare with what I hope looks like a fierce glare, but it's fruitless as he ignores it, guiding us both over to the bar.

I plop down in my seat on a huff, and as I do, I encounter a pleasant surprise. In the haste to get up and dance, not all the wine in my glass was consumed. I extend my hand, but that too is swiftly hauled away from me. A groan rumbles up my throat as I lay my head in my arms on the counter.

'How did you manage to get yourself into this state within half an hour?' he asks, finding it all rather amusing as he settles himself on a stool next to mine.

'I had many shots. It also might have something to do with the fact I haven't eaten since Midday,' I slur into my arms.

'Well, then I have no sympathy.'

I lift my head, and with squinted eyes, watch as he passes me the water Billy had left in front of him. Billy is a kind egg.

'It's a good job I'm not asking for it then, isn't it?' I respond, pushing his hand away, instead reaching for the now near empty bottle of wine. 'Are you following me?' I grumble when he thrusts it further down the bar to meet the glass.

'Might be,' he replies, prying open my hand. He places the water in my palm and forces my fingers to clasp the glass, giving me no chance to contest. 'Look at me,' he orders as his fingers gently grip my chin. Our eyes lock and his shift from side to side as he studies mine. I'm finding it hard to focus, but there's no doubt that his twinkling emeralds are the sole incentives to try and break through the haze in my vision. 'Believe it or not, I was heading back to my car when I heard a racket coming from inside here, I thought someone was dying, but it turns out it was just your singing.'

'You're hilarious,' I mock, taking a sip of the water to entertain him, I would never admit that it is a refreshing change from the dryness of the alcohol. So, after one mouthful to satisfy my throat, I place it back down on the side.

'I like to think so.' He grins cheekily before drawing his fingers off my chin, however his eyes remain on me. 'I don't think you have concussion, but if you want to go to hospital, I can take you.'

'I can't feel anything,' I reply on a shrug.

'You wouldn't, but that was one hell of a fall.'

'Okay, Grandma,' I quip on a giggle. He's awfully concerned for a condescending jerk.

He smiles. 'I'd quit while I was ahead, if I were you,' he says, gesturing to the accumulation of shot glasses and the wine glass and bottle he moved closer to him. 'We wouldn't want you wandering off and drowning.'

I blink my weary, glassy eyes, and desperately try to focus them on the empty glasses in front of me, but it doesn't work – the intoxication is getting worse by the minute. 'Good job you're a lifeguard,' I taunt, flicking my head in his direction.

'Yeah, but I don't feel like saving anyone tonight. It's late and I've just eaten.' He taps his stomach and my eyes follow his hand as he rests it on his thigh, his rings and the ring on his pinky yet again drawing my attention. I've always loved rings, William refuses to accessorise his hands, saying no man should wear them unless it's a wedding band, which I think is utter nonsense. They're... attractive.

'You really do think you're incredibly witty, don't you?' I snap out of my ring daze and swivel to face the old, rustic bar again.

'I don't think, I *know*.'

'Wow.'

'Seriously though, you should slow down, you'll feel it tomorrow.'

'I didn't realise you cared so much,' I say, expressing my sarcasm and chancing another glance at him.

'I'm a caring person,' he responds on a shrug of his shoulders.

I find myself watching him. He has an answer for everything. 'I thought you were on your cliff.' Instinctively, I pick up the water, my thirst now crying out to be quenched.

'I got bored. Thought I'd search for the frowning girl and annoy her some more.' He observes my movements closely.

'Well, this frowning girl is a tad busy at the moment, so if you don't mind.' I shoo my hand toward the doors behind him, before sliding the water away from me and swiftly snatching the wine glass from next to him. He doesn't attempt to seize it, most likely fed up with trying, which is exactly what I need. The novelty of him coming to my aid and me ogling his rings is wearing off, and I want to carry on partying.

'You're staying at Maple Cottage?' he half asks, half states, clearly having not received the message.

'And he's still here,' I utter before chugging back the rest of the wine. 'What's it to you?'

'I just want to make sure you get back in one piece. Knowing Mags, she'll be worrying.'

I stare through my fuzzy vision at his furrowed expression. 'Since when were you my dad?'

'I'm a lifeguard, I have a duty of care.'

'And here's me thinking I was special.' Locating the empty shot glasses, I then find my friend. 'Billy, two more please,' I yell over the music, shaking one in the air.

Billy looks across before starting toward us, but the party pooper to my right throws his hand out.

'We're fine, Billy,' he says resolutely. He slides off his stool with ease, swiping my jacket from on top of the bar and inching closer to my floppy frame. 'Let's get you home, come on.' He holds out his palm, but again he's causing irritation to grow inside of me. I didn't ask him to come and babysit me, and now he's preventing me from having fun.

'I don't want to go yet,' I slur, attempting to push his hand away, however he catches my arm effortlessly. His long fingers glide down my skin, leaving a trail of goosebumps as they find their way to my own. My eyes fix on them, his hand has practically engulfed mine; it's big and warm and smooth and… big. I can't help but be totally absorbed by it. I can feel his eyes boring into me, but I'm so concentrated on our hands that I fail to pay attention to anything else. I fail, for instance, to acknowledge my swaying body and being able to keep myself upright, so by the time I'm aware that I'm tipping further to the right, it's too late. I feel myself falling, but I never hit the ground. His strong arms are steadying me once again. Managing to snap out of my trance, I stable my wobbly legs, placing my feet safely on the ground.

'You're drunk,' he asserts, the quick switch in demeanour shocking me. 'You can either walk with me,' he lets go, and the absent support means I have to grip the bar with one hand to stay upright, but he remains incredibly close, so much so, I can feel the soft tickle of his breath on my cheek, 'or I'll have no other option but to carry you.'

I feel like I'm a child being scorned by their parent. My face hardens. 'You touch me, I scream.'

He stares down at me, and I stare up at him; both completely serious, both extremely adamant. With neither of us moving, I start to think we're going to be here for hours. That is, until he breaks his glower and makes to grab me. I throw my hands up in surrender.

'Alright, alright. I'm going.' I step past him and clumsily make my way to the doors. 'Bye, Billy. Thank you,' I call, but keep my eyeline focused forward, trying not to fall flat on my face.

'You take care, petal.'

The fresh air hits me like a ton of bricks, the breeze feeling like I've stepped into another world. Luckily, it's dark now, so I don't have any bright light to contend with. I hop off the patio, rotating on the spot and scanning all the vehicles. 'Where's your car?' I ask, hearing his footsteps behind. My jacket is draped over my shoulders with a gentle squeeze of my arms before he strolls past me.

'We're walking it off!'

My heart sinks, knowing what lies ahead.

'But… there's a hill,' I grumble, not liking this idea one bit.

'I'm aware.' He nods, turning to my frozen figure as he continues to tread backwards. 'This way, alky.'

Smiling, he spins on his heel, clearly back to his facetious self.

I blow out a long, unimpressed breath and glare at him before reluctantly following. 'I am *not* an alky,' I gripe, struggling to push my arms through my jacket holes.

'Whatever you say,' he calls as marches past Maggie's Surf Shack.

'Dick,' I curse, giving myself a mental pat on the back when my arms are successfully pushed through.

'I heard that!'

'You were meant to,' I mumble this time as I toddle after him.

He eventually slows down as we cross the bridge, allowing me to reach him. We fall into a slow and steady pace – well, waddle, on my behalf.

'You don't like me very much, do you?'

My thoughts seem to stop as I leave the silence to answer – although something inside tells me I'm not sure it speaks the truth.

'I feel as though we may have gotten off on the wrong foot,' Jackson declares, and I watch my shoes, one step, two step… the third takes me astray as I stumble to the side. 'What do you say we start a fresh?'

The next footstep stables me, and that's when I realise; there's always another step to adjust you if the last one didn't steer you right.

My head snaps to look up at him. It's getting darker as we move away from the glow of the shack's outside lights and begin up the narrow lane. I'm relying purely on him to make sure we avoid any bushes or trees, or even, as we get higher, the edge of the cliff. What's more, as my vision is far from 20/20 right now, I'm struggling to even make out his face to tell if he's being serious. I feel him stop, so I do too.

'Jackson Turner,' he states, and I vaguely register him holding out his hand.

'Emily Lambert,' I say, following his lead and taking that adjustment step. His grip is firm and strong, yet snug and comfortable. 'This would feel a lot more real if I could see your face,' I admit, trying to hide my titter at the invisible man I'm holding hands with.

'You know, I was thinking the exact same thing.' He sniffs as he drops our hold and scuffles about before a small, but effective, white light illuminates our path. He holds the phone under his chin which highlights his face dramatically. 'How's this?' He smiles, pulling a waggish expression.

It takes everything inside of me to keep a straight face, but somehow, I manage. 'I think I preferred it when I couldn't see you. Can you turn it off?'

'Oh, well in that case I'll let you fumble your own way home.'

I try incredibly hard, but the toothy grin breaks through and I can't control the giggles which follow.

The corners of his eyes crinkle. 'So, she can smile.'

I stare back at him. It's strange that just moments ago I was dancing on a table in front of a crowded pub not caring what anyone thought, but now, when it's only one person looking at me, I feel inexplicably shy. 'Just shine the light, Pennywise,' I order, breaking out of my brief timidity.

'Yes, boss,' he breathes before aiming his phone light ahead. Our feet start moving again, but with our truce now in action, we're heading forward on the right foot. 'Do I really look like a clown?' he asks, furrowing his brow.

'Of course not,' I chorus. 'More like a court jester,' I add, keeping my attention focused on the ground as my lips uncontrollably curl upwards.

He snorts but remains quiet as we continue our leisurely pace. Unlike back in the pub, he doesn't seem to be in such a hurry now, and I'm wondering why. After all, if he wanted to get me back quickly then he could've driven us. No, he wanted to walk. And as much as I hate this hill, it isn't all that bad; it's pleasant. Just as Jackson mentioned about walking it off, the fresh air does seem to be clearing my head. I'm not angry or wanting more alcohol. I'm strangely content.

'It's Emily Rose, by the way,' I mention, the thought randomly passing my lips. 'Which, not to be big headed or anything, but I kind of like, it rolls off the tongue. Emily Rose Lambert,' I say, making exaggerated movements with my mouth. 'It's funny how some words just sound good, you know, they have that edge, like wean, that's a great word,' I finish, staring ahead in my own world. 'Plume, there's another.' I feel his eyes on me as my stomach growls angrily and I clutch it. 'I really hope Aunt Maggie has chicken nuggets.'

'You talk a lot when you're pissed, don't you?' His tickled tone brings me out of Emily-land.

'Do I? I've never noticed.'

'I hope you're not going to make a habit of this. I can't be pealing you off the floor every Friday night,' he laughs, and I notice how the phone light is revealing his scruffy black and white Vans. My gaze drifts to his side profile as his brow contorts in thought. 'Excuse the blunt question, and by all means tell me to shut up, but how come you've never visited before? I mean, you may have, it's just, I've never seen you.' His eyes meet mine fleetingly before I tear them away, finding the spinning floor.

My heart sinks. The things I'd forgotten in The Marshlyn and up to this point come racing back. There are feelings of guilt for not seeing Aunt Maggie, anger toward Dad, and the most overwhelming, loneliness. Because I've never properly felt like I belonged. Ever. What am I meant to say to him?

I'm terrified that whilst being in my current intoxicated state, I'll end up divulging more than I probably should. And how do I answer in a way which doesn't make him think I'm a completely terrible person?

'It's complicated,' I opt with. *Keep it simple, you'll be fine.* 'I'm only really here because my dad messed up.'

I'm aware he's studying me, but I keep my head down, silently begging him not to dig any deeper. He must notice my despondency because mercifully, he doesn't.

'Well, if you ask me, Emily Rose Lambert, family is way overrated.'

My head darts up, eyes wide. 'You don't get on with yours?'

'Something like that.' He shrugs, gazing ahead as though he's staring into the darkness before us and beyond the short range of the phone light. Like me, he seems as though he's reluctant to discuss the topic of immutable relatives. However, the steam has been building inside of me and Jackson's question has forced my resentment to its edge, and all I want to do is rant. Before I can think better of it, I'm doing just that.

'It's the damn secrecy,' I huff. 'Adults and their bloody enigmas!'

'Everyone has secrets, maybe it's our way of dealing with things,' he offers rationally, and my weary eyes narrow.

'You're talking like you're an expert in secret keeping.'

'Maybe I am.' His eyes twinkle as he flashes me a small smile.

'Like some sort of secret keeping God.'

'I wouldn't go that far.' He shakes his head on a chuckle.

My will to stop is surpassed, drunk Emily taking full control. 'Are you good at keeping secrets?'

We pause in our tracks, and he turns to face me, shining the torch to the ground so we're both dimly lit. 'Depends on what it is,' he ponders teasingly, stepping a little closer.

'What if I told you a secret?' I ask gently, almost as a whisper.

Somewhere, awfully deep inside, there's a rational part of my brain screaming to stop this illogical Emily, but there's also the uncontrollable inebriated version, which is screaming, yes!

Tell him that you can't get the image of his intense watchful gaze out of your head. Tell him the reason you're so cold and hostile towards him is because it's your protection, and the reason you need that protection is because you're attracted to him. You're physically attracted to him even though you can't be. Yet, as you're staring at him, as he's standing there looking utterly breathtaking in this low light, you're realising that even though you have a boyfriend back home, he's evoked more feelings and emotion inside of you in three days than William has in three months. Tell him you think his hair is wildly perfect, and that he constantly drives you crazy with infuriation, but not as crazy as the thought of his soft, kissable lips do… and it's taking every ounce of rational you not to press yours against them right now.

'I think… I am a tiny bit drunk,' I murmur, fighting the devil on my shoulder and stepping back.

He smiles. 'That's not a secret,' he says, raising his brow.

'It is if no one else knows, for instance, my aunty.' I purse my lips with what I hope to be a pleading expression. She won't be happy with me being out for so long without her knowing my whereabouts, and most certainly would be livid if she knew what I'd been up to.

'Are you asking me not to tell your aunt you're pissed?'

'Now that you mention it, that's a very good idea.'

'You do realise that's something else you'd owe me for,' he says, and I flash him a big, cheesy grin. He rolls his eyes in response. 'I'll add it to the list.'

I hear a creaking noise behind me and spin around a little too quickly. Jackson grips my arm, stabling me. I watch with wide eyes as a porch light flickers and a pink, fluffy, raging lady with a cluster of rollers in her hair storms up to us.

'Where on earth have you been?' she snaps as she works the latch on the gate and shuffles with purpose across the road in her pink slippers. 'Is she drunk?' She points at me, but glares in Jackson's direction. I'd been so invested in Emerald Eyes, I hadn't realised we'd reached the cottage.

'Yes, yes I am,' I admit without thinking and with my head held high whilst swaying on the spot.

Jackson leans down. 'I take it you're not an expert in secret keeping,' he whispers in my ear. I ignore the warm flurry in my tummy and glare at him.

Aunt Maggie narrows her eyes and I shrink under her daggers, genuinely quite frightened. 'Guy has been out looking for you, young lady.' She tuts as I peer at her with the best apologetic eyes I can muster, but I wouldn't be surprised if I just look constipated. Her lips pucker before she sighs. 'Come on,' she says in a calmer tone before grabbing my arm and hauling me towards the gate. 'Thank you for walking her back, Jackson. I appreciate it.'

'You're welcome, Mags,' he replies cordially, but I could definitely hear a hint of laughter in his voice.

'Do you have any nuggets, Aunty?'

She scoffs, her grip on me remaining firm. 'You're lucky I'm a forgiving woman.'

'Is that a, yes?' I gleam hopefully.

She scowls down at me.

'Can I have ten, please?'

'You'll get what you're given,' she asserts without malice, and I may have been imagining it, but I even think there was a flicker of amusement on her lips.

I gaze over Aunt Maggie's shoulder as Jackson begins his journey back down the hill. However, what I didn't expect was for him to turn around and glance at me too. He smiles kindly, and I do something I thought would never happen from our first encounter in the shop and our mishap meetings thereafter.

I smile gratefully back at him, keeping that adjustment foot on the right path.

# *FIFTEEN*

I hadn't seen Lily or Vicki since the party. Lily text me that night and asked where I'd disappeared to, but I didn't tell her about the episode. I apologised and said I wasn't feeling well so went back to Aunt Maggie's. Luckily, she didn't ask further questions, so I assume Jackson hasn't told anyone about what happened either.

Jackson.

I haven't been able to get him out of my head. I woke this morning, not only with a splitting headache and a heavily bruised back, but also wondering what in the hell I said to him last night, because for the life of me I can't remember. I'm hoping it wasn't too embarrassing. Him seeing me in such a state was bad enough, and I know I'm never going to be able to live it down. Aunt Maggie wasn't best pleased with my behaviour either. This morning I was met with about ten dozen missed calls, Anadin Extra, and an intense scolding about how worried she and Guy were, so I promised not to do it again and I intend to stick by it. Alcohol doesn't agree with me.

'She won't tell me who it was, maybe you could get it out of her?'

'How are you so certain she slept with someone?' I ask Vicki, who is leaning across the till desk as I hang up a bunch of T-shirts on the back-wall rack. My headache is very much present and booming.

'She's one of my best friends, Emily, I can tell,' she claims. 'Plus, she disappeared at the end and wasn't at home yesterday morning when I called to drop her at work.'

Lily went to grab more stock from out the back a few minutes ago, and that's when Vicki took her chance to fill me in on the gossip from the beach party. Apparently, she thinks Lily went home with someone but can't work out who. Personally, if she did, I wouldn't be surprised if it was with Dex, which could be why she's so reluctant to tell Vicki. I bet she's embarrassed, seeing how much she rattles on about how annoying he is.

'I'll ask her, but I doubt she'll tell me.'

'Tell you what?' Lily wobbles in from the back with two large cardboard boxes covering her face. She dumps them on the floor by my feet with a huff and a puff. The flaps are tossed aside before she picks out and folds a blue and white polo neck top.

'We want to know who you went home with on Thursday night,' I say, watching her closely as she concentrates on placing the material on the shelf perfectly. After tweaking the edges and flattening the creases, she straightens and folds her arms.

'My mouth is shut; my lips are sealed.'

'Ha!' Vicki cries, banging her hand against the counter, and making Lily and I glance over with eyes wide. 'So, you did sleep with someone!'

Lily holds her hands up in surrender. 'I'm admitting to nothing,' she declares as she picks out another top. 'Anyway, you're not getting off the hook,' she announces, shooting me a knowing look. 'We heard about your antics last night.'

I recoil. 'What! By who?'

'It's a small bay, Em, people talk,' Vicki says. I throw her suspicious eyes, challenging her to tell me who spilled the beans. Was it, Maggie? Jackson? 'Billy came in this morning and told me.'

'Ugh!'

'It's alright, we've all had alcohol lapses. Good stories never start with, 'This one time I was drinking water,'' Lily says, I'm sure with good intentions, however it's failing to make me feel any better.

'I'm not sure this story is so good, more pure shame,' I reply, dropping my head in disgrace as I fiddle with a hanger in my hand.

'Oh, come on, it's not that bad,' Vicki attempts.

'I fell off a table in front of a pub full of people!'

Her pause is long and notable. 'Yeah, that is quite bad. But at least Jackson was there.'

'Mmm.' I get back to my job at hand and place a T-shirt onto the hanger.

'Sooo…' Lily pipes up as she folds a second top.

'Sooo… what?' I ask. The hangers slide across the

rack on a screech as I slot in the new addition. Her suggestive tone is patent, but I'm not quite sure what she's suggesting.

'Anything you want to tell us?' She waggles her insinuating eyebrows at me and I turn to her.

'What?'

'Mr Turner's what.'

I pause, running the name through my mind. It clicks. 'Me and Jackson?' I exclaim.

'Absolutely. Handsome guy, gorgeous girl.'

'I have a boyfriend,' I explain, unamused at her hints of getting with someone else.

'Sure, but you're not married,' she says on a shrug.

My eyes widen in bewilderment.

'Lily!' Vicki scolds from across the room.

'I'm just saying.'

'Well, don't,' Vicki warns.

'Alright, sorry. I won't bring it up again.'

We both go back to work, but I don't miss the sly wink she throws me without Vicki noticing. I roll my eyes, hanging up another shirt. She is being ridiculous.

It's as the shop falls quiet when my mind starts running amok. I freeze, it's like my brain has been restored and it's sending forgotten memories around in circles. I remember my thoughts. I remember standing there, looking at him in the dim light and thinking those irrational things about his hair, his lips, his eyes. My fingers clench around the hanger in my palm as I cringe.

That's it, categorically never drinking again!

'Afternoon, girlies!' Aunt Maggie's sprightly tone flurries around the shop as she steps inside.

'Hi, Mags,' the girls say together.

I muster up a smile, still embarrassed about last night's actions. Keeping my head down, I return to organising the T-shirts in order of size, whilst Aunty scurries over to the till and pulls out a large brown book from underneath the desk, plonking it on top.

'Why don't you girls take a break while I do the accounts, go get an ice cream,' she suggests, waving her hand towards the door.

'You sure?' Vicki asks as Aunt Maggie opens the book to her bookmarked pages.

'Yeah, we're quiet. You've been working all morning and you should make the most of it. Apparently, there's a storm coming tonight.' Her eyes then lift to meet mine. 'Besides, Emily looks like she could use one.' She winks and I tut.

'Ha ha,' I mock, placing the final hanger on the rack. In all fairness, she's not wrong, I need the fresh air to clear my hungover, Jackson filled, throbbing head.

'Thanks, Mags,' Lily calls as she skips out the shop with Vicki and myself trailing behind.

We wander onto the jam-packed beach, meandering around the groups of people set up on almost every inch of the dry sand. The sky is clear, giving the sun no barrier as she beats down in full force on the masses of half-naked, glossily sun-creamed tourists. I'm thankful to be wearing my new flowy summer dress I bought in St Iven, because unlike this morning, the fresh air has turned so thick you could cut through it with a knife, and along with the heat from the blazing sun, my current hangover situation is not being helped one bit.

We decide to perch on the rocks which are, much to my utmost delight, shaded by the cliffs behind us.

As though it saw us coming, the ice cream van makes its way up the beach, stopping only a few metres away. On cue, hordes of kids bound towards it as the parents amble behind with their change at the ready.

'Ice cream?' Vicki asks, standing with her purse in hand.

'Calippo, please,' Lily responds excitedly.

'Em?'

The thought of something ice cold and fruity running down my throat makes my dry mouth water. 'Same, please!'

'Three Calippo's coming up.' She spins and treks down the beach, joining the back of the already shrinking queue.

Up ahead, my eyes zone in on two familiar bodies as they jump out of a lifeguard truck parked down by the sea. It's facing the ant-like surfers and bodyboarders in the water, and one lifeguard marches over to a red and yellow flag, unscrews it from the sand, and shuffles it backwards away from the incoming tide. The other is a female in shorts and a red top which is tied at the front, flaunting her toned stomach. Even if I was partially sighted, it would be obvious as to who it is. She leans her arm against the side of the truck as she watches Dex fix the flag in place.

I turn to Lily who has been abnormally quiet and as soon as I do, I get my reason why.

'You should tell him.'

'Hmm?' Her eyes maintain their focus on the truck – or rather, a certain someone who is stood chatting to Olivia beside it.

'He clearly likes you too,' I say, nudging her arm. The action seems to bring her out of her daze as she looks at me through unconvincing puzzled eyes.

'Who? Dex!'

I nod encouragingly with a grin on my face, but her head is instantly shaking. 'Don't be ridiculous, Emily.' Her attention rests back on the smiling lifeguard. I study her before watching them myself.

'I may have only been here for a few days, but I know ogling eyes when I see them.'

Her head whirls in my direction and I can tell she wants to hit me with a retaliation, but nothing leaves her mouth, or maybe it does, I just don't hear her.

The revving of my own distraction comes to a gradual halt as the engine of the quad bike ticks over when it stops in front of Dex and Olivia. Sat with both hands extended out and gripping the handles, a shirtless Jackson lifts his toned arm up to point at the window of the truck. Dex reaches inside and pulls out a blue and red jacket before hooking it over the front handles, he pats Jackson's muscular back; both faces painted with wide grins.

'So do I,' Lily says. I pull my gaze away to see her smirking at me.

The purring of the idle engine is replaced by a cavernous growl as he whizzes off, flicking sand in the air and leaving doughnut shapes in the ground before vanishing up the beach.

I take a breath. 'I have a boyfriend,' I repeat for the second time today.

A wave of revelation punches me smack bang in the chest. I don't know what senseless Emily was thinking last night. Alcohol is a sin and Billy was right; it does make you forget who you are. Your thoughts are thrown completely out the window. I don't want to think about *his* hair or kiss *his* lips. Why would I? He was simply there at that particular moment when I felt vulnerable, frustrated, and alone. Yes, he's easy on the eye, but I was also drunk. I wasn't thinking straight, and I'm missing William.

William…

'And where's he?'

I turn away from her in thought.

Sod his lack of communication, hectic lifestyle, and poor ability to stand up to my father. He gets me, and he knows how I'm feeling. Why else would he have been apprehensive about telling me I have to stay longer? He cares. He understands how much my freedom means to me. I need to talk to him. I need to apologise for the way I've acted. He needs to know how grateful I am to have him in my life – how important he is to me.

After work, I raced back to the cottage, leaving Aunt Maggie with her account book in the shop. Guy sent me a text, letting me know he was back at the hotel doing his daily checking in with Dad, so I'm curled up on the grey corner sofa with Buddy lying at my feet.

My phone is clasped in my hand. I draw a deep breath, pressing his name.

It rings, and rings, and rings. No answer.

I re-check the time on the screen. Three o'clock. He might be in the office. Tapping the number below his personal mobile, my phone is pressed back to my ear. This time it rings twice before I hear fumbling on the other end as he picks up. I don't give him a chance to speak.

'William, I'm sorry I was short with you the other day, it's just been a lot to take in and–

'Emily? Is that you?' a deep voice interrupts which doesn't belong to my boyfriend.

'Oh, hello, yes,' I reply, vaguely recognising the hoarse tone.

'It's Steven Andrews.'

I knew he sounded familiar. Steven works in William's office; the man William goes out drinking with on the regular. Not my most favourite person.

'Yes, of course. How are you?' I ask, putting on my fake happy phone voice.

'Not too bad, how's everything with you?'

'Oh, you know,' I reply briefly, brushing the question off. After all, I can't really say it's utter shit, because when people ask that question, they're doing it to be polite, when in reality they couldn't care less about you or your problems – something I'm guilty of doing too.

'William's gone to fetch us a coffee,' he reveals in a tone of jolliness which grates on me. He's so oblivious to how many arguments we've have had because, 'Steven suggested we go for a drink,' which always turned into several, with 3 a.m. being last orders on many a weeknight – 4 a.m. on weekends.

'Ah,' I reply, annoyed at my bad timing. I'd rather not be stuck on here making frivolous chitchat with him.

'Have you sorted everything out?' he asks when I don't offer anything else. I'm not really concentrating, I'm thinking about everything I want to say to William

– when I eventually get the chance to speak to him. 'I have to say he was a little upset that you both hadn't been talking.'

'Oh, he told you?' They're obviously close enough for William to be discussing our relationship troubles with him, so I start to wonder how much Steven knows. He works for Dad and he's William's partner. Does he know what happened to me? 'Well, there wasn't really much to sort, I know we've both been a little off recently, but it's nothing we can't work through,' I say simply, not wishing to dwell on the matter. I just want to talk to my boyfriend.

'I'm glad, everybody makes mistakes. I know I had a part to play, it was my idea after all, and honestly, I can't apologise enough. But when you've had a few drinks, everything seems like a good idea, right?'

My body tenses. His words grasping my full attention.

'I'm sorry… I'm confused. What was a good idea?' I question, my tone is composed, but my jaw automatically clenches as soon as it's asked.

'The Penthouse.'

My heart sinks. The Penthouse is a club which sits on Sealey Street. A club for a particular type of male.

'Look, I'm sure you can understand, sometimes working in this industry can become tiresome, shall we say, and we needed time to relax and let loose.' Sympathy is present in his voice, but I get the feeling he's not all that sorry.

I gather myself, swallowing in order to speak. 'William went to The Penthouse?' I have a horrible feeling in the pit of my stomach.

'He said he was going to tell you, I thought he had.'

No, he has not!

'Just as well he had to leave early; some drama the boss called him with. Something about an attack on a client. I swear your father works him to the bone.' He chuckles. *He chuckles!*

My stomach turns and I can feel bile forcing its way up my throat. It's like someone's taken a hammer and is striking me in the gut over and over again. My heart is pounding in my chest. I can't tell if it's been mere seconds or minutes since Steven's admission before he speaks again.

'Here he comes now. It was nice to talk again, Emily,' he says, none the wiser about the blow he's just dealt.

'Yeah, it was definitely enlightening,' I mutter, my grip tightening around my phone.

Muffled words travel down the line.

'Em? Everything alright, babe?'

His voice causes tears to prick in my eyes.

'I don't know, you tell me.'

'What?'

'Have you got anything you want to tell me?'

A pause. 'No… why?'

'In that case, let me refresh your memory.' I muster a sharp breath. 'The night your home was broken into, Steven just informed me on your wonderful time together.' My tone is harsh. Unrelenting. Bitter.

There's silence.

'Oh.'

'Yeah. *Oh!*'

'Jesus, I'm sorry. It all got a little out of control, drinks were flowing. I didn't even want to go. It was just a stupid kiss, it wasn't–

'What!' I gasp. 'Kiss? You kissed someone!' Buddy's ears prick as I bolt upright.

'Shit! I thought Steven told you?'

'He said you went to a strip club, no mention of you sticking your tongue down someone's throat!' My hands are shaking in utter rage. This keeps getting better.

'Ah, fuck!'

My mind is racing, but nothing is making sense. Why? How could he? Who! 'Just a kiss?'

Nothing.

'William, just a kiss?' I push again.

'She was a lap dancer,' he eventually admits on a sigh and I grit my teeth, my hand meeting my forehead as I wait for his explanation which I know is only going to cut into me further. 'After the… performance, I was at the bar, and she came over to me.'

'And…'

'And I was in shock at first.'

'At first?'

'It was less than five seconds.'

'Did you kiss back?'

'I…'

I scoff. 'You did.'

'I pulled away.'

'Bullshit!'

'After I realised, I pulled away.'

'How long does it take you to realise another woman's lips are on yours?'

'Emily–

'I feel sick!' My hair is gripped, my jaw physically aching from how much I'm clenching and tensing it.

'I was going to tell you the other night on the phone,' he declares, but I'm finding it hard to listen. I'm fighting with myself not to hang up on him, a part of me wanting to hear his futile apologies and excuses.

'Then why didn't you?'

'You weren't giving me the chance.'

'So, this is my fault now?'

'No, I'm not saying that!'

'It's a good job I may have to stay down here longer,

or I swear to God, I'd kill you. I bet you knew about that, didn't you? Another fucking thing to add to the list!'

'Emily–

'You should count yourself lucky Dad doesn't know about this.' As much as the man turns my stomach, if Dad knew what William had actually been up to that night, there's no telling what he would do, and I would be in full support.

'I'm so incredibly sorry. I love you. I truly do.'

'He should throw you out to the wolves, take everything from you and leave you with nothing.'

'Are you going to tell him?' he asks, his voice quiet… nervous.

I bite my lip, pondering my options. 'I don't know. What would you do if I did?' I reply, curious to know how he would react if I did go crying to Daddy.

'Nothing. I deserve it.'

'Yes, you do. I… I hate you!'

'What can I do? Emily, please.'

His voice is like sandpaper, grinding me down and grating on my boiling skin. 'You left me alone,' I remind him on a murmur. The damage has been done. There's nothing he can do to make this better. There's no going back now.

'I know.'

'You left me for some dirty strip club and a slapper

with no shame. Was it worth it?' I ask, raising my voice once again. The anger pulses through my veins, leaving my words unfiltered.

'Don't do this.'

'Was the drink and the tits on tap worth my life?' The line is silent. 'Well…' I push.

'I'm sor–

'You're sorry? Okay, then all is forgiven.' I laugh lightly.

'Tell me what I need to do to make this better.' His voice is beseeching, carrying regret. It's almost pitiful, hearing him so weak.

'I'll tell you what you can do, go fuck yourself and leave me alone!'

'Can we just talk about this?'

'There's nothing to say. You disgust me,' I gag before ending the call. My breath hitches in my throat and the tears spill. With an ear shattering scream, I launch my phone across the room before collapsing back in a heap, my sobs consuming me as my limbs tremble.

A cold nose grazes my knuckles. Buddy nudges my hand covering my face and I let the tears fall as I bury my head in his fur. My dog is more of a man than he will ever be.

I got it so completely wrong. He wasn't apprehensive because he cared, he was afraid to talk to me because he's a lying, deceitful bastard. I'm seething. Not only does his betrayal hurt like a knife to my heart, but the fact that I could've lost my life while he was out making selfish decisions makes this a thousand times worse.

After several gut-wrenching sobs, the tears eventually subside, like the tap behind my eyes has been tightened. My face hardens as numbness takes hold.

He is dead to me.

I sniffle and brush away the wetness from my nose and cheeks before stalking over to where my phone is lying on the carpet. Two missed calls. I ignore them, pulling up my contacts. His name makes my stomach churn, but it's only for a brief moment, because just like that, his numbers are blocked and wiped, his messages, erased.

I'm still angry, my hands clutching the phone in a death grip. I want to hit things, throw things, kick and scream!

Then, as though it heard my cries for help, something out the corner of my eye catches my attention.

That will do just fine.

# SIXTEEN

It didn't take long to find Aunt Maggie's stash of firewood logs. The hardest part was locating the key to the shed – which, after about fifteen minutes of searching all the drawers and cupboards, I found to be underneath the middle plant pot on the kitchen window ledge.

I arrange the kindling in the open fireplace and kneel down. Taking the gas cooker lighter from the floor beside me, I hold yesterday's newspaper which I found in the recycling bin over the wood. There's a click and the flame lingers under the corner of the paper, it smokes into action and I watch the bright yellows and sizzling oranges dance their way across. I hold the blackened, crimpling newspaper for as long as possible before dropping it onto the wood.

The embers glow, flicker, and crackle as they play on the kindling, building in strength with every second that passes. When spending many cold evenings on my own in Dad's mansion with an open fireplace, I taught myself the art of crafting a good fire. I came to understand just how calming it can be, however maybe not so much on a scorching afternoon in August. With my body temperature rising, I stand.

Brushing my hands over his hoodie draped on the end of the sofa, William's face forms a vivid image in my mind and my blood boils once again. I swipe it up and storm back over to the fire.

'Fuck you.' It's tossed onto the blaze without a second thought. The flames immediately engulf the material, swallowing it up like a starving lion who has just caught its prey. Tears brim my eyes with one escaping, trickling down my cheek. 'Bastard,' I whisper, letting the glow absorb all distractions, hypnotising my senses.

A cough startles me from behind, I spin on a gasp and Buddy stirs from his place at my feet. My eyes are wide before I note who it is and wipe the tear away. 'What are you doing here?'

His white T-shirt reveals the bottom of his toned stomach as he leans his forearm above his head and against the living room doorframe. A jangling sound draws my eyes to his hand by his side, where a set of keys on a keyring hang from his index finger. My focus then lifts to meet his glistening emeralds, an annoying smirk settled on his lips.

'Came to fix Mags' bath tap.' He shrugs on a relaxed tone. Buddy scampers happily over to him, his bushy tail high and wagging when Jackson crouches to fuss him.

'Do you like to wander into all the cottages in town of your own accord?' I ask accusingly, folding my arms across my chest.

He lifts the keys up to rattle them in the air. 'Mags gave me a spare set, I'm not a trespasser.'

So, he's the reason she had to get me an extra key cut. He shoots a glance behind me.

'Nor am I an arsonist. Want to tell me what you're doing lighting a fire in Saharan heat?'

My reply is curt. 'No.'

I whirl back around on a frown. It's not long before I feel his towering presence approaching. He lets out a prolonged whistle of astonishment and I peer up at him, his eyebrows quirked. 'Someone really did piss you off,' he pauses, 'or are you just having a clear out?'

'Don't start, I'm not in the mood.'

'None of my business,' he says on a shake of his head.

'No, it's not.'

Silence settles in the room, the only sound coming from the snapping and crackling of the fire. Both of us are focused purely on the flames which are completely obliterating William's hoodie.

But then he sighs. 'Fancy cake?'

My face contorts in confusion. 'I'm sorry?'

'Cake. Cake makes everything better,' he insists, briefly locking eyes with me before they shift back to the fireplace.

'We don't have any cake,' I reply, puzzled by his suggestion.

'Oh, don't worry. I know a place that does.' He nods confidently.

He's serious?

'What about Aunt Maggie's tap?' I ask, watching him from out the corner of my eye.

'I'm sure she'll understand, besides I think the happiness of her niece is more important, don't you?'

I feel his eyes drop as they study my side profile. With my hair tied up, little make-up on, and red puffy eyes, I'm very aware of how much of a mess I must appear, but I manage to muster every scrap of courage – which William hasn't destroyed – in order to not shrink under his fulgent stare.

'I doubt she'll be taking any hot and steamy baths in this weather,' he continues. 'Well, not unless the man who's got her all doe-eyed gets involved.' He chuckles.

'How do you know there's a man?' I question curiously. The only man in Aunt Maggie's life at the minute, as far as I'm aware, is Guy, and they're not together – far from it. Okay, she tries to impress him at every opportunity she gets, but when you've spent so many years away from male company, you're bound to act differently when a, let's be fair, particularly robust man is suddenly presented to you.

'She mentioned someone's name last night after your drunken escapade, and she's perked up. She's always been perky, but she's got a glow about her which is different. Must be all those steamy sessions.' He winks at me, and I try to bite back a smile. Annoyingly it fights through, creeping reluctantly onto my face. 'That's more like it,' he says, nudging my arm.

I roll my eyes to disguise the rosy tint I know is colouring my cheeks. 'Okay, sure, why not?' I agree, returning back to his previous question and dismissing the mental image of Aunty caught up in a *steamy session*. Right now, I'll do anything to take my mind off my arsehole of an ex. I swallow the lump in my throat which forms at the thought of the word, *ex*. I haven't been single in over a year, and although it's by no means the lengthiest of relationships, I've grown accustomed to having someone by my side. Now I'm going to have to re-adapt to being on my own.

'Great!' Jackson exclaims. 'Cake it is. Buddy can keep us company too,' he says as he strides over to the living room door.

My eyes narrow. I hear him fumbling around in drawers and running the taps before he strolls back in with a jug of water. He bends down, grabbing the fire poker resting against the back wall, and spreads the embers in the fireplace before pouring the jug over the firewood. The flames hiss, almost like they're protesting as they rapidly diminish, turning to smoke. Jackson straightens to observe his work, his eyes momentarily catching my questioning blues.

'I don't particularly want to be on the receiving end of Mags when she comes back to a well-cooked cottage, do you?'

I shake my head, imagining her wrath. Those pink slippers and that fluffy dressing gown would be no more, and that's enough to start a civil war.

He leaves the room again as I look down at the remnants of what was a thunderous fire. You would never be able to tell I'd thrown anything on there, it's just a pile of black kindling, smoke and dust. As soon as that hoodie was thrown on the fire, it didn't stand a chance.

I scoff at the irony. That hoodie is me, and that fire is the mess I call the world. As soon as I was born it had a plan for me and decided I would be damned. My life has been one set back after another, it's been a constant emotional battle and doesn't appear to be getting any easier. In fact, it's so much worse. I've lost my mum, my dad, my boyfriend, my independence. Above all, I've lost me. I have no idea who I am, all I know is that I'm broken and charred. I'm constantly waiting for the next bad thing to come up from behind and suffocate me and it's exhausting. This world has consumed and smothered me into total darkness. Just like those flames, it is insatiable; it's burning me out and there's nothing I can do to escape it. I'm exactly what that hoodie is now. Irrefutably fucked.

'Ready?' Jackson's expectant voice calls from the hallway. I hear Buddy trot across the room, the jangling of his collar distinct as Jackson attaches it around his neck.

I take a breath and gulp down my pain.

'Yeah.'

I grab my shoulder bag from the sofa and follow them out the front door. Much to his certitude, I don't quite believe his statement. I'm not so sure cake will make this better. But I'm willing to give it a go, because the other option is to sit on my own, with nothing but taunting thoughts left to fester and drive me crazy.

My feet carry me onto the porch step as Jackson passes me Buddy's lead while he locks up. I notice an old Jeep parked where Guy's Mercedes usually sits. Jackson steps past me, but halts when he notices my lack of movement.

'What?'

'Where are we going?' I ask curiously.

'If you get in the car, you'll find out,' he replies, turning again, his long legs carrying him to the gate. He waits there, his back to me. 'You'll find your feet at the end of your legs, they do move if you allow them to.'

'You're not going to murder me, are you?' I sound pathetic, but with my recent experience, I wouldn't be surprised. I hardly know him, and isn't this something they warn you about as a child? When a strange man offers you sweets and tells you to get into his car, you run as far away as possible?

He frowns at me over his shoulder. 'Do I look like a killer?'

I shrug. 'You don't have to look like a serial killer to be one.'

He glances down before exhaling and marching back over to me and my pooch on the step. Our eyes never leave each other's, and my neck has to tilt in order to keep the contact. Even though I'm stood on the porch step, he still manages to tower over me. He peers down, his emeralds curious, sparkling as the light strokes them. He edges closer, his face only inches from mine.

'Emily Rose Lambert,' he murmurs, and I find it hard to ignore the tingle his voice leaves as it filters up my spine. He pauses for a moment, searching my face deeply as if taking in every detail, and it's as though this action captivates me. I don't want to look away. 'I promise I'm not going to murder you,' he says, stepping away swiftly, his demeanour switching from intense to sarcastic in a heartbeat. The air held in my lungs is released. He holds out his hand and I study it. Silver rings are positioned on his index and pinky fingers, with several leather bracelets dangling loosely on his wrist.

Gathering myself, I smile up at him on a hum, snubbing his gesture and strutting past him. 'Just remember, you'll have Buddy to answer to if anything happens to me.'

My smile only widens when I hear him sigh, picturing his eyes rolling as his footsteps follow after us. I hear his soft voice travel over my shoulder.

'Buddy's not the one I'd be frightened of.'

# SEVENTEEN

The journey has been in silence so far. A comfortable silence. I tried to prise where we're going out of him, but he wasn't letting on, so I gave up. After winding down my window, I've simply been admiring the sunny view as he drives us around the country lanes.

My hand unconsciously strokes Buddy's head resting on the centre console, his bum perched on the back seat. Jackson's car is surprisingly clean for a frequent beach visitor, I was expecting sand and food wrappers and old clothes, but it's spotless – for a timeworn Jeep at least. A coconut scented air freshener swings with the movement of the car on the rear-view mirror, letting off a calming aroma, taking my mind to a deserted beach in Hawaii.

I flicker my sights to the grazing sheep on his side, but I'm quick to be distracted. His large hand is wrapped slackly around the steering wheel as his elbow rests on top of his open window. The other lies on his jean covered thigh, his fingers tapping his knee in a random rhythm. My eyes drift up his toned arm to his neck, and then to his sharp jawline, all the way to the little crease in his forehead as he concentrates on the road ahead. His lips are puckered, his eyes narrowed as if he's deep in thought. I lean back against the headrest and begin to wonder what's running through his mind. Hopefully not ideas of how to cover up my murder.

We've been driving for ten minutes; the quiet lanes have now turned into a main road and before long, we're cruising down a steep hill at a steady speed.

'Are you going to tell me now?' I ask as we turn a sharp corner and Jackson works the gears.

'Just wait and see.'

We continue our descent as the view opens out. I watch as groups of tourists come into sight as they saunter down a pathway. I then see where they're heading.

The road eventually narrows, and Jackson slows to a crawl, avoiding the masses of people, dogs, and seagulls when we enter a town. Buddy springs to life, his head jerking left and right as he takes in the new and exciting environment. His pants fill the car as I shadow his nosiness. My attention is captured by the open cafes, gift shops and ice cream parlours, and then by the harbour on Jackson's side, where boats of all different sizes bob up and down in the water. He comes to a steady stop, finding a space on the quay which overlooks the entire harbour square.

Our windows are wound up, the engine is cut, and we sit in the quiet, admiring what's in front of us. With the bright blue sky and sun gleaming down, along with people sat with their legs dangling over the wall, admiring the scenery, eating fish and chips, pasties and ice creams, it feels like a dream town. To me, at least. For a girl who has rarely stepped foot outside of London, I've never seen a place so busy and full of life, yet so peaceful and relaxed at the same time. It's beautiful.

'Welcome to Rockstone,' Jackson says. He pushes his door open and hops down. A hint of a smile plays on my lips. I like it already.

I copy his lead and jump out, but I'm immediately re-thinking my previous thoughts as my nose crinkles. He meets me on my side with Buddy and spots the look on my face.

'You brought me to a place which stinks to high heaven of fish and seaweed?'

He takes a big sniff and releases on a contented exhale. 'Invigorating, isn't it?'

'It's definitely something.' I grimace as they idle away.

'It's not so bad further on in the town. Come on, city girl!' He motions his head towards the main part of town, and I don't hesitate to obey, keen to get away from the overwhelming aroma.

It's impossible not to take in every single detail around me. This quaint town is buzzing as we meander through large groups of people sauntering in and out of independent shops and cafes. My eyes light up, bouncing between all the dogs on leads, and I notice how Buddy's head is flicking left and right, ogling every dog and seagull around us. The smell of the harbour is now overshadowed by the scent of freshly made pasties and fish and chips, which I'm pleased about, but it's also reminding my stomach it has only been fed a Calippo today.

I'm so lost in what's going on, I forget that the main purpose of coming here was for cake. That is, until I bump into Jackson's side when he comes to a sudden stop.

I gaze at the café. Stylish rose-pink calligraphy writing on a giant white sign sitting above the door reads, *Traci's,* adorned with a floral and butterfly design in each corner. Flowerpots hang and rest on the small balcony above the entrance, and a hatch to the left of the door has a similarly designed sign for takeaway treats. A couple of people are already sat in the outdoor seating area, where white roses in silver mercury jars are placed in the middle of each patterned graphite table.

'Traci's,' I read aloud.

'*The* very best.' Jackson nods staring at the café too.

'Best in Cornwall?' I ask, turning to him, my eyes squinting as the bright sun beats down with the smallest of smiles painted on my lips at how comfortable he looks.

'Nope,' he says popping the 'p'. He meets my gaze. 'Best in the world.'

I chuckle. 'Don't let Albert hear you say that.'

'Who's, Albert?' he asks on a frown.

I give him a pointed look. 'The best cake baker in the world, according to him.'

'Well, trust me, you haven't lived. Come on, dogs allowed.' He hands me Buddy's lead on a wink and strolls inside, my eyes rolling at his snide remark.

As soon as I enter, I know immediately by the smell

that this is going to be sugar heaven. It's relatively small width wise, but with a single isle in the middle, the tables seem to stretch down for miles. The counter is directly to my left and behind the glass display are rows of sweet treats, from lemon meringues, strawberry cheesecakes and mountainous gateau's, to smaller cupcakes and cookies, but all equally designed to perfection. My mouth waters, my eyes running hungrily over them all.

'Here's my handsome chap! I haven't seen you in ages, Jackson.' The woman behind the till beams as he saunters over.

My neck is craned forward, examining all the cakes, but I subtly peer over at the woman. She looks around her fifties; hair blonde and bobbed, and her rose pink apron shows stain marks on the front – it makes me think about the bakery back in London.

'Don't tell me, you've been watching your figure?'

Jackson beams at her quip, and he laughs a genuine laugh. I notice the dimples on his cheeks and the crinkles by his eyes as the contagious sound escapes his mouth. I can't help but smile at his moment of natural happiness, keeping it on my face when he turns to look at me.

'Who's this stunning girly and handsome chappy?' Traci asks and my attention flickers from Jackson to her, her kind blue eyes are focused on me with an endearing smile on her plump lips.

'This is Emily and her boy, Buddy,' Jackson responds for me.

'Hi,' I say, stepping closer to them both.

'It's nice to meet you, Emily. I must say, you're one lucky man, Jackson, she's beautiful.'

I glance to the floor, fiddling with the lead in my hands and feeling heat rise to my cheeks. Awkwardness always seems to run through me whenever I'm paid a compliment, and I have no idea why.

*Wait*, is she insinuating–

'We're not together,' he states, quick off the mark. 'We're just… friends, I guess,' he stutters, looking to me for support as he scratches the back of his head.

'More like acquaintances, really,' I add, and he nods in agreement.

Friends? I only met the boy on Tuesday, and it has hardly been a smooth sailing friendship.

'Oh, that's a shame,' she expresses, the disappointment clear. 'Your children would be dazzling.'

I'm too shocked to even glimpse in Jackson's direction, my eyes are wider than Buddy's when he spies food. Neither of us speak but Traci appears unaffected by her words.

'Now, what can I get for you both?'

I eventually muster up the courage to risk a peek up at him, and apparently, he has the same idea as his head shifts to gaze down at me. However, whilst my face is the depiction of utter disbelief, his holds amusement; a smirk playing on his lips with his eyebrows arched. He's entertained. He just loves awkward situations, or rather, awkward situations where I'm at the heart. It's really quite irritating.

We pick our cakes and select a table outside to admire the view. I ended up with something called Dreamers Delight and a chocolate milkshake, I had my eye on a couple, but in a bid to get away from matchmaking Traci, I simply picked the first one I saw.

Jackson tucks into his four layers of chocolate cake, or as Traci named it, The Devil's Sponge, and slurps on his strawberry shake. Buddy is also happy with his doggy cupcake and freshwater bowl. I, on the other hand, can't bring myself to start eating.

My stomach is turning, a horrible sicky feeling settling inside– and it's not because of the good looking children remark… well, not totally. Thoughts of William have prompted their way into my mind, and the fact that this cute little café reminds me so much of the bakery back home is making it ten times worse. Because it's not home, not anymore. Nowhere is. Not London, or here. I feel lost. Aunt Maggie is the only family I really feel I have, and I can't even talk to her about any of it, because she has no idea of the real reason I'm here. I don't see why Dad thinks it's best to keep the fact it wasn't a chance attack from her. She'll be angry, and she'll worry, I realise that, but it's better than all the secrecy. I can't stand it.

'So,' Jackson says, grabbing my attention. 'Do you want to tell me why you were throwing clothes into a lit fireplace in the middle of August?'

I shoot a look over the table as he shovels a mound of cake into his mouth.

'I felt like it.' I shrug, moving my own sponge around absentmindedly with my fork.

'You'd be amazed at how easy it is to open up to a stranger, especially a stranger who won't judge.' I flick my unconvinced eyes up to him. He stares back, but as I wonder if he will concede his hard gaze, after a moment, he recognises that I'm not going to open up, so drops his fork to his plate. 'You don't want to talk about it, that's fine,' he says, resting both arms on the table as he leans in. 'But at least eat your cake, Traci won't be happy to see it wasted.' I glance down at my dessert and then back up, his eyes seeming to draw mine to his to make certain I'm hearing him. 'I promise you'll feel better.' He nods encouragingly before collapsing back and slurping on his shake.

I study the cake; it's red velvet with swirly icing and sprinkles, and I have to admit, it does look rather tasty. Fighting against my inner feelings, I break a little bit off with my fork and lift it to my lips. The texture is light and fluffy, and it melts away in my mouth as an explosion of sweetness runs down my throat. My delighted expression is hard to subdue. Jackson watches me intently, chuckling as I dive in for more.

'Told you,' he remarks proudly.

We finished our cakes, drained our milkshakes and decided to have a stroll, visiting the different little shops. Strangely, the delicious snack has given me the energy my body needed, and I've pushed the thoughts of William to the back of my mind, instead focusing on the charming town. It seems dogs are allowed in most of the establishments here; a quirk I've now fallen completely in love with.

After wandering into a hospitable clothes shop, Jackson headed over to the men's side with Buddy in tow, so I took my chance to have a browse in the women's section.

Skimming the neatly hung clothes on display, I admire a black lace skater dress in my size. My eyes then scan the room, finding Jackson engrossed in a pair of jeans. With the temptation of the changing room only two feet away, I scurry over.

My summer dress is pulled over my head, replaced with the garment on the hanger. As always when trying on new clothes, my breath is held, my brain scorning the rest of me for overindulging in certain devil treats. This time it's put to rest quickly, because the dress fits perfectly.

The floor length mirror reveals off-shoulder lace sleeves falling loosely to my elbows, and a sweetheart neckline keeping my boobs in check – with no risk of an accidental spillage. The fit and flare design means the ruffles fall daintily down to the middle of my thigh. It's flattering, pretty, and I'm in love.

But my mood is quick to drop.

I undress, throw my original attire back on, and pull my ponytail tighter to the crown of my head before brushing the curtain aside, returning to the shop floor. He's leaning against the wall with his arms folded, Buddy lying at his feet. Ignoring him, I wander over to where I found it and hook the dress back on the rack.

'Did you not like it?' he asks, pushing himself from the wall and moseying up to me. I run my hand down the front of it once more feeling its soft material.

'Actually, I loved it.'

'Then why aren't you buying it?' His tone is laced with confusion.

'Because there probably will never be an occasion to wear it,' I retort, giving it one last look before walking away. I don't have a boyfriend to impress anymore, and it's unlikely I'll be going to any university parties now. Besides, I bought a couple of dresses in St Iven, another one would be unnecessarily greedy.

A shiver runs over my body when I step out of the shop. The weather has completely turned whilst we've been here, it was gradually growing cooler as the afternoon progressed, but the wind has picked up a lot now with the sun disappearing behind the darkening clouds. Aunt Maggie was right about an approaching storm.

Jackson appears behind me. I offer to take Buddy's lead back, but he objects as we wander away, heading nowhere in particular. 'Where to next?' I ask as we saunter past a couple of shops down a quiet cobbled street.

'Why don't we have a walk along the harbour before it starts bucketing it down?' he suggests, glancing my way.

I smile in response and follow his lead. He takes us down an alley which brings us out on the opposite side. We stroll for a little while, the sea in the distance is choppier now and the boats are rocking rather fiercely. I notice there seems to be fewer people down this end as Jackson tosses a few coins into an old busker's hat, the old man – who looks like a stereotypical fisherman with a long white beard – nods kindly to us as he continues to strum his guitar and sing in a deep, husky tone.

The sound of the busker gradually becomes a pleasant background sound as Jackson takes a perch on the edge of the quay, letting his legs dangle down the wall. He taps the space beside him. The floor is cold, despite the sun having shone on it all day, but it's not uncomfortable, it's really rather relaxing as I make the most of the fading sunlit sky. Buddy peers over the edge, wagging his tail before sliding down in between us. My fingers find his fur as I close my eyes, opening up my senses to the soft splashing of the water against the wall, the clinks of the bells on the boats as they bob back and forth, and the calls of the seagulls resonating around us.

A deep breath is drawn, and on its release, the answer Jackson has been so keen to know and the words I've been building myself up to say. 'My boyfriend kissed someone else.'

The energy around us shifts. I peel my eyes open to see his wide on me. 'Shit,' he says on a gasp.

'A stripper of all people.'

'I'm sorry,' he offers, a concerned look on his face.

'Don't be. It's not your fault,' I say, glancing idly around the boats in front of us, doing well to keep the knowledge of my own whereabouts at that time trapped inside.

'How long have you been together?' he asks with his head down as he watches his legs sway backwards and forwards.

'I've known him for two years, but we've been together for just over a year.'

'Dick.'

'You can say that again.' I scoff.

'Is that why you've been so temperamental?'

My eyebrows raise at his blunt question, his eyes crinkle at the corners and I feel my mood lift ever so slightly at his teasing. 'He's part of the reason,' I confess. My brief shift in mood soon plunges. 'I'd be lying if I said everything's been perfect up until this point. Don't get me wrong, there were good parts, but the bad always seemed to outweigh.'

William and I became friends at first, but on my seventeenth birthday last year it all changed, and months later William asked me to move in. I was incredibly relieved and, of course, grateful. I fled Dad's hell hole of an empty home as fast as anything, unaware I'd only be moving into another. I thought it would mean we'd be in each other's company almost all the time and it would be a new and exciting experience for the both of us. I never expected the total opposite. We're still so young, yet we've been living like middle aged people whose marriage is drying up. His long hours and stressed-out work head, along with both our fathers' work philosophies having been schooled into him since the beginning, set the foundations of so many heated arguments. I gave so many excuses to protect us, but the truth is it just hasn't been okay for a while.

'This is probably a silly question, but do you love him?'

I swallow when he looks my way, his face carrying an expression I can't read. 'What makes you ask?'

He shrugs. 'Sometimes love runs dry.'

My brain ticks as I focus on the rocking boats, as if they'll provide me with the answer I need. I honestly don't know. I believed I did, but this act has only made me realise just how crappy these past few months have been whilst living with him. Do I even know what love is? I'm so young. I was so young. I was sixteen when we first met and I thought he was my world, but things change, and I honestly can't remember the last time I said those words to him.

I sigh. Therein lies my answer.

'I did, once upon a time. I used to idolize him. When

we met, he was this wealthy businessman at twenty-one; smart, kind, head strong. He knew what he wanted. He was free, everything I'd always wanted to be.'

'What changed?'

I ponder my response, before settling with the truth. 'For some time now, I've been feeling like something hasn't been right. I couldn't put my finger on it, I brushed it to the side and carried on as normal. But now I know,' I admit. Turning to look at him, my eyes catch his, they're soft and gentle as he encourages me to continue. 'We've both been kidding each other.'

As a besotted sixteen-year-old with a crush on an older guy, I didn't understand it then. But maybe deep down I knew. William was my way to escape, to be free from my father and the never-ending loneliness I felt. The years of being neglected by Dad, maybe I was crying out for some attention. Maybe, I loved what he was able to give me, rather than him as a person. And maybe he felt that too. Could it be, that's why he did those things? That's why he was constantly out drinking, rarely having time for me, and why he went to that strip club. Because he knew my love wasn't truly genuine.

But then if he did, why didn't he end things? Why continue to make our relationship a miserable place?

I fumble with my hands in my lap as the revelation washes over me. 'I could be wrong, but I think towards the end he was with me just to keep my father sweet. And I was waiting, filling time.' I shake my head at how awful that sounds. 'When I moved in with him, I had a year of finishing my A-levels, but I knew after that, I could go to university. I would be free too.'

'Free from what?' he asks softly.

'Feeling trapped, my dad, bad memories. You name it and I'm escaping from it.' My head lowers as I study my hand which finds Buddy's fur again, reality reminding me that I might have to wait yet another year for that. 'But nothing's ever that simple.'

'What do you mean? You're still going, aren't you?' I feel his stare on me.

'I don't know.'

'But all this talk of being free, I wouldn't have thought it would even be a question?'

'It's complicated.'

'So it appears. Everything about you seems complicated.' He pauses, his hand I hadn't noticed settled in Buddy's fur, brushes against mine. I watch as his finger caresses my pinky with the lightest of touches. 'You're a little enigma, Emily Rose,' he murmurs softly.

I flash a small smile, peering into his eyes. They show a kindness which I've been reluctant to see up until this point, he looks genuinely interested in what I have to say.

'What are you going to do about him?'

'I'm finished. I can't go back to the way it was, and William,' I close my eyes and take another breath as his name passes my lips, 'William's going to have to accept that,' I state strongly.

He watches me for a moment. 'Well, it's his loss. You can do better.' His gaze flickers out to the harbour, his hand retracting back to his lap. I focus on him, the loss of his touch igniting a question in my mind. He helped me at Leo's party, again last night, and he's done the same today. He didn't need to, but he did, willingly.

'Why are you doing this?' I ask. 'Helping me? Buying me cake?'

The wind blows through his hair, causing a few strands of the unruly waves to fall onto his forehead. He lifts his hand and brushes them back, the brown curls sliding effortlessly through his long ringed fingers. He turns to me, and I can see the cogs ticking behind his eyes as he conjures a reply. His lips part, but what he settles on only prompts more questions. 'I'm intrigued.'

My eyes narrow. 'Intrigued by what?'

His chest expands, his gaze narrowing as though he's studying me thoughtfully. And that's when I catch my breath.

'You.'

I don't get a chance to respond as the heavens open without warning. Light droplets fall to begin with, but they soon pick up. Thunder rumbles across the sky, and I gasp as the heavy rain pours down on us.

'Looks like fun's over,' he calls as he heaves himself up.

Jackson offers his hand and I take it, letting go as

soon as I'm on my feet. My hair is already beginning to drip, and with a quick glance down, I'm reminded that my dress is white; it'll be see-through if we don't hurry up! My chest is hugged as we make a dash for the car.

It seems to take forever to get there, the rain only growing heavier. As we scramble to the Jeep, Jackson hands me Buddy's lead and rummages in his back pocket for the car key. I bounce my legs up and down to try and keep myself warm as he rushes over to the driver's side. I try the door over and over again desperately, but it doesn't release.

'What are you doing?' I yell over the noise of the wind and rain.

'Fucking thing,' I hear him curse. 'The battery's going.'

I groan, my shoulders now shivering, my patience wearing thin. 'Just do it manually!' I shout, there's not a part of me which is dry now.

His key meets the lock and I watch him climb in. He reaches over to pull on my door's latch, and I don't hesitate to clamber in, letting Buddy sit at my feet.

'Ugh! I'm soaking wet,' I complain, slamming the door and flicking my hands out to make a statement.

'I tend to have that effect on people,' he remarks, shoving the key in the ignition.

I shoot him a *don't test me* scowl, but he simply smirks, clearly proud of his inappropriate comment as the engine trembles to life. He places his hand on the back of my headrest, reverses and pulls away.

I'm trying to keep as still as possible, my dress is sticking to me, and as much as I love him, Buddy's soaking wet fur is pressing against my bare legs which isn't the pleasantest of feelings in the world. Jackson also informed me earlier on that the car's air con is broken, so I'm getting colder by the minute. But no matter how wet and uncomfortable I am, his words are failing to leave my mind.

He's intrigued by me.

No words have left us since we began the drive, and although I want to eventually question him about it, right now all I'm concerned about is getting dry.

I recognise the road Jackson turns onto, it's the lane which leads to Marshlyn Bay, meaning I'm only minutes away from the cottage and therefore, civilisation.

I barely hear the bang before my body is jerked forwards with my legs wrapping tightly around Buddy. An arm dashes across my body, and I don't delay in grabbing it tight. The Jeep screeches to a halt and we both collapse back.

'Shit…' Jackson breathes over my deep pants.

'What the hell!'

My heart is planted firmly in my mouth and that cake is making its way back up. We stare wide-eyed out the windscreen which continues to take a beating from the rain. My heavy breaths fill the car, but unlike my shaking, panic-stricken body, Jackson is totally calm and entirely composed.

'Are you alright?' he asks coolly, flicking a glance across. I can't take my eyes away from the road but I manage a nod in response.

'How are you not in shock?' I eventually question, finding my voice.

'I mean, it didn't hit us,' he says, and that's when I realise my hands are still holding his arm for dear life, and so does he. We gape at our contact before I unpeel my fingers, his arm retracting back to his side.

'Oh, only five inches away from death,' I fire back.

Out of nowhere, what can only be described as a monstrous, killer tree, collapsed across our path, causing the whole car to shake. Its trunk is almost the width of the lane and it's blocking the entirety of it, there's no way we're getting past it.

'It wasn't five inches,' he replies on a shake of his head. 'More like four,' he jests.

He receives an unimpressed glare.

'What are we going to do? We can't exactly move it.'

'We'll have to reverse up,' he says, twisting to assess the view out of the rear window.

'And go where? We can't get to my aunt's another way.'

'No, we'll have to go to mine,' he proclaims, his body now facing my shocked and irritated form.

'Yours? I haven't got any other clothes, Jackson, and I'm freezing.'

'I have clothes you can wear. What else do you suggest? Wait here until someone with a massive truck turns up and catch pneumonia in the process?'

It's as though the staring match from the pub last night has been resumed for round two, his adamant eyes are fixed on my stubborn ones. But the longer I sit here with my hair dripping down my neck, and my wet dress clinging to every inch of my skin, the sooner I'm crumbling. He wins again.

'How far is it?' I huff.

'Only a couple of minutes down the road.'

'Fine,' I agree. Anything's better than staying here like this. I lean forward, hugging Buddy to me as his head rests on my leg; his damp fur suddenly no longer a bother to me.

'Okay,' Jackson says, thrusting the Jeep into reverse.

# EIGHTEEN

The rain pelts down as the wiper blades work hard to give us a glimpse of the murky road ahead. It's strange how the weather can turn so suddenly, the beautiful clear blue sky now feeling like a distant dream.

Thankfully, Jackson was right, and within a couple of minutes we're pulling onto a driveway. The lights are on inside the detached house, illuminating the front drive with a plush silver Evoque parked outside. He doesn't stop next to it, instead driving up to a garage door attached to the side.

'Home sweet home,' he says as the engine shuts off.

'Are your mum and dad in?' I ask, watching how the house in front of us is becoming more and more blurred as the wipers are halted, allowing the rain droplets to coat the glass. I wonder what his parents' reactions will be when they see a wringing wet girl they've never met before stroll into their home unannounced, with their equally saturated son.

'No idea, but Dex's Mum and Dad probably are,' he replies, leaning over to my side. I flinch as his arm grazes my knee when pulls out a set of keys from a small holder. His eyes peer into mine and I can't help but remain fixed. 'Ready to run?' he murmurs before shifting back, opening the door, and sliding out.

My brow furrows. *Dex's Mum and Dad*? My focus follows him as his blurry figure jogs over to the garage. Summoning the courage, I pull on the door handle and let Buddy hop out first. The callous wind and rain hold no remorse, thrashing my body as soon as my feet hit the ground. Forcing the car door to shut, I dash over to him, keeping my arms locked together. 'What's wrong with the front door?' I ask as he turns the key in the cam lock and bends down.

'Nothing, if the house is where you want to go.' The door lifts up and out slowly, but what I see inside is in no way a storage room for cars. He strides in without a thought and flicks a switch on the wall, the room instantly lighting up to give me a clear outlook of its entirety. My feet squelch forwards before he pulls the hefty white door down with a bang, making me jump and Buddy grumble.

'Sorry, mate,' Jackson coos, taking on the task of unfastening his lead and collar as my confused eyes scan his place.

First of all, it's much bigger than it appears. It's all one large room and I've just stepped straight into the living area. A cream, L-shaped sofa faces a flat screen TV attached to the cloudy grey wall, whilst a square glass coffee table sits in front of it.

Placing my bag onto the sofa, I peer further ahead as Buddy follows Jackson into the corner where the kitchen is set. The marble tops are spotless, there's not a dish, plate or mug in sight – just like in his Jeep, it's all so very clean. The oak floorboards appear new under my feet, and I instantly cringe at the moody footprints I've trailed behind me. Realising he's taken his Vans off and placed them together next to the wall, I slip off my Converse, positioning them beside his.

My wet socks slide across the skiddy floor as I follow after him. Tossing his keys onto the kitchen side, he moves to a wardrobe towering over his double bed, which is positioned to face the kitchen area. He sifts through a shelf at the top and tosses a couple of items onto the perfectly made covers.

I rest my hip against the kitchen counter and watch his actions. 'You live in a garage?'

'Yes,' he replies plainly, kneeling down with his back to me, delving into a drawer.

'Okay,' I say, a little discouraged, expecting more of an explanation.

'It's not really a garage anymore,' he adds and my ears prick. He stands holding boxer shorts, before grabbing the white T-shirt and towel he'd previously thrown onto the bed. 'They were converting it into an annex when I first moved here and said I could stay, but I liked the door, so they kept it,' he says, flicking his eyes over to the white garage door. 'It's different.'

'They?' I ask, picking up on his choice of wording.

'Dex's Mum and Dad,' he answers, strolling towards me. It's now, as my eyes travel his looming body, that I notice his now transparent shirt sticking to him too. Attaching itself to every muscle. I adjust my stance, my hip leaving the counter as I straighten and try with all my might to lift my focus. His curls are the next distraction, damp, and straying onto his face.

'You live with Dex?' I probe, my eyebrows raising in question.

'And his mum and dad, yeah.' He holds out the white T-shirt and towel with the boxers on top. 'Bathroom's through there.' He gestures to the door ahead as I take hold of the items, my hands melting into the softness of the towel. 'Sorry, all my other bottoms are in the wash, will these do?' he asks, and I study the black boxers draped over the towel before nodding. They're going to have to. 'Take as long as you need,' he says on a smile, the intensity of his gaze drawing me in again.

'Thanks,' I breathe, desperately fighting the urge to ask more questions.

He's intrigued by me? I'm the one who's being tied down whilst he prods my curiosity with a big stick. The more time I spend with him, the more he seems to surprise me in different ways, and I want to delve deeper. I want to know more. Right now, though, the priority is getting this sopping dress off.

I shuffle past him and push the door he motioned to open. Finding a string hanging from the ceiling with a metal handle, I yank it, and the room brightens with a subtle warm glow. But just as I go to close the door, I catch an accidental peek of him standing by his bed. He hauls his dripping shirt up and over his head, the muscles in his toned back and arms stretching and contracting as he chucks it to the floor. After a ruffle of his hair, his hands find his jeans and they begin to unbuckle. Whether he senses me staring, or whether I'm paranoid that I'm doing something I shouldn't, and my mind is playing tricks on me, I feel him begin to turn in my direction, so I hastily, but quietly, click the door shut. My head falls back against it. What the hell am I doing?

My eyes wander the space. It's a small bathroom complete with modern décor, there's a luxury glass screen shower in the corner, and a smart floating vanity unit which sits below a light-up mirror on the white tiled wall.

I don't waste time in stripping. The damp material is peeled from my skin and thrown to the floor before I scurry over to the shower. The lever is pulled towards me and the welcomed warm water cascades onto my head and over my body, instantly providing it with the heat it so desperately desired. The water drips down my back, splashing onto the ceramic basin before trickling down the drain and disappearing, along with my thoughts. Steam clouds my vision as my brain fades into a foggy abyss, forgetting all my worries and focusing purely on how good the water feels as it beats down on my skin.

After five minutes of absolute heaven, I bite the bullet and cut the shower off. I grab the towel from the floor and wrap it around my body, cuddling its softness tightly. My feet guide me over to the mirror, and as I take in the girl staring back at me, I'm thrown off balance at just how tired she looks; the bags under her eyes dark and noticeable. It's the first time I've properly studied my face since I arrived in Cornwall. It's stripped back, bare, exposed and completely exhausted. All the stress and worry my body has been dealt this past week is taking its toll, and I try to think back to a time when I didn't have any angsts weighing me down, but it's impossible. I can't seem to relieve the pressure pads in my head carrying everything I'm feeling: anger, fear, loneliness, anxiousness, to name but a few.

It's times like these when my need for Mum is overwhelmingly painful. I would bury my head in her calming embrace as she stroked my hair and told me everything would be okay. And even though she wouldn't know that for certain, it wouldn't matter, because she would be there, which would be enough to carry on.

I run my fingers over my washed-out cheeks, but before the tears can fall from my misty eyes, I'm drying myself off and pulling on Jackson's clothes. They're baggy, as expected – the shirt falling to my thighs and the boxers threatening to tumble down my legs if I move too quickly – but I'm finally dry and comfortable, which is everything I'd been so desperate for.

I fold the towel and gather my damp dress and underwear from the floor before pausing by the door. I'm nervous and I don't know why. *Possibly because you're about to parade around a man you barely know in next to nothing, the same day you break up with your boyfriend,* my rational subconscious tells me.

Taking a deep breath, I decide to simply act normal, as if this isn't a very unfamiliar and strange situation. So, before my current mindset disintegrates and leaves me feeling like an exposed, self-conscious mess, I grip the handle and step back into the large open room.

Jackson is perched on the edge of the sofa, drying Buddy off with a towel – whose face is creased, enjoying the motion of his rubdown. He splays the towel on the floor and as he relaxes back into the sofa, Buddy circles the fluffy material, flopping down and curling into a ball. The room is lit with flashing blues when Jackson punches the remote for the TV, dressed in nothing but loose grey shorts.

I can't help my eyes which gape at his bare torso, observing as his chest rises and falls slowly with the pattern of his breathing as the chanting of a football crowd echoes around the room. They then drift up to his. They're engaged, intently studying the screen in front of him, but I can hardly hear it now, my attention too fixed on his flawlessly sculpted face and dampened curls.

He hasn't noticed my re-entering, and I'm stood awkwardly fiddling with the items in my hands. I clear my throat. Immediately, he glances over and flashes a smile in my direction. The screen turns off and he chucks the remote to the side before pushing himself up.

'Better?' he asks, his long legs reaching me in a matter of seconds.

'Much,' I reply, making a conscious effort to keep my eyes raised to his face.

He takes the pile from my hands, but my cheeks promptly redden when he holds up my nude coloured bra by its strap. 'Cute,' he says on a quirk of his lips. I try my best to appear unbothered, my eyes rolling at his remark.

'Yes, that's why I bought it,' I quip, the sarcasm radiating off my tongue as he chuckles.

'I reported the fallen tree, they said a crew will clear the lane first thing when it's safe.' I nod as his long pins carry him over to a door hidden in an archway. 'I'll put these in the dryer in the main house, they'll be ready by morning.' He calls back over his shoulder. 'Make yourself at home,' he encourages, before disappearing through the door.

I stand unmoving, not really knowing *how* to make myself at home. I remember that I need to let Aunt Maggie know where I am, she's probably already stressing out. Pacing over to my bag on the arm of the sofa, I send her a brief text:

*You were right about the storm, Aunt!*
*It's blown over a tree which is blocking the lane to the cottage.*
*Don't worry, I'm fine. Buddy and I are*
*staying at Jackson's tonight.*
*See you tomorrow.*
*E x*

She must've been waiting anxiously, because her reply is almost instant.

*It's so dangerous out there tonight.*
*I'm glad you're okay, Pidge.*
*See you tomorrow.*
*Be good and don't do anything I wouldn't!*
*M x*

My mouth parts before a smile dances on my lips. That woman. As I stuff my phone back into my bag, I hear shuffling behind me. I spin to see Jackson avert his gaze, avoiding my own. Was he watching me?

'Tea or coffee?' he asks as he meanders around the kitchen counter.

'Tea, please. I'm not a lover of coffee,' I answer as he flicks the kettle on. Buddy trails behind me as I make my way over, perching on one of the bar stools. Jackson grabs two mugs from the cupboard above him and then milk from the fridge. I frown, the questions from earlier coming back to mind. 'So, how come you live in Dex's annex?' He freezes before placing the carton of milk down on the side, his head lowering.

'It's cheap,' he replies on a shrug, seeming to gather himself. His head lifts. 'Being a lifeguard doesn't exactly earn you millions, and Dex's parents are good people, they let me stay here for basically nothing. It's not much, but it's home, for now.'

I hum in response as the room falls quiet, the only sound coming from the juddering kettle as it boils. 'What about your parents?' I break the silence, but quickly realise, maybe I shouldn't have.

His fingers drum the side. 'Sugar?' he asks, with an obvious evasion of the question. He grips the steaming kettle, focusing on pouring the boiling water into the mugs. As much as I'm dying to know the answer, I am, after all, going to be staying the night, and it's evidently not a subject he's keen to talk about. I don't particularly want to upset my host when there's a raging cyclone with killer trees happening out there, so I answer simply.

'One, please.'

After stirring in the dollop of milk and sugar he passes me a plain grey mug. I blow the steam before taking a sip, relishing in the warmth trickling down my throat.

'So,' he declares, 'tell me about you. How is it we've never crossed paths before?' Jackson delves into a biscuit tin, whistling Buddy around the counter. He breaks a Digestive in half, dipping one into his steaming tea and giving the other to Bud.

I almost forget his question, watching him intently and finding a strange feeling of fondness taking over me. His sensitive side is hard to mistake whenever he's around my pup. My eyes narrow, the subject sounding familiar. 'I seem to recall a similar question being asked last night.'

'Oh, you recall, do you? Forgive me, because I recollect you being a tad intoxicated,' he teases, offering me a biscuit before fastening the lid when I decline. 'If you do recall, then you must remember you never actually answered properly.'

I eye him over the top of my mug as I take another sip. He really has a way of encouraging you to talk, even if you don't want to. I think it's in the eyes, and the way he seems to peer so deeply into your soul, putting you on the spot. 'It probably has something to do with the fact I haven't been to Cornwall since I was four years old,' I admit.

'How come? You and Mags seem pretty close,' he says, guzzling his tea.

I keep my vision lowered in thought, my fingers unconsciously twiddling my mug. 'We're family. She's always been good to me and I always meant to visit, I just never did. My family's kind of–

'Complicated?' he finishes, cutting me off on a smirk.

'Complicated,' I confirm on a nod.

The tiniest of memories break through the surface of when Mum and I used to visit the old house. Since I can remember, Aunt Maggie has lived in Cornwall, and I can see why, because it's beautiful. I was too young to retain every detail, but slight musings of us running around and playing in her garden, along with Uncle Jerry, will always be planted in my mind. When things were good and happy. It was our monthly trip, and I suppose, as I got older, it was a sad reminder of what once was. I could never muster up the courage. I felt it would hurt too much. It also didn't help that after Mum died, Aunt Maggie's contact with Dad deteriorated, and with Cornwall being so far away and me never learning to drive because of living in congestion city, the excuses just made visiting all the more difficult and impractical.

'I thought you were supposed to be cheering me up, you won't achieve that if you carry on asking about my family history,' I say, shaking the memories.

'Okay, what would you like to talk about?' he complies, a twinkle in his eye.

'You,' I reply quickly and before I can stop myself.

The twinkle fades as he scoffs. 'Fair warning, there's a risk you'll fall into deep depression.'

'I'm sure your life can't be worse than mine at the minute.' The truth is I have no idea what he's going through. I know nothing about him, and despite appearances, his life may well be worse than mine. But people like to object to opinions or presumptions made about them – at least, that's the tactic I have grown up seeing in Dad's world – so in expressing that sentence, my hopes are it encourages him to give me even just a hint into his mysterious life.

However, this isn't just another person, this is Jackson.

He peers back at me intently, holding my attention. So much so, I just can't bring myself to look away. So much so, I don't want to.

'Oh, Emily, you have no idea.' His voice is low and soft, his face unreadable.

'Then give me one.' We're silent, our stares never straying as I watch him watch me. He doesn't respond, and the quiet atmosphere is starting to unnerve me. My word vomit is forcing its way up my throat, yet I find myself wanting to ask the question, even if it will make things incredibly awkward. I want to know. 'You said you were intrigued by me. In what way?'

His focus remains, but his jaw is set tight. I try not to blink in fear of missing any indication of him satisfying my curiosity. He leans in, his dampened lips parting. 'Scrabble.'

'Pardon me?' I frown.

'You want to be cheered up. Nothing like a little healthy competition to stimulate those endorphins.' He shifts, pushing himself off the counter and strolling over to his bed. He reaches for something underneath, and when he pulls out an old, tattered box, his head turns to me as his eyebrows waggle.

'I didn't pin you as a Scrabble kind of guy.'

Jackson brings the box back to the breakfast bar, and I'm trying my best not to show my disappointment at his reluctance to elaborate.

'I wasn't, until Eleanor introduced me. Now I can't get enough.' He places the game on the bar before picking up the stool next to mine and carrying it around to the other side.

'Eleanor?' I question, whilst he plonks himself in his seat, lifts the cardboard lid off and sets out the game.

'Dex's little sister.'

My eyes widen in amusement, I can imagine Dex being a pest of an older brother. 'Eleanor has good taste.'

'We played once when she was bored, and somehow, I've ended up with it. She comes to have a game every now and then.' Jackson glances up at me as we both take turns to shuffle through the bag and pick our tiles. 'So, I must warn you, I am a pro. I've had a lot of practise.'

'You're talking to the girl with an A in A-level English language.'

'That means nothing in the world of Scrabble,' he dismisses, a profoundly high level of confidence radiating off him.

'We'll see,' I retort, positive in my Scrabble ability.

'Alright, let's make this interesting.' He thinks for a moment then flashes a smirk. 'The winner takes the bed.'

His playful competitiveness is influencing me, and I'm determined to beat his self-assured arse. I take a look at my letters I've arranged on my rack and my confidence only grows. 'You're on,' I say, giving my best game face. I'm having that bed.

He organises his tiles and then rests his chin in his palm as his fingers tap his cheek. 'Ladies first,' he offers, and I don't complain. Ignoring his devilish grin, I focus on my first word.

I smile as it's pretty much given to me. Picking up my tiles, I place them down vertically to spell the word, 'queues', positioning them perfectly. I'm inwardly pleased that my tactics to get my Q to fall on the Double Letter Score whilst still landing on the centre star worked. 'Twenty-five,' I announce satisfied.

'Nice start.' He nods as he jots down my score on his pad.

I grab six more tiles from the bag, eyeing whilst he ponders for a moment, his finger drumming against his lip. But then he looks at me with a cheeky grin and picks up all his tiles. 'Thanks for the 'S',' he says, and I watch him with incredulity as he places his letters down. Although 'savaging' only makes fifteen, I'm now a little on edge as he has just proven his skills. This is going to be harder than I thought.

My next word only totals ten, whilst Jackson manages to bag himself fifty-one with a Triple Word Score. I gaze down at my rack with a frown as he writes out his result and I chew on my thumb irritably, knowing this turn is going to be crap. Having to use one of the blank tiles, I only manage 'surf', which gives me a measly six points.

I can hear the rain pattering on the roof as Jackson concentrates, flicking his eyes from his tray to the board. 'Can you?'

'Can I what? Beat you at Scrabble? It would be my pleasure, Jackson.'

'Surf,' he retorts with a roll of his eyes, but a smile dances on his lips as he keeps his focus on his letters.

'I've never surfed in my life,' I reply, studying him with my chin rested on my knuckles.

'Maybe I should teach you one day. It's thrilling once you get the hang of it.'

It takes me a moment to process. I can't gage what he means by those words, and I don't want to ask him with the risk of sounding like an idiot if I've taken it the wrong way. This can't be his way of implying a date, can it? Surely, he's not asking me out the day he knows I've broken up with my boyfriend. Surely, he's just being kind, making conversation in offering me his lifeguarding services. I mean, a surfing lesson is hardly what I'd call a date. So why am I even considering it could be what he's implying?

I have no idea what's going on inside my head at the minute, it's all fuzzy and dishevelled. I shouldn't be thinking this. I shouldn't be watching him undress or studying his face and body when he isn't looking, and I most certainly shouldn't be wanting to say *yes* to his offer just so I can spend more time with him, because it's not sensible and it's not what I want. My mind is simply all over the place.

Then why am I finding myself doing those things? And worst of all, why am I finding myself liking it?

'No, that's okay, I'm more of an observer anyway,' I reply, choosing the sensible option. The safest option.

'Suit yourself,' he says, but whilst I had been locked away in my thoughts, I failed to notice him placing his word on the board to meet several others. 'Erogenous,' he reads aloud. I stare at him, my mouth agape. 'It means parts of the body sensitive to sexual stim–

'I know what it means,' I cut him off, my eyes darting straight to my tray as my cheeks flush. I really don't know what it is about this boy, but whenever I'm around him, my body betrays me, and control is outright destroyed.

'Good. Thirty-three.'

My head shoots up to the board and my prior embarrassment vanishes, replaced with utter frustration. He landed on another Triple Word Score.

'Your turn.' He grins when he notices my dismay. I shoot him a glare as a vexed sigh escapes me.

Several long words and many aggravated huffs from both competitors later, the game has been packed away and the loser is sat on the sofa.

The cushion seat bounces up and down underneath me, the aim to evaluate how much back pain I'll be suffering with tomorrow. It doesn't seem too bad; a lot spongier than it appears.

'What are you doing?' Jackson asks as he shuts the door to the bathroom behind him. He observes me bobbing up and down before sliding open the wardrobe and pulling out a blanket.

'Testing the sofa,' I answer in an obvious tone.

He paces over to me, holding the blanket in front of him with both hands. He comes to a stop and I peer up at his looming form. 'Now, what kind of a gentleman would I be if I let you sleep on that?'

I'm taken aback. He's being serious. My eyes widen. 'You wouldn't be…' I retort, smiling at him when my shock tapers.

'Exactly.' He throws the blanket onto the sofa. 'Say what you want about me, but you can't deny that I am a great host. You should count yourself lucky, Miss Lambert.'

'Are you sure? I don't mind.' I was so determined during the game to win the bed, but now he's willingly offering me the better option, I feel guilty for taking it away from him.

'I'm sleeping on the sofa, Emily. Up you get before I change my mind.'

My eyes drop to the floor and I smile before pushing myself up. 'If you insist.'

I kiss Buddy's head, who is lying on a mound of towels below the bed and glance up. The clock tells me it's just gone nine and although it's early, I'm officially drained of energy. As I pull the crisp covers back and climb in, a real sense of relief and comfort wash over me as my exhausted body finally relaxes into the unfamiliar sheets. It's snug but spacious, and it smells like his sweet aftershave. I turn to see him placing his cushions together. His fingers run through his messy hair before he paces over to the light switch on the wall, leaving the lamp beside me as our only source of visibility.

I stretch my arm out. 'Hey!' I call. His gaze lifts as he arrives back at the sofa, and with all the strength I can muster, I toss one of my pillows across the room. Much to my surprise, it reaches him with minimal movement on his behalf, he scoops it from the air, flashing me a grateful smile and a wink.

Moving my now only pillow into the middle of the bed, I sink into it and stare up at the ceiling. Today has been a complete whirlwind. When I woke this morning, the only thing I thought I'd be battling was a hangover, but again the universe had other plans. In twelve hours, I've lost a boyfriend, a perfectly convenient hoodie, and a tiny piece of my protective barrier has been chipped away. I revealed things to someone who is basically a stranger, but in doing so it awoke thoughts I probably wouldn't have realised if I hadn't opened up. He made it so easy and natural. I admitted hidden feelings to Jackson, but I also admitted them to myself too. And if there's one emotion above all the others swimming around my body, it's one I never thought I would feel when I lost the man I've known for two years. It's not anger or hatred or even sadness; it's relief.

There's still a part of me which cares for William. He's been such an important part of my life. He was my first. And as much as I hate that it has fallen apart the way it has, I don't know what I would've done without him. After all, he pulled me away from a lonely place. And that tiny piece of respect is why I'm not planning on telling Dad about his actions.

Nevertheless, today has allowed me to process and understand the truth I was reluctant to admit, because I was so terrified of being left alone. I'm not in love with him. He's not the one. I don't know who that guy is, or if there even is one out there for me, but I know one thing is for certain, a whole weight has been lifted, and for the first time in what seems like forever, I strangely don't feel overwhelmed with thoughts and emotions. I'm content.

'Jackson?'

'Yeah?' His low voice travels from the sofa.

I roll my head. He's watching me too, lying on his back, the blanket pulled up to his bare chest with his arm positioned behind his head. 'Thank you.'

'For what?' he asks, furrowing his brow.

'Just being there.'

His face remains neutral, indecipherable, his eyes focused deeply on mine. The corner of his mouth curls ever so slightly. 'You're welcome, Emily Rose,' he replies softly. 'Goodnight.'

I smile back. This is possibly the most relaxed I've been in months, and it just so happens to be in the bed of the guy who irked me to no end at the beginning of the week. I pull my attention away from him and reach over to the bedside table, shutting the light off.

My eyes close straight away.

# NINETEEN

The room is dark. There's nothing around me but empty space, I'm alone and I'm scared.

'Hello?' my small, timid voice calls. 'Is anyone there?'

Nothing.

The darkness seems to be closing in on me, but there's nowhere for me to go. I search around desperately as it crawls up my skin, touching every fraction and cell of my body. A deep snicker echoes around the room, but before I have the chance to locate where it's coming from, I hit something solid, my back throbbing with immense pain.

'Please,' I squeak as the footsteps grow closer and louder. 'I don't want to die.'

I can't see his face, but I can hear his dark chuckle as it rings in my ear, becoming louder and louder until I'm dropping to my knees.

The brown carpet is visible now. It's rough under my hands. I stare across the landing and see her. She smiles and my hand lifts, reaching for her. But she doesn't reach back. A deafening scream makes me slap my hands over my ears as I squeeze my eyes closed.

'No,' I whimper. 'No, no, no,' I continue to sob.

My eyes open and I see her fall. Tears stream down my face as I remain helpless and unmoving on my knees. It's *then I succumb to my emotions and let out a harrowing wail, crumpling into a heap on the bristly floor.*

I gasp as my body jolts awake. My breaths heavy and my cheeks wet. I'm disorientated and it takes me a moment to gather my bearings. The environment is unfamiliar. It's not until I see Jackson across the dim room that I remember exactly where I am.

It was just a nightmare. Another disconcerting nightmare.

The room is dark, but my eyes are adjusting, and although it's fuzzy, I can make out his sleeping form; one arm is dangling off the sofa, while the other rests on his stomach, the blanket now only covering his legs. I swivel my body around so I can read the clock above the bed. It's half three. Like a yo-yo, my chest rises and falls, my heartbeat mercifully beginning to steady itself.

Will they ever stop?

My hair is sticking to my dampened neck, so I quickly scrape it all up into a loose bun and tie it with the bobble on my wrist. *Every goddamn night.* I throw the covers off my hot, sweaty body and swing my legs over the edge of the bed, taking several deep and calming breaths.

When I've gathered enough strength, I stand and tiptoe softly over to the kitchen, trying my best not to disturb a slumbering Jackson or snoring Buddy. I reach the sink, opening a couple of cupboards above my head before discovering what I'm in need of. Clasping the small fishbowl shaped glass, I carefully lift it down, however with the room being so dark, I make the mistake of overlooking the glass placed on top of it, and my quivering hands have to make quick work of catching both as they tumble.

'Shit!' I curse. I manage to save them, but a clang ricochets around the room as they smack together. Giving a wary glance over to Jackson expecting his eyes to fly open, I breathe a sigh of relief when he mercifully remains sound asleep. Buddy lets out a huff and stretches his paws, rolling onto his side. Being extra careful, I place one of them back and run the tap at a gentle speed before filling the glass halfway and cutting off the flow.

I rest my back against the counter and swig the cold water, appreciating the refreshing liquid which instantly reduces my body temperature. Maybe I should consider therapy, because even though my dreams haven't been haunting me long, I know the nightmares aren't planning on easing up anytime soon, and I'm not sure how much longer I'll be able to take the sleepless nights before I break.

Cradling the glass to my chest, I stretch my neck, rolling it around to ease my tense muscles. It slowly centres as something ahead comes into view, something which I hadn't spotted before. My eyes narrow.

As gently as possible, I place the glass onto the side. It's right in the corner of the kitchen and I give in to my inner nosiness as I tread silently up to it. The door is solid oak, and as I try the handle, I realise it's locked. I don't know why I want to look inside, it's most likely just a boiler or a storage room or something tedious. Nonetheless, now I know it's inaccessible, my interest is only fuelled.

My forehead meets the wood. It's just a door to another room, Emily. Who cares? I'm over tired.

With that thought, I give up, throwing the remaining water into the sink before swilling the glass and popping it back in the cupboard, being hyper-aware of any other smashable items this time.

The light taps of my bare feet on the laminate floor carry over to the bed where my body collapses onto the mattress. Drawing the duvet up to my chin, my eyes are left to stare at the ceiling, praying the nightmares leave me alone for the rest of the night.

My fluttering lids open. It takes me a few seconds to work out where I am, the room I'm not accustomed to confusing my awakening mind. My cheek is pressed against the pillow, and I'm lying on my front as I gaze over at the vacant sofa. I'm about to roll over when I hear the door to the bathroom creak open. I don't move, listening closely as he fumbles through the wardrobe behind me.

Jackson comes into view, but I remain still, observing his actions. A towel is draped around his waist and his hair is dripping as he throws some items, including a black T-shirt and jeans, onto the sofa. His back is to me and I can't help but study his flawlessly muscular shoulders, his tall frame and strong build making him look like a giant. I'm now understanding why those boys surrendered to him at Leo's party so easily, I certainly wouldn't want to get into a punch up with him.

I'm caught off guard, my breath hitching in my throat as he turns to the side and drops the towel without any hesitation. My eyes squeeze shut, but the temptation to look is too much.

Just a peek, a tiny peek won't hurt. I peel one eye open.

*Holy shit!*

My other eye unbolts in pure shock. That thing could do some serious damage.

*Put your tongue back in. Stop being a perv, Emily!*

But I can't, he's too damn enthralling.

He pulls his boxers up, followed by his jeans, and I push down the unwarranted displeasure. Grabbing his towel, he ruffles his hair with it creating a matted mess, but somehow, he still manages to make it look good. After pulling his shirt over his head, he turns in my direction and I quickly close my eyes again. I follow his movements with my ears, trying to work out the best time to fake my awakening.

A few minutes pass, the sound of the kettle boiling and cutlery clinking against each other signals his engagements in the kitchen. Soon afterwards the smell of bacon engulfs my senses, making my stomach growl.

I make my move, stirring in the bed and sitting up sluggishly.

'Morning, sleepy head,' his chipper voice calls as he stands with his back to me, facing the pan.

My eyes scrunch, feeling like sandpaper when they're rubbed. 'Morning,' I say through a genuine yawn.

'Sleep well?'

'Yeah,' I lie, smacking my lips together. I'm exhausted. I didn't get back to sleep until gone five. I just couldn't shut my mind off, and I was scared that when I did eventually close my eyes, the horrid nightmares would come rushing back. Mercifully, they held off. 'You?' I ask, even though I know the answer, he's too cheery to have had a bad night's sleep.

'Like a log,' he replies, pouring steaming water into two mugs. He waves one in my direction and places it down on the breakfast bar. I realise I haven't moved as I gawp at him, the image of his naked body still very much present in my mind and showing no signs of disappearing.

I snap myself out of it and push myself up, adjusting the skewwhiff boxers which had fallen down my leg. Padding over to the bar, I perch on the stool I've apparently claimed as my own personal seat. 'Where's Buddy?' I ask, suddenly realising the towels where he lay are missing. Jackson points at his feet and I hoist myself up, peering over the worktop to see him gobbling what looks to be chopped up sausages in a bowl.

'I went for a quick jog with him while you were sleeping. You looked peaceful, so I didn't want to disturb you. I hope you don't mind?'

I feel my tummy flip. Peaceful. 'Not at all.' I shake my head in reply to him, but also to cast away the images of him watching me sleep. Dear God, I hope my mouth was closed. 'You've taken a liking to him, haven't you?'

'He's just so darn adorable, aren't you, Buddy boy?' He dives to the floor, fussing behind his ears, but Buddy takes no notice, too busy with his sausages.

'The sofa wasn't so bad, then?' I ask, sipping at my tea.

'Surprisingly, no,' he replies, resting his hip on the side and swigging his own steaming brew. 'But I can't lie, I look forward to getting my bed back tonight.' He throws a wink over his mug and I smile. 'I'm making breakfast, I hope you're hungry,' he says, turning to crack several eggs into a bowl, the bacon sizzling happily in the background.

'Starving,' I answer eagerly, my eyeline shifting to the door behind him which grasped my curiosity last night.

'Are you working today?' he asks, glancing over his shoulder as he whisks the mixture before pouring it into a saucepan.

My head shakes. 'Day off. Are you lifeguarding?'

He mimics me, jerking his head and smiling. 'Day off.'

'Convenient.'

'Quite,' he retorts, a hint of amusement to his tone.

I'm fascinated as I watch him meticulously prepare our food. First, he spoons the scrambled eggs precisely, *very* precisely, onto the middle of the two plates, before placing the bacon in a crisscross on top. He picks up one, whilst grabbing the ketchup and brown sauce on his way over. It looks delicious as he lays it down in front of me. My knife and fork are already on the side, so I don't hesitate in squirting a dollop of ketchup next to the eggs before tucking in. I instantly recoil. 'Oh, holy crap!'

'Yep.' He nods casually as he leans on the other side of the counter tucking into his own.

'These are the best eggs I've ever tasted,' I exclaim, diving in for more, not caring that I'm boosting his already huge ego. These are too good to hide my feelings.

'Special recipe,' he admits, grinning as he stabs his food with his fork.

'Does that include a mound of butter?' There's no way he could make them so flavoursome without some kind of fatty ingredient.

He feigns a hurt expression. 'I'll try not to take offence to that. We lifeguards have to watch our diet, keep our bodies in tip top condition,' he defends. 'Minus a couple of sweet treats every now and then.' A cheeky glint sparkles in his eyes.

'Come on, you have to tell,' I plead, scooping some

more up with the bacon this time, my taste buds in utter bliss. 'In fact, no, don't,' I say, waving my hand manically. 'The mystery makes them all the more delicious.'

He laughs, most likely at me, but I'm not bothered, all my concerns and worries have been put on temporary pause, all that matters is this beautiful breakfast.

We eat the rest in a comfortable silence. Surprisingly, he finishes first and I can feel his eyes on me as I take my final bites.

'The storm's blown over and hopefully that tree's been dealt with. I'm meeting Dex on his shift in about an hour, so I'll drop you and Bud back at the cottage when I go,' he informs me, leaning forward and sipping his tea.

'Okay, thank you.' I give an appreciative smile, but a feeling of dejection washes over me. Because, whilst the idea of him bringing us back here last night was initially opposed by me, my emotions have spun a complete U-turn. Now it's time to leave, I'm finding myself not wanting to. This place is like a hideaway; a den for a boy who wants to escape the world and shut out its brutality. It's his home. A place where he can be himself. And I like the fact he's allowed me into it. I've always said that people are different at home, it's a personal space, and Jackson opened the door for me to step through. Sure, he seems to be incredibly popular in this town, but there's so much of him which is closed off. His walls are up, and I get the feeling he doesn't let many people in. So the idea that he's given me even an inkling into the tiniest portion of his life by allowing me to stay here, I can't help but feel privileged. On top of that, I've inadvertently seen the side profile of his manhood, so I don't think I could leave here not feeling that little bit closer to him.

Just before the images of his naked body once again devour my mind and turn it into mush, a muffled chime sounds from behind me. Saved by the bell!

He raises his brow as I hop off the stool and scamper across the room to my bag. 'Hello?' I answer and Lily is quick to speak.

'You, me, Marshlyn Bay, one hour,' she rambles off. The connection is crackly, and judging by the echoing of her voice, I'm guessing I'm on speaker phone. I can imagine her running around her bedroom frantically throwing her clothes on.

'What's the urgency?' I ask as I try to wake my brain up.

'Don't ask questions.' Her voice becomes clearer and I can tell she's now holding the phone to her ear. 'I'll explain when I see you. Vicki's on another lifeguard training day so she'll be there.' She pauses. 'I need you both.'

My eyes lift to catch Jackson watching me curiously from the kitchen. 'Okay,' I agree, rubbing my forehead. What could be so pressing that she's getting in such a state about and can't tell me over the phone?

'One hour,' she stresses.

'One hour,' I echo with a nod even though she can't see me.

'Thanks, Em. Don't be late!' she warns before hanging up.

Jackson's focus is bold as I slowly peel the phone away from my ear.

'Lily,' I say, answering his questioning gaze. 'Looks like I'll be seeing you at the beach,' I proclaim, throwing my phone back in my bag.

'Convenient.' He grins into his mug.

'Quite,' I shadow on a smile.

After Jackson returns my clothes from the main house, I quickly change and the three of us clamber into his Jeep. The weather has revived itself, with blue sky peeping through swirls of white cloud as the sun shines down brightly, providing a welcomed subtle warmth. Apart from the fallen branches and leaves, there's no hint that a storm ever hit the town.

The time on the dashboard says it has just passed eleven. All four windows are rolled down and Buddy's head is protruding out in the back. Through the wing mirror I watch him, smiling as his tongue flaps in the wind. Constant air is blustering through the car causing a few wayward strands to fall out of my ponytail, with trees and bushes whizzing past us in a speedy blur.

We're both quiet as we pull up outside the cottage, with Guy's Mercedes parked in its usual spot in front of us.

'Who's that?' Jackson asks, and I stare intently at the

Benz, trying to work out if Guy is behind the blacked-out windscreen watching us.

'It's Guy, one of Aunt Maggie's old friends,' I lie, and it pains me to do so. I hate dishonesty, and I just wish this whole mess would go away so I wouldn't have to be.

'Ah, so he's the one who's got Mags all doe-eyed,' he says, glancing at me briefly with a noticeable smirk on his face.

'No,' I argue on a small smile. 'He's just a friend.'

He throws me a knowing look before turning his attention back to the Mercedes. 'If you say so.' He pauses in thought. 'Nice car,' he adds, pouting and raising his eyebrows in admiration.

*Curtesy of working for 'Mafia Fighters Anonymous',* I so desperately want to say. 'I should go and prepare myself for Lily,' I flippantly settle with instead as I reach for the door handle, but his arm is thrown out, barring my movements.

'Just a minute.' He opens his palm. 'Give me your phone.'

'Why?'

'Just.' He motions to my bag, flexing his fingers. I frown but search for it anyway and after unlocking it, place it in his hand.

His fingers tap away before he hands it back to me, and when I study the screen, I see he's added his phone number. 'Just in case you have any more breakdowns,' he explains when he notices my hesitation.

I smile back at him, trying desperately to ignore the warmth in my tummy. He's resting his right hand slackly on the steering wheel, his emerald eyes twinkling as the sun gleams through the windscreen, hitting them enchantingly. There's a faint but pleasant breeze entering through our windows, causing a couple of stray waves to drift onto his forehead.

'Thanks, Jackson,' I offer. We've only been sitting here for less than a minute, but the grasp he has on my attention makes it feel like we've been here for hours. 'For everything.'

It's beginning to concern me that whenever he looks at me, those eyes seem to consume me. It's not his eyes per say – although they are too striking for their own good – which are bothering me, it's the way I don't want to look away. Every time I fall into the trap of getting sucked into them, I get this feeling of warmth and serenity, but each time I do, I'm also made aware that behind those eyes, hidden in the depths, there is so much mystery. Maybe that's why I can't seem to tear mine away, because maybe I believe that if I stare into them long enough, I'll find out who Jackson Turner really is.

But why do I care so much? I shouldn't. I barely know him, and in a few weeks' time – if by some miracle Dad gets his act together – I'll probably never see him again, or for only a few days of the year when I come back to visit Aunt Maggie. I need to stop being so bloody curious.

'Don't mention it,' he replies, bringing me back to reality.

I finally get a hold of myself and break our stare, climbing out of the car. I open the back door for Buddy to hop out. Jackson watches me through the opened window. 'See you at the beach,' he calls as I back away, observing how he turns the car around with ease and takes off the way we came.

His car disappears, and on a deep sigh, I hoist the thin strap of my bag onto my shoulder, unlatching the gate. Buddy trots through, but I don't get the chance to enter. Guy's gruff voice is calling me.

'Good morning, Miss Lambert.'

I spin to see his face through the open window. He *was* watching us.

'Morning, Guy,' I retort, bending down to peer inside.

'If it's alright with you, I'm going to head back to the hotel and take care of some business, check in with your father, that sort of thing,' he says on a calm tone. He's dressed in his casual attire again, and I'm slowly growing accustomed to him not being in his formal bodyguard suit.

'That's okay, I'm heading to the beach soon anyway.' My voice is composed, and I note how the nerves I previously felt about him leaving me on my own are gradually easing away with each passing day.

He nods. 'Thank you. I just wanted to make sure you were okay.'

I smile in response and begin to straighten, but his words pull me back down.

'Before you go, I hope I'm not overstepping the mark, however I wanted to give you a piece of advice.' He pauses briefly, and I watch him curiously. 'Be careful with who you let in.'

My eyes narrow in puzzlement. 'What do you mean?'

'The lifeguard,' he replies, and I try desperately to understand what he's getting at as he continues. 'Ms Taylor said you stayed over at Mr Turner's last night?'

'Yes, but it was the only option. I barely know him,' I defend, even though I'm not sure why I'm under interrogation.

'Exactly. Just be vigilant. Some people are not all they seem.'

My lips part as I stare at his unwavering expression in confusion.

'I'll be at the hotel if you need me, have a good day, Miss Lambert.'

By the time I'm confident enough that words will form comprehensible sentences when I speak, he's already pulling away.

What the hell is he talking about? Who's not all they seem? I tell myself he's probably just channelling his inner security consciousness, making sure he's doing his job in keeping me safe. Still, it doesn't stop me wondering.

'Aunty, I'm back!' I call as I flick my shoes off. A head peeps into the hallway from the living room.

'What did you do to my fireplace, young lady?'

Crap! Buddy bounds past, scooping his new tennis ball up from the floor as he goes. A guilty look washes over my face before she disappears. I reluctantly enter the living room to see her with her hands on her hips, flicking her eyes between me and the ashy mess where the fire had roared, which was entirely unsoiled this time yesterday.

'Long story,' I say, avoiding any eye contact.

'Sit.' She points to the sofa.

'It's not that long,' I try, not wanting to go over what happened again, I really just want to forget about it. She flashes me a stern glance, and realising there's no escaping from it, I give in, sitting my bottom down.

With Buddy chewing his ball at my feet, I place my hands in my lap as she lowers down beside me. Her brow raises, encouraging me to explain.

I tell her everything, from my feelings about my relationship these past few months, all the way to the dreaded phone call which revealed his sickening actions while I was home alone the night *it* happened.

Her mouth falls agape. 'You're joking!'

I shake my head, now looking her dead in the eye.

'Oh, Pidge, are you okay?' she asks, her mood shifting entirely. There's not a hint of annoyance to her tone anymore, it's been replaced by compassion, and I know that barrel of disapproval she was pointing at me not a moment ago has now been turned in William's direction.

'Actually, I am.' I bob my head, recalling the conclusion I came to yesterday. 'I've realised that I don't need him. I don't need a man to be happy.'

She grabs my hand in a forceful but supportive grip. 'No, you don't.' Her arms fly around me and I relish in her comfort as she strokes my back. 'I'm proud of you, Emily.' We stay in this position, neither of us wanting to pull away. Eventually she does though, gripping both of my arms firmly. 'Hold on, how does that explain my fireplace?'

'I burnt his hoodie.'

Her brow raises before she grins. 'That's my girl.'

My appreciation for her is only growing the more time I spend here. Whenever I need a hug, she's there, even when I don't even know I'm in need of one. She's kind, caring, loving – everything I've been missing out on because of my silly fears and reluctance to face them. I'm glad I have her now.

She pulls me into another brief embrace before patting my leg and standing. 'You're cleaning that mess up, madam,' she points.

'Fair enough,' I comply as she leaves the room.

Firm but reasonable. That's why I wholeheartedly respect her.

# TWENTY

I struggle up to Lily and Vicki, my bare feet trudging across the uneven sand. They're sat in a hidden cove away from the crowds.

'What's the emergency?' I ask, my hands carrying my Converse flying out as I reach them. Lily's dressed in hot pants and a white and blue stripy crop top, whilst Vicki looks like someone out of Baywatch in a red swimming costume with denim shorts over the top, her blonde locks pulled into a high pony.

'I'm going to tell him,' Lily blurts.

I pause for a moment, fumbling to wrap my head around her words. Have I missed something? 'Tell who, what?' I turn to Vicki. 'What's going on?'

'Dex,' Vicki answers, giving me a knowing look. My eyes widen in realisation as I mouth, 'Oh,' in response before plopping down next to Lily.

'I'm going to tell him I like him,' she confirms, nodding as her focus zones ahead, as though she's psyching herself up.

'About bloody time,' Vicki snorts. Usually, she would be met with a glare, but this isn't usual circumstance. Lily's unease is present and very much out of character.

'What are you going to say?' I ask, studying her face.

She looks scared to death and I feel bad for finding her dramatics amusing.

'I don't know. I've never had to do it before, boys always come to me.'

I shoot Vicki a look and she gives me an eloquent nod. Lily's not exaggerating. Being popular with the opposite sex is a dangerous game, because as I have found out, men are made to break hearts. I should be encouraging Lily to stay well clear.

'All you can do is be honest,' I advise, against my better judgment. Lily's old enough to make her own decisions. Besides, maybe it's just the men in my life who turn out superficial. Maybe Dex is different.

I find the surf hut in the distance, studying him as he stacks a couple of surf boards. Jackson is beside him, his arms folded across his chest as they chat, but there's another person with them too. Olivia has her arm linked through Jackson's. I clench my jaw when he drops his arms and drapes one over her shoulder. There's something about her which really bothers me, only I can't work out what.

'Be honest... right,' Lily echoes, drawing me back to her.

'I'm curious, how did you finally figure out what we've all known since forever?' Vicki asks as she hugs her legs.

'Ever since you went to get ice cream yesterday and me and Emily were watching him on duty, I've been thinking about it a lot,' she spills. 'He's like a little puppy and he's really cute, but incredibly stupid and ridiculously annoying. I don't know why I like him, but I do, and I've come to the conclusion that life is too short, so fuck it. I'm going with my heart before my head talks me out of it.' She's a little out of breath from her reveal, but I can see as well as admitting it to us, she's also completely reassured herself that this is what she wants and is exactly how she feels.

Vicki and I flick a glance to each other behind Lily's back, our eyes wide with big grins on our faces. 'Then what are you sitting here telling us for? He's right over there! Go get him,' I squeal with a light smack to her arm.

'Exactly! Go, before I drag you there myself,' Vicki exclaims, gesturing with a curt nod towards the hut.

On a deep inhale, Lily pushes herself up, brushing the sand from her butt and turning to face us. 'How do I look?'

Without any communication between the two of us, Vicki and I rise to our feet, immediately tending to her appearance. Vicki takes her hair; fluffing and zhooshing. I work on straightening her crop top and brushing all the sand from her shorts. We stand back, admiring our work before nodding in approval.

'I love you girls,' Lily declares on a sigh and wraps her arms around us, holding us close.

I giggle as Vicki rolls her eyes. 'For heaven's sake, woman, go!' she cries. Lily releases us before flashing a nervous smile and taking off up the beach. I inch closer to Vicki. 'Tenner she bails,' she says quietly.

'You're on,' I reply, keeping my eyes on Lily as she grows closer to where the three lifeguards stand. Dex is leaning against the hut now, and his head turns when he spots her marching up to him. We don't hold back on the gasps as she lunges.

So much for fretting about what to say.

He's rigid at first, his arms down by his side in utter shock, but within a couple of seconds he seems to relax. They wrap around her waist as he picks her up and spins her around. Jackson's arm drops from Olivia's shoulder and I don't miss her subtle unapproving frown as he does so, however he doesn't notice, he's too busy gawping at Dex and Lily attacking each other's faces.

I glance at Vicki. 'I'll put it on your tab,' I say on a smug smirk as Vicki puckers her lips, subduing a smile.

They finally pull apart and Dex's eyes couldn't be forced wider if they were being yanked open with string. His mouth falls agape before he presses his lips together and Lily's begin to move. I squint hard, trying my best to lip read, but it's proving impossible from this distance. I don't have to concentrate for too long though, because he's soon grabbing her face, kissing her once again.

Without any thought to possible shame and embarrassment, Vicki and I throw our arms in the air and let out several whoops and cheers of utter delight. Taking hold of each other's hands, we dance around on the spot, laughing like complete idiots.

This inevitably catches their attention, as well as everybody else within a two-mile radius. Vicki's elation is contagious, and in the moment we simply don't care. My own joy being fuelled in knowing that this is quite possibly the happiest I've been in a while.

Our twirling stops, but our laughs remain as Lily shakes her head at our stupidity, a beam on her face. Dex is smiling too as he pulls her to his chest, and when my eyes flick to the side, I realise so is Jackson. But not at them. At me. My grin only widens when I catch him chuckling, neither of us looking anywhere else but at each other. I feel an arm on my shoulder as Vicki jerks me closer to her.

'You'll have to get your boyfriend to visit, we could triple date,' she says and my face drops. My stare turns to the floor and I know Vicki is sensing something's off, because her arm loosens, dropping to her side. 'Is this one of those, open mouth, insert foot, moments?' She visibly cringes, gnawing on her knuckle.

'No, it's okay.' I shake my head. Yesterday I probably would have burst into tears at her suggestion, but today, I couldn't care less. So many months of feeling so desperately undervalued have taken their toll and when I think of William, I'm entirely numb.

'Are you sure? I'm sorry.'

'It's fine, Vicki, honest.' I nod, placing my hand on her arm, giving a reassuring squeeze. She relaxes under my touch.

'So you're not upset?' she asks, her brow crinkling.

'I was, but now,' my eyes flicker over to Dex and Lily cuddling, and then to Jackson. His expression has changed; the smile it held is now neutral, yet his attention still remains on me, 'I'm actually really good.'

Buddy's head lays in my lap. My fingers tickle behind his soft ears as he fights the desperate urge to close his eyes. It doesn't take long before he's giving in.

'Look up,' Aunt Maggie urges as she begins on the right side of my French plaits. Having just washed and dried my hair, I plopped myself on the sofa ready to watch TV when Aunty peered over the top of her magazine, asking if she could braid my hair. It was definitely a silent plea, because it's currently a freshly washed wiry mess, but she would never admit it. Sitting on the floor below her, I relish in the relaxing sensation of her weaving hands through my long locks.

I follow her instruction, my head tilting and my eyes drawing back to whatever soap is on the TV. It could be Emmerdale, or it might possibly be Coronation Street, I haven't been paying much attention. My mind keeps drifting back to Jackson and his words. I'm still yet to find out what he meant when he said he was intrigued by me, but I guess I'm going to have to get over it, because I can't see him ever telling me. Every time I ask him a question, he shifts and swerves, either avoiding it entirely, or turning the conversation around on me. It's extremely frustrating.

'Your hair is so lovely and thick. It's just like your mum's, I was always so envious,' Aunt Maggie says softly, bringing me out of my daze as she pulls more hair from the side of my face into the braid.

'Do you miss her?' I ask, glancing out the corner of my eye, careful to keep my head as still as possible.

'Every day.'

I covertly smile to myself. 'Sometimes it feels like I imagined her, like she was just a beautiful dream,' I admit sadly. I wish I'd had longer with her. It's unfair that she was taken from me before I had the chance to properly know her. All the memories which could have been, never became.

'She was very real, Emily. She loved you very much, and if she were here now, let me tell you, that slimy boy would need to go into hiding. She would've done anything to protect you,' she pauses for the briefest of seconds. 'In fact, she did.'

'What do you mean?' I prevent her fiddling hands from plaiting as my body twists in her direction. She doesn't tell me to turn back so she can continue, instead she studies me, as though she's thinking very carefully about her next words.

'I just mean, for every moment you were with her she was there, loving you and protecting you, and she still is. She's up there somewhere with a glass, or several knowing Marie, of the finest Rosé, watching over you. She's probably spying on us now, making sure I'm looking after you properly.' Her lips quirk but her eyes carry a sadness, a sadness I've never seen behind them before. It still pains her. I know she was my mum, but Aunt Maggie lost her younger sister; that's a completely different type of pain, and it's a pain she's living with every day. Yet she never ever lets it show. She always puts others before herself no matter how she's feeling, and that's why she's the strongest person I know.

'She'd be so thankful for you, Aunty,' I say, placing a hand on her knee. 'I'm so grateful for everything you've done for me. You've been nothing short of amazing.'

She lays her free hand over mine. 'I always said, even though she was younger, she had a far older head on her shoulders, and if I could be half the woman your mother was, then I would be satisfied.'

'Trust me, Mum would be so proud. I know I am.' I show her a warm and honest smile.

'And she would be immensely proud of her beautiful daughter. As a matter of fact, I *know* she is.' Her thumb strokes my hand and I have to force down the lump in my throat. 'Now turn around and let me finish before my arm falls off.'

I do as she says, my hand finding Buddy's ears once again, a small, sad smile planted on my lips.

A quiet chime and a repeated buzzing wake me from my slumber. I wince as an ache works its way up my neck when I shift from the awkward position it had fallen into. I rub my eyes, moving my other hand around to aimlessly feel for my phone in the darkened room, which I could've sworn I was using to play games on before sleep took over. I'm not sure at what point in the evening it happened, but the three of us fell asleep on the sofa, with Buddy nestling himself in the middle.

A wave of relief washes over me when I eventually grip it under the cushion beside me. Without reading the name on my screen in a hurried bid to halt the chiming, I answer.

'Hello?' I groggily murmur. Standing, I notice that the opened curtains reveal an eerie pitch-black view of outside and I wonder what the time is.

Late. It's very late.

I tiptoe past the two sleeping bodies on the sofa. 'Hello?' I repeat when there's no response, and quietly exit the living room, soundlessly closing the door behind me. I knead my delirious head before shifting the phone away from my ear, glancing at the time. In doing so the name of the silent caller is exposed to me. I swallow. 'Jackson?'

'Did I wake you?' His voice is low. It's so soft I can barely hear him.

'No,' I lie. 'No, it's okay. What's up?' I ask with all manner of questions running through my drowsy mind. Why is he calling *me* at this time? I thought he only gave me his number in case I needed to phone him. Has something happened? But if it has, why would he want me specifically?

'Can we meet?'

I squeeze my eyes together, feeling very dazed and groggy. Am I hallucinating? I take another look at the time on my phone. 'Right now? It's one in the morning,' I murmur, knowing that Aunt Maggie's walls are paper thin and fearing the slightest noise might wake her.

'I know, I'm sorry. I just…' he falters, taking a breath.

My body stiffens. He doesn't sound like Jackson, he sounds tired… fragile.

'I nee…' His voice trembles and my head seems to clear itself, suddenly feeling wide awake.

'Where?' I ask without hesitation.

He sighs a sigh filled with relief. 'The clifftop bench. Ten minutes?'

'Okay,' I agree, not even considering how uncomfortable the walk will be in the dark on my own. For whatever reason he sounds desperate.

'Thank you, Emily,' he manages before we disconnect.

I sneak a glance through the glass in the door to see Aunt Maggie and Buddy still sound asleep. With as minimal noise as possible, I slide on my shoes at the bottom of the staircase, unhook my jacket from the banister, and quietly slip out of the cottage.

It's the feeling of both curiosity and concern which is carrying me through the chilling, creepy darkness towards our meeting place, because I can't seem to grasp why he wants to talk to me. Why not go to Dex who's basically in the same house? What made him choose my name – a name he's known less than a week – over the hundreds he probably has in his phone? But the most prominent question: what could have possibly made the man who doesn't seem to give a damn about anything, sound so troubled and anxious? My answer: something bad. It has to be if he's calling me in the middle of the night, struggling to get his words out.

I don't know what I'll be confronted with in ten minutes time, but what I do know is, if I can be there for him in any way, just like he has me, then I'll try my utmost to make sure he's alright.

# TWENTY-ONE

It takes seven minutes to reach the car park, and as I march across it, my eyes locate the silver Wrangler sitting on its own in the darkness. The headlights aren't gleaming so I know he's already up there.

My crappy phone light feebly guides the way as I climb the steps up to the clifftop path. It's so quiet, there's no noise apart from the sea below as it crashes against the rocks and plunges onto the shore. I can barely see anything in front of me, the carved footpath and the three millimetres of light are the only aspects preventing me from wandering off the edge, but they don't deter the unnerving feeling creeping around my gut as the darkness touches every part of me – just like in my nightmares. A shiver creeps down my spine and I can feel the goosebumps on my arms, so I push myself forwards. However, I'm now beginning to question my decision in agreeing to meet him at this time of night.

A darkened figure is occupying our meeting spot up ahead. My feet come to a stop as a feeling of apprehension takes over my body. It's the fear of the unknown, and I've now realised that I've left the cottage alone, in the dead of night without telling anyone, to meet a man who phoned me in a distressed state, on top of a cliff. Something in my mind tells me to turn around and get somebody to help, but I don't have the chance to consider it, because his head turns in my direction.

I gulp down the ball of uneasiness in my throat before carefully treading towards him.

'Hey.' His voice is husky, slightly broken. He's been crying.

'Hi,' I reply slowly. Warily.

I move to stand in front of him, his neck cranes as he peers up at me. He pulls his grey hood down, the sight confirming my thoughts. Eyes red and blotchy, hair a wild mess. He scoots over, gesturing me to sit, and I do without a word.

We remain in silence, looking out into the dark abyss as the ocean swooshes below us. I don't know what to do. I'm not sure if he's waiting for me to speak, or whether he wants us to sit in the quiet, or if he's trying to think of what to say, so I'm uncertain as to why I say it, possibly because it's my way of making light of an unusual situation, but the words spew nevertheless. 'We're making a habit of this, isn't it the fourth night in a row now?' I laugh, and my body relaxes a little when he lets out a husky chuckle. But the relaxed state is short lived.

My body tenses again when his face falls into his hands. They slide through his curls and drop into his lap. He sighs and his eyes meet mine, pulling me in as usual. 'Do you ever have dreams where you're aware that you're dreaming, but you have no control over what's happening?'

I nod. It's safe to say, I've experienced this more than

I'd like. But they're not dreams, they're nightmares, and they're haunting.

'It's called a lucid dream,' he says, and although I already know this, it's like I'm learning all over again. His voice holds my attention, and his eyes are making sure it never dwindles, and even though I'm wondering where he's going with this, in my absorbed state, I go along with it. My previous apprehension evaporates, nothing else seems to matter but the syllables he's speaking, and they're affecting me. It's like I'm following his words, but I'm also feeling his discernible pain. 'Those aren't the bad ones,' he continues. 'The bad ones come more frequently and are ten times more intense. Your subconscious is so powerful in its persistence, that you can't override anything as it manifests your worst thoughts and feelings. All your fears and anxieties you hold deep within reveal themselves, and you can do nothing but face what's being thrown at you until your subconscious decides it has tortured you enough and wakes you up.' He pauses on a sigh. 'That's a lucid nightmare.'

His stare lowers, and I feel my shoulders drop as some of the tension I overlooked holding in them is relieved as our connection temporarily breaks. A part of me though, is begging him to raise his head so I can feel connected to him again. So I can fully understand and feel what's running through his mind.

'My life, Emily, is one big nightmare.' He does as I've been silently pleading, his red eyes lift to my tired ones. My eyebrows furrow and I know concern is written all over my face. 'The only problem is, I can't wake up from reality, I have to live with them.'

'Them?' I ask softly, afraid that if I'm too brisk he'll completely crumble.

'My demons,' he breathes. 'No matter how far I go or how hard I try, they still manage to follow me. They'll never leave, they're always there,' I can feel the heaviness in his chest as it expands, his eyes glassy, 'and they always will be.'

I sit in shock, my eyeline remaining in place as his shifts away, moving to the perpetual darkness in front of us. I swallow, my body freeing itself from its frozen position and inching closer to him, studying his profile. 'Talk to me. What's happened, Jackson?'

He doesn't answer for a moment, but then his eyes close. 'August seventeenth. Six years ago, today. It's the anniversary.'

'Anniversary of what?'

'Of the worst night of my fucking life.' His head turns and his gaze is intense, his sad eyes building my tautness back up as I brace myself for his next words. 'It's the night my father left.'

My mouth opens before I realise, I don't know what to say. His revelation is making me reflect. I'm trying to put myself in his shoes, to imagine exactly how he's feeling right now, because even though I know what it's like to live your life without a father figure, I'm used to it, and it's different for me. My father was still around, he was a shit Dad, and he did his best to stay away, but he was there. I was also a little girl when we drifted, so I've essentially grown up without one, whereas Jackson, he would've been–

'I was sixteen,' he says, as though he can read my mind. His voice is brittle. I'm terrified that whatever I reply will send him over the edge, but then again, maybe that's what he needs; to let it all out. Because I get the feeling he doesn't very often. I place my hand on his arm, encouraging him to continue and reassuring him that I'm here and I'm listening.

'I thought everything was okay, I mean, we didn't have a lot of money, but things weren't bad. Then one night, he comes home drunk, saying he's got this new job in Devon and that whilst he'd been going down for interviews and training shit, he'd met another woman.' He scoffs, shaking his head. 'Fucking prick.' His fists curl into balls in his lap and I notice his knuckles turning white. 'I resent him,' he hisses. 'I resent him because he left behind a broken home… a broken boy. He walked out that door and we never heard from him again, my whole life turned upside down. We didn't have much money coming in, so we had to move to a grotty flat in a fucked-up area, my mum started drinking heavily. It broke her. The night he left changed everything. It changed me. I became someone I hated, and I got caught up in some fucked-up shit, all because of him, because he left us.'

My vision is blurry, my eyes welling as I watch him scrunch his face up, struggling to keep his tears from falling. It's strange to see how a man who first appeared so strong and intimidating, can now look so sad and so utterly broken.

'And then,' he gnaws down on his bottom lip, 'after months of watching her fall apart… of watching *myself* fall apart… it all ended. My life took another turn, because of my own decisions.' He sighs deeply, turning to me. 'I made some bad fucking decisions, Emily. And that's on me, I have to live with them, but they were decisions I wouldn't have had to make if things hadn't changed. If he hadn't left us with nothing.'

'Jesus,' I murmur in shock. 'I'm so sorry, Jackson.' I want to ask more. I want to push further. I want to know what those decisions were and what happened to him. But something tells me I shouldn't, that if he wanted to, he would tell me on his own. However, there is one thing which is running through my mind, one thing which has been bothering me throughout his admittance and since I discovered he lives in Dex's annex. So, with the risk of sending him over the edge, I ask. 'Where's your mum now?'

He visibly tenses, but his gaze never shifts from me, and I don't dare break from his hold as I wait for his reply, hoping that he won't lash out and tell me to mind my own business. He's been so open and honest with me, letting his emotions and thoughts out, and in doing so he's put himself in a vulnerable position. I think that's the reason I'm not afraid to ask, because he's already confided in me about parts of his past, so he must feel as though he can trust me. Which he can.

He eventually unclenches his jaw and as he does, his whole face softens. 'She's gone,' he breathes.

A tear escapes his eye. It doesn't even make it halfway down his cheek before he's wiping it away with the sleeve of his hoodie. He steers his gaze away from me. That's when I know not to push any further. He leans forward, resting his forearms on his thighs as his knee bounces up and down. My heart aches for him, with empathy consuming my entire body, because I definitely know how he feels in this instance. I feel myself wanting him to know, I want him to know that I get him.

I mirror his actions, facing the unnerving pitch-black ocean. Slumping against the back of the bench, my legs are hoisted up and crossed in front of me. 'I lost my mum.' I don't fully look, but out the corner of my eye I see his head turn back in my direction. 'She died when I was four. And my dad,' I scoff, 'my crappy excuse of a dad was never the same. I lost him the night I lost her and I've been alone ever since.' My head remains still, but my eyes flicker down to him. He's watching me closely. 'If there's one thing we have in common, it's that our dads are total fuck ups.' The corner of his mouth quirks, and even though it's the tiniest of desolate smiles, it still manages to pump warmth around my heart. 'But trust me, I know how you feel. If there's anyone who understands feeling like a lost soul, it's me.'

'I'm way past lost, Emily,' he rasps. 'I'm irretrievable.'

The compassion and understanding my heart is feeling as I hear his sorrowful words work up to my face, because I've felt exactly how he's feeling before, like there's no way out. In fact, I still do. But there's always been one thing in the back of my mind which has kept me going, that will always keep me going. Hope. Hope that things will get better.

'I don't believe that,' I say on a shake of my head. He sits back, studying me closely. 'I'm not claiming to know everything about what's happened in your life, Jackson, but there's one thing I can reassure you on; there is always a way out of the dark. Yes, sometimes the light is hard to find, but it's definitely there. It's waiting for you to find it and step through to the other side, you just have to unearth your glimmer of hope, and once you've found it, hold it tight and never let it go, because it will show you the way.'

His expression doesn't hold any emotion and I can't tell what he's thinking. I glance to my lap as I absentmindedly play with my fingers. 'I don't necessarily believe it myself all the time, but I'm trying to see a light at the end of the tunnel, because whatever it is,' my eyes flicker up again to see he's still watching me carefully, 'it won't last forever.'

He doesn't move or speak as we simply observe each other. His eyes lower for a split second before they meet mine again. 'I hope you're right, because I'm riding through one long tunnel,' he retorts softly.

My lips curl up. 'Oh, I'm always right.' I nudge his arm and his own smile draws on his lips. He glances away, but I keep my focus on him. 'Can I ask you a question?' He turns back. 'Why me?'

Pondering, his puffy eyes narrow. 'Honestly, I don't know.' He sniffs. 'I like talking to you. I don't know what it is, but it's nice, I feel comfortable around you. I thought that,' he pauses, scoffing at himself and shaking his head in the process, 'it sounds so stupid.'

'Go on,' I urge.

After a second, he obliges. 'I thought that being around you might help me feel some ease, some comfort.'

His words engulf me, but they also confuse me, because they unearth a feeling that I'm not used to. It's a foreign feeling for me, being wanted by someone. 'And has it?' I ask, holding my breath, scared that I haven't been the person he'd hoped for. The person he needed.

His eyes are the window to his soul and it's clear that his sadness hasn't diminished entirely, but his mood has noticeably brightened, and that, along with his answer, puts a small smile on both of our faces. 'Yes.' Silence ensues, filling the air, though it's a contented silence. 'So,' he breaks the quiet, clearing his throat, 'what about... William, is it?'

'What about him?' I ask on a groan. I'm tired of the whole thing and I'm annoyed that he has come up in conversation once again. The mere mention of his name is a waste of brain power.

'How are you feeling? You're not beating yourself up, are you?'

'Not in so many ways, but I can't help feeling like a puppet, you know? He made me feel as though I was never enough, like I was just there for whenever was convenient for him. It's the same with my dad.' I look down to my twiddling hands. 'Sometimes I feel like there's something wrong with me. I've never felt as though I belong, not truly.'

'Don't take this the wrong way, Em, but boys like him really don't deserve women like you.'

'Women like me?' I echo on a frown.

'Yeah, caring, understanding,' he stops his list, raking his eyes over every inch of my face before settling back on my eyes, locking me in place, 'beautiful,' he finishes on a murmur. My breathing seems to stop as I feel the air around us shift. I'm not quite sure what it is, but it's making my heart beat that little bit quicker. 'And don't ever feel like you're not good enough for anyone or any place, because you are.'

In listening to his words, I failed to fully acknowledge that he's managed to yet again turn the conversation around on me. 'There you go again. I thought it was my turn to help you.'

His expression softens. 'Emily,' he says as he inches closer, with his body eating up the space until there's only centimetres between us. He seizes my fumbling hands with his, leaning in. His emeralds never deviate from my blues, the sadness in them now long gone, but what's taken its place is something I'm unable to read. One hand reaches up to cup my cheek, his thumb brushing over it with the lightest of touches. 'I told you, you already have.'

It's like my body has gone into shock, because it doesn't move. My eyes remain open, with the ability to blink entirely disregarded. My heart is pounding and it's like my cheek is melting under the heated touch of his giant hand. A breath passes through my parted lips. 'What's happening?' I whisper.

His piercing emeralds flicker slowly from side to side and then down to my mouth. 'I don't know,' he breathes, 'but I think we should let it.' And just like that, his lips are pressing against mine.

An explosion of warmth stems from deep inside and it doesn't hesitate to spread as it dances around, touching every cell. I close my eyes, and my body finally responds, thawing from its initial shock and relaxing into the kiss. We're moving in sync, just like we've choreographed the whole thing before now. Everything in this moment feels so right. He feels so right. In this moment, nothing else matters but him and his soft lips. The sadness we have both been feeling is being released, driven out of our system as we move together. And I'm now realising the reason he hasn't left my thoughts, why those penetratingly, mesmerising, green eyes have been a constant picture in my mind; I've been yearning for him, wanting him… needing him.

He slowly pulls away, both of us breathless. My eyes flutter open to see he's already gazing back at me, his hand still on my cheek, his lips parted just as mine are. The twinkle in his eyes, which I've grown so accustomed to, is back as a smile forms, lighting up his whole face.

'Not a condescending jerk anymore, then?' he murmurs.

His smile is contagious and I'm entirely powerless as I let one spread on my own face. 'It seems I got you wrong.'

He brushes his lips over mine. 'Hmm, can you say that again?' he whispers against them, and it's like fireworks have been lit in my stomach.

'Don't push it,' I say before he captures my lips for the second time.

This wasn't what I was expecting when I set off to meet him. I hadn't planned on this *ever* happening, but I'm glad it has. We've both been alone, we've both been left in the cold, and we've both felt gruelling pain. However, as our kiss deepens, that loneliness fades away; as I move into him, warmth purges the cold; and as his fingers stroke my skin, that ruthless pain withers. It's all pushed away by his lips, his hands, his body. It's all pushed away by him.

Here with each other, we know we're both wanted, we know we're both needed, and we know that together, in this moment, neither one of us is alone.

# TWENTY-TWO

My ponytail swishes from side to side as the surprisingly encouraging burn in my legs increases as I push on; faster and faster. The balls of my feet dig firmly into the sand, each step becoming harder to drive on with every dip in the profoundly soft surface, but I keep going, cranking the volume up. I want to see how far I can push myself.

The wind isn't helping, it's blowing towards me, acting as an invisible wall I'm fighting against in a bid to get to the other side of the beach. If I wasn't so focused on keeping my breathing as steady as possible, I would laugh at the irony of having something trying its absolute hardest to prevent me from reaching my end goal. Keen to get the image of my father out my head, I transfer that frustration into energy for my legs to feed on. My vision blurs as my mind blanks, the only thought: *get to the rocks before you pass out!*

Buddy speeds ahead, using the advantage of his four legs to spur him on. I use him as my motivation, because the impossible idea of catching up to him is enough to keep my feet moving. The rocks grow nearer, and within minutes I'm flopping onto the ground fully fatigued and breathless as Buddy licks my salty face.

My hand manages to lift and stroke him for a second before it falls weakly to the floor. I'm shattered. My body collapses back, my arms and legs like jelly as they slump down into a spread-eagle position.

I lie, staring up at the cloudy sky. The rising sun peeps through as the fluffy, candy floss-like shapes drift across my line of view. Tilting up my cap, purchased from Maggie's Surf Shack, I wipe away the beads of sweat from my forehead before repositioning it as I try to regulate my heavy breathing. In hindsight, maybe a long run on the beach wasn't the best way to break in these trainers, but I decided to brave the sand, and they've proven successful, giving me one hundred times more support than Aunt Maggie's old ones.

The upbeat song playing through my ear buds dips in volume as my alarm chimes over the top. It's half eight; the original time I'd planned to get up and go for a run, but the events of last night rendered me sleepless. I was unable to shut my brain off after Jackson dropped me back at the cottage.

We didn't really speak much after the kiss, in fact, neither of us spoke a word until Jackson turned to me as we pulled up and said a simple, 'Thank you for coming out so late.' I don't think either of us knew how to react. I still don't.

My mind keeps replaying the moment over and over. It was electric. Gentle yet powerful. But most of all, it gave me butterflies – something I haven't felt in a very long time. I'm not sure what it was or what it meant, and I sure as hell am not certain on what I'm feeling right now, but after the couple of hours sleep I did manage to steal, I woke up with a smile on my face, and that's something which is extraordinarily rare for me. So, I'm not taking it lightly.

I could lay here all day with the gentle morning breeze cooling my sweaty, exerted body, the blowing clouds and calm sound of the crashing waves in the distance relaxing my over-used mind, but I know I have to get back and shower before heading to the shop for ten, so I reluctantly haul myself up. Swatting the sand from my bum, I prepare myself for another jog back as I stretch out, what in my mind, is a sad excuse for a pair of legs. *Maybe not so fast this time.*

'C'mon, Buddy, let's get going.' With a bark and a leap off the rocks, he darts away.

I make it across the beach – just about. It's as I'm slowing down when I gaze ahead to the exact spot I've been reluctant to focus my attention. The bench on top of the cliff is vaguely visible, and as I envisage us sat next to each other, all the feelings I felt when he pushed his lips against mine come racing to the surface. The warmth I felt in my core surges once again. However, I have to give my head a shake, because I've come to the conclusion that if the situation just so happened to arise again, I would let it happen. And therein lies the problem.

Questions have arisen in my mind. Questions which I've been deliberating. Should I be moving on so quickly? Does it make me a bad person for not only doing it, but for liking it too? Even though I feel nothing for William, we were in a relationship for over a year, maybe I shouldn't be feeling this way. But I can't help it.

My focus diverts away from the clifftop and I have to blink several times, my already tight chest tensing further, because, as if prompted, he emerges. The all too recognisable Jeep pulls up to the edge of the bank and my feet unthinkingly slow to a walk. I'm too far away to see him through his windscreen, but it's half eight in the morning and I'm the only person – bar a couple of early morning dog walkers – on the beach. I'm also directly opposite his car. He must be able to see me if he hasn't already spotted Buddy trotting way out in front of me.

I suddenly feel nervous. When I was replaying every single second and every single detail in my head, I didn't think about how it was going to be when we next came face-to-face. I don't know how I should act or what I'm going to say, and above all, I don't know what's going on inside his head. Will he want to talk about it? Will he dismiss it and try to forget it ever happened? He was, after all, in emotional turmoil. He wanted comfort and I gave him that comfort, but in the moment, people get carried away. He may have said things he didn't mean or told me secrets about his past which were never meant to pass his lips. Is he regretting the whole thing?

My thoughts add to the nerves and the back of my mind is making me second guess everything.

He may have seen me, but he doesn't have to know that I have seen him.

I chew on my bottom lip, debating with myself, before coming to the conclusion that choosing the cowardly way out and running back to the cottage to sidestep the no doubt awkward encounter, is only going to delay the unavoidable. So, my big girl pants are hauled on as I will myself forward.

I whistle for Buddy who skids to a halt before racing up to me. Unhooking his lead from around my shorts, I clip it to his collar. But as I straighten and my eyes flick back up to the Jeep, his door opens, and I'm forced to catch my breath.

Brown curls are the first to take my attention; as unruly as ever and blowing over the sunglasses which are resting on top of his head. I watch his movements, his arms crossing as he grips the bottom of his hoodie and hoists it up and over his head, revealing his finely sculpted torso. He throws it into the car before grabbing something off the seat, he pulls on a red lifeguard shirt, and I study as the bottom comes to rest just below the waistband of his shorts.

He closes the door, ambling around to the front of the Wrangler. I start to wonder if he has seen me, but then he pauses on top of the bank, his eyes roaming the open beach. I'm too far away to grasp whether he's clocked us, or whether he's just taking in the view. I turn my head, scanning the perimeter – there's four people at most around us. My focus rotates back to him, and it's as though he's pensive for a moment before he draws his sunglasses from his head to shield his eyes. He marches across the bank and jogs down to the surfer's hut, proceeding to unbolt the wooden doors. Not once acknowledging my existence.

A frown paints itself on my face. Maybe he didn't see me after all. Or maybe he didn't recognise me with a cap and my workout gear on. Buddy nudges my leg with his paw, bringing my attention down to him. Huh. Surely, he would've noticed the dog he's taken such a strong liking to.

As my feet begin in his direction, a voice halts my tracks. Olivia appears out of nowhere, bounding down the bank and up to the hut. Dressed in an oversized red jacket, her hot pants appear almost invisible underneath. Jackson hobbles into view, lugging two surfboards under each arm. He flashes her a grin and after the boards are laid on the sand, she takes her chance, throwing her arms around him to give him the tightest of hugs, to which he returns.

I sigh, my breath has been caught and my nerves have faded, being replaced by something I know far too well. Disappointment. I glance down to Buddy who is sat patiently waiting for me to move. A small, dejected smile forms on my face.

'Come on, Bud.'

We begin the trek back up to Maple Cottage, bypassing the two lifeguards.

The musings in my head return. Maybe it's a positive that Olivia interrupted my chance to go up to him, because at least now I have more time to think logically about how to go about this.

It hits me like a punch in the throat. Through all the shock of that unforeseen kiss, I seem to have completely overlooked the reasoning which led to our lips connecting. Jackson trusted me enough to unlock a gate into his past, he opened up to me about something which is evidently extremely difficult for him and has affected him since the day it happened, and that's a big deal. I'm worrying so much about what I'm going to say, when in actual fact, it's already been said.

He called me to meet him despite having so many other options, and I did. He trusted me to confide in about his past, and I listened. He instigated a kiss, and I kissed back.

Last night has revealed to us that we are into each other.

Shit.

I like Jackson Turner.

And there's a strong possibility that he likes me too.

No!

I can't catch feelings. Not now. Not when my life is utterly fucked up and uncertain. I'm going to have to find a way of keeping these feelings strictly limited to pure attraction, because if it goes any further, I'm afraid of what might happen. As I've discovered, nothing in my life ever runs smoothly and I can't drag someone into that. I can't drag *him* into that. I'm not sure how much more drama my heart and head can take.

I exhale a frail breath as Buddy tugs me up the hill, my feet dragging along the tarmac.

Something tells me that what was once meant to be a short and simple refuge trip to a safe and quaint town, is going to become far more complicated than first anticipated.

I don't remember getting to work, or in fact, the past two hours I've been here. I keep waiting for him to walk through the doors in his shorts, his chest on full show and with his hair as shaggy and attractive as it always is.

'Your head has been in the clouds this morning, Pidge.'

'Sorry,' I reply, toying with a pocket-sized lip balm tub in my fingertips. My eyes keep inadvertently flicking across to the door every time I sense movement, and it's driving me crazy.

'You okay?' Aunt Maggie asks, her focus lowered as she studies her account book on the counter.

Well, apart from the fact I don't know whether I'm coming or going, or have a place to call home anymore, and there's people out to end my life, which is, to add to it all, in complete tatters, not forgetting the uneasy feeling presently pulsing through me from being extremely anxious that the guy I haven't stopped thinking about, who I snuck out to meet, ended up kissing whilst you were sound asleep and none the wiser, could walk in at any minute. Yes, aside from all that, I'm wonderful.

'I'm fine,' I answer.

'You seem distracted.' She glances up from her book and I meet her concerned gaze. 'Has your dad said anything to you?'

I cringe at the mention of him.

'Guy told me that you might be staying a little longer than your father first thought,' she admits, watching me closely.

'I'm sorry.' I feel awful, I feel like I'm invading her home.

'Don't you dare apologise. I'd much rather you eat all my food and use all my washing powder, and be safe, than to go back to London and for whoever attacked you to come back, and heaven forbid, do far worse than they managed last time.' Her tone is stern yet soft, and I know that sternness is directed at my attacker. But she has no idea who that is, or to the big fat lie surrounding us. She believes my attack was from a random crazy person. She's not aware that there are others out there, and the reasoning behind it is somehow related to Mum and Dad.

'You'd tell me if I was getting under your feet, wouldn't you? I could always ask Guy to find us a place elsewhere,' I offer with my head bowed as I examine the multi-coloured lip balm tub in my fidgety fingers, fearing that if I look at her, I'll break down.

'Don't be silly. You could never get in my way, I love having you here, Pidge. To be entirely honest with you, it's the company I've been needing. I know that cottage is small, but it sure does get lonely living on my own sometimes.'

I lift my head, meeting her warm grey eyes and smile gratefully, placing my hand on her arm. I didn't know she felt like that. I pull her in tight, squeezing my eyes shut and burying my face into her shoulder. Her comfort is soaked up with every stroke of her hand on my back, and I begin to relax, until a chirpy voice interrupts our moment.

'Awww, aren't you two just adorable!'

I pull my face up and rest my chin on Aunty's shoulder, a smile tugging on my lips.

'What are you doing here on your day off?' I ask. Untangling our arms, I turn to Lily, my eyebrows arching when a long arm flopped over her shoulder leads my line of vision to Dex, who's grinning like a Cheshire cat as they stroll up to the counter.

'I want an ice cream. If I have to sit around and watch these trials all afternoon, I'm going to need sustenance.' She wriggles free of Dex's embrace before skipping over to the chest freezer. There's a moment as Lily bounces away where I catch Dex's eyes drifting up and down her body, before fixating on her arse as she bends over to inspect the ice cream selection. I clear my throat which soon brings him out of his daze. He tears his wide eyes away, appearing very pleased with himself.

'Oh, of course!' Aunt Maggie exclaims, seemingly unaware of Dex's actions. 'It's the lifeguard initiations, how could I forget?' She tuts, slapping her hand to her forehead.

'It's that brain, Mags, it's not as young as it used to be,' Dex jokes and I'm forced to bite the inside of my cheek to stifle a laugh.

Aunty scowls back at him. 'Don't come it with me just because you've got my girl on your arm, young man.'

'What can I say?' He shrugs just as Lily reappears, completely oblivious with her chosen ice lolly. He slings his arm back over her shoulder pulling her closer. 'I've won the prize, Mags. Better luck next time.' Dex leans in to kiss Lily's cheek but she's quick to slide out of his grasp.

'Excuse me, I'm not some prize in a competition,' she retorts, raising a finger.

'If I agree, can I have a kiss?' he pleads, his arm still positioned in the air as if Lily hasn't moved two feet away from him.

She ponders on a pout. 'Fine, but you're paying for this as well,' she says, waving her rocket lolly in the air.

He tugs her back to him, kissing her hard. I throw a knowing glance over to Aunt Maggie. They seem to have forgotten they are in a public space, standing in front of two people – one of them being a middle-aged woman.

After a few more agonising moments, I decide I can't take the smacking noises any longer. 'Jesus, let her breathe, Dex.'

They finally break away and the pleased look resurfaces on his face as he flashes a wry smile. Lily seems unbothered as she dives straight into unwrapping her lolly.

'How's the lady of the hour feeling?' Aunt Maggie asks, keen to move the conversation on.

'A little nervous, but I've told her she'll smash it,' Lily replies, sucking on her icy treat.

'Of course, she will,' Aunty agrees, taking the sticky wrapper from Lily and throwing it in the bin at our feet.

'What are these trials for?' I flick my narrowed eyes between them.

'The lifeguard trials. This will determine whether Vicki becomes one of us, a part of the big team,' Dex answers as he rustles in the pocket of his baggy red shorts, before placing some change on the counter.

'It's what she's been training so hard for, and let's be honest, she hasn't got much competition,' Lily says as she licks a melted droplet running down her stick.

'I wouldn't be so sure, Ethan stands a good chance,' Dex argues.

'Please, Vicki is going to wipe the floor with those boys!'

'Did I hear someone mention *boys*?'

I internally sigh when the person responsible for those words marches up to Lily and wraps their arms around her waist. Lily clocks me and grimaces. 'Liv!' she sings. 'I thought you were setting up?'

'We've finished,' she replies casually, but then I hear the voice I've been anticipating. My whole body stiffens.

'You mean *you've* finished, thanks for leaving us to shift all the boards.'

He saunters straight past the group and up to the fridge in the corner, where he studies the selection of drinks.

'You had Leo,' Olivia retorts.

'Not the point.' He shakes his head.

'Don't be angry, I'll buy you a celebratory drink later for working so hard.'

His face remains set, holding irritation as he peers over his shoulder in her direction.

While my focus hasn't drifted from him, he's yet to glance my way, and I realise I'm holding my breath, awaiting our first exchange since the kiss. His shift in persona is unmistakable; the fragile voice and puffy eyes now long gone, the strong guise and penetrating emeralds are back. Almost as though last night never even happened.

'I'm just popping to the loo,' Aunt Maggie says, which causes Dex's ears to prick.

'Is that a hint, Mags?'

'Oh, stop it,' she snaps on a light chuckle as she shuffles away.

I'm already willing her a hasty return, my unease is flooding my veins and causing my tummy to flip and having her beside me is a massive safety blanket. *Fuck!*

'They're all warming up by the hut.' A face I haven't seen since the party emerges as he jogs straight up to Dex, patting him on the back. 'Vicki's got some tough competition.'

Lily rolls her eyes at Leo's remark, pointing her rocket ice lolly in his direction. 'I've said it before and I'll say it 'til I'm blue in the face, Vicki is going to smash it!'

'I don't doubt it, she's one hell of a woman.'

It's nice to see him sober and able to stand on his own two feet today. I try to refrain from glancing his way. I'm not sure if he remembers me, but I certainly remember him, and I distinctly recall that our previous encounter wasn't my most favourable of the year.

'I won't tell James you said that,' Lily says. I snort as she slurps noisily, sucking up the melting ice.

I'm aware that Leo's eyes are on me now and it's almost as if I can hear the gears ticking inside his brain as he works out why I must seem familiar. It remarkably doesn't take long as he ignored Lily's absent-minded reply. 'We have definitely met, haven't we?' he asks, pointing his long finger in my direction.

I reluctantly shift my line of focus from Jackson, who is studying two bottles in his hands by the fridge, to Leo. 'Yes, I believe we have.' I nod casually, refraining from shrinking under the stares which are homing in on us.

'Emily, right? We were sat by the fire at my party.'

My eyes widen in surprise. 'Good memory, I'm surprised you remember.'

'Yeah, you were pretty pissed, mate,' Dex adds on a mocking laugh.

'It was my birthday,' he defends innocently. Just as

those words leave his lips, Jackson joins the group. I'm searching his face, but he keeps his eyes lowered as he pulls his wallet from his shorts, passing me a five-pound note.

'And anyway, hammered or not, I never forget a pretty face,' Leo pauses as if something comes to mind, 'or a pretty thigh,' he finishes on a smirk. I shrivel under his fervent stare, recalling his hand creeping up my leg.

'What are we talking about?' Jackson asks on a frown.

'Emily,' everyone calls nonchalantly in unison.

He's quiet, but I do notice the slight tightening of his fingers around the bottle in his grip, it's too subtle for anyone who isn't studying him closely to see, but I do, because I am.

'Oh, right,' he replies evenly, seeming to let the comment wash over his head. Unscrewing the cap, he sips at the Citrus Punch drink.

Although I'm dying to ask him what's going on, I can't with everyone standing around. I open the till drawer – now fully competent of its temperamental side – and scrape out the correct number of coins, my eyes never straying from him as I hold my hand out.

He finally flicks his gaze to me. For a fleeting moment. It carries no emotion, his face straight and unreadable as he steps back once I hand his change over. He manages to mumble a 'cheers,' before gulping more juice.

What the hell? I frown, my lips parted. I'm trying

to convince myself that last night and the past few days have happened, because right now anyone would think we've barely spoken two words to each other.

Olivia unwraps her arms from around Lily's waist and subtly shuffles over to his side.

'Fancy coming to watch, Em?' Dex brings me out of my gawping state as my attention shifts to him, my mouth opening as I take a breath.

'Err.' I ponder, my concentration lost; my mind only aware of the frustratingly blasé man in the circle.

'I'll save you a seat, we can share a towel if you'd like,' Leo says, but I don't wholly acknowledge his jesting remark as my focus is once again brought back to Jackson. Olivia is on her tiptoes, whispering in his ear. He scoffs, a smile on his lips. His arm lifts before it rests on her shoulder. She pulls his face down with her hand and pecks him on the cheek.

My stomach turns.

No one else seems bothered, and of course they're not, this affection is normal between them. But it's bothering me, and up until this moment, I hadn't realised just how much it actually has been. I'm beginning to wonder whether he's told Olivia the things he told me. Has he opened up and cried on her shoulder? Is this just a typical Jackson Turner trademark I've stupidly fallen for? Or is what happened something he's only ever done with me? Clearly, it's irrelevant now anyway, because he's obviously forgotten all about it.

Her giggles, along with the fact he hasn't once properly looked in my direction, are beginning to rattle my bones.

Two can play that game.

I give Leo my full attention, smiling in response to his offer. 'How big is the towel?' I ask flippantly, trying to be as outwardly playful as possible. 'Given our last meeting I'd expect you'd find the smallest one possible.' I don't have to look in their direction to know I've now pulled them both into the conversation.

'Who needs material, you might as well sit in my lap, it'll save space,' he replies.

'There's a two-mile beach out there, Leo, I think somewhere as far up the bank and away from you will be more viable,' Lily intercepts as she sucks up the last of her lolly.

'That hurts, Lily, really, that cuts deep.' Leo feigns an offended expression causing Dex to laugh and Lily to fire back a mocking grin. I know she's joking, but in truth, if I am to go to the trials, that's where I'd rather be. The idea of sharing a towel with Leo doesn't particularly appeal, especially if he's as handsy sober as he is pissed.

'Are you sure she'll be able to keep up?'

My eyes snap to the other person in the room who also seems to be the handsy type. Olivia has her arm slinked sloppily around Jackson's waist as she gazes around the group.

*She?*

'It's hardly University Challenge, Liv,' Jackson retorts, and if I wasn't so confused and irritated by him there's a small, minute possibility I would've found it funny.

'I know, I'm just being realistic, she's not from around here. No offence, Emily.' She turns to me. 'I'm only thinking of you, it can be boring when you don't know what's going on.'

My jaw clenches.

'I can teach her all about it,' Leo suggests.

'Of course, you will,' Jackson snickers, as if he has the audacity to comment.

I fear my teeth may shatter from the force of my clenched jaw. I'm riled, and it causes my words to escape without proper processing. 'Do you know what? That sounds like a plan, Leo. I finish in an hour.' I'm purposely not looking at Jackson, but for the first time he's acknowledging my existence as I feel both his and Olivia's eyes on me.

'Perfect.' Leo smiles.

My lips curl up, though inside, that guilty, terrible feeling is swirling. I'm using him out of frustration. Lily raises her brow in question as the group begin in idle chit chat. I simply shrug back, both of us wondering the same thing.

What the hell am I doing?

# TWENTY-THREE

It's been three days. Three days since the kiss, and three days since Jackson Turner has spoken to me.

I tried so desperately to concentrate and give Vicki my full support at the trials, but it proved difficult. It was difficult, because no matter which way I turned, all I saw was him.

Him with her.

Sitting with Lily, Dex, and Leo in the cornered off area of the beach, we were shortly joined by James after he'd finished giving Vicki a good luck smooch. Despite the initial skepticism of sharing a towel with Leo, it turned out to be not so bad. He kept his hands to himself, and the five of us, for the most part, had a good time.

Leo kept his word and explained to me the process of each stage of the trials; three phases, five trainee lifeguards, competing for two places on the team. Fitness levels, lifesaving skills, and a demonstration of surfing abilities for Marshlyn Bay's Surf School all seemed to prove Lily right, because Vicki smashed them all.

The only issue being, Jackson and Olivia were the main assistants, along with the head supervisor. They were professional, of course they were, but it seemed as soon as they were able to take any breaks, she was by his side. And by watching them throughout the whole trial experience, I came to realise that it's not Olivia I have the apparent problem with. After all, she likes him and she's doing nothing wrong. It's because I'm attracted to him. He's making me feel things and I hate it, for one of those feelings happens to be jealousy. I'm generally not a jealous person, I became so used to William receiving female – and occasionally male – attention, that I'd brush it off. But when I see her with her hands all over him, the jealousy burns in my veins and I get the urge to tear them off.

But I can't, because he's not mine, and at this particular moment in time, I don't want him to be. There were plenty of opportunities to come up to me, yet he didn't. He's deliberately ignoring me for reasons unknown. And it's been like that for three whole days. I've hardly seen him. I've noticed he's been avoiding the shop, and when I have clocked eyes on him it's because I've been walking Buddy on the beach and he's been on shift, but he doesn't glance my way, even when I know he knows I'm there.

The keys in my hand jangle as I shuffle through the set to find the one Aunt Maggie showed me to lock up shop, before she left to go and do whatever Maggie does of an evening. Once I locate it in the mass of metal hanging from the keyring, I attach the chain lock and push and pull the handles, double checking they're fully secure. Once satisfied, I make my way up to Maple Cottage.

My emotions are running amok; I'm confused and embarrassed.

The factor which is trying me the most is that he's doing exactly what I need him to do. He's staying away.

This is good, this is what's best.

So why do I feel so hurt?

Maybe if he'd set me straight. Maybe if he'd come up to me and told me he doesn't like me then I would be able to deal with it. But he's said nothing, not a word.

How am I supposed to take that?

He did his best to make me feel better when I felt shitty, he confesses things about his past which hold shadows over him, then he kisses me, and now he's ghosting me. There's keeping your distance and not allowing anything more to happen but letting that person know how you feel, and then there's being a complete and utter dick.

I thought I was beginning to see a different person, but he's back to how he was at the start. Maybe he is just a jerk after all.

It was a kiss, a simple, little kiss. It was in the heat of the moment and he's probably done it with hundreds of girls before you. I shouldn't be hurt. But I am. I'm upset and I'm ashamed that I allowed myself to be sucked in by his luring charms.

My shoulders are slumped as I open the door and step into the hallway. Kicking my shoes off, a strong wholesome smell drifts through the hall, and my nose promptly follows the aroma to the kitchen.

'Is that you, Pidge?' Aunt Maggie calls as I enter.

My eyes widen in surprise, spotting the other figure in the room.

'Guy?'

'Good evening, Miss Lambert,' he says on a nod in my direction.

The table is laid out; for three. Three sets of knives and forks, and three placemats. Aunt Maggie waltzes about in her spotty apron, stirring saucepans and shuffling food on trays in the oven, whilst Guy is leaning against the counter sipping from a wine glass. Buddy is perched near the table, oblivious to my arrival as he ogles Aunty handling all the food.

'What's going on?' I ask, frozen in the doorway, utterly puzzled.

'You're just in time, Emily. I've cooked us up a storm.'

'Okay...' I murmur, going along with it. 'I didn't see your car outside, Guy,' I say, a part of me worrying if it's been stolen. Despite the unlikeliness in this neighbourhood, it's hardly a cheap model and you never know.

'No, I left it back at the hotel,' he confirms coolly.

'I told him he must have a drink, so he walked here. You can't begrudge the man a night off, Emily.' Aunt Maggie blithely stares into the oven before opening the door and taking out a tray which I now see is covered with parsnips and roast potatoes.

'I'm not supposed to be drinking at all, but your aunt offered to cook us a meal. I'm sorry if I'm overstepping the–

'Nonsense!' Aunty interjects.

'You need to relax too, Guy. It's okay,' I encourage. I'm glad Aunt Maggie has done this, it's just a bit of a shock, that's all.

His lips curl up in response as he guzzles down his red. I stand awkwardly, not really knowing what to do, until I realise that I'm still holding her keys. 'Here,' I offer.

'Oh, thank you.' She takes the bunch from me before turning her back and marching up to the back door to place them in a small box. 'Did you lock up okay?'

'It's safe and secured,' I reply, scooting Buddy's bum along the floor to pull a chair out from under the table. He stretches his head, his tail swishing along the tiles, but that's about all the greeting I receive as he sets his sights back on the food. I spot the deliciously succulent, steaming beef joint on a plate, half wrapped in tin foil beside the oven, making my mouth water. That, and the combined aroma of everything else cooking, as well as the large bottle of Pinot next to my arm, has persuaded me to wait a little bit longer before going into hibernation for the rest of my stay. I now desperately want to eat my emotions away in food and drown my sorrows with a sizeable glass of wine.

I reach for the bottle as Aunt Maggie places a glass down in front of me. 'You go easy on that.' She points a rigid finger at the bottle. 'I heard about your alcohol infused antics from Billy.' She doesn't look amused as she sets about piling our plates up with food. Bloody Billy and his gossiping ways!

Guy shifts from his position by the sink. He picks up a carving knife and fork from the side and begins slicing up the meat.

'I'm putting it out there so there's no animosity, but I'm not particularly pleased that the favour he owed me went on offering you free drinks. I've had a word with him and I'm giving you my warning now, nothing good ever comes from drinking yourself silly.'

'Trust me, I've learnt my lesson,' I retort as I fill the glass up to just above halfway and take a big gulp.

'Hmm.' She gives me a warning eye over her shoulder, the metal serving spoon in her grip drumming against a crockery plate.

I gasp as the liquid trickles down my throat. With wine I find it has an acquired taste, and the more you drink, the more you get used to it, so I take another swig – purely to warm up my taste buds. The clearing of a throat halts me in my sipping as a plate is laid down in front of me. Knowing she's standing over me, I reluctantly put the glass back on the coaster.

'All in moderation, Emily.'

I hardly hear what she says, my eyes wandering over the mountainous plate which has been piled high and neatly arranged to perfection. Roasts, mash, honey-glazed parsnips, stuffing balls, veggies, beef, and of course, a *mahoooosive* Yorkshire pudding to complement, all covered in delicious gravy. I didn't know how much I needed this.

Guy and Aunt Maggie take up their seats with Guy sitting to my left and Aunty opposite me. 'This looks incredible, Ms Taylor,' Guy politely offers as he shakes some salt over his meal.

'Oh, please, call me Maggie, I've never been one for formalities.' She shakes her head, dolloping English mustard beside her meat.

'Very well.'

'I can confirm it tastes just as good,' I mumble as I shovel in my second forkful. I glance down to see Buddy's head resting on my leg, so I break a piece from my Yorkshire which he takes gently from my fingers.

For the next couple of minutes, the meal goes well, with mindless chatter and chuckles – mainly between Aunt Maggie and Guy – but on the third minute, until Guy turns the conversation onto me.

'So, how are things going with that young man?' he asks, flashing me a pointed look as he cuts up his food.

My hands stop their movements, suddenly going off what's in front of me. 'They're not,' I mutter, dropping my knife and outstretching my arm for my glass. Aunty reaches out to take a sip from her own.

'Is this Jackson? I thought you were getting on well with him?'

My head shakes, my tongue lapping the liquid. 'Not anymore.'

'Why ever not? He's a lovely boy, Emily,' she continues, but I wish she wouldn't.

'Can we change the subject, please?' I beg as politely as possible, my left-hand tightening around my fork handle.

'I'm only expressing–

'Well, please stop expressing,' I snap more sharply than intended which catches Aunt Maggie off guard, nevertheless, she persists.

'I'm only expressing my opinion,' she repeats, unperturbed. 'He's been good to me these past few years since he arrived.' She's on the defense, but she doesn't know what he's done, she's clouded in a perfect Jackson mist, and I'm not surprised; he has her fooled too.

'I'd rather not talk about him.'

'Why not? What's happened?'

'It doesn't matter.'

'Pi–

'Aunty, please just leave it!'

'Okay, okay,' Guy interrupts, holding his hand out. 'Whatever's happened, maybe it's for the best, Miss Lambert. Let's talk about something else, hey?'

'Good idea,' Aunt Maggie says, tipping her glass up to her lips, but I can tell she's aggravated that I'm not expanding on the subject.

It goes quiet. Placing my chin in my palm and resting my elbow on the table, I prod a parsnip with my fork. Then I frown, because I begin to register what Guy has just said. *Maybe it's for the best.* I think back to that strange conversation we had after the night I'd slept over at Jackson's, where he warned me that people may not be all they seem and to be wary of who I let in. By *people*, did he mean Jackson? Is he truly that good at his job to have seen the type of person Jackson is from the get-go?

I jump, my thoughts halted when several raps of the front door echo down the hallway. Aunt Maggie thrusts her chair back, but Guy beats her to it.

'Don't worry, I'll go.'

Her eyes follow him out the room. 'He's such a gentleman,' she whispers. I watch her as she returns to her own world, slicing a section off her Yorkshire pudding to eat with her roast potato. I sigh quietly, my appetite lost.

The wine yet again meets my lips.

'Miss Lambert!' My eyes find Aunt Maggie who glances up from her food. 'You have a visitor.' Guy's gruff voice travels down the hall, circling the table.

Confusion is etched on my face and Aunt Maggie shrugs, answering my questioning frown. She's not expecting anyone either. I gulp down the last of what's in my glass before reluctantly shifting my chair and moseying into the hallway. Guy is stood by the door, blocking my view.

I grit my teeth when he steps to the side.

'I'll leave you two alone.' He turns towards me,

flashing what I can only take as a warning glance as he passes by, strolling back into the kitchen.

I remain in place, my arms folded across my chest.

'Hey,' he says softly.

I roll my eyes and check behind me before forcing myself to the door, preventing any prying ears from making out the impending exchange. 'What the hell are you doing here?' I hiss as quietly as possible.

'I was around, thought I'd come and say hello.' Jackson's eyes are strong, never moving from my face, but I keep myself together, instead focusing on the freshly mown lawn behind him.

'Wow. Now he wants to talk. That's funny, seeing as you've barely looked at me for three days.' He stays silent. 'Where's Olivia? Isn't she usually stuck to your side?' A bit harsh and infantile, but in the moment, I don't care.

'I let her have the day off.'

If I could see my face, I'm sure it would be radiating hostility, and I think he finally registers that I'm in no mood to joke.

'She's not my girlfriend, you know.'

I crack, my eyes lowering to meet his; as captivating and mesmerising as they always are.

*Bloody hell!*

'No? Does she know that?' I keep my stony exterior,

satisfied that I've made my point when he doesn't reply. 'What do you really want?' I push.

'Dinner, tomorrow.'

'Dinner?'

'Yes.'

'With you?'

'Yes.'

I rub my lip with my index finger, laughing in disbelief. 'Let me get this straight, you tell me that you feel comfortable around me, that you can talk to me, you tell me things which have clearly pained you, then you kiss me, but after decide to flirt with another girl and act like I don't exist for three days. Now you've turned up out of the blue expecting me to go to dinner with you?'

He sighs, breaking our stare. He runs his fingers – which are adorned with his usual rings – through his curls, before taking a breath. 'Look, I know it's a big ask–

'Fuck you.' I stand back, ready to swing the door in his face, but he throws his hand out.

'Emily, just hear me out.'

'Move your hand!'

'Not until you agree to come to dinner. What do you say? You, me, delicious local cuisine?' His eyebrows waggle.

'Takeaway fish and chips?' I mock, because I bet he came here, thinking he'll click his fingers and I'll fall at his feet. Well, he's got another thing coming.

'Emily, I'm sorry.'

I glare back, my eyes narrowing.

'Okay? I'm sorry. I can explain everything now, but I realised I haven't thanked you properly for the other night. So… I'll pick you up at eight and explain then.'

'I have plans.' I don't, in the conventional sense, but I'd much rather hide in bed watching back-to-back episodes of *Peaky Blinders* than do anything with him.

'No, you don't, I asked Mags.'

'You… I don't believe this,' I say in utter astonishment. That conniving woman!

'I'm not moving until you accept. I'll answer all of your questions, I promise.'

I don't say a word. I'm angry. I'm angry at myself for being so enticed by him, just standing here looking at him now in his plaid flannel shirt and black jeans with his intense eyes, unruly curls, and kissable soft lips, I can feel myself melting away and I hate it.

*Arrrgghhh!*

'I know I don't deserve it, but one chance, that's all I'm asking for. One chance.'

My eyes shift behind him as I sigh. I'm going to regret this.

'You get one hour.'

'One hour.' He nods, his brow lifting with relief.

'This doesn't mean I forgive you. Any bullshit and

I'm gone!' I want it known that I'm not being pushed around. I'm going to hear him out, but then that's it.

'One hour, no bullshit,' he repeats. 'Thank you.'

'I don't know what you're thanking me for, you're paying.'

He chuckles and finally lowers his arm from the door. 'See you at eight.'

I watch him stride back down the path before he disappears inside his Jeep. Pushing the front door closed, my forehead drops against it.

One hour. No bullshit. You can do it.

Just stay strong, Emily!

# TWENTY-FOUR

7.50 p.m..

There are two deep impressions on the sofa. The marks, the result of kneeling anxiously to peer out of the living room window for half an hour. I have repeatedly told myself – so much so I think it's now safely engraved in my mind – to be calm and listen to his excuses. All I have to remember is any bullshit, I leave. I must not fall for his charms!

Having apologised to Aunt Maggie for my bad temper yesterday, she agreed not to question me on the matter and said she was sorry for prying, as much as it kills her not to be in the know. I asked her for help on what to wear, and after sifting through my crumpled pile of clothes, she picked out a casual and reserved button front tea dress. I also put my hair up in a messy bun and applied minimal makeup. I need to appear natural and indifferent, like I haven't spent all day fretting about the whole thing.

I catch a glimpse of movement behind the hedgerows and my mouth dries, my stomach flipping with nerves. I'm not sure why I'm so uneasy, this isn't a date. But for some reason the idea of being alone with him in a very 'date-like' situation is putting me on edge.

The Jeep pulls up in front of the gate. He slides out the driver's side and my body forces a sharp breath. I feel a presence enter the room, and the nosy parker who I'd told to wait in the kitchen with Buddy comes up behind me, kneeling on the sofa and joining me in surveying – along with my four legged boy who takes a perch on my other side.

'Sorry, I heard a door and couldn't resist.'

I'm too busy watching Jackson stroll up the cobblestone path to reply. He brushes his hands together in front of him as my eyes rake up and down his tall figure; black jeans, white T shirt, his usual plaid jacket and black boots, all combine to make him intimidatingly striking. My nerves continue to bubble as I feel myself sinking deeper into the sofa, unable to move.

'He's come to impress I can tell you that,' Aunt Maggie muses, but I don't respond. I feel a shift in her gaze as she searches my face when she receives no response. 'Don't write him off straight away, Pidge, he has a good heart. You should give him a chance.'

My eyes lower before they meet her warm and encouraging greys. I know the effect he can have on me, so giving him a chance means opening up a gateway which right now is locked and bolted. Behind it: my vulnerability. A vulnerability which if unchained, could dampen my strength and trample all over it. Just as William did.

'That's what I'm afraid of,' I retort just as the door is struck. Our eyes shoot behind us. Moment of truth. On a shallow exhale, I push myself up and flatten the creases which have formed on the bottom of my dress, before lifting my head. It's held high, hopefully disguising the fact I'm withering on the inside.

'Good luck,' Aunty whispers as she shuffles closer to Buddy, and I leave the room.

With the front door in my sights, I come to a stop in front of it. Knocks echo down the hallway again and my apprehension is swallowed back, the handle pulled. I'm met with twinkling emeralds. His lips quirk with his wandering gaze taking in my appearance.

'Hello, beautiful,' Jackson says, leaning his arm against the porch wall.

My chest expands, my eyes narrowing, outwardly pretending like the words haven't sent waves of tingles around my body. 'I thought we agreed no bullshit?'

'We did.' He gives a curt nod, the smile falling from his face.

'Right, because I didn't agree to play games, I agreed to hear you out.'

There's a pause as we stare one another out.

'Okay, I'm sorry.' He eventually backs down. 'Hello, Emily.' His smile returns with his hands slotting into the front pockets of his jeans, rocking back and forth on his heels.

'Better,' I state appreciatively.

'Ready to go?' he asks. I nod in response, unhooking my shoulder bag from the banister. He steps to the side as I close the door behind me. 'Your carriage awaits.' A faint cloud of his aftershave drifts through the air and tickles my senses as I follow him down the path. I have to force my nails into my palms to subdue the trail of tingles the sweet scent leaves on my skin.

Taking the moment of privacy, and in a bid to distract my unhinged pheromones, I peek over my shoulder, knowing Aunt Maggie will be watching with keen eyes. She is, and she doesn't hesitate to throw me a thumbs up with a wide grin, I flash her a nervy but grateful smile and turn around. Jackson reaches the gate, unlatching it and moving to the side, allowing me to pass through. 'Thank you,' I say as I reach for the handle of the Jeep.

'Hang on.' He rushes over, tugging the door open himself.

I ogle him curiously. 'You're really taking this apology thing seriously, aren't you?'

'I don't know what you're talking about, I'm always polite and gentlemanly. Besides, I can feel Mags' big grey eyes on me, and I don't fancy a clap around the earhole for not treating you like an angel,' he says on a wry smile.

'And the truth comes out.'

'I'd take full advantage of my kindness, if I were you.'

'Oh, I will.'

My palm is held out as I watch his eyebrow quirk. Slowly he lifts his own and I take hold, using it to hoist myself up.

'Where are we going?' I ask when he ducks into his side.

'You'll see,' he replies, turning the key in the ignition.

I sigh. 'Really? Again, with the secrecy.'

'What's wrong with a little surprise? Keeps things interesting.'

My arms fold across my chest. 'I don't want interesting! I want an explanation.'

'And you'll get one, I promised, remember?' he remarks, his strong jaw clenching when he punches the gear into reverse.

After a couple of seconds my glare relaxes, and I take my focus from him to outside my window. I can still see Aunt Maggie's snooping head spying on us. 'I hate surprises,' I grumble.

'I think you're going to like this one.' He cocks a grin, the sight causing my eyes to roll – but my skin to heat.

We take a familiar route, making a sharp turn down the recognisable steep hill as the road opens out to reveal Rockstone. My eyes flicker to him and I notice the little crease in his forehead, positioned just as it was when he brought me here on Saturday. He drives into a main car park this time and easily backs into a gap between a blue Kia and a white Peugeot. The engine switches off, and we're left in a deafening silence.

'So, what is this delicious local cuisine, then?' I ask, repeating his words from last night.

All I receive is a quick flick of the eyes and a smile before he reaches for his door handle and climbs out. A deep exhale fills the empty car as I observe him strolling around the front. I wish he'd stop dilly dallying. He's enjoying this game of mystery and the fact he has my attention, and I don't like it one bit. He arrives at my side, holding the door still to prevent it knocking against the Kia whilst I clamber out.

'Tight squeeze,' I mutter as I flatten down my dress and sidestep from between the two vehicles.

'Just how I like it,' Jackson replies, but I snub his mindless remark. 'Come on, angel, it's this way.' He strolls on ahead, leaving me to watch his broad shoulders as he meets the footpath leading to the harbour front.

I have to jog along to keep up with his pace, his long gaits carrying him much farther much more quickly. 'Can you slow down a little?'

'I only have an hour, need to make speedy work,' he retorts, his steps unfaltering, instead I think they even hasten.

'Are you trying to be funny?' I poke, but there's no reply, and I'm quickly beginning to question my agreeing to this. 'Can you at least tell me where we're going?' I ask, falling behind.

'I told you, it's a surprise.'

'And I told you, I hate surprises.'

There's a brief pause before he spins on his heel,

facing me as he treads backwards. 'Berrittini's,' he says, and I frown, confused.

'That sounds Italian?'

'It is Italian.'

'I though you said *local* cuisine?'

He pivots around, walking normally again. 'Well, it's a local restaurant and it's Italian cuisine. Are you going to nit-pick all evening?' he asks, glancing behind him.

I pinch my lips together in a tight line. 'I'm not nit-picking, and even if I was, I think I have every right to.'

'You are definitely Maggie's niece.'

I stop in my tracks. 'What's that supposed to mean?'

'Nothing,' he says on a shake of his head. He pauses and spins to face me again, his loose curls falling onto his forehead. 'If you're quite finished, the restaurant's this way,' he declares, gesturing behind him.

'You're such a… *ugh*! I should turn around and walk back to the cottage.'

'Then why are you still here?'

Words fail to leave my mouth. I can feel my thumping heartbeat and heavy breaths, and the cause isn't all because of the mini workout I've been forced to do. His demeaner has shifted to his conceited self once again and I'm not liking it. He sighs, his head turning to the side before he brushes the stray curls away. His focus shifts back to me, his features softening.

'Come on,' he offers gently.

I thought this was supposed to be an apology, already he's pushing the boundaries and meeting the line of bullshit territory. Nevertheless, against my better judgement, I want to hear his excuses. And I'm absolutely starving. I march right up to him and then straight past him, his narrowed eyes following as I pass. 'I thought you were in a hurry!' I call as the square comes into view.

I didn't think this town could get any more beautiful than when I saw it for the first time in the afternoon sun, however looking around now as daylight fades, and the different lights from the shops and restaurants illuminate the whole picturesque town, I can't help but be in complete awe.

The multi-coloured reflections on the calm ripples of the still harbour water from the combination of burning reds and oranges low in the sky, and the bright lights streaming down and out from the old-style buildings around the square, shimmer and dance on the trapped seawater surrounding each and every bobbing boat. There's a gentle buzz, the atmosphere as calm as it was during the day, though the vast flurry of people has evaporated, leaving only a few groups milling around. The soft background hum of the restaurants and the clinking of cutlery echoes from left to right, with smells of all different foods coming from every direction; but the more flagrant is that of garlic bread. My mouth waters as I let my senses absorb everything around me.

Jackson catches up, his long legs needing to exert little effort as we stroll in sync, the pace now steady and manageable for my shorter limbs. 'There it is,' he proclaims, pointing to the second floor of a building above an ice cream parlour. The restaurant is opened up as a balcony setting, with people sat on tables overlooking the harbour, and plant pots adorned with red flowers decorate the bottom of the railings which run all around the front of the upper establishment. 'Not quite takeaway fish and chips, but I hope it'll suffice.' He throws me a quick knowing glance, picking fun at the comment I made yesterday. My smile is small, yet uncontrollable as we reach the bottom of the entrance. Stairs are to the left, and to the right, a large black and white menu is pinned to the wall with, *Since 1973 Berrittini's,* written boldly above.

As we climb, the noise from the restaurant grows louder, the aromatic food smell enhances, and my anticipation peaks as my mind drifts to what our conversation might shortly entail. We hit a long line of people queuing through a set of double doors. I knew it was going to be busy from the view outside, so I'd already prepared myself for a wait, but apparently, I needn't have bothered. As I join the back of the queue instinctively, he leans down, his breath fanning my ear. 'What are you waiting for?'

I glance up, watching him with dumbfounded eyes. 'There's a line,' I say obviously.

'I know, but we're special.'

I feel his fingers brush lightly over my wrist, causing goosebumps to rise on my arms. His touch drifts down to my palm and then to my fingertips, before he intertwines both our hands together. I can't help but stare at them, my hand seeming tiny in his giant grip, though I don't get to ogle at them for long, as he pulls me behind him. We squeeze through the small space, feeling the waiting people eyeballing us as we skip the queue. We're soon at the front, stood before a wooden stand.

A waiter peers up from a sheet resting on top of the small desk and Jackson drops my hand. I try to ignore the feeling of dejection washing over me as he does.

'Good evening, sir,' the waiter says in a very strong Italian accent, smiling in Jackson's direction.

'Evening, Giovanni,' he replies, and I quickly notice the name badge pinned on the waiter's white shirt. 'Come va?'

Giovanni appears, as I do, taken aback for the briefest of moments at Jackson's Italian speech. 'Va bene, signor,' he responds on a smile.

'Que bella sera,' Jackson continues.

'Si è bellisima.' I stand awkwardly as the Italian waiter replies, not knowing what on earth is being said as they pass comments back and forth.

'Gli affair vanno bene.'

My eyes drift up to Jackson, gaping at him in utter bewilderment.

'Si, non ci lamentiamo.'

They both chuckle and I smile clumsily. Thankfully Jackson returns to the only language I'm fluent in. 'There should be a booking for Mr Turner?' he says as Giovanni runs his finger down the sheet in front of him.

'Yes. Mr Berrettini made sure to reserve specific table you ask for. One moment, I go see if it's ready for you.'

'Grazie, Giovanni,' Jackson finishes. My eyebrows raise as I stare incredulously at his nonchalant expression. 'What?' he asks obliviously, finally giving me eye contact.

'You speak Italian?'

'Yes.' He shrugs casually, like it's the most normal thing in the world. Of course, it's not the most absurd thing, but I wasn't expecting to hear it and it's making me wonder what else he's got secretly hidden away.

'Okay…' I blink just as our waiter returns.

'If you would like to follow me.' He guides us over to a table in the corner next to the open shutters, giving us a perfect view of the harbour, and with the sun setting in the distance along with the soft breeze blowing through, it makes for a beautiful backdrop. Jackson shrugs his jacket off and drapes it over the back of his chair as Giovanni pulls out two menus, placing them down in front of us. 'Our chef's top recommendations this evening are the Antipasti Platter along with the Funghi Ripiene, and as special treat, Mr Berrittini wanted to give you our complimentary champagne as thank you to you, sir.'

My eyes narrow as I shift my gaze from Giovanni to the composed man opposite, who is running his eyes over the menu in his hands. A thank you? For what?

He avoids my stare, but I can tell he's aware of the direction my eyes are pointed when his momentarily shift. 'Is he here tonight?' he asks, glancing up at Giovanni.

'Yes, he is with another guest, but I tell him of your arrival,' he answers kindly, his hands clasped in front of him.

'Thank you.'

'I come back in few moments to take orders.'

I smile my gratefulness at our waiter as he backs away. Jackson scans over the menu like it's the most interesting thing he's seen in a while. My eyes copy, focusing on the black and grey book in my hands, but my attention is still very much concentrated on him. 'You're loved everywhere, aren't you?' I say, glossing over the options but not fully taking them in.

'I'm a loveable person, Emily.' He peers across and I briefly meet his luring gaze, before mine falls back down to my menu.

'Hmm.'

'To all except one it seems.' He places his menu onto the table and leans forward.

'So, what's the bubbly for? What has Mr Turner done to deserve special treatment?' I question, my focus never deviating from the words on the page.

'I know the owner. Well, I know his daughter.'

I immediately shift my attention to him, mirroring him in resting the menu down on the table. 'Oh, yeah?' I retort, quirking an eyebrow.

He shakes his head. 'Not like that.' He pauses, and my silence tells him to elaborate. 'She was a pupil in one of my surf schools; it was during the school holidays last year, I was teaching my class the basics, and she was doing well, until we got into the water. She went in too deep, got herself sucked under by the current, and–

'You saved her.'

'I pulled her out,' he confirms, 'she was unconscious, she'd taken in a lot of water. I gave CPR and fortunately she was okay. Her mother watched the whole thing. All I remember is her screaming… wailing. She was helpless. She could do nothing but hold her daughter's hand as I tried to bring her back.' His face loses the smug, cheeky look it's been holding for the most part of our evening as he reminisces. It's solemn, and images in my mind are flashing back to the night on the clifftop; the night he opened up and showed me a part of him I hadn't seen before.

'But you did,' I say softly.

'Yeah, I did, luckily.'

'You're a hero.'

He swallows, watching me closely. 'I wouldn't go that far.'

'To that family you are, you saved their daughter's life.'

'I just did my job; I did what I had to do.' He holds my attention, our eyes completely fixed on each other. He's being modest, brushing off my compliments, and that's when I'm reminded that he hates talking about himself. It's all fine to joke about him being an amazing person and everyone adoring him, but as soon as the conversation digs a little deeper or reaches further than he'd like, he dismisses it, and then– 'So, what looks good?' … changes the subject. He clears his throat, picking up his menu again.

I choose not to push, after all, the reason we're here is for an entirely separate matter, so I'd rather not start an argument before he's even begun justifying his actions.

We choose our mains with mindless chitchat about what the different meals are, and shortly Giovanni returns with our champagne in an ice bucket. Where Jackson asks for his pasta dish perfectly, I opt to pointing at my choice, knowing I'll only get the pronunciation wrong resulting in sheer embarrassment. Just as Giovanni finishes scribbling down our orders, a large, jolly man appears from behind him.

'Ah, Jackson!' he exclaims ecstatically, his arms extended on either side.

'Hello, sir.' Jackson stands immediately and they shake hands, both grinning widely at one another. 'This is Emily, Emily, this is the owner, Mr Berrittini.' Their gazes shift over to me. I take the opportunity to stand and greet the chipper man politely.

'Hello.' I smile as my hand lifts to shake his, but instead he takes it gently, bringing it to his lips and kissing my knuckles.

'It's a pleasure to meet you, Emily. Giovanni, please make sure our guests are well looked after. I hold Mr Turner in very high regard.'

Jackson makes to sit, and I follow as Giovanni nods curtly. 'I will, Mr Berrittini.'

'Please, anything you want, free of charge,' the delighted owner affirms.

'You don't have to do that.' Jackson shakes his head tightly.

'But I do. This man is very special. My family will forever be in your debt.' His Italian accent is strong as his demeanour switches to that of a far more serious manner. He pauses for a moment, seeming to muse over his thoughts, before he snaps back to his jubilant persona. 'We leave you in peace now, enjoy your evening. It was wonderful meeting you, Emily. You make beautiful couple,' Mr Berrittini calls on a grin as he ushers Giovanni away. My mouth parts automatically as I go to correct him, but Jackson cuts in before any words can spill.

'Grazie, signor!'

I give in, realising it's easier to go along with it. 'Grazie,' I echo on a small smile. My eyes fix on Jackson as he sighs, reaching for the already popped champagne bottle. The bubbles hiss and fizz, splashing my hand on spirited bounces when he fills my glass. 'So that's why you brought me here; it's free.' He doesn't look up as he pours his own.

'No, I didn't know he was going to do that. I brought you here because it's the best restaurant around, and I want to impress you.' He fixes the bottle back into the ice and picks up his glass as his eyes flicker to me.

'Oh, you do?'

'I do,' he retorts, clinking his glass against mine. 'Cheers.'

We watch each other closely, bringing the liquid to our lips. 'Best not tell Olivia, then,' I taunt as I set the glass back down. A nice restaurant and champagne are not getting him off the hook so easily.

Jackson gulps down another mouthful of bubbly before setting the glass down, his exterior unruffled by my remark. He intertwines his ringed fingers on the table as he leans on his forearms. 'I seem to recall you were getting rather cosy with Leo yourself.'

My lips part in disbelief. 'Don't be a dick, you know why I did that.'

'Do I?'

I scowl at him. The bullshit sensor is rising. He notices my distaste and drops his complacent expression, clearing his throat as his gaze meets the harbour. 'I'm sorry,' he breathes.

An awkwardness falls over us, and I find myself staring listlessly around the restaurant before bringing the champagne to my lips again.

'You know, your stubbornness is a quality I find very endearing.'

I halt, watching him over my glass as he brings his focus back to me.

'It's why I'm such a cocky bastard toward you. I like winding you up.'

I laugh lightly. 'So, you're only a sarcastic, condescending jerk to me? Thanks for clearing that up, I was wondering.' My tongue laps the bubbles, but then I hesitate as something comes to mind. 'Wait a minute, during one of the first times we met, and I couldn't get that bloody till to open, you were being a smug arsehole. That was your attempt at flirting?' He stays quiet. 'You watched me squirm and panic in front of a shop full of customers because you found me *endearing* and wanted to wind me up?'

'Okay, there were three people tops, and I was observing. Did you know you stick your tongue out when you concentrate?' He waggles his finger in the direction of my mouth.

'Just as you have a little crease in your forehead,' I shoot back, pushing his hand away.

'So you've been observing me too?'

'It's hard not to, you're everywhere I turn, you never

leave me alone.' I bite my tongue, realising what I just said as I was saying it. 'Well, apart from the last few days.'

He averts his eyes, gazing down as he twists his silver band ring around his index finger. I study him closely, and I can tell he's clearly bothered by what he's done, but as the silence between us expands like pressure to a balloon fit to burst, my mind travels to something I've been thinking about since he said the words. I allow them to fill the air, even though a part of me is apprehensive about what I'm about to ask and the answer which could follow.

'The last time we were here, and you bought us cake, we sat just down there.' I gesture over to the harbour wall, where we were perched last week and his head lifts. 'When I asked you why you were helping me, you said you were intrigued by me. What did you mean?'

He watches me carefully, his expression blank and unreadable. 'I saw the look on your face when you were stood in Maggie's living room. It was desolate, like the whole world was against you. I know that feeling well. I know when a person is crying out for help. I may be a smug arsehole because I like to try your stubbornness, but it's also a very good technique for distracting you from reality, and I want to distract you, Emily. I want to help you.'

It's a very rare occasion when I'm rendered speechless, but right now, my words are nonexistent as I listen, staring at him with his emerald eyes holding me in place as they always seem to do. The world around us is a total haze of distorted colour and blurred noise.

'There's a fire in you; a fire just like Maggie's. But there's also a vulnerability. There's more to you than you allow the others to see; they don't notice it, but I do. And that's why you intrigue me. I…' he falters, his eyes narrowing as he leans in closer. '… I want to know you. All of you,' he murmurs.

My breath hitches ever so slightly, and I wonder if he senses my nervousness. 'That may take a while.'

The corners of his tempting mouth curl upward. 'I've got time.'

I gather myself, shifting in my seat, my fingers mindlessly rotating the bottom of my champagne flute. 'The thing is, I don't know how much time I have. It's all a bit up in the air,' I reply vaguely. He's pulling me in, turning my mind to mush.

And with a soft hum and confident words, he tilts his glass to his lips, leaving me entirely powerless.

'Best not waste anymore, then.'

# TWENTY-FIVE

The girl in the mirror gazes back at me. She looks confident, classy and strong: which is the absolute opposite to how she's feeling.

After our food, I made a quick escape to the ladies, needing a break from the intense atmosphere around us which was making the air unbreathable – despite the open backdrop. I don't know if he's aware of it, but I certainly am, and it's exhausting. As soon as the door to my cubicle closed, I felt my shoulders drop and my neck relax as I took a few minutes to loosen up.

So much for being strong. My fears of the consequences which I knew would come from giving him a chance are looming, and I'm crumbling.

Fixing the thin bag strap on my shoulder, my eyes complete a once over. Satisfied, I take a deep breath and strut back out into the jam-packed restaurant. Waiting by the bar next to the entrance, I see him take his wallet from the back pocket of his jeans. He pulls out a couple of notes before grabbing his jacket and starting in my direction, meeting Giovanni in the middle. Jackson shakes his hand and pats him on the back, and I don't miss him slide the money into Giovanni's palm who thanks him in return, before he strolls over to me.

'I thought Mr Berrittini said everything was free?'

'He did, but like you said, I'm loved by everyone, we have to keep it that way.' He winks and I shake my head at his cheeky confidence. As we're about to head out the double doors, we hear a call from behind.

'Goodnight to you both!' Mr Berrittini shouts from the far side of the bar. We wave our thanks before making our way down the stairs.

As soon as I reach the bottom step, I instinctively hug my arms across my body, the breeze shocking my system with the loss of the restaurant's warmth. It's dark now, the glow from the surrounding restaurants and the bright full moon, our only sources of guiding light. I flinch as I feel something touch my shoulders, but as I turn, I see Jackson draping his jacket over them.

'You look cold.'

I smile sheepishly, pulling my arms through the sleeves and relishing in the fact that it's ridiculously big on me as I embrace it closer. 'Thanks,' I offer coyly.

We wander along the harbour, the peaceful sound of the bells clinking on the boats and background noise from the restaurants with the added warmth from the jacket, relaxes my tense body as I prevent my eyes from drifting up to him. I'm afraid to ask the question, but it's the reasoning behind us being here and it still hasn't been addressed. 'Is this slow walk going to lead to an explanation?' I ask, finding the confidence. I glance up and watch his burly shoulders drop as he sighs.

'I was secretly hoping you'd forgotten.'

'You kissed me, then ignored me; how could I forget? I was promised a reason and I gave you an hour. You have...' I lift my wrist up, catching the time on my new rose gold watch, '... five minutes left before time's up.' I wait expectantly for his reply, my focus remaining when he draws his bottom lip between his teeth.

'I was scared,' he breathes quickly, almost as though he rushed the words before he could stop himself.

'Scared?' I ask, my nose crinkling at the surprisingly truthful response.

'I was scared of getting too close. I have a bad history of pushing people away, Emily, and I don't know how to handle it.' Our steady pace has slowed considerably to a crawl, his head is heavy as he keeps his focus on the floor, but I can't take my eyes off him, noticing how his frown has brought back the small crease in his forehead. 'I've never allowed myself to become too attached to any girl ever, because I've always been terrified of getting hurt, of feeling those feelings I did when my dad left.' He stops in front of me, lifting his gaze to meet mine. 'I've been selfish out of fear.' His body inches closer, and my heart begins to beat that little bit quicker when his hand brushes the stray strands of hair away from my face. My eyes are locked on his emeralds as they appear to sparkle more than I've seen before. 'I don't want to be scared anymore. I tried to stay away from you.'

I draw a short breath, trying and failing to ignore the fact that his face is so close to mine. 'What changed your mind?'

A smirk forms on his lips, overthrowing the serious look it had been holding. 'You're too damn irresistible, angel.'

My eyes lower, somewhat embarrassed as I sniff. 'I wouldn't go that far.'

'You really don't see it do you?' I give him a questioning glance, maintaining composure when inside I'm falling apart. 'How beautiful you are, and not just on the outside.' He strokes my cheek, his soft thumb running gently across my now rosy skin. 'I can't stay away any longer.'

His touch, his eyes, his words, they're all blending together, and the fight I have to not get close to him is fading with every passing second. I can't control it. All restraints and self-control are being melted away, once again he has me under his spell. Against my better judgement, I let my body take over as I step into him. I want to feel his lips on mine. I roll onto the balls of my feet, my tippy-toes allowing me to lean in, leaving my lips inches from his parted mouth. 'So, don't,' I whisper, and in an instant, I'm feeling them.

He takes my face in both of his hands as I place my palms on his chest. The kiss is gentle, soft, and my stomach flutters, sending a surge of warmth through my whole body. Our champagne tasting lips work together as I enjoy every moment they're connected.

I pull away first, my breaths light, and as my eyes flutter open, I see what I was expecting: his gazing down, observing my face as they shift from my lips, to my nose, to my eyes, and back again.

'Your hours up,' I say faintly, but he shakes his head, his eyes flickering down.

'Not quite.' His hands slide from my cheeks, leaving light, teasing tingles down my arms. He lifts my wrist up to his chest, rolling back his jacket sleeve to unveil my watch. The hour hand is dead on nine, but the minute hand has a microscopic margin before it reaches the twelve, and having drowned out any background noise whatsoever, I can vaguely hear the ticking of the second hand as it almost aligns at the top of the face. My wrist remains in the air even when Jackson lets go to rest his hand on my hip. I keep my eyes on the watch, observing the ticking hand as I feel my senses prickle when he presses his lips on the side of my neck. 'Three,' he mumbles... the hand ticks. 'Two,' he utters, moving to my jaw as the hand beats again. 'One.' He kisses the side of my mouth lightly, and the second hand makes its final tick along with the minute as they meet the twelve simultaneously. My breath is shaky when he moves across to my ear. 'Now it's up,' he whispers, sending my senses into overdrive. He pulls back, watching me intently.

Without any indecision, I throw my arms over his shoulders and wrap my hands around the nape of his neck, pulling him to me and losing myself in his lips.

Losing myself in him.

The drive to Jackson's was agonising. Every minute my want for him grew, and when he eventually pulled up outside his annex, not a second was wasted.

He yanks up the old garage door and I scurry underneath, immediately heading to the light switch on the wall as he wrenches the metal back down with a thud. My chest rises and falls, attempting to catch my breath whilst watching him turn on the spot, his hungry eyes growing closer and closer as he stalks toward me. My bag is dropped to the floor when his hands grab my hips which slam me into the wall, his lips crashing down on mine. Our kiss is voracious, desperate and unbreakable as my hands feel up and down his strong arms before sliding into his hair. I run my fingers through his curls and grab onto them, which earns me a soft moan.

Making quick work, he tugs on his jacket still covering me, and I help slip my arms out before he throws it to the floor without breaking our connection. His hands run up and down my body, feeling every part of me as his mouth moves to my neck, kissing just below my ear. He knows what he's doing, and what he's doing is branding me helpless and giddy as that all too familiar flurrying warmth leaves me totally breathless.

'You have no idea how much I've been wanting to do this,' he murmurs eagerly. 'You're driving me crazy, Emily,' he moans into my neck.

'Jackson,' I gasp.

His mouth leaves my neck as we gaze into each other's eyes, his consuming emeralds hypnotising me whilst my fingers brush over his clear-cut cheekbones. They worm their way into his hair again, and it's like my need to study him is growing with every second I spend looking at him. But that connection is quickly cut, replaced with a different form. He pushes his lips back onto mine, his big hands grabbing my trembling thighs as he hooks his grip under my leg, drawing me up and carrying me over to the sofa, my dress riding up as he does so. One hand is placed on my back when he lays me down, his body hovering above my weak form.

Our kisses turn laxer, the pace slackening as we take a few minutes to breathe. My legs remain wrapped around his waist, his hand stroking down the back of my thigh. He grips it tight which causes my hips to jerk up into his groin. He groans against my mouth.

I tug on his T shirt, encouraging him to discard of the material, and he obliges, pulling away for the briefest of seconds to haul it over his head. His defined torso is revealed to me, drawing the smallest of gasps from my throat. Throwing it behind him carelessly, his eyes fix on me as I tug him back down, my ravenous hunger for him consuming my entire body.

I lose my breath again when he grazes his mouth down my neck, using his hands to craftily unbutton the front of my dress whilst leaving a trail of kisses as he works his way down my chest. He lifts his head, gifting me a peck before his hand leaves my dress to cup my face. His thumb strokes my cheek softly and I become transfixed on his piercing eyes. Eyes I'm not accustomed to seeing in this way.

'I've only ever been with–

'Shh, it's okay,' Jackson coos. 'Are you sure you want to do this? We don't have to.' His thumb continues to trace my skin as his eyes wander the entirety of my face; the hungry, intense look they held mere moments ago showing a more tender side. My hand reaches up to brush away his curls as he holds my gaze, and a small smile forms on my lips, providing him with my answer. I've never felt so absorbed and so powerless by one person, yet so incredibly safe that my willingness to submit to him suppresses any other feeling in my body. 'Tell me what you want,' he whispers, leaning in and stopping just above my mouth.

'You, Jackson. I want all of you,' I beg, surrendering to him completely.

His mouth quirks before he claims my swollen lips again. His hands move to my wrists, pulling me up as my knees position themselves on either side of him, giving me the control to grind my hips teasingly against him. His touch glides under the material covering my shoulders, making it slide effortlessly down my arms to bunch at my hips, before it snakes around my back, unclasping my bra with seamless ease.

'Fuck, look at you. You're so sexy,' he moans, the sound drifting up my breastbone as he kisses it tenderly.

My hands discover his chest, then his abs, distracting myself from any shyness that I feel from revealing myself to him, and I find I'm becoming overwhelmed with just how attractive he is. All the sexual tension which has been building, not only tonight, but for the past week, is bubbling to the surface as we both give in to our temptation.

He may be cocky, and I might not know everything about him and his mysterious past, and he's undoubtedly had many a girl, but as I straddle his lap, his eyes locked on my own, I know that for tonight he's mine. Completely. Utterly. Entirely mine. And I'm all his.

Moving his palms underneath my bundled dress at my waist, he hoists me up and stands. I take the opportunity to pull the bobble from my hair, letting the curly blonde mess fall down past my shoulders before we collapse back onto his mattress. I kick my Converse off as he slithers the rest of my dress from my body. My eyes watch his every movement, his hands running up my legs as his head follows, trailing kisses up my thighs, heating my core and sending my pounding heart wild. His emeralds flicker up to my face as his fingers brush along the rim of my knickers. I'm begging for his touch, silently pleading, squirming under him.

'Please,' I gasp.

'Patience, angel,' he croons, and I groan in frustration when he grips my hips, squeezing them tight. 'I want to savour every part of you.'

And so, he does – driving me crazy in the process.

His lips travel to my tummy, kissing across it delicately whilst his eyes hold my own, distracting me from the movement of his fingers. That is, until he slips two under the black material and my hands instantly grasp his hair. He is slow and patient, his fingertips lightly running up and down, teasing me as my hips jerk upwards, but he pushes them back down.

Much to my displeasure, he draws away his hand before crawling up my body, taking both my arms and pinning them above my head. Teasing me. He's a vision of perfection and my pulse doubles with every second he spends gazing into my eyes. I push myself up, capturing his mouth and my tongue battles his, but he wins when I recoil, whimpering against his lips as I feel his hand sneakily slipping entirely under my knickers, his thumb circling around and working its magic.

'Jesus, Jackson.' My core is pulsing, aching for him. I fumble with his belt, doing my best to unbuckle it blindly as my lips consume his. He chuckles into them and I practically die on the spot at the deep sexy sound as his free hand meets mine, helping me in my task whilst still maintaining his painfully pleasing rhythm down below. 'Condom?' I ask breathlessly, when the belt has been successfully unbuckled.

He shakes his head, telling me 'not yet', and I huff with impatience just as he lightly traces his fingers down my entrance, making me writhe underneath him. Snaking down until his face is comfortably between my legs, he smirks up at me, taking the only material left on my body into his fingers and gliding it off. My head is thrown back into the mattress when waves of torturous pleasure are sent through me. The sheets are clasped, my moans filling the room. I'm building, and I'm not sure how long I'm going to be able to last.

My bent legs are quivering, my breaths are chaotic, and my skin is burning. '*Oh… ooh… fuck!* Jackson, please,' I beg, and he complies, halting in his rhythm after a few more seconds of torture, moving back to linger above my face.

'In the drawer,' he says softly as a flash of relief followed by eagerness blossoms in me. Whilst he swiftly rids of his jeans and boxers, I reach across the bed, swiping up the blue packet. I turn back and he's already taking it from my hands, tearing the wrapper with his teeth as I collapse back, watching him keenly.

He balances his hands on either side of my head before leaning down and placing a gentle kiss on my temple, my nose, and then my lips. My eyes bore into his beseechingly. He lingers, his bright emeralds searching my face, silently asking if I'm okay. I nod encouragingly, getting lost in the sparkle that they hold, my mind and body unequivocally ready for him.

Everything tenses and I gasp, gripping his arms firmly when he loses himself in me. He rocks slowly at first, and I know he can sense my slight discomfort as I adjust to him, because his thumb brushes my cheek, whilst his lips kiss my jaw sweetly, and after a few seconds, I relax.

'You're so fucking sexy, Emily,' he murmurs, his pants growing heavier. It's like my body reacts to his voice as

I feel myself loosen entirely, and I know he feels it too when his pace increases.

My cries, mixed with his groans, combined with our hot and sweaty bodies only intensifies just how much pleasure my senses are being engulfed in right now. I don't care that this is probably a really bad idea, and that this might cause a problematic awkwardness afterwards. All I care about in my greedily aroused state is Jackson Turner. Jackson Turner, and the need to have every single part of him tonight. So, I put the thoughts which are swimming around my mind behind bars, pushing them back into the deepest depths of my brain as I concentrate solely on him and let myself go completely.

The words threaten to break down the barriers I've placed in front of them, but as my heart races and the feeling in my centre begins to climb, I ignore them, focusing on the sensation building within caused by the handsome lifeguard whose muscles are tensing and flexing, his touch sending me into overdrive.

My hips arch as we move together and he goes deeper, our pants and moans loud and chaotic. The bed is creaking, the headboard knocking against the wall, and if I wasn't so consumed with the mounting feeling below, I would be concerned about Dex and anyone else in the main house overhearing. But I'm not worried. Because everything around me is a complete haze of blurriness. The only thing in the room in focus, and the only thing that matters, is him. My legs tighten against his waist as my hands dig into his brawny back, trying to hold off my impending orgasm, wanting this to last for as long as possible.

'I'm close,' I wheeze just as he claws on my thighs. He is too.

'Shit,' he cries.

And with one final thrust, I let go as that warmth explodes. My world goes blank and I fall limp underneath him with his moans in my ear, rocking slowly through his release.

Jackson collapses on top of me, panting erratically into my neck as we allow our climaxes to devour us. But as he finishes and my high begins its inevitable descent, as he rolls off me and we're both left in a state of breathlessness staring at the ceiling, unable to move our dripping, exhausted bodies, the trapped thoughts release themselves from confinement, travelling all around my mind. I close my eyes, trying to overlook them, but they're too powerful to restrain.

My head shifts to the side as I watch him pant. His chest rises and falls rapidly and the waves around his face stick to his dampened forehead, but when he brushes the strands away, running his long fingers into his hair and resting his muscular arm on the pillow beneath him, I realise that my thoughts hold the truth.

This man is going to ruin my life.

# TWENTY-SIX

*It's dark. As it always is. There's nothing around me, it's like a black void of nothingness, and as usual, I'm alone and I'm scared.*

*'Hello?' my small, timid voice calls. 'I know you're there, you're always there.'*

*Nothing.*

*I hold my breath as the darkness closes in with nowhere for me to escape. I search around desperately as it encapsulates me, touching every fraction and particle of my body. That deep snicker echoes throughout the room, and I brace myself for the inevitable. It comes quickly as my back hits solid wall. 'Let me go,' I yelp as the footsteps advance. 'I'm tired, I'm so tired,' I sob.*

*'Oh, gorgeous girly. This is your father; this is all your father. He's the one who's killing you.' I can't see his face, but I can feel his towering presence. His deep chuckle rings in my ears, louder and louder until I'm falling to my knees.*

*The brown carpet is visible. It's rough under my skin. I stare across the landing and see her. She smiles, my hand slowly lifts, reaching for her. But she doesn't reach back.*

*Something's different. My eyes snap to her side to see him. His face is blank, his cold, dark eyes sending shivers through my body, like snakes slithering down my spine. He's not usually here. 'Why!' I yell, trying to find the strength to stand, but I can't.*

*Her deafening scream pulls me back, and I slap my hands over my ears, squeezing my eyes closed. 'No,' I whimper. 'Not again, no, no,' I continue to weep. No matter how hard I try, it's like I'm not in control of my body as my eyes open and I watch her fall. Tears stream down my face, I'm helpless, motionless on my knees. The man remains still. But his face has shifted, he's smirking at my pain.*

*'Stop, stop, stop!' I cry as his sickening laugh echoes all around, trapping the air in my throat... suffocating me. 'STOP!'*

'Hey, hey, Emily. Wake up!'

I jolt, my eyes flying open. My brain juggles as I peer frantically around the room, trying to fathom where I am. Jackson's hands are on my arms, his face close to mine as we sit up. 'Wha– where...'

'Are you okay?' he asks gently, but with the pounding in my ears it's difficult to hear. I finally glance at his concerned face, his eyes narrowed, and his forehead creased.

I nod feebly, attempting to catch my breath and scrape the damp hair off my neck. Breaking our stare, I try focusing on anything except him, but he continues to watch me, his hands still gripping my shoulders, almost like he's frightened to look or move away. 'Yeah... bad dream. Happens sometimes.'

*More like all the time.*

His fingers loosen and he clears his throat on a short bob of his head.

'Was I talking loudly?'

'Emily, you were screaming.'

My wide eyes flicker to his.

'I thought someone had broken in. You scared me to death.'

'I'm sorry,' I sigh, glancing down.

He sniffs. 'Don't apologise. Do you want to talk about it?'

Immediately my head shakes and his brow furrows at my adamant expression, before accepting and rubbing my shoulder reassuringly. 'Alright, well, if anyone understands what a nightmare does to you, it's me.' He shuffles back, resting against the headboard, and I'm happy he's compliant, because I don't fancy explaining my nightmares to him in grim detail.

'Do you have them often?' I ask.

'No. Hardly ever now, and when I do, I've become so used to them that I've learnt to block them out,' he replies nonchalantly.

Confusion must be etched on my face. 'But the dreams you were describing to me, the lucid dreams, they're so real, how do you not let them faze you?'

'Because nothing fazes me anymore.' He shrugs, scrunching his nose.

'You seemed pretty fazed the other night,' I say, remembering his profound descriptions on the topic.

'Oh, that was just a special occasion,' he adds lightly, and I roll my eyes, turning to gaze around the dim room. How he manages to be so flippant all the time is beyond me. A faint light shimmers through the garage door window.

'What time is it?' I ask, eyeing the dust particles floating in the sunbeam.

'Six.'

My fingers fumble with the duvet covering my tummy and my eyes dart down as my suspicions are confirmed; I'm as naked as a jaybird. I shift my body to face him, manoeuvring the sheet up to cover myself and noting that he is entirely nude too, however he's making no conscious effort to shield his manhood. I avert my eyes, not really knowing where to focus. His face is usually distracting enough, now I have his whole exposed body to contend with.

'So…'

'So…' he echoes.

'Last night.'

'Yep,' he replies, popping the 'p'.

'Not what I was expecting.'

'You can say that again.'

I scoff, shaking my head. 'Oh, shut up.'

'What?'

'You knew that was going to happen.'

'I did not,' he says on an innocent tone, but his eyes deceive him. I stare at him pointedly. 'I mean, best case scenario, obviously, I hoped it would, but I knew you'd be a tough nut to crack,' he jokes and I tut.

'Arsehole,' I fire back, lowering my head sheepishly to hide my growing smile.

'Seriously, though, I am sorry for ignoring you.'

My eyes lift to catch his remorseful gaze. 'It's fine,' I offer softly.

He shakes his head. 'No, it isn't. You're right, I am an arsehole. I deserved a slap not a shag.'

'Yeah, you did.' I smile teasingly. 'Lucky for you, I'm too nice of a person.'

He smiles back, a warm smile which melts me inside. 'Too good for me.'

Taking a breath, I frown. He's far too smooth for my liking. 'Is this what you do, then? Say some flattering things to girls and immediately they drop their knickers?'

'No,' his face contorts, 'well, not all the time.'

'So bloody smug,' I scorn as a question comes to mind. 'How many girls have you actually had?'

'That's a bit personal for six in the morning, Emily Rose,' he says, feigning a solemn expression which causes my eyebrow to arch. He holds my gaze for a moment, almost as though he's deliberating his answer. 'Not as many as you probably think.'

'But Olivia's one of them?' I ask quickly, before I allow myself enough time to bite my tongue.

He doesn't say anything, he just studies me pensively, like he's reluctant to reply. He clears his throat, his line of focus drifting away from me. 'Yes, she's one of them. But there's nothing more to it, it's just sex.' He's swift to defend.

'And you're both okay with that?' I push.

'Yeah, it's purely physical.'

Either he's completely oblivious to the world around him, or he knows, and he doesn't want to admit it to me. I know it's more than sex, for Olivia at least. I'm simply curious as to whether he's aware and is willing to acknowledge it. But going off his relaxed body language and expression, I'll take it as he clearly has no idea that Olivia is one hundred percent in love with him.

'You have no clue, do you?'

He licks his lips as he peers at me through narrowed eyes. 'About what?'

'Womankind.' I trace my fingers over the creases in the duvet, contemplating my next question. 'Have you done anything with her since our kiss?'

There's no hesitation as he gives me a definite answer. 'No.' My eyes flicker up. 'We haven't for a while now, my mind has been a little distracted recently,' he says on a smile, but then it falters as he watches me intently. Apparently, I'm not doing a very good job in hiding the tentative feeling I have in the pit of my stomach, because his face turns bleaker. 'You don't believe me.'

'Before last night I had all manner of things running around my mind, Olivia being at the forefront,' I reply truthfully.

'And now?'

I sigh. 'I don't know.'

'Well, you can believe me.'

'Is there anyone else?'

'Is this 'twenty questions'?'

My lungs fill. I know I have no right to ask him, like I have no right to be angry with him if there is, because in truth, I'm probably just another number. And when I leave here, he'll forget about me and find comfort in some other lost soul, and I'm going to have to be okay with that. Nevertheless, for the moment, I'm going to appreciate and enjoy soaking up his view, no matter the ache I may feel when we eventually part.

His gaze wanders my face, a glint in his eye, like he's thinking deeply. 'No, there isn't anyone else.'

I decide to believe him, because that idea brings far more solace than the idea of questioning him further, only to find he's being untruthful.

'Now,' he says, leaning forward and taking my wrist, encouraging me with a gentle tug to move closer to him, 'let's talk about something else.'

I can't control the smile which forms on my lips, his face only inches from mine as the duvet falls from my body. 'Like what?'

He pulls me so my legs straddle his lap, our naked bodies pressed together, once again sending flutters around my tummy.

'I want to talk about you,' he murmurs, staring up at me as my hands cup his face and his rest on my hips.

My nose wrinkles. 'I'd rather do this.' I connect our lips, kissing him deeply. I know it's only been a few hours since I tasted him, but as our kiss becomes increasingly more heated, I realise just how much I'm craving him. He's like a drug, and I'm insatiable.

Disappointment rushes through me and it comes out in my groan when he pulls back, looking at me with encouraging eyes. I roll my mine on a huff.

'I like the smell of coffee but hate the taste. I'd much rather listen to slow, sad songs, because they allow my mind to drift somewhere else, but I never disregard crap pop music. I would pick a homemade roast dinner over pizza, but a Chinese over a roast. I'm not one for receiving compliments or being made the centre of attention, I shrivel up under the pressure of trying to act a certain way which is considered normal in those situations. I'd choose flats over heels and casual over glam. When I go to sleep, I have the most horrible nightmares.' … *I also have bad people out to kill me and a gun hidden under my bed…* 'And last night was the most connected I've felt to another person in a heck of a long time,' I finish, gazing down and knowing that that final admission should have remained safely trapped in my mind, yet for some reason not regretting allowing my mouth to take over. 'Is that good enough for you?'

'Wow.' He pauses thoughtfully. 'You'd really choose a roast over pizza?' he says with incredulity. I swat his arm, but only end up giggling like a schoolgirl when he chuckles. This time he pushes his lips to mine as we laugh into the kiss. I shriek as he flips me onto my back, his hands running up and down my waist as our mouths move together.

Pulling back, he props himself up with his head in his palm and his elbow on the pillow as he sucks me into his eyes. My fingertips lightly graze up and down his burly arm as his do across my tummy. 'Tell me your hopes and dreams.'

'That's a bit personal for six in the morning, Jackson,' I mimic on a grin.

'Oh, come on. Enlighten me, angel.'

'Okay... The biggest is to see the world. I want to travel: Europe, America, Africa, all of it. And I want to do it all before I'm too old and decrepid.'

'I like it.' He smirks as his eyes run from my face, down my body, and back again, whilst continuing his soft strokes of my skin.

'My dream job would probably be travelling the world as a journalist or as some form of writer. I used to read these blogs when I was younger and there was a woman who reported on stories wherever she went, I think that would be my ultimate dream. Think of how amazing it would be to wake up somewhere faraway doing something you love. That's my goal for after university anyway.'

He hums quietly and contentedly. 'Will you do something for me, Emily?'

My eyes narrow. 'Depends what it is.'

'It's a promise.' He holds our stare with a sparkle in his emeralds. 'A promise that you won't give up. No matter how many setbacks come your way, no matter how many no's you receive, you keep going, because in a thousand no's, there will be one yes. And that yes could change your life.'

My lips part, whether it's from shock or captivation I'm not sure. His words always seem to lure me in, and the most enticing thing about them is that he has no idea just how much they're affecting me.

'I promise,' I reply without any effort or control, the agreement falling from my mouth mechanically.

'You have to pinky.'

'Really?'

'Really. Pinky or it doesn't mean anything.'

He halts his light tracings on my skin and holds up his little finger in front of my face expectantly. Without taking my eyes from his, I link our pinky's together, and that's when I feel his ring. I flick my line of vision down and watch as he slides the rest of his fingers between mine, intertwining them, but my focus is on the engraved silver band which has grasped my attention several times before.

'This ring,' I say, my eyes drifting over the markings. 'These symbols. Do they mean anything?'

Jackson glances to our connected hands. 'It's runic lettering,' he explains as my fingers on my free hand brush over the engraved writing. 'It means, My Seraph. It was my mother's.'

I study his face which seems to have darkened. 'She gave it to you?' He nods but with no reply, and my heart sinks at the sadness in his eyes. 'You miss her.'

It's as though my words go straight through him, like my voice is white noise in his ears as he stares at the ring. Although desolate, I take in his relaxed features and smile sadly at the grief he's had to endure, wondering how the world can be so cruel to someone so undeserving of it. 'What's, My Seraph?'

His chest expands, but he doesn't meet my gaze. 'It's a religious being to do with light and purity or something like that.'

I watch him with obvious notice that the air around us has turned heavy. So, deciding that's enough sorrow for the morning, I untangle our hands which wins me back his attention. 'Your turn. What are your dreams?'

He snorts, collapsing back onto the mattress, tucking his hand under his head. 'I don't really have any of those.'

'Why not?' I ask, my eyes narrowing, rolling onto my side and gazing at him as he stares at the ceiling. Everyone has dreams.

'Just don't. Maybe when I first came here, but I'm happy now, comfortable, you know?'

'You should never be comfortable when there's so much out there, Jackson. Always aim high. There must be something you want to reach for?' His head shifts as he watches me, puckering his lips and pondering. 'What?' I press, keen to understand what's ticking inside that mysterious head of his.

'Can I show you something?'

My lips quirk as a large plume of interest and a sprinkle of excitement swells within me. 'Of course, you can.'

On my approval he rolls over and pushes himself off the bed, my marveling eyes observing him raptly the whole time. He opens his wardrobe, tossing a black shirt onto the bed so it lands over my legs, before tugging his grey shorts up. Happy that I still get to ogle his bare torso, I stand from the bed and haul the shirt over my head, feeling it trickle down to my upper thigh. Without a glance towards me, he steps up to his bedside table and yanks on the drawer handle. He pulls out a single key.

Neither of us speak as I follow him over to the kitchen, and then, to my surprise, to the door which captured my attention the last time I slept here. He stops with his back to me when we reach it, the anticipation, I'm sure, glowing in my eager eyes.

'No one's ever been in here apart from me.' He sighs. I watch closely as he holds up the key. 'That's why I keep it locked; it's my own space.'

'I take it it's not just a storage cupboard,' I joke, a part of me trying to lift the sudden somber atmosphere which has fallen upon us, and the other trying to hide my restlessness to see inside.

'No, not a storage cupboard. I suppose you could say this room holds all my aspirations.'

He stands unmoving, almost like he's gathering confidence to lift his hand and unlock the door. 'You don't have to show me, Jackson,' I say, noting his uncertainty, even if it would kill me not to know.

There's no reply, only the click of the lock retracting and the sound of the handle being turned, before the door is pushed open. He treads forward slowly, but considering my prior keenness, for some reason I'm now nervous, my legs reluctant to move.

I'm the first person to see whatever's in here, which means everything in this room is incredibly personal and not something he shares around freely. Which makes this moment a big deal.

I force my feet to carry me in. He shifts from the doorway, stepping into the room and turning on the light. My eyes wander over every single element, every single detail, and a smile dances on my lips.

My toes sink into the cushiony cream carpet, my feet feeling like they're floating on feathers as I tread further inside. There are a diverse range of drawings pinned to the walls all around the room; some colourful, some left shaded in grey pencil, some of animals and wildlife, and some of landscapes. Several tall wooden easels are dotted in different places, but unlike the drawings on the wall, these look like designs for buildings and houses; lines and shapes all coming together to form plans for not only outside structures of homes, but gardens as well. A long rectangle table is situated in the middle of the room with papers in piles, and silver pots of crayons and pencils aligned along the top. Above, there are wooden beams decked with skylights which cascade around the room radiantly, giving it a warm and calming feeling. And at the back next to a large window, which from where I'm stood looks like a view into a garden, is a bookcase with many thick and colourful spines lined up on asymmetrical rows.

My eyes widen as I leisurely pace around the room. 'You can draw?'

His hands are together behind his back, his lips pursed as he nods slowly. 'Yeah,' he replies, almost as though he's ashamed. I walk over to one of the wooden easels which has a large piece of card balancing on it. On the card, a design of what appears to be a construction idea for the outside of a modern home – this modern home.

'Is this what I think it is?' I ask as my eyes take in every feature of the sketch. I hardly hear his footsteps on the soft carpet, and only register that he's beside me when I feel him press against my back.

'That depends on what you think it is.'

'It's this house, the annex part which Dex's parents were building when you first came to live here.'

Glancing up, I see his face scrunch. 'I may have been telling a little porky.'

'What do you mean?'

'They were thinking about extending and turning the garage into something, but they hadn't started when I arrived. Anne and Jeremy let me stay, but in Dex's room. This annex didn't exist when I first moved in. I heard them talking about it one evening and decided to draw out a plan to show them what it could possibly look like, just to see what they thought and whether they would like it – which they did.'

'So, you designed this whole place?'

'Have a look behind the card,' he says, gesturing to the drawing on the easel.

I turn back to the design and feel the corners of the card, only to find another piece underneath. Lifting the first off, my eyes widen at the second plan; the whole layout of the annex's interior, including what the garage looked like before the extension.

'Jesus Christ, you're talented!' I affirm, spinning around to gawp up at him.

'I just have an eye for a good-looking building,' he says indifferently, and I scoff in disbelief.

'Why the hell are you not pursuing this? Architects would snap you up given half the chance.'

'Like you say, it's complicated.' His voice is calm and collected, quite the contrast to my shocked and ardent tone.

'How? Come on, Jackson,' I hold the card in my hand up to his face, waving it in front of him. '*this* is amazing, why let your talent go to waste?'

He stays quiet, his lips in a straight line as he takes a breath, but he doesn't respond. Shaking my head, I return the sketch, neatly placing it back onto the easel before continuing my lap of the room. I go to his desk, musing over the drawings, seeing half drawn birds and brightly coloured plants all scattered tidily in different piles. My eyes then zone into something past the table and on the floor.

'What's this?' I ask, picking up the crumpled piece of paper from the carpet and beginning to unravel it. The flicks of pencil reveal a well-sketched drawing of a dog who looks exactly like Buddy. Erratic lines show his fluffy fur blowing backwards as his wide stance illustrates him running on a sandy beach with a calm sea in the distance. My mouth parts, but I'm at a loss for words.

'I was drawing that the night I called you,' his deep voice says, and I can feel him edging closer. 'I haven't been in here since.'

'It looks like Buddy,' I murmur, studying the vivid drawing in my hands.

'He's a good model to draw,' Jackson replies, and I'm surprised he's making no effort to deny it. My head lifts as he halts in his tracks, registering the confusion on my face. 'I said that I brush off the bad dreams, well the way I learnt to do that was through putting pencil to paper and letting my hand take over. It would ease my mind and calm me down, so now, whenever I have a nightmare or when something which bothers me happens–

Something springs to mind. 'Like the tree which nearly killed us?' I remember him being so unruffled and composed, whereas I reacted like a startled cat.

'Yeah, like that,' he confirms on a small smile. 'I just think about the motions of the pencil and I somehow manage to stay in control. But, very rarely, there are times when it doesn't work, the night I saw you being an example, and I get overcome with emotions. Probably because I'm suppressing them all the damn time.' When I don't say anything, he looks down at his feet sheepishly, shaking his head. 'It's fucking ridiculous, isn't it?'

He's mistaken my silence for judgement, but he couldn't be more wrong. I run my eyes over the picture and note how I feel myself drawn into every detail. 'No, it isn't. It's really good, Jackson. They're all really good.'

He smiles his appreciation, but still a shyness peeks through. 'I've never told anyone about this, let alone shown them.'

The tiniest of smirks appears on my lips. 'Does that make me special?' I gaze at him cheekily, seeing him reach out for the paper in my hand.

'I guess it does.'

'Why are you showing me?' I ask as he places his drawing onto the table behind us and takes both of my hands into his.

'I don't know,' he replies softly. 'Maybe because I know you won't judge.'

'How could anyone judge you for this? These drawings, those plans, are incredible. You should put yourself out there, who knows what could happen.'

'Hmm.' He takes his bottom lip between his teeth, his face unconvinced.

'Why are you so hesitant?' I question. He shouldn't be letting what is quite clearly a God given talent and knack for design and drawing go to waste.

His eyes flicker above my head and then to the door as his chest billows. 'Because if I put myself out there, there's a chance I fail, that's just the way the world works, Em. I don't want to end up hating the one thing that helps my sanity.'

I flash him a pointed look, because how can he tell me to never give up on my dreams and not attempt to pursue his? 'Maybe you should tell the world to piss off.'

His piercing yet warm eyes gaze longingly back down into mine. 'Maybe you should too.'

I lower my focus, the realisation of my statement coming to light inside my mind; I've tried telling the world to piss off, it never listens.

His finger hooks under my chin, drawing it up, but

as he does, my eyes narrow. I flick them curiously from him to the cabinet on the far side of the room and back again.

'What?' he asks as I break our contact and pace around him.

As I approach the oak cabinet I turn back to his tall, shirtless frame and point to the object perched on the top. 'Is that a Polaroid?' I pick up the baby blue instant camera, studying it closely.

'Yes. I like visual things,' he replies as his head nods, and it's when I glance up that I register he's gesturing to the lines of Polaroid photos pegged to long strings hanging either side of us.

'I've always wanted one, I think they're so cool. It doesn't matter what you take, every photo will come out enchanting and special,' I say, entirely fixed on the vintage camera.

'Here.' Stepping forward, he takes it from my clasp and holds it up in my direction, snapping a picture. The film rolls out of the bottom on a whir and Jackson watches it develop. He grins down at the picture, before letting me get a glimpse of it. 'See. Beautiful.'

I snort. I'm not sure if he's taking the Mickey. He sees beautiful? I see a dishevelled mess. My hair looks like I've been dragged through a hedge backwards, and my face is hideously tired and pale. Yet, proving my point, the vintage look of the photo adds its special enchantment, rectifying my dreadful six in the morning, sleepy state.

He retracts the picture, instead holding out the Polaroid camera. I glance at him confused. 'You can have it if you like.'

I recoil ever so slightly. 'What?'

'Oh, I want it back, it was expensive.' He chuckles and my heart skips a beat. 'Capture some memories,' he says, extending his arm.

I reach out for it, a small smile playing on my lips. 'Thank you.' As my fingers worm around it, I gasp when he jerks me into his body. His eyes capturing mine.

'Where on earth did you come from?' he asks as his fingers trace lightly over my cheek, making me melt on the spot. 'You're turning me into a big softy, angel.'

'Guess you're just going to have to deal with it.'

And with that, our lips connect once more.

# TWENTY-SEVEN

*I'm seeing you after your shift. When do you finish?*

I smile down at the text, my fingers hovering over the letter keys. They begin tapping away a response when I feel a thump on my arm. The small soft ball bounces off me, rolling around my feet.

'That was unnecessary,' I say, flicking my eyes up to Lily who is filling a basket with beach balls by the entrance. She flashes a mocking smile in my direction.

'Got your attention though, didn't it? The place has been dead all day, you've had your head down on that thing… I'm dying of boredom over here!' she groans, tossing a ball diagonally onto the floor so it lands perfectly in the tall wicker basket.

'How can you be bored when you're occupied with your most favourite things in the world?' A smirk snakes its way onto my lips as she glares back at me, but I know she's doing her best to hide her amusement.

'Now *that* was unnecessary. Who are you texting anyway?' she asks, dragging her feet over to the counter before flopping on top of it with her chin in her palm. I send my reply.

*And what makes you so sure I want to see you?*

'No one special,' I retort on a shrug.

'No? You sure?'

'Yeah…'

Lily looks at me pointedly and my defense rises to the surface.

'What?' I ask as my phone pings again.

*Because I've been to Traci's…*

'Your smile would beg to differ,' she says which brings my focus back to her, causing my lips to pucker and my brain to tick.

'It's just Maggie.'

*You win! I finish in half an hour.*

'I love Maggie and I think she's the funniest woman ever, but that smile isn't on your face because she's told you one of her gardening jokes. There's a boy.' Her body perks up and I cringe.

Not that Jackson and I are even the slightest bit of a *thing,* but if I told Lily what has happened between us, she would freak out, and soon every person in this town would know and make something out of what is basically nothing. He and I are simply enjoying each other's company, that's all, but having to explain that to people will automatically cause assumptions, despite what would be my denial. It's best to keep it on the down low, and I'm planning to talk to Jackson about it, so I know we're on the same page.

'I'm right, aren't I? There's a boy.'

'Lily, I've just broken up with my boyfriend,' I say, because even though William is completely out of sight and mind, I'm hoping playing on that factor might help my case and put her off the topic. But, being Lily, of course it doesn't.

'So?' She shrugs.

My brow raises.

'I'm not prying, I promise. All I'm going to say is that if he's making you smile, then remember, that ex is an ex for a reason. You deserve to be happy, Em.'

Despite her snooping and perseverance, my lips curl. 'Thanks, Lily.'

'But you have to give me the goss!' I shoot her a warning glare again. 'Okay, sorry,' she says, her hands surrendering as she steps away from the counter, 'backing away to my balls.'

*Perfect. Meet me by the hut.*

I tap the back of my phone with my finger and sigh as the butterflies dance around in my tummy. It's not a thing, Emily. It can't be a thing. Yet, all I've been able to think about today is him, and I'm scared, because the more time I spend with him and the more I get to know him, the more I like him. But I can't. We just can't. Once feelings are involved, things become far too complicated. And I refuse to even acknowledge complicated right now.

*Oh, and bring Buddy!*

Buddy hauls me to the beach, his excitement has been building since the moment he saw me pull out his collar from the drawer, the twizzle turns and barks his way of telling me to get a move on.

Up ahead Jackson is perched on a white crate next to the locked-up surf hut. It's around 5 p.m., and the sea's in at its highest tide, leaving only a small patch of dry sand with no people around, so it only makes sense that all the lifeguards have gone home.

With my arm one more yank away from escaping its socket, I stop and unclip the lead from Buddy's collar. He darts over to Jackson, who drops to his knees and opens his arms for Buddy to run into. I laugh as my dog jumps on top of him, licking every inch of his face.

'I think he likes you,' I say on a grin, holding my hand out to help him stand. He takes it and I have to use both hands and all of my strength to heave him up as Buddy breaks off to sniff around the hut, his tail wagging happily.

'What's not to like?' He beams back as I snort and shake my head.

'You're ridiculous.'

'Ridiculously hot.'

'Please, stop.' I have to bite back my smile and glance down, his cheeky expression annoyingly infectious. He is, in fact, looking ridiculously hot with his flannel shirt and wavy hair, but there's no way I'm going to increase the size of his already ginormous head. 'You mentioned Traci's?' I say, gathering myself enough to direct the conversation to one of greater importance.

'Yes, I did.' He sinks his fingers into his hair, before picking up a brown paper bag from the crate and shaking it in front of me. I waggle my eyebrows.

'Gimme, gimme!'

He retracts his arm. 'Ah, ah, ah.'

'What?'

'Let's go down there.' He gestures to a giant rock being kissed by the sea across the beach.

'What's the difference between that rock and this crate? Other than the fact this crate is probably *exceedingly* more comfortable.'

'Just, trust me.'

I give in, knowing the more I argue, the longer it'll be before I get my cake. 'Fine. This way, pup!' I call and Buddy dashes over, racing ahead as we begin our stroll across the beach.

'I think he's got the right idea,' Jackson says and my eyes narrow. Without warning he sprints off. 'Last one there has to run into the sea naked!' he cries over his shoulder.

'Wait! Jackson!' I throw my head back on a groan before pushing the balls of my feet into the grooves in the sand and forcing myself forward. My little legs are no match for his ludicrously long and robust pins, and it takes me until I'm halfway there to realise. So, I give up. I hunch over, trying to regain my breath, but the little oxygen I manage to inhale is lost again when I yelp. My feet leave the ground as I'm flung over his shoulder. 'Hey! Jackson put me down!' I'm self-conscious of the fact my high waisted shorts have ridden up and my arse is now in his face.

'Nope.' He laughs and once the shock of being swept off my feet clears, I can't help the giggles as he manages to keep up his fast pace, even with my weight on top of him. Buddy jumps up, running circles around us, and it doesn't take long for Jackson to reach the rock and place me back on my feet. He sighs, out of breath.

'Thanks for that.'

His cheeky grin is infectious. 'I hope you realise you lost.'

'I'm not getting into the sea naked,' I affirm. It's hard to tell if he's being serious, but I am deadly.

'It was the forfeit, them's the rules.'

'Just give me the cake,' I say, impatiently reaching for the bag which I successfully snatch.

'Alright, bossy.'

I try and suss a part of the rock which looks the least pointy, but it's a losing game, it'll be uncomfortable wherever. Plonking myself on the flattest section, I dive into the bag as Jackson steps up next to me and takes a perch.

'Yours is the red velvet.'

My head flicks to him. 'You remembered?' I ask, a flurry of warmth hitting me.

'I did.' He nods on a proud smile.

I grin as I pull the boxes out, checking which is mine and handing the other chocolatey one to Jackson along with a wooden fork. At the bottom of the bag I notice a smaller box.

'Buddy's got a doggy cupcake too.'

My eyes glance over, he's too busy eyeing his cake, but my lips curl up at the handsome man beside me. He told me that I'm turning him soft, but deep down, I think he's always been this way. It's just been hidden away, waiting for a reason to escape.

I feel my throat thicken. I'm his reason.

Distracting my thoughts, I open up Buddy's box to see a cupcake with miniature dog biscuits stuck around the edge and a large one wedged in the centre. I break it up, place it down on the rock in front of us and call Buddy over.

'How was the walk of shame this morning?' Jackson asks, shovelling in a mouthful.

My nose wrinkles as I wince, thinking about the encounter with Aunt Maggie when I got back to the cottage earlier. 'Hideously painful. She didn't even say anything to me, just gave me the eye over her coffee mug when I went into the kitchen to get water.' He chuckles, lifting another forkful of cake up to his mouth. 'Don't laugh! It was awful, I couldn't get out of there quick enough. I'm waiting for her to bring up the safe sex talk.'

He snorts and I only have to glimpse over at him before we're both laughing uncontrollably.

'It was a good night, I had fun,' he says, his laughter simmering, and I smile, looking out at the horizon. My mind drifts, thinking about his tall, muscular body carrying me over to the sofa and lying me down on the bed, making me feel things in the most intense of ways. His lips consuming mine, every touch sending my senses into overdrive, leaving me breathless and entirely under his spell.

'Yeah, so did I.' My thoughts switch, changing to the softer, more vulnerable side of him, when he unlocked the door to his secret room, showing me his drawings and sketches. Exposing a part of him nobody else knows about. A part of him he doesn't want anybody else knowing about. Apart from me.

Our delicious cakes are eaten in minutes, the tranquil view capturing our attentions as we stare out in a contented silence. I feel a tickle and my eyes flicker down to see his pinky lightly brushing my own on the rock. I swallow the lump in my throat and lift my gaze, but I'm not really concentrating on the beautiful blue sky, the only thing I'm focusing on is how I'm going to word this.

'Jackson?'

'That's me.'

'This thing that's going on between us…'

'Oh, there's a thing?'

We glance at each other and his eyebrow quirks cheekily. I press my lips together.

'I don't know, is there?'

A beat of silence fills the air around us. It needs to be brought up, otherwise it's going to be a nagging thought whenever I'm around him.

'What's on your mind?' he asks more seriously, and I have to look away, his intense stare too much for me to think in a logical sense.

'We've been spending some time together, and for the most part it's been good, and last night was amazing. But, I guess, that's the problem.'

'There's a problem?'

Out the corner of my eye I see his body angle itself towards mine, and I'm tensing even more. My words fail to form in my head, but I open my mouth regardless, praying they'll find cohesion when released into the air.

'This isn't my home, Jackson. I'm going to be leaving at some point, and London's quite far, the University of Sunderland even farther, and I don't think I could get into anything too serious. I know how long-distance things work… they don't. But I also know that it's fairly obvious we can't stay away from each other.' My skin is burning under his gaze and I'm trying desperately not to shrivel up entirely as I express my thoughts. Knowing full well I'm rambling utter nonsense, I reach my point. 'Despite first impressions…' I take a breath. 'I like spending time with you. So, maybe it's best if we just live in the moment, have a bit of fun and enjoy each other's company before I have to leave. I'm probably being presumptuous and overthinking the whole–

'Okay.'

I catch my breath. 'What?'

'Okay.'

'Okay?'

'I agree,' he retorts on a chuckle. 'You're right, we have been spending a lot of time together and I'm enjoying your company too, be it a bit nutty at times, but I agree, let's live in the moment and enjoy what time you have left here. Let's create some happy. God knows, I think we both need it.'

'Yeah?' I wait for his reply, for his final validation that he is truly okay with what's happening between us. His eyes shift from mine to the view pensively and I'm about to ask again, but he replies before I open my mouth.

'Yeah,' he answers, drawing his head back to me on a nod.

I smile gratefully, a weight being lifted. This is good. Like he said, this is what we both need: not serious, but happy. Happy and not serious. 'And can we not mention anything about last night to anyone? I don't want people to get the wrong end of the stick, or start making comments, or get too involved in something which is just between you and me.'

'Emily, you have my word that nothing about last night will pass my lips.' His words match the sincerity in his eyes and I feel myself melt under them.

'Thank you,' I reply, lowering my gaze.

'So,' he says strongly, 'speaking of living in the moment, fancy a dip?'

'I'm not stripping off,' I reply firmly. Imagine if someone were to pass on the clifftops and see me butt naked, I'd be a viral hit before the day was out.

He chuckles. 'You can keep your clothes on, angel.' My eyes follow him as he stands, shaking off his flannel shirt followed by his black T shirt, revealing that strong upper body which renders me extremely weak. 'Although they might get a little wet,' he adds before encouraging Buddy to follow him into the ice-cold sea. I'm thankful he's left his shorts on, otherwise I may have had heart failure. He's far too attractive for his own good.

His yelps and cries make me giggle as he charges into the water, pulling his arms across his chest. 'Nice?' I call.

'Oh absolutely, you don't know what you're missing, Em. It's really lovely and warm.'

Watching him playing around with Buddy brings a big grin to my face, and although just looking at the freezing cold water conjures a shudder, seeing him without a care in the world makes me want to join in.

Fuck it!

I slip my Converse and socks off and charge over. As soon as he sees me coming, Buddy darts over and jumps up, splashing me in the process before dashing between Jackson and I excitably. My waist is gripped and I'm shrieking as my body is swung around. As soon as I'm up, I'm dropped, the cold striking me like sharp pins. In return, I catch him by surprise, thrusting a torrent of seawater over him, soaking his chest.

His mouth falls agape. 'If it's a fight you want, then it's a fight you shall have.' Squatting down, his arms vanish, and my eyes widen when he looks up at me with a cheeky glint. I suddenly regret my decision.

'Ah, Jackson, I'm sorry, please–

His arms drive the water up and I instantly recoil, my white top and shorts drenched. My angry glare meets his amused face and he shrugs casually.

'You asked for it. You can't say I didn't warn you. I said they might get wet.'

Over his shoulder, Buddy is eyeing a seagull next to the rock, and from past experience, I know what's about to happen, so I concoct my plan. On cue, Buddy's barks echo around the open air and Jackson's head darts to the commotion. It's then I take my chance. Running at him – as fast as my legs under the water will allow – I leap onto his back. The surprise blow catches him off guard and he tumbles to the floor, taking me with him.

I land on top of him, the small but strong waves crashing over us and making it incredibly difficult for me to move, let alone stand up. It's not helped by the fact that we're both laughing hysterically.

I manage to roll off him and he finds a way of getting to his knees, his hair dripping as he flicks his amused emeralds down to me, sparking more laughter. He finds his feet and I lift my arms in the air. His palms secure themselves on my own before hauling me from the sandy ground with so much ease it's scary. My clothes are sopping, my hair is ringing, but I'm still laughing. His eyebrows raise on his grinning face and I shrug.

'You asked for it,' I say brazenly.

'How are you going to explain that to Mags?' he asks, pointing to my soaking clothes.

'I'll say I fell over.'

He snorts. 'Right, good luck with that.' He ruffles his hair, but it's his eyes running over my body which causes me to shiver. 'Nice bra, haven't seen that one before.'

I look down, covering my see-through chest with my arms, but then remember he saw way more than that last night, so drop them, punching his rock-hard abs when he laughs.

He captures my eyes, locking me in place. A couple of wet curls have fallen on either side of his face and I smile, because simply looking at him, just gazing into his sparkly eyes, fills me with a joy that I can't explain. His wet hands snake around my soaking waist as I feel us inching closer. My body instantly reacts to him; my heart beats faster and my breaths turn heavier as his lips brush against mine. I stand on my tippy-toes to press them together, but frustratingly they never meet. Instead we break away, grumbling in distaste as Buddy shakes his wet fur vigorously, covering us both in wet sand.

'Lovely, Bud, thank you,' I say, and he stares up at us, panting happily and obliviously.

Jackson grins down at him. 'Come on, Buddy, I'll race you back!' His enthusiastic tone resonates with my pup, because his tail starts wagging frantically as he jerks into a stance as though raring to go. And they take off.

'I'll carry everything back, shall I?' I call out as I watch them race away.

'Thanks, Em!' he cries back.

'Don't let him get too close to the road!'

Jackson throws a hand up in acknowledgement. A small smile forms on my lips as I pick up our rubbish, my shoes and Jackson's clothes before sauntering back and eyeing them playing in the distance.

It's best to keep him at arm's length, away from the crap in my life. He can't know why I'm here or be involved or associated with me when I do leave, because everything I touch goes wrong. I intend to keep him well away from the world I've been forced into. His life has already been beyond tough, I can't drag him down further. But along with that, I must selfishly protect my heart. I refuse to feel the pain of leaving him only to be a forgotten memory – another number to his list of girls.

Yet, I also know that he's right. I do need happy in my life, and he might just be the key. He agreed that we should live in the moment and not let whatever this is deepen, but I can't help feeling apprehensive.

Spending time with him is dangerous… however it's impossible not to.

I'm at a crossroads. The smiles, the excitement and the happiness he creates which bubble inside all fuse together, and that's when I realise something.

A part of me doesn't want to leave.

# TWENTY-EIGHT

The happiness grew over the coming days. Secret meetings on the beach of an evening, taking Buddy for walks, playing Scrabble at his place – which has bumped up my score, we're now even at 3-3 – and watching him surf on my morning runs as the sun rises has been the best of all. I know Aunt Maggie is aware of how much time we've been spending together, but she hasn't mentioned anything to me about it, and I'm relieved she's trying her best to stick to her word about not prying, even though I know it's killing her.

I have spoken to Han a number of times – she's been keen to inform that her relationship with Shawn is slowly blossoming – and my friendship with Vicki and Lily, and consequently Dex and James has also grown, they've taken me in and looked after me. We've been for dinner in Rockstone and to the cinema – which was basically me and my popcorn sat in the middle of two couples snogging, but the movie was enjoyable, not that they would know. Dex crafted a joke about me fifth wheeling, which cued Lily's beady nose. She said I should invite *mystery guy* to hang out with us. I declined, obviously, repeating over and over that he's from London and it's still early days. Little do they know he's already a big part of their lives.

Jackson's Polaroid has come in handy, and I now

have a sizeable collection of photos. My favourite is one of Jackson and Buddy on the rocks; Buddy perched between Jackson's legs, the latter grinning as my happy boy smothers him with sloppy kisses.

I read in a woman's magazine a while ago that sex is the biggest contributing factor in making a woman fall deeply in love with a man. And I'm very conscious of how he can make me feel, so I've been holding out with all my might to fight that urge. However, I'm only a teenage girl, and in a moment of weakness this morning, he was too bloody hard to resist.

Our pants echo around the room as I collapse from on top of him.

'Fuck,' he gasps, running his hands through his hair.

'Yep,' I puff, staring at the ceiling. I can feel my heart pounding in my chest. Who needs to run? This is far more enjoyable cardio.

'Food?' he asks, his head shifting to glance at me.

'Food,' I agree with a curt bob of my head.

I pick up his crumpled white T shirt from the end of the bed, slipping it over my head as he pulls on his boxers. Believe it or not, I only came round to pick up my watch I left here yesterday after a very intense Scrabble game, but his continued jokey behaviour of him treating me like an angel led to him attaching the watch to my wrist himself. All it took was a stroke of my hand, tickles of his fingertips running up my arm and one intense locking of our eyes for it to spiral. Worst of all… I don't feel any regret.

'What would, Madam, like?'

I follow him to the kitchen and rest my back against the breakfast bar. 'Scrambled eggs and bacon wouldn't go a miss,' I reply, smiling as I watch him fumble about in the cupboards.

'Coming right up.' He pulls a packet of bacon rashers from the fridge and takes the frying pan from the drawer before flicking his eyes over to me. There's an expression on his face and I can't tell what it is, which bothers me.

'What?' I ask as he drums the side with his fingers, watching me intently.

'Nothing.'

'Jackson,' I press.

'You're glowing.' He steps up to me, resting his hands on my hips. My skin naturally heats under his touch. 'I like seeing you in my shirt... you look irresistible,' he whispers close to my ear, making the warmth transform into tingles which dance up my spine.

My lips curl as my eyes dart down sheepishly.

'I know you hate compliments, but I can't help it. How am I supposed to control myself when you're like this?'

I laugh flippantly. 'You channel your inner human, rather than the animal.'

He ponders. 'Animal, huh? Like a bear?' He smirks.

'More like a crazed ape.'

'I think I'm more like a lion, you know, majestic, strong...' he hooks his hands under my thighs and hoists me onto the side, 'fierce,' he rasps into my mouth.

I giggle as he growls before attacking my neck with kisses.

'Okay, okay,' I laugh uncontrollably. After gripping either side of his head, I pull him back to look at me, he pries open my legs with his, stepping between them. They react automatically, wrapping around his waist as he leans down, pressing his lips into mine. My senses dance. Feeling his hands running up and down my back, mine move to the nape of his neck, pulling him closer. They run down to his chest, grazing over his nipples, to his abs, before travelling behind and resting on his bum. He squeezes my hips making me moan into the kiss. That's when I have to force myself away.

Breathless, I move my hands to his shoulders and hold him back. 'Are you on one today?'

'Emily, it has been almost four days since I had you, you're killing me,' he declares, brushing the top of his nose across mine.

'We've just done it.'

'Once isn't enough,' he says, shaking his head as he kisses along my jaw. I have to fight back conceding to the pleasure he's engulfing me in.

'We're in agreement. We said we wouldn't get too deep,' I breathe feebly.

'Yes,' he murmurs, 'but we also said we'd live in the moment and have fun. This is fun, isn't it?'

Damn, he has me on my own words.

I feel his hand slither up my thigh, up his shirt to cup my breasts. He's pushed against me, and I'm melting into him, his tongue rolling around my neck. 'Fuck, okay. You win,' I gasp, unable to find my will to stop. Surrendering, I pull his lips back to mine once again.

'I'm telling you, Eleanor, I heard Mum mention it.'

Our kissing halts, Jackson drawing back as we stare at each other, listening closely.

'Dex, you're not getting a car for Christmas,' a female voice says as their footsteps grow louder.

My eyes widen and Jackson scrambles backwards before helping me off the side. We stand in silence, watching Dex and a young girl stride in through the door behind us and around the kitchen counter. They're both arguing about something, but I'm too busy trying to figure out how to stand to listen in. I decide on clasping my hands in front of me, covering the vitals which I'm scared may be visible through Jackson's white shirt. The awkwardness hits like a snake slithering around my neck when the girl clocks us, but Dex is still blissfully unaware of our presence as they approach the fridge. The brown-haired girl is smiling clumsily as he rummages through Jackson's food, rambling about how there's nothing to eat in the house. Jackson's hands are clamped over his crotch, and I have to bite the inside of my cheek to stifle a nervous giggle.

Eventually, Dex turns around, a flapjack square held to his mouth. He pauses, his eyes flicking between us. 'Right. I take it from the happiness that is radiantly showing downstairs,' he points the hand holding the flapjack down to Jackson's enveloped hands, before moving it across to me, 'and your attire, Emily's not just here to say hello.'

We're silent and I purse my lips, lowering my uncomfortable gaze.

'Don't look Ellie, it's perversion gone mad, not for the delicate eyes of a fourteen-year-old.' He throws his hand over her eyes, but Eleanor appears exasperated by his actions and pushes it away.

Jackson jumps straight in, completely ignoring the fact his friend, who seems far too relaxed, has caught us. 'Why are you stealing my food? What's wrong with your fridge?'

'Did you not hear me over your sexual fondling?'

Eleanor butts in, rolling her eyes at Dex before answering for him in a more pleasant manner. 'It's big shop day and Mum still hasn't been.'

'Our fridge is bare. Just like you two,' Dex points, chomping down on Jackson's flapjack.

'I'm Eleanor, by the way, Ellie for short,' Dex's sister says, grinning in my direction.

'Emily.' I smile back.

'Sorry about my brother, we think he was dropped on his head as a baby… several times.'

'That has never been proven,' Dex defends, pushing her arm lightly.

'The proof is standing right next to me,' Ellie fires back, shoving him harder.

'Alright, come on, take your food and go,' Jackson says, bravely moving one hand from his excited manhood to shoo Dex away.

Thankfully, he surrenders. 'Okay, okay… you're coming to the barbeque later though, aren't you?' he asks as he treads away.

'Yes, I'm coming.'

'You're coming too, Emily,' he affirms, taking another bite of the snack as his sister ushers him to the door.

'Nice to meet you, Emily,' she says.

'You too, Ellie,' I call.

'Bye, Em, love you,' Dex cries just as he's pushed into the main house.

'Bye, Dex,' I giggle.

How can his fourteen-year-old sister be so much more mentally advanced than him?

I turn to Jackson who shakes his head as I laugh. But my eyes soon narrow as a spark lights a thought in my mind. 'He wasn't surprised,' I ponder aloud. Jackson is silent and I sigh. 'You told him, didn't you?'

He looks at me guiltily, his eyes wide like a lost puppy.

'Jackson!' I groan.

'I'm sorry. He came down to watch the match last night and saw your watch on the side, I couldn't think quick enough. Besides, he's like my brother, I tell him everything.'

'So much for keeping it between us,' I say, cursing myself for forgetting it.

'He won't say anything to anyone, I promise.'

'You're sure?'

'If he does, I'll put his head on a stick.' He grins, stepping into me and I roll my eyes, a smile dancing on my lips. His fingers gently grip my chin, tilting my head to meet his gaze before taking me by surprise. He scoops me up, spawning squeals as he throws me onto the bed. 'Now, where were we?' he asks, propping himself up on his elbow and hovering above me.

'I think you were about to cook me some lovely eggs.'

'I've got a better idea.' His big hand finds my thigh as his mouth lowers to my neck, kissing it sweetly. I have to dig extremely deep to find my inner will power, after all, my stomach is grumbling.

'I think I'll take the food. You can cook whilst I powder my nose.' His displeased face lifts. 'Do you want to be the cause of my UTI?'

His eyes tighten as he grouses into my shoulder. Struggling to hold back my amusement, I push him away and roll off the bed, smiling smugly as I stand and face him with my arms folded. He sighs, flopping face down into the mattress before rolling himself off too. His feet reluctantly drag him back over to the hob. My smile widens, because he's like a stroppy child who's just been told he can't play with his toys.

'Who knows,' I say, my eyes lowered as I trace the outlines of the marble specks on the counter with my fingertips, 'if the breakfast is up to scratch, there might be a little reward.'

He swivels on the spot, his eyebrow quirked. I laugh, enjoying the sight of him dancing around the kitchen, preparing our food with incredible speed.

# TWENTY-NINE

The bed frame creaks as I balance my knee against the wooden back. With my left foot on its tiptoes, my arm stretched as far as it can go, I wish I'd listened to my nanny and eaten my greens as a child. I could really do with being an inch taller, at least while I try and complete this arduous task.

I grunt as I smooth the tape down on the wall over the middle section of my fairy lights. My hand flops onto the bed frame as I sigh, pushing myself into a standing position on the mattress with my hands on my hips. After a satisfied exhale, I leap off the bed, bouncing over to the plug socket in the corner and flicking the switch. The subtle lights twinkle above my bed, making the room noticeably prettier. My eyes glance over to the collection of Polaroid photos stuck to the wall on my right, and then to the glowing candles on the freshly dusted window ledge.

'Perfect,' I say, smiling proudly. My own little touches to my own little room.

Knowing I'm going to be here for the foreseeable future, I decided to take matters into my own hands, making my bedroom homier and cosier. And I reckon I succeeded. I even unpacked my suitcase.

A rather startling feeling has taken over my body quite recently, and it's been strengthening over these past few days. Happiness has been a relatively distant emotion for the most part of my life, but right now, it's never been stronger. Settling contentedly in my gut.

Never wavering though, is the feeling of doubt. The feeling that because I'm finally cheerful and contented, there is something bad lurking in the shadows ready to jump out and gobble me up. As small as it may be, it's still there. But I'm desperately trying to overlook that doubt. However strong it may become, I refuse to let it ruin my decent mood. As agreed, not only with Jackson, but with me, myself and I also, I'm living in the moment, and for now, that moment is good. Screw anything else.

I grab Aunt Maggie's gas lighter borrowed for the candles, and sellotape from the window ledge, before sauntering out. My phone buzzes in my back pocket.

'Hello, Lily,' I answer, putting her on speaker as I stalk across the landing and begin my descent down the stairs.

'Hey, Em. Dex told me he told you about the barbeque later.'

I freeze, biting my lip in fear. I hope that's all he told her. 'Yeah, he did… well, he mentioned it.'

'We're all meeting on the beach at six.' Her tone is her usual chirpy self, there's nothing to suggest any different and I'm satisfied she doesn't know. That means though, that because Jackson is going too, we'll have to act normal, which may prove difficult. My body responds to him automatically, even when I'm trying my best to control it, and I don't want to let anything on, especially in front of a big group of people. I'm suddenly tense.

'I'll have to see if Aunt Maggie's got anything planned for dinner.'

'Come on, Em, you have to be there. There'll be free booze,' she tempts.

Oh, what the hell! I'm sure it'll be fine. 'You've convinced me, I'll see you there!'

She whoops and I laugh. 'You're the best, love you!'

'You too,' I call before we hang up. I'm thinking of it as another way to shake off the shadow of doubt and build up 'the happy', a barbeque on the beach will be nice. And now I've put a stop to my overthinking, I'm excited to be spending time with the people I can call my friends.

I reach the bottom of the stairs, but my feet pull up. Leaning against bannister post, I hear Aunt Maggie's voice travelling down the hallway from the kitchen. And it's not her usual chipper tone.

'You said you would stop this,' she hisses. 'If I had known I would never have left her with you. You've put her in danger and you've lied about it, not just to me, but to your own daughter.'

I hold my breath, trying to stay as quiet as possible as I listen to her words.

'It's time you told her the truth.' She pauses as she waits for the person on the other end to reply. 'And what if the same thing happens to her? Tell me how you would live with yourself. You finish it and you finish it now!' Her anger is mounting. Anger which might see a glass or plate thrown at the wall. I tread carefully down the hall and stop just before the kitchen door. 'Don't give me that, you're the one...' Buddy's yelp halts Aunt Maggie's scolding and makes me gasp as I jump in surprise. I was so conscious of not being heard or seen, I wasn't fully concentrating on my surroundings and as my foot moved forward an inch, I trod on Buddy's tail. 'Oh, Pidge,' she says cautiously, throwing the landline onto the side.

'Who was that?' I question, trying to mask my confusion. I know who it was.

Buddy drags himself over to his bed in the corner as Aunt Maggie's mouth parts, but there's no response. She stands awkwardly. It's scaring me a little, because she's usually so quirky and quick-witted, but I'm looking at her now and it's like her character has shifted entirely. Her shoulders are tense, her fists clenched, her eyes narrowed; she's on edge. 'It was your father, he was just checking in,' she says, unconvincingly blasé.

It didn't sound like a casual checking in. And since when does Dad speak to Aunty directly? Guy's the middleman and has been throughout this whole trip. Dad and Aunty don't speak. Ever. It just doesn't happen, and I can see why. He clearly makes her very angry. So why now?

I swallow the lump in my throat. I'm slow, I'm so slow.

*If I had known I would never have left her with you. You've put her in danger and you've lied about it, not just to me, but to your own daughter.*

*It's time you told her the truth.*

She knows. Somehow, she's found out that the attack wasn't a one-off by some crazy loon. That's why she's so angry, Dad's just confessed something, if not everything.

I want to ask her. I want to know every single thing, every single secret. It infuriates me that he won't tell me. But that's exactly the point, I want *him* to tell me, to grow some balls and take some responsibility. I don't want to push Aunt Maggie and make her feel any worse than she probably does now. I don't want to make her madder or more upset, because if she now knows who attacked me, then there's a possibility she knows what they have against Dad and how they relate to Mum.

So, I hold back. I nod passively, a small smile tugging on my lips as I try with all my might to let my thoughts wash over me. Don't let this ruin your mood. Forget about it. You know Dad only causes issues and drama, what else is new? Push it away.

'I was about to make Guy a cup of tea, do you want one?' She sniffs, filling the kettle and placing it back on the gas ring. She's trying to act normal, but there's now an awkward air around us.

I clear my throat, relaxing my neck and shoulders before moving over to the drawer to put the lighter and Sellotape away. 'Yes, please,' I reply, keeping my vision lowered to avoid any uncomfortable eye contact.

'Go and put your feet up, I'll bring it in,' she says, watching the kettle boil. She sounds more like herself, but there's still a hint of something in her voice, there's still something wrong. 'Guy's in there already.'

My eyes dart up to her. 'Guy's *here*? As in, in the house?'

She turns around, meeting my wide eyes. 'Yeah.'

'In the living room?'

'Yeah,' she echoes, nodding indifferently.

'Okay.' I smirk, my eyebrows raising.

She strains to bite back her smile but fails. 'Stop it,' she says, throwing her hand at me, a grin on her face.

'I'm not saying a word.' I back towards the door, smiling at her reply.

'Good.'

I step into the hallway and my face falls, thinking back to Dad and the mess surrounding him which he's managing to burden us all with.

I take a deep breath before entering the living room. My eyes catch Guy sat to the oak table at the back of the room. He's sifting through several pieces of paper which look like separate newspaper cuttings.

'You're slowly becoming part of the furniture, Guy.'

He glances across the room abruptly, gathering up the pages and stuffing them in his trucker jacket pocket. 'Sorry, Miss Lambert.'

'It's okay, I didn't mean anything by it. I don't think Aunty has any qualms with you being here, do you?' My lips quirk and he mirrors. 'May I?' I ask, pointing to the chair next to him at the head of the table.

He nods, offering with his hand. 'Please.'

I shuffle the chair back and plop down. 'What were you reading?' I ask, tucking myself under.

'Oh, just some old newspaper stories I found in the hotel,' he brushes off, clasping his hands together in front of him.

'Anything interesting?'

'Marginally.'

'Can I see?' I question, simply to make conversation more than anything else. His nose wrinkles and he shakes his head.

'It's probably nothing of interest to you, miss. Ten-year-old sports results, that sort of thing.'

'Ah. Well, I happen to be into sports. Watching, not playing, mind you.' I grin, expecting one back, but he just releases a short chuckle, avoiding eye contact. My eyes lower. He's off too. I'm starting to wonder if I should take my tea upstairs and occupy myself before the barbeque, but a shift in my gaze and a search of the face of the casually dressed man prompts another idea. 'Do you have a family, Guy? Wife and kids?' I have no idea where the question comes from, it's something I've been curious about, but I never planned on asking him.

His small brown eyes meet mine. 'No, miss, the wife and I divorced a long time ago. No children, she never wanted them. Always said they would ruin her figure.' His facial expression remains neutral, and it's unnerving just how poised he can be even when discussing the most personal and paining of topic.

'I'm sorry,' I say, purely because I don't know what else to offer back.

His head shakes faintly. 'Don't be, these things happen.'

'You loved her though?' I receive a blank look and immediately scorn myself. 'Sorry, that's private, I don't know why I'm asking. Ignore me.' My hands run along the smooth oak table, now wishing I hadn't opened my mouth at all.

'Yes, I did.' My surprised blues meet his composed brown eyes. 'Very much. But sometimes it doesn't work out, and for most people, like in my case, it's for the best. We weren't right for each other, and that's okay. There was a point where I couldn't do enough for her, but things change and that can't be helped.'

I'm shocked at his depth, and the reasoning as to why I even posed the question is revealing itself to me. 'Did you ever lie to her?'

His gaze lowers, but when he nods they lift again, as if he took a second to collect himself. 'Yes, I'm ashamed to admit, I did. Nothing big, just little white's, but, I suppose, in the end they all add up, don't they?'

'Did you ever confess those lies to her?'

He scoffs, laughing lightly. 'Oh, she already knew, she could always tell when an untruth passed my lips.'

'If she didn't know, though, would you have told her?' I keep pushing, searching for the comforting answer I want; that this is something everyone does to the people they love. That it's not just me who has been left in the dark.

'What's this about?' he asks, his disorderly eyebrows furrowing.

I swallow. 'Nothing. Nothing, I don't know.' My vision drifts to the table finding interest in a random black marking engraved in the surface.

'Something, or rather, someone is playing on your mind. It's your father, isn't it?'

I don't reply, instead I rest my chin in my palm and stare across the table to the cream coloured wall. He's right. He's always right.

'Listen,' he leans forward, 'stop me if this is too intrusive, but I've seen the resentment you have for him, and I honestly believe deep down he's not the man he comes across as being. He cares about you an awful lot, and I've seen first-hand the worry and pressure he's felt to keep you safe. After all, all a father wants is the safety and happiness of their child.' He pauses, musingly. 'No matter how formidable and unrelenting a man can be.'

My eyes flicker to his straight face. 'I wish I could see him the way you do, Guy.'

His chest expands as he sighs. 'Your father has been kind to me. He took me under his wing during one of the darkest times in my life through my divorce. In fact, if it wasn't for him, I may not have been here to talk to you today, and for that, well, there is no greater debt. I have a lot of respect for him.' I sense a waver in his voice and I have to double take, glancing back over at him. His expression is the same as it always is, but his eyes are no longer unreadable. There's sorrow behind them, and I feel awful for making him think back to what was clearly a terrible time.

'That makes one person,' I murmur, not dwelling on his admission for my own selfish reasons, I'm not sure what I would do if he broke down in front of me.

'I believe there is good in his heart, it's just been so long since it's made an appearance that he's forgotten how to show it. Nonetheless, it is there.'

I never thought anyone would make me feel differently towards my father, but this man I've known only three weeks, who I've spoken to very little, through the power of his words and the strength in his tone, has sparked a glimmer of hope in my heart I never knew could exist. And this shocks me. 'You honestly think so?'

He nods curtly, his eyes now welcoming and warm. 'I honestly do.'

A small smile appears on my lips. 'Thank you, Guy,' I say gratefully. 'And call me Emily.'

'Of course… Emily.' He chuckles. 'I appreciate it.'

My fingers drum the table. I can hear Aunt Maggie pottering about in the kitchen, no doubt piling a plate high with an ensemble of biscuits.

'Emily,' my focus aligns back on Guy, my first name sounding foreign in the air, 'while on the concept of good hearts, I'm going to admit that I told one of my white lies.'

My eyes try to read his face – they fail. 'When?'

'When you walked into the room.' He reaches into his breast pocket, rustling the newspaper cuttings. 'These aren't old sports results.' I watch him intently as he places them in a line in front of me. My mind ticks, racing to understand what he could possibly be showing me, but as he begins to elaborate and I start to read, my mouth dries and my pulse quickens. 'Being a security protection guard to one of the most influential and highest ranked lawyers in the country, means if there's one skill I have mastered, it's being able to read people. I know when someone's lying, I know when someone is hiding something, and I know when a situation or a person is suspicious.'

My eyes scan the articles, my chest tightening as I try to not only listen, but hear exactly what Guy is saying whilst attempting to process the words on the three jagged-edged pages.

'I get a certain feeling,' he continues, 'and there's one person in particular who's sparked my interest, and apparently, yours too. I've been looking into the lifeguard, Jackson Turner.'

My chest expands as I grapple with the air to ease my aching lungs. What is this?

'Before I go any further, I want you to know I only have your welfare at heart, and this is only to make you mindful, I'm not claiming to know everything about him.'

'What are these, Guy?' I press, not taking my eyes away from the dirty, old and partly smudged words.

'They're news articles from November 2015.'

I read over the words in bold – over and over and over. However, it's like my mind is spinning as I try to grasp what they're telling me.

*Woman in critical condition after incident*
*in London tower block.*
*Woman rushed to hospital with stab wounds.*

His voice forces its way into the forefront of my mind. His words from that night on the clifftop.

*'My life took another turn, because of my own decisions. I made some bad fucking decisions, Emily.'*

'There was an incident in London, Shoreditch. A woman was stabbed several times, and there were two arrests made that night. Now, it doesn't name anyone on the earlier articles, but I found one online published at a later date.' Guy slides the relevant news article frontwards. 'It identifies one of those arrests as–

'Jackson,' I breathe, barely. I don't even have to glance at the page to know what it says. It's like my throat has closed up. 'Who… who was the woman?' I struggle to ask.

'Her name was Collette Bridges, however searching online I couldn't find very much on her fate, going off where the incident took place, I'd say a lot of these types of cases occurred there. The press would have most likely moved onto the next story. But there is something else, the police found drugs in the flat at which it happened.'

I can't speak. I knew he was mysterious. I knew there was a history behind those deep emerald eyes, but newsworthy history? It seems absurd that the man I've come to know and genuinely like has this horrifying story associated with him, yet it's sitting right here, right in front of my eyes.

'As I said, I'm not claiming to know who he is or exactly what befell here, all I can go off is what I've read. I'm not telling you to stay away, all I'm asking is that you be vigilant. My duty of care is to you. *You* are my priority.'

'Are you saying he's a threat?' I ask, managing to find my voice, although it's shallow.

'No,' he points at the torn article closest to him, 'but there's a past here, Emily, and in my years of working for your father, I've come to learn that it doesn't matter who you are or what type of person you become, pasts catch up to people. So, I'm asking you to be careful.'

I stare blankly at the articles, not taking anything in. My mind not allowing information to be processed. Aunt Maggie calls from the hallway. Guy swiftly scoops up the papers from under my nose, putting them securely back into his pocket with my eyes remaining on the table where they had been.

'Everything okay in here?' Her tray rattles as her footsteps approach from behind. 'What have you two been nattering about?'

The tray is placed down in front of us. My eyes follow it, but my mind is elsewhere. It's recalling the night he told me about his father leaving him and his mother... he looked haunted. I had questions then; I have even more now. Including the major one: who was Jackson Turner before he came to Marshlyn Bay?

'Nothing really, just chewing the fat, weren't we, Emily?' Guy replies as Aunt Maggie hands out our mugs and my head bobs slowly.

I gulp down my tea, but it doesn't wash away the swelling doubt circling my core.

# *THIRTY*

'Hello!'

I shoot up from the sofa, switching the TV off. I'd been so engrossed in some random animal documentary I hadn't heard the front door being opened. I rush out of the living room and the accustomed warmth swirls in my tummy when our eyes lock.

'Hey,' I say, grinning widely.

'Anyone home?' he asks, shifting his eyes cagily around the hall and up the stairs.

'No, Maggie and Guy left about ten minutes ago.'

It's around four in the afternoon, Aunt Maggie needed to get a couple of things from the supermarket and Guy offered to take her, so apart from Buddy, I have been home alone. And I desperately wanted to see him.

'Good.' Stalking up to me, Jackson's hand jerks my arm, tugging me into him. His moistened lips consume mine, kissing me hungrily like it's been days since we last touched rather than hours. My hands travel up his body and back down his arms where they knock something, making a crunching sound. I pull back, my eyes narrowing as they lower.

'What's in the bag?' I ask, searching his smiling face.

'A present,' he murmurs, and I can't help the cheeky grin which spreads on my face.

'For me?'

'Who else?'

He reaches into the brown paper bag. At first I'm confused as to what it is, because all I see is a white feather, but when the whole object is unveiled my heart swells.

'It's a dream catcher,' he says, holding it up in the air with the string at the top hooked around his index finger. 'For your bad dreams. I know it's all superstitious crap and it's more decorative than anything else, but I thought it would be nice to have above your bed, and it might give you some comfort.'

The circular centre connects tiny intertwining gemstones with long white feathers cascading off glistening crystals attached to short cotton strings. It will go beautifully above my bed.

'I love it, thank you,' I say, beaming up at him. This is why I wanted to see him, because in spite of everything Guy showed me, this is the person I know. I needed to remind myself of the Jackson I've come to understand and appreciate. Whatever's happened to him in the past, as curious and intrigued as I am, I know the person he is today, and that person is good. If the moment arises and we talk about it then fine, but as of now, I'm not going to let it discourage my opinion of him, because I don't know the full story. I don't know what happened, and as I gaze up at him, all smiley and happy and handsome, I don't want to know. All that matters is now. Living in the moment, we agreed. So that's what I plan on doing.

'You're more than welcome,' he says as I press the tip of my index finger to his. He tilts his hand, the string sliding smoothly onto mine. Squeezing my hips, he connects our lips again, humming into the kiss. He slowly breaks away, scanning my face with a smug expression before stepping backwards and leaping up the stairs two at a time.

I'm left breathless and puzzled. 'Where are you going?' I shout, hoping he's going to say the bedroom. But that hope diminishes very quickly.

'Might as well fix this hot tap while I'm here, she's been badgering me about it for weeks,' he calls down.

My lips pucker and with a roll of my eyes I slog up the stairs behind him.

'So, you're a lifeguard, an architect, and a plumber,' I say, leaning against the bathroom door frame with my arms folded across my chest. Jackson's sitting in the bathtub, fiddling with the tap.

He mumbles something around the screwdriver clenched between his teeth.

'Pardon?'

He takes the tool from his mouth casually. 'A man of many talents,' he repeats, screwing the back of the tap.

'Oh.' I'm bored, and watching him concentrate whilst skilfully using his tools is very much a turn on. When I messaged him to come over, this wasn't what I had planned. 'How long is this going to take?'

Muffled noises become trapped in his mouth which is holding the screwdriver once again.

'Excuse me?' I press, more exasperated than the previous as I lean forwards and scrunch my face. He garbles something in reply and I huff. 'Can you speak properly?'

He frees the tool. 'I'm finished now,' he says just as a gush of water leaks from the tap, soaking his work shorts. 'Bollocks!' His hands fly out and he jolts back from the shock.

My giggles fill the room and I'm met with an unamused scowl. 'At least they're designed for water,' I laugh. 'I'll get you a towel.' He grunts as he hoists himself up.

Opening the drawer to where the towels are usually kept, my brow furrows when I don't see any fluffy white material. Aunt Maggie must've done a wash. 'I'll check the airing cupboard.' Leaving him standing like he's crapped himself, I amble onto the landing and over to the door in the corner, before searching the shelves for anything which resembles a towel. Finding nothing other than some old clothes and a sewing kit, I roll onto the balls of my feet and stretch my arm to fumble around the top shelves above eye level. Satisfied when I feel something soft, I yank it down, but what I wasn't prepared for was the clatter of a solid object.

My feet scuttle back in surprise. With the towel in my grasp, I bend down to pick up what looks to be a hardback book face down on the carpet. Only, when I turn it over, I find that it isn't a book, not in the literature sense, but an album. A photo album. On the front, waves of bright colour drift from left to right, and in the middle the word, 'Memories', is inscribed in bold lettering.

Vaguely aware of what might be inside, my heart begins to hammer in my chest. My legs find the strength to straighten, but as I turn to the first page, I fear they're going to collapse in a heap. There's a picture; the left side black and blank, but on the right, a single photograph, sealed behind a sheet of cellophane. Aunt Maggie, me... Mum. My lips part as a shaky breath escapes. I turn to the next page, this time Mum is sat on a bench outside Aunt Maggie's old house, holding me as a newborn in her arms; her long blonde hair curly and blowing across her face, her dazzling smile wide, making her look naturally beautiful.

I'm only aware that my feet have intuitively moved back to the bathroom when I faintly hear Jackson's voice. 'The things I do for that woman,' he mumbles as I throw him the towel whilst remaining transfixed on the photo album. Picture after picture of Aunt Maggie, Mum, Dad, Uncle Jerry and me. As the pages turn it shows me growing up, from a tiny, wrinkly babe, to a cheeky, energetic four-year-old. And then the photos stop.

'What's that?' Jackson asks, patting down his leg.

'A photo album,' I reply dejectedly, studying an image of Dad and I feeding the ducks by a lake somewhere.

'Don't tell me there are pictures of a young Mags in there? I bet they're hilarious,' he chuckles, but I don't reply or even glance up. My legs finally give in, my back sliding down the bathroom cupboard until I'm sat on the cold tiled floor. 'Em?' he utters, the humour in his tone vanishing.

'I've never seen these before,' I say, flicking my eyes over the pages.

'What are they?' he asks softly, joining me on the bathroom floor, the towel scrunched in his lap. He peers down at the album resting in the middle of my legs.

'That's my mum,' I say, pointing to the blonde woman laughing next to a younger looking Maggie in a kitchen I vaguely recognise. I feel his gaze lift to my face after studying the page.

'Now I know where you get your good looks from.'

The shortest of scoffs leaves my mouth and my head shifts to focus on him. His face is close to mine, a small reassuring smile is present on his lips and my eyes draw up, taking in his warm sparkling emeralds. I know he's empathising with me, he doesn't need to use his words, because the sad but gentle and encouraging look in his compassionate eyes tells me that it's okay. And after a couple of seconds of losing myself in them, the pain in my heart, although still there, lessons, creating a soothing feeling, a consoling feeling that I'm seeing Mum in images I've never seen before. That she's not a figment of my imagination. That she truly existed with me.

I swallow, glancing back down. 'I never had any photos of her at home. Only one, on my bedside table, it was of me and her. I took it with me when I moved in with William.' I gather myself, not allowing my thoughts to drift to him.

Jackson seems to tense briefly at the mention of my ex-boyfriend, but he soon relaxes, brushing the comment away. 'What happened to the others?'

A pump of pain circles my heart as I try to remember a time when our home wasn't empty; before any trace of her vanished. But I can't. The memories have been washed away, just as she has. 'Dad got rid of them all. I don't know where he put them, but I guess it was too painful for him to see her face around the house.' I turn to the next page. There's a print of me where I must be around two or three. I'm sat on a big brown sofa, my face smothered in chocolate as I shovel more of the treat into my mouth. Jackson chuckles and I grin at the state of myself.

'Nothing's changed,' he says, and I elbow him in the side playfully.

My smile drops when I turn to the last page; the final photo causing a lump to form in my throat. Mum, Dad, and little Emily in the middle, all stood next to a very short and stout snowman, but we're all beaming proudly at our creation. This is the first time, from which I can remember, I have seen Dad's genuine smile. I sniff, the emotion building within me until Jackson nudges my arm.

'Hey,' he murmurs. I tear my focus away from the photo. He offers me a small smile and I return it, extremely thankful to have him by my side. My eyes narrow when I see his shift into quizzical squints. 'What's that?' His fingers pinch something sticking out from the back of the album, something which, whilst being so consumed by all the images, I hadn't spotted. He slides out a folded piece of paper. Opening it up, the bright, scraggly strokes of colour pull my lips up, but also manage to conjure threatening tears. My eyes sting, my vision blurring as I stare at the drawing held delicately in Jacksons fingertips, like he's scared it's going to break or ruin in his grip.

I don't completely remember doodling this, but it is ringing some bells. The very chaotic lines craft up a little girl with short, scruffy blonde hair and a pink triangle shaped dress, she holds hands with an equally shambolic taller figure underneath a squiggly sun in the top corner.

To anyone else this drawing would seem trivial, most likely seeing it as nothing more than a child's attempted portrait, but to me it's so much bigger than that; Mum and I bonded together for a lifetime through my younger self's scrawled masterpiece.

'Little Emily was incredibly cute,' Jackson says, grinning down at the paper in his hands, before I feel his head jerk in my direction when he hears me sniffle. 'Do you want to talk about her?' His voice is low and careful.

'It's impossible to remember all the details, I wish I could, because I know she was an amazing person.'

'I bet she was,' he retorts softly.

'There was a loose flap.' I feel those eyes deeply fixated on my face as I stare vacantly at the photo of the three of us next to the snowman in my lap. It's a photo of her last Christmas. 'It was a few days after New Year's,' I say, sucking in a deep, encouraging breath. 'Dad was out getting fuel and a takeaway for him and Mum, and I was in bed. It must've been just after that, after she'd tucked me in, as she'd walked out and turned to go back downstairs. There was a piece of carpet at the top that had come loose, Dad told me he had been planning on fixing it that weekend. She must've not seen it or forgotten it was there.' I gulp, closing my eyes and allowing a couple of tears to escape. 'Dad said he came home and saw her lying there, at the bottom. He didn't know how long she'd been like that, but given my bedtime and from when he'd left us, he reckoned about an hour or so.'

'Fuck.'

I vaguely hear his whisper over the drum of my heartbeat as he places his hand on top of mine resting on my thigh before squeezing it lightly.

'I don't remember hearing a thing, all I recall is waking up early the next morning to Dad sitting on the end of my bed. His eyes were red and swollen. When I asked where she was, he told me that she wasn't here anymore, that she was in the sky now, looking over us.' My eyes zone in on his large hand over mine as I bite down on my bottom lip, trying to hold back from breaking down entirely. 'There have been moments throughout my life where I've blamed myself and thought it my fault, sometimes I still do. If she hadn't put me to bed… if I hadn't been born.'

'No, Emily,' he tries.

'It's fuzzy, but it's like I remember the dream I had that night. It was as though someone was in my room with me. I like to think it was Mum, coming to say goodbye in my dreams.' I sniff, shaking my head. 'I don't know. It's just so sad. There's not a day that goes by when I don't wish she was still here with me.' My head lifts as I glance up at the white ceiling on a lingering exhale. 'God, I'd give her the biggest hug.'

'She's here.' Our eyes meet, his expression filled with a glowing warmth and compassion. But it's as his fingers wipe away my fallen tears, our gaze entirely locked on one another, when I feel a swell in my chest. 'She'll always be here with you, Emily.' His free hand drifts up my body, stopping over my heart. 'She's your angel.'

I push my cheek into his palm, feeling his comfort transfer itself into me from the heat of his touch. From his chiselled jaw, strikingly mesmeric eyes and boisterous brown hair, to his caring and understanding heart and soul, I'm suddenly envious of all the people who have known him before me, infuriated at anyone who may have disregarded his kind spirit, and resentful over those who have ever gotten this close to him.

I've tried to keep myself emotionally detached from him, but it's becoming increasingly harder to fight. I feel protective over him, I want him all to myself, and every time we're apart I get a powerful urge to be close to him. With his touch on my skin and our eyes connected, it's proving impossible to hold back.

Nevertheless, I won't allow the walls around my heart to collapse, because once they do and I let our closeness intensify, there's a chance I lose him. And you can't lose something you never had. Everyone around me disappears, and I refuse to let him fade from my life now. Not when he's the one holding it together. I've got to be careful.

'Who's that?' he asks, and I notice his eyes have lowered to the picture above the snowman image. Uncle and Aunty.

'Uncle Jerry. He was Aunt Maggie's husband. He died a couple of years after Mum: heart attack. I think that's why she moved here, to get away from the big empty home holding too many memories.' He nods understandingly as I observe Aunty's happy and youthful face. 'I don't know how she's coped all these years, all this death.'

'She's a strong woman,' he says gently.

'Stronger than I'll ever be,' I murmur. It's true, she's been on her own for all this time, she's lived a life far crueler than I, and not once have I heard her complain.

'No, don't you dare. We're all strong, in our own way. You've grown up without your mum, and from what I've gathered, with a pretty shit father, but look at the person you've become.' He hooks his finger under my chin, drawing my head up. 'Love yourself, Emily, because you genuinely deserve to.'

My lips part, my body once again feeling the pull. 'No one's ever said that to me before.'

'Well, now they have.'

My neck cranes before I even register its movement. Hovering in front of his face, our eye contact remains, before my focus is flickering down to his lips. They press together like two pieces of a jigsaw puzzle, the kiss slow and delicate as I savour him. His hand snakes down my body, coming to a stop on my thigh before I blindly close the album and place it beside me. As our kiss deepens, I shift from my position on the floor, Jackson pulling me closer so I'm kneeling in between his legs. My lips move to his neck, kissing and sucking up to his jaw. Every part of me is on fire, his soft moans only intensifying the heat.

The emotion within me seems to be feeding on his touch, every kiss and every graze of my thigh making my need for him grow. Our lips connect again as my fingers grip the bottom of his grey hoodie, briefly pulling away to rid of it before he jerks my face forward, joining our mouths hungrily.

'So fucking beautiful,' he mumbles into the kiss, causing explosions in my chest. I fiddle with the buttons on my white shirt as he begins untucking it from my denim shorts. His hands slide underneath, and a small shiver carrying sweet desire works its way up my spine when he feels every part of my tummy and back. They move to my now revealed bra, cupping my breasts over the thin material. We're in the moment, so consumed by each other, nothing else matters but him.

'Cooey!'

We freeze. Our heavy breaths the only sound in the room. The front door shuts and the thudding of feet on the stairs grows louder. We unfreeze.

'Shit,' we pant, scrambling off the floor.

I quickly slide the photo album under the bathroom cabinet whilst fiercely buttoning my shirt back up. Jackson scurries over to the bathtub, harshly yanking on his hoodie. He climbs in and grabs the screwdriver from the side as he pretends to mend the already restored tap. As I flatten my shirt down, I notice that his hair is messed up more than usual and I pray she doesn't take any notice.

As expected, a sunny face peeps around the door. 'I thought I heard movement, I'm about to put– *Oh*! Jackson.' Her eyes widen as they shoot over to his seated figure in the bathtub.

'Hey, Mags.' He waves and I can tell he's trying to keep his breathing as steady as possible, much like I am.

'How's that tap coming along?' She takes a step into the room.

'Almost done,' he replies, nodding whilst playing with the screwdriver in his hand.

'Fabulous. I'm about to put dinner on, are you staying?' she asks, flicking her gaze between the two of us.

'No, it's okay, we're going to a barbeque later,' I speak for the first time. I feel like I've got guilt written all over my face, we've just been getting frisky on her bathroom floor and although there's no way of her knowing, my mind's conjuring thoughts of her reaction if she found out. I inwardly cringe.

'Alright then, I know when I'm not wanted. Don't go drinking too much, young lady,' she says, pointing a long rigid finger in my direction.

'I'll keep an eye on her, Mags,' Jackson responds with a wink and an irresistible beam. My stomach flutters.

'I know you will.' She smiles back. 'Okay, I'll let you get on.' Her feet shuffle around, but she quickly twizzles back. 'Although, you might want to fix your shirt and hair before you both leave.'

My head darts down to see my buttons askew and immediately my cheeks redden. Aunt Maggie flashes me a knowing glance as she exits the room and I purse my lips, pressing them together as if the force will somehow make this embarrassment more bearable. I glance over to Jackson who is puffing out his cheeks to contain himself. 'As long as you're being safe!' she calls as her steps drum back down the stairs. My mouth is wide open.

The horror!

That's when he blows, the snort and the chortles coming at once. Seeing him in hysterics seems to momentarily overshadow the mortification as it stems my own giggles. My lips stretch into a grin, my shoulders lift, and I throw my head back, the laughter flowing out.

# THIRTY-ONE

The Jeep comes to a halt beside James's black Honda on the car park bank. I watch as he, along with Vicki, Leo and Olivia, climb out. Turning back to Jackson, my pulse quickens as I meet his twinkling eyes zoned in on my face, however I'm swiftly gathering myself appropriately.

'Right. Remember, no touching, no standing or sitting alone together, no lingering stares; eye contact must be kept at two seconds maximum, and most definitely no talking to anyone else specifically about the other – apart from Dex, if you're unaccompanied by everyone else. Okay?'

No sound of acknowledgment passes his lips, only a tiny smirk loiters on them.

'What?'

'Nothing,' he replies with a slight shake of his head, his smirk growing.

'Why are you looking at me like that?'

His body shifts forwards. 'You said no lingering stares, I'm getting it all out while I can.'

'Jackson, it's only for a few hours, I'm sure you can manage,' I try to assert, but my damn lips betray me as they quirk.

'Maybe I can survive the eye contact, but the

touching,' he reaches over, placing his palm on my thigh as his fingertips draw circles on my skin, making my senses tingle, 'that may prove *exceedingly* difficult.'

'Well, you're going to have to control yourself,' I say, grabbing his hand, and as much as it pains me to do so, I push it back over to his side.

He sighs. 'Remind me again why we have to act like strangers even though we have just driven here together.'

'You were fixing Aunt Maggie's tap and offered me a lift. Would you like to deal with all the questions about what we've been getting up to?'

He ponders for a moment, his eyes drifting to the near vacant beach beyond the windscreen. 'Not particularly, but–

'Besides, I don't think Olivia would be best pleased to find out that I've stolen her sex buddy away from her, and I'd rather not have scowly eyes being aimed at me all evening.'

A knock on my window makes me gasp and jump as a face appears.

'Are you coming, or what?' Vicki's muffled voice calls impatiently.

Unbuckling my seatbelt, I shoot one final warning glance to Jackson who rolls his eyes, but complies with a brief nod. 'Alright, fine, but it's going to be damn difficult, angel.'

'I know.'

Vicki yanks me into a hug as soon as my foot is out of the car. Olivia flashes me a surprising smile as we catch each other's gaze over Vicki's shoulder. She strolls around the Jeep to hug Jackson, and I have to force down my displeasure.

'Hey, Emmy, Emmy!' Leo cries, high fiving me.

'Evening, Leo,' I reply, laughing when he stumbles. He saunters up to greet Jackson who is passing Olivia the bags of food we just made a pit stop to purchase from the boot. 'How many has he had?' I ask, and Vicki raises her brow, puffing out her cheeks.

'Knowing Leo and given that it's just gone six, I'd say he's about hitting double figures.'

James strolls over with a big blue cooler in his hands and offers me a nod and a grin. 'Hey, Em, you hungry?'

'Starving!'

'Goooood, I see the lovebirds have set up camp.' He winks at the both of us before starting down the bank towards an embracing Lily and Dex, who have already lit up two disposable barbeques. Vicki links my arm and we follow.

'Sooo, how's being a fully qualified lifeguard for Marshlyn Bay?' I ask, nudging her side.

'A lot harder than you might think.'

I bob my head. 'Aunt Maggie said you're working long hours.'

She hums as we focus on treading carefully down the uneven sandy slope. 'I'm trying to earn and save my pennies. If James and I want to move into our own place, it's something I have to do, and it's not like I don't enjoy it. So, whilst I'm looking for a proper full timer, this and the shop are helping me save, along with James's job at his uncle's air conditioning place.'

'It's so nice,' I comment on a sigh.

'What is?' she asks, glancing over with her orderly furrowed eyebrows.

'Watching you two. You have your shit together; I'd love to be in that place.'

'Oh, I in no way have my shit together, trust me. You're eighteen, Emily. James and I weren't even together three years ago. It's crazy how fast things progress, but it'll happen for you, in your own time.'

My head turns subtly over my shoulder to see Jackson and Olivia together, carrying the bags of food.

'I suppose.'

We join the others at the hut and Lily greets us with big hugs as Dex, James and Leo grab the beers and ciders from the cooler. Lily mentions to Vicki that she still has her hair band from the other day, but I'm not focusing on their tedious conversation, because I catch Jackson's eye as he tosses Dex the packets of burgers and sausages over the barbeques. Dex is chatting away, but Jackson doesn't appear to be paying attention.

A smirk is playing on his lips as he mouths, 'One... two,' before we draw our heads away and I try to hide the smile creeping onto my face. My eyes travel up to find Vicki staring at me, with Lily now heading over to the cooler.

'What?' I ask innocently.

She shakes her head, her beady eye trained on me. 'Nothing,' she replies just as James calls her over for a drink. She leaves and I lightly kick the sand with my shoe, lowering my gaze to floor as I attempt to collect myself. Why does he have to look like such a damn snack all the time? He was right, keeping our eyes away and hands off might prove to be painfully more difficult than I thought.

'Emily!' The knowing voice pulls my head up sheepishly. He's strolling my way with two drinks in his hands. 'How you are you?' Dex asks as he reaches me.

'Fine,' I say, trying my best to not let my embarrassment show, even though I'm crumbling on the inside. Dex saw me in next to nothing this morning in his best friend's kitchen, and because I'm thinking about it, I know he definitely is.

'Good, that's good.' He pauses for a second, his eyes floating around in avoidance of mine. He clears his throat. 'Here,' he says, offering me a can of cider.

'Thanks.' I take it from him and immediately slurp the overflow after flipping the seal. Another moment of silence develops between us as we stand awkwardly. My eyes narrow when Dex turns around in search of someone, he scratches his head and my lips curl as Jackson mouths what looks to be a push of encouragement from across the sand. Taking another swig of my sweet cider, I await Dex's words.

He spins back, a pained look in his eye caused by the topic he's about to pull from the awkward air and bring to light. 'Listen, about you and Jackson, you've got nothing to worry about. I won't say anything to anyone, not even Lily.'

'Did he tell you to come over and say that?' I ask, now finding the funny side.

'Yes, yes he did. But I wanted to reassure you anyway. Your secret's safe with me.'

'Thanks, Dex,' I reply on a genuine smile.

'You two look good together.' He pouts with a confident bob of his head before gulping back his beer. The unease within him has vanished with his task now complete. Though it seems to have drifted into me.

My mouth parts as a tentative laugh is released. He idles back over to the barbeque and I turn my face towards the sea. Tilting my can, the fizz hits the back of my throat when I attempt to swallow down the uncomfortable feeling which has suddenly arisen. We can't look good together, because we're not together, and we won't ever be.

I notice that Vicki has taken a perch on a large rug laid over the sand, so I join her. Gasping in satisfaction as my bum hits the ground, I observe the others around the cooler and watch how Dex is taking charge in flipping the sizzling burgers over with a spatula, James beside him. Olivia, Lily, Leo and Jackson are stood as a group, each with their backs to us, though one member keeps flicking his eyes in my direction. His face holds a twinkle, but I can't tell if that's due to their conversation, or because he knows he's not supposed to be looking at me.

'He's been doing that a lot recently.'

My head spins around to Vicki's relaxed form, she's leaning back on her hands with her hair blowing freely behind, her long legs stretched out in front. 'Doing what?' I question, not bothering to ask who, when her focus drifts over my shoulder.

'Smiling.'

I take in the creases by his eyes and the sparkle they hold as his smile widens into a grin when my lips curl up. My attention is fully on him and it's not until Vicki speaks again that I notice her eyes have now turned to me.

'Correction,' she says, 'smiling at you.' She pauses, and I gather she's finally realising. 'That boy you've been talking to, who you're always texting at work. The one *from London…*'

My shoulders tense and I risk a glimpse out the corner of my eye. Her gaze is accusing, yet encouraging at the same time. 'We're just having fun.'

'Okay, so how would you feel if he got with someone else? Olivia, for instance.' I don't reply. I would hate it, there's no denying. 'Point proven.'

Naturally, my gaze lowers as I twist the can around in my fingers. I thought this was what was best, not letting myself become emotionally involved. Other than the fact that I have an alternative life with someone out there who wants to kill me, there's the fact that this isn't my home, I don't live here, and at some point, I'm going to leave and do my own thing, and so is he.

But somehow, that pain of leaving doesn't seem nearly as cutting as the pain of not knowing what we could be.

Lily plops down on the rug with a big cheesy grin on her face.

'Why are you so cheery?' Vicki asks.

Lily stares at her with pursed lips and wide eyes. My own flicker to an equally gleeful Dex working the barbeques. 'Is love in the air?' I probe, which earns a scoff from the blonde beside me.

'Lily doesn't fall in love,' she retorts.

Lily grimaces. 'Well, I wouldn't be so sure about that anymore.'

Vicki's mouth falls agape as she bolts upright. 'You love Dex!' she cries and I instantly wince.

Lily waves her hands about frantically, shifting closer to us. 'Shhhhhh! Keep your voice down, I don't want the whole world knowing.'

'This is huge, Lil,' I say on a grin.

'Yeah, so don't say anything, please. I haven't actually told him yet.'

Vicki and I catch a glance.

'Promise me,' she presses.

Through pointed expressions, we reply in unison. 'We promise.'

Lily breathes a sigh of relief before a smile spreads on her lips. The three of us let out small and controlled, yet extremely excitable, squeals.

'Burgers are up!' Dex calls.

We rush over and I fill my paper plate with a juicy burger in a bun and a kebab stick on the side. Reaching out for the ketchup bottle laid on a towel with the rest of the condiments, a hand, adorned with two rings on its index and pinky, makes contact with mine.

'Ladies first,' Jackson says, holding his plate piled high with food. My brain tells me to keep my focus on flavouring my burger as I ignore him. After a good shake, I flick the lid. I feel him inch closer, his torso pressing against my back, his breath fanning my ear and making my stomach flip, but again, I do my best to pay no mind. 'If you're lucky you may even get dessert.' His hand squeezes my bum and I gasp just as the ketchup squirts from the bottle. It shoots out, missing my burger entirely and landing on the sand below. I groan, but also check around to see if anyone noticed. Thankfully they're all too engrossed in their own food. Jackson snorts which brings my irritated expression to him.

'Thanks for that, I thought I said no touching.'

He swipes the ketchup bottle from my grasp and squeezes a neat line along his hot dog before passing it back to me. 'Slip of the hand, angel. Couldn't be helped,' he says with a glint in his eye and a whopping bite into his bun. I roll my eyes, dolloping some sauce onto my plate before throwing the bottle down, grabbing my drink from its balanced position in the sand and strutting away, knowing exactly where his eyes are trained.

I take a seat beside Lily on the rug, she grins at me with her mouth full. Before I even reach my second bite, the person I least expected approaches without any hesitation.

'May I?' Olivia asks, her plate in hand.

'Sure,' I reply, shuffling up and eyeing her warily as she sits. It's not that I dislike the girl, after all, I hardly know her, I've barely spoken two words to her, the only thing which bugs me is her possible feelings for Jackson. And I don't particularly want to be the cause of confrontation.

'Thanks.'

Dex soon follows and takes his place next to his girlfriend. I idly stare around, aware of Olivia delicately eating away. Leo's gulping down his beer with his arm hung around James who is trying to eat by the cooler. Vicki and Jackson are with them, and I use this moment of peace to let my eyes wander, casually observing his beauty; how his jaw moves, clenching as he takes his bites; the fact he appears so utterly irresistible and huggable in his grey hoodie; and the way his tall frame makes him look like a giant, so big and powerful, yet I know there's so much softness underneath.

'It's always interesting,' Olivia says, taking me by surprise. My neck twists, glancing at her through questioning eyes. 'Seeing what Leo will get up to every time he drinks,' she confirms.

'Oh,' I retort on a nod. 'I'm now realising he's not someone who just goes out for one drink.'

'Does anyone?' she says on a smile, her jet-black bob blowing off her face in the breeze.

'That's very true,' I reply as she giggles. I'm very conscious of my awkwardness, but maybe that's because I know what I'm doing with the guy she indubitably likes. Unlike Jackson, I'm mindful of her possible feelings, and right now, even though I have no reason to, I feel like a sly bitch.

On a sip of my cider, I decide that maybe it would be a good idea to go against my rules and bring up Jackson. Only in a casual manner, just to find out exactly how she feels. And even though I know it won't make the slightest bit of difference to my situation, and it'll either spike my possessiveness or put it to ease, I hope for the latter, because at least there's a chance I'll have one less thing to worry about. The risk is worth it. 'I bet it's fun having Vicki with you as a lifeguard now,' I ponder nonchalantly.

Olivia bobs her head slowly. 'It is, and it's good that

she has James, because I still get all the male attention.' My eyes widen as she takes a bite into her sausage. 'I'm joking,' she adds on a smile which I mirror, but rather more clumsily. I have a feeling she's not.

'Are things not good with Jackson?' I go in for the kill.

'You're kidding, right?' She sniffs as she glances down, fiddling with the half-eaten sausage on her plate. 'When are things ever good with Jackson?'

'Didn't you used to get on well?'

'Let's put it this way, he can say the sweetest words when he has one thing on his mind.'

I swallow, watching her carefully, knowing I have guilt written all over my face.

She flicks her eyes to the group by the cooler. 'Just look at him. Standing there, knowing he's the best looking out of everyone here. *Ugh!*' She shovels in the rest of her sausage, grinding her jaw and chewing with anger. I don't know if she's forgotten it's me she's talking to, because she carries on like she's venting to a best friend, and not someone who is practically a stranger. 'I might become a lesbian.' I keep my eyes low, sheepishly using my teeth to slide off a chicken piece from my kebab stick. 'Why men feel the need to toss girls about like they're nothing but a good shag, I'll never know. We have emotions, we have feelings.'

I nod, too afraid to open my mouth to interrupt. I'm scared she's about to charge over there and rip Jackson's head off.

'He knew my feelings went beyond fucking, yet he still treated me like shit.'

My mind travels back to mine and Jackson's conversation in his bed – about the girls he's had. When I asked him about Olivia, he told me the relationship was purely physical, that there were no feelings on both sides. I stand by my thoughts now, which is he's clearly got a case of oblivious male behaviour, going off all the affection she's visibly shown him.

'Sometimes boys can be dumb,' I say, now feeling bad for her.

'You can say that again. I just feel like a mug. I should've pulled back the minute I told him and got no reaction, but silly me, I can't ever be subtle.'

I shoot her a glance. 'You told him you liked him?'

'Yeah, one night after we'd had *the* most amazing sex, but he didn't say anything. I tried to show it through my actions after, a little touch here and a flirt there, but I never got anything back. Ever.'

'When did you tell him?'

'I don't know, a few months ago now, does it matter?'

He lied to me. 'I was just wondering,' I say with a sluggish shake of my head. 'Do you still like him?'

She shrugs, her resentment seeming to subside. 'It doesn't really make a difference if I do or don't anymore, he's not into me. He never was. He used me for sex, but he's obviously found someone better because he hasn't made a move on me in weeks.'

'I'm sorry,' I say, now feeling horrifically awful.

'What for? It's not your fault he's a dick.'

No, but it's my fault he hasn't been around you.

'I'm just sorry for how he's made you feel.'

'You're acting like he's your responsibility, Emily. The man's responsible for his own actions. Whoever he's moved on to, I wish her luck, because the guy can pull you in and make you fall with a single glance, but he can drop you just as quickly. He's a dangerous game, and not one I'm willing to play anymore.'

Her anger seems to have passed through into me. I'm aware he's not good with his emotions, the fact he ignored me for three days after our first kiss tells me clearly, but if what Olivia's telling me is true, the way he's treated her is awful. And the way he's relayed it to me isn't any better.

'You're completely over him, then?' I ask, my fingers tightening around the paper plate.

She scoffs. 'Emily, I spent so much time under the boy thinking he was the best person in the world, now, I'm glad to be over him.' She sighs as I contemplate going over there and ripping his head off myself. Though there is a part of me which doesn't quite believe her. Her tone is resolute, but if she truly is *over* him, then why is she always draped over him whenever they're together? 'I need another drink.' She rises on a huff. 'Do you want one?'

'No, I'm okay, thanks,' I reply, following Jackson with my eyes as he leaves the group, jogging up the bank towards the Jeep.

Olivia heads for the cooler. I shift, leaving my plate on the rug and striding over to Vicki.

'Where's Jackson gone?' I question quietly, making sure the others can't hear.

'We wanted more booze, so he's gone to get the rest of the beers from the boot.' She looks at me through narrowed eyes. 'Is everything okay?'

'Yeah, everything's fine.' I scoot past her and march up the bank. He's reaching inside the boot as I tread up to him, my temper steaming.

'Hey! Come to have a cheeky snog?' he asks as he wrenches the door down.

'You lied to me,' I say, crossing my arms tightly.

'What?'

'Olivia. You knew she liked you, because she told you to your face.'

'Hang on, Em.'

'Yet you still fucked her, lead her on, and then you lied to me.'

He sighs and reaches forward in an attempt to grab my arm, but I flinch away.

'Listen, I didn't say anything because I didn't want a big thing made out of nothing.'

'So you thought lying to me would be the better option?'

'I don't know what I thought. All I know is that I feel nothing for her, and I didn't want you to get the wrong end of the stick.'

I laugh incredulously. 'That's completely not the point. You strung her along even though you knew how she felt and you didn't care.'

Is this what he does? Uses girls and then tosses them aside when someone new comes along? Have his caring mannerisms and kind words all been one big ploy?

'I did. I do care, I'm just shit at handling situations like that.'

'You don't say,' I snipe. 'We're playing with feelings here, Jackson, and I don't like it.'

'Emily, I don't like her, that's not playing.'

'But the way you've treated her… Jesus, the way I've treated her.'

He holds my gaze with big regretful eyes. 'I don't claim to be a good person, Emily, but I'm trying to be better.'

Despite my best efforts, water swells in my eyes. He sighs, stepping into me.

'What's this really about?' he asks softly.

'It's about the fact that we're going behind her back. She's hurt and you lied to me. Of course you knew how she felt. I was stupid to believe you didn't.'

'No.' His voice is strong, and it sends a wave of shock through me. 'This isn't about her.' Jackson's eyes are troubled, they're watching me, hardened on me, as if I'm the only thing he sees. 'You're scared,' he murmurs.

'What?' I recoil back.

'You're scared because you don't want to get hurt. I may have made bad decisions in the past, but I'm not him, Emily. I'm not William. It's different with you.'

I shake my head disbelievingly. 'I…'

'Don't pretend like you don't feel it too.'

He's sucking me in again with his eyes and his words. He's doing exactly what Olivia said he does. He's pulling me in with one glance. Only I don't want what comes next. I don't want to be dropped. He's right… I'm terrified of him.

If he lied to me about this so easily, how else has he fooled me? What other secrets does he have hidden away? Thoughts of Guy's newspaper findings about the attack in London cross my mind.

*'Don't tell me to calm down!'*

My attention darts to the commotion coming from down the bank. James has his hand pressed against Leo's chest, but Leo's pushing it away, raging as he spits his words at the group who are looking on horrified. I begin to step towards them, only I'm tugged backwards. Jackson's hand is wrapped around my arm as he jerks me into his chest. I try and pull back, but his grip is too strong.

'Emily, you need to know–

'Jackson, stop! Can you not hear them?'

'It's just Leo, he always gets rowdy when he's pissed. We need to talk about this,' he tries more softly, but my eyes shoot to the beach when I hear James calling Jackson for help just as Leo shoves Dex in the chest.

'Not now, Jackson,' I say, ripping my arm from his grasp and taking off down the bank. My feet can't carry me fast enough as I see the two of them in each other's faces. 'What's going on?' I ask, coming to a stop next to Vicki and Olivia who are comforting Lily, her fingers fidgeting in front of her.

'I don't know, Leo just flipped out,' Vicki replies.

'She should be kept on a leash!' Leo shouts, pointing a finger in Lily's direction.

'Shut your damn mouth!' Dex yells back as James tries to keep them both apart when Leo attempts a daring step forward.

Jackson comes bounding past, immediately getting in between them as he hauls Dex away from the situation. James keeps a firm hand on Leo's chest.

'Here he is, the big man,' Leo says through a mocking cackle, a beer clasped loosely in his hand.

'You're drunk, Leo,' Jackson declares in a jaded tone, as though this is a common occurrence he has to deal with.

'And? Sounds like you were too the other night,

didn't do you any harm, in fact, I think it worked in your favour quite a bit,' he slurs before taking a swig from the glass.

'What's he talking about?' Dex asks, pointing to Leo as Jackson shakes his head taking a step towards the drunken boy.

'I don't know. Listen, shut up and calm down,' he hisses.

'Or what?'

'Simmer down, bud,' James intercepts, patting Leo's chest.

'No, go on, what are you going to do, London boy?' Leo tries, his hands flying out in a challenging manner.

'I'm not doing this, I think it's best if you go home, Leo,' Jackson replies, turning his back. His body is tense, his fists scrunched by his sides in tight balls, and I know why; he's trying to channel his anger through them, trying to think of his gentle pencil strokes.

'Or *what*?' he demands again more forcefully.

Jackson spins. My heart drums in my chest at the rage which has taken over his face, his technique failing with every testing word Leo's throwing at him. 'Or I'll fucking drag you there myself!'

'Confidence, I like it.' Leo grins which seems to irk Jackson even more. 'Is that what she liked about you too?'

My mind starts to race.

'Leo, just go home, mate,' Dex says. He's seemingly calmer as he approaches us four girls, flinging an arm around Lily consolingly.

'I don't know why you're sticking up for him considering what he's done.'

Questions whir in my brain.

'What in the hell are you talking about?' Dex asks half-heartedly, seemingly over the conversation.

'Dex just leave it,' Lily says quietly.

'No, I think he has a right to know,' Leo retorts.

'Know what?' Dex questions, becoming more riled over Leo's persistence.

'You better shut your big fucking mouth,' Jackson warns, and I suddenly feel a wave of nausea engulf me. My breaths become heavy as my pulse quickens. I'm scared. I've never seen this side of Jackson before, his eyes so unwelcoming and dark, his whole body so rigid it looks like it might burst. And there's a reason for that, because he wouldn't get so angry over nothing. With Lily's worried face and Leo's words… it can't be…

'Know *what*, Leo?' Dex pushes again.

Leo stares back at Jackson, his smirk growing. 'That Jackson has been fucking your girl.'

I hear the gasps around me. My heart sinks to the deepest depths of my stomach.

'Leo, go home!' Lily cries, but it's like my mind has shutdown, it's indistinct and muffled.

'He what?' Dex breathes, his arm dropping from Lily's back lifelessly.

'You mean they didn't tell you? Well, this is a spectacle.' Leo flicks his attention to Me, but my eyes are trained on an enraged Jackson staring him down. 'Emily, work your magic, we could sell tickets.'

It happens in a blur, Jackson's hands fly out, grabbing Leo's shirt. He balls up the material near his neck, clenching it tight. He uses so much force that for a brief moment it looks like Leo's feet leave the ground. 'Why don't you shut the fuck up,' he sneers at the boy who still has a smug smile painted on his lips.

Leo simply chuckles, showing no fear as he stares back indifferently into Jackson's furious eyes. 'Go on then, show them your true colours. You play the nice guy but we both know who you really are.' He's snide which only causes Jackson's grip to tighten as he shakes him firmly.

'You little fucker,' Jackson spits. Dex and James tear into action, Dex ripping Jackson away as James forces Leo back.

'Stop, mate. Calm down,' James tries.

'Why are you on his side?' Leo asks, slapping James's shoulder with the back of his hand.

'I'm not on anyone's side, I just think we all need to take a step back and calm the fuck down,' James replies rationally.

Jackson rips himself out of Dex's grip, tightening and releasing his fists.

'That's not true, is it? He's just pissed, isn't he?' Dex asks dubiously, staring wide-eyed at a crumbling Lily. She gazes back vacantly, giving no answer, or indeed, providing the answer Dex is reluctant to see. He spins around. 'Jackson?'

Jackson doesn't look at him, instead his daggers are locked on Leo. My head is pounding yet my mind is blank with only one word decipherable. Everyone was right. He pulls you in and just like that, you're used and forgotten. He pretended to care. It's all true.

'You're a liar.' The words burn up my throat. I feel a comforting hand on my back from Vicki, but it does nothing to ease my aching body. As soon as those emeralds meet mine, their fury diminishes. Instead, all I see is guilt. I'm too hurt to care about every pair of eyes which are now on me. He says nothing, which I suppose is a good thing. There's nothing he can say.

'Oh…are you two a thing?' Leo's voice fills my ears, which is really beginning to grate on me.

I wish I could, but I can't bring myself to look away from Jackson, as if staring at him will drive all this out of existence. As if it'll bring back the man I thought I knew.

'My bad. Well now he's fucked it up, how about me and you give it a go, Emily, huh?'

Before I can blink Jackson is leaping for him. His fist flies out and the thump sounds in time to the throbbing in my head. Leo stumbles back, clutching the side of his face as Dex and James race towards them, once again yanking them away.

'It was you all along,' Olivia's appalled tone airs beside me. 'You're the one he left me for.'

I swallow back the bile. 'I thought you implied you were never together.' I stare emptily over to the girl who is leering at me through a scowl. The sorrow I felt for her has vanished, she's pinning the blame on me even though one of her so-called friends has also been sleeping with him behind her back. Only I owe her no loyalties, and evidently Jackson feels the same way towards Dex… and me. 'Well, you can have him, Olivia. It's finished.'

My feet carry me forward in a hurried sprint. I don't look at anyone or anything apart from the path ahead leading me off this damned beach.

# THIRTY-TWO

'Emily!'

*Keep running.*

'Em, please!'

*Don't turn around. Keep your feet moving.*

'Emily!'

'Leave me alone, Jackson!' I shout as my feet slow to a fast walk, eager to get off the tough sand and onto the smooth tarmac, even though my tight chest is restricting my sprints.

'Let me explain,' he cries and the anger inside of me forces my body to stop in its tracks and spin around.

'He's your best friend! How could you?' I feel physically sick at the fact he could do that to anyone, let alone someone he calls his brother. Someone who gave him a home.

'I–

'You lied to me! I asked you if there was anyone else and you lied to my face... again!'

He holds his hand out cautiously and takes a small step forward. 'Please, listen to me.'

I don't.

'What was it? You didn't want to say the wrong thing just so you could get into my pants? I'm so bloody stupid.

Vicki even warned me, you do it as a pick me up. Is that what this whole thing was? You were feeling a bit low, so you serenade me with a load of crap to tempt me into bed. Did I seem that easy to you? She's just broken up with her boyfriend, so she'll be easy and vulnerable.' My whole body is trembling with anger. I've been so foolish.

He shakes his head. 'No, it wasn't like that at all. I just didn't want you to think any less of me, especially because it involved Lily.'

'I've been surrounded by secrets my entire life, Jackson, and I am not putting up with it anymore. I can't.' I pause as my heart pounds in my chest. 'I'm done.'

'With me?'

'Especially with you!' I tear my eyes away from his tense form.

'I made a mistake not telling you I've been a complete dick to Olivia, and even more so about Lily, but I thought that if you knew–

I interject his excuses with a scoff. 'I wouldn't want to sleep with you anymore?'

'You're not listening,' he says through a frustrated groan.

'I've wasted enough time *listening* to you.' I turn my back with silence looming the blustery air.

'So what if I was sleeping with her?'

I grit my teeth as I whirl around, despite my better judgement to walk away. For some reason I want to hear what farcical words are about to pass his lying lips.

'It's not like we're together. All you wanted was a pastime and that's what you got. You thought you'd claim me for a few weeks, have your fun and then toss me away like nothing when you leave and expect me to be true to you? You tell me that I string people along, why don't you take a look at yourself?'

My fists are clenched tight as I glare at him in utter disbelief. The truth hurts, but it's a truth which he's taken the wrong way, because that was not my intention, and his words are only pouring more fuel to the fire in my veins. 'Don't you dare turn this around on me. I'm not the one fucking my best friend's girlfriend!'

Jackson runs his fingers through his hair, roughly tugging on the ends as he grumbles. 'I haven't slept with Lily since they've been together, this was going on way before they even realised they liked each other. You think I could do something like that?' His chest expands as he sighs, his tone turning limp to match his slumped shoulders. 'The last time was at Leo's party, I didn't think anyone knew, but Leo has his ways of blowing things out of proportion.'

'You expect me to believe that? You're a disgusting liar, Jackson. You use girls! Vicki told me. Olivia told me.'

'Believe what you want, it's the fucking truth.'

I laugh lightly as my eyes drift to the cloud covered sky. 'Do you know what hurts the most? Despite what I know you think of yourself deep down, I really thought you were special. I thought you were a good person.'

His expression softens at my confession, those emerald eyes are peering deep into my soul and I can't look away, because I want him to see my pain. I want him to know what he's done to me. 'I shouldn't have been selfish; I should have stayed well away from you.'

'Emi–

'They disappear, everyone always disappears and I'm sick of it.' I sniff, reaching my limit. 'I'm done.' Turning myself around for the final time, I walk away, my pace quickening with every step.

'Emily, please!'

'*Done*, Jackson!'

The adrenaline is pumping through my veins, but it doesn't help to numb the pain in my heart. It grows with every second I spend walking away from him. Tears brim my eyes and I've lost the strength to hold them back, so I let them fall. One after the other. I turn my strides into a jog, wanting to get back to the cottage and under my covers as quickly as possible.

I got so caught up with trying to keep the dark side of my life away from him, but with just being around him, close to him, connected to him, I forgot about the possibility of me being hurt because of his. And yet, deep down I knew. From that first kiss, and the first time we slept together, I knew he was going to ruin my life and my fears have been made reality. I've become another number to his list. Just like Olivia… just like Lily. I've lost my self-worth, my dignity. But more than that, I let it happen. I was so scared of feeling this pain, and it cuts deeper than I ever could've foretold. I've lost him.

I scurry down the cobblestone path of Maple Cottage, not bothering to attempt to wipe away my tears, I'm past caring what Aunt Maggie will have to say. My phone buzzes in my pocket but I ignore it, knowing the only options are Jackson, Lily or Vicki; and none of them I wish to speak to. Slamming the door behind me, I stride up the stairs two at a time before Aunty's voice pauses my movements.

'Is that you, Pidge?'

'I'm going to bed,' I call back numbly.

'It's a bit early, isn't it?'

I place my foot down on the next stair, but my heart sinks for the second time this evening. That wasn't Aunt Maggie. I gulp down the lump in my throat before my body unthinkingly directs me back to the hallway. My breaths are heavy, and a sickly feeling is planted in my gut as my small steps carry me warily through the living room door and onto the cushiony carpet. And that's when I know my ears didn't deceive me. As if my day couldn't get any worse, the unexpected is sat in Aunt Maggie's living room with a cup of tea in their hands.

'Hello, sweetheart.'

I gaze back at the smartly dressed man and my jagged breath clogs in my throat when I register what I'm witnessing. 'What the hell are you doing here?'

'We need to talk, Emily,' he says, placing his mug onto the coffee table.

'You're thirteen years too late,' I throw back with not a care in my tone. I turn to Aunt Maggie, ignoring him entirely. 'Why did you let him in?'

'Pidge, I think you should hear what he has to say,' she replies, shifting from her position on the arm of the sofa to stand with her hands enveloped in front of her.

The weight of everything is finally overwhelming me. 'You like to pick your moments, don't you, Dad? How long have I been waiting for you to *talk* to me? And you choose today of all days to come here presuming I want to waste my time hearing what you have to say. Well, I'm sorry to disappoint, father, but I'm not up to listening to your crap right now, I'll call you at my own convenience.' I march away.

'Sweetheart, this is important.'

I stop, my chest billowing as I spin around in a rage. 'So was getting first prize in my year six spelling competition, so was finishing my A-levels, so was turning eighteen, so was being accepted into my first-choice university, but you didn't give a shit about any of that, did you? Like I said, I'll let you know when I'm ready to waste my time listening to you.'

I wipe my tears with the back of my sleeve as my feet carry me into the kitchen. Heading straight for the fridge and grabbing the wine, a small amount glugs into a glass and I swallow it back like a shot. The dryness thrashes my throat, but only makes me want more. The glass is filled higher this time as I gulp it down, before it's slammed onto the side and my head drops into my arms on the counter. I try to breathe through my anger, hoping it'll subside quickly before I end up throwing the wine bottle and glass across the kitchen. That's when the sound of shuffling slippers enters the room and I have to work even harder to bite my tongue.

'Emily…'

'Why?' I mumble into my arms before lifting my head to stare absently out of the window into the small but immaculate garden. 'Why have you given him the time of day?'

She sighs, before dragging a chair out from under the table. 'Look, God knows I've loathed that man for so many years, he's ruined my niece's life and I would never allow him into this home under normal circumstances,' she pauses, 'but these aren't, Pidge. I think you should give him a chance to talk.'

'Is this about what he said to you on the phone?' I ask, scraping the courage to turn and face her. 'I heard, and I know that he probably told you everything about what happened to me.'

Much to my surprise her eyes are fixed confidently on mine as she takes a sharp breath. 'Yes, I know it wasn't an arbitrary attack. Your dad was never going to explain it to you, but I convinced him that it's only fair you should know. I told him that if he cared even the slightest bit for you, he would tell you everything.'

I look away, my eyes glassy once again. 'I've been thinking about this over and over. I've been so confused and I've hated him for keeping me in the dark, but now the time's come when I can finally get my answers, I'm not so sure I want to hear them.'

'You don't have to do anything you don't want to, but it's very rare when your father takes the chance to do the right thing. So if I were in your shoes, I'd grab the opportunity with both hands.'

The lump in my throat feels like it's cutting into my skin and the pounding in my head is hammering into my skull, making me dizzy. 'I'm scared,' I admit. My voice wavers and Aunt Maggie's sad eyes aren't helping, but she does her best to offer me an encouraging smile.

'I know, and that's okay. Being scared and fighting through that is what makes us brave, it's what makes us stronger. And I'll be here. Always.'

There's a tug on my lips as I allow my head a small nod. I straighten up, wipe away the remainder of the tears and take a deep breath. 'I hope I'm not going to regret this,' I murmur before treading out of the kitchen to take my opportunity.

# THIRTY-THREE

His back is to the door as he stares out of the living room window with his hands in his suit trouser pockets. I observe the flecks of grey in his hair and how even from behind, he still gives off the aura of importance.

'I'm ready.'

He spins, his eyes wide as though he wasn't expecting me to comply, and to be honest, neither was I. And as the seconds tick by, I'm quickly questioning if it is such a good idea. He eventually regains his composure. 'Okay,' he replies on the smallest of smiles.

'Should we sit?' I ask when he offers nothing more.

'No.' He saunters towards me in the doorway, stopping at the edge of the coffee table. 'We'll go somewhere else. There's a nice restaurant in St Maryl, I'd like to take you there, if that's okay?'

My eyes flicker down, I'd rather get it over and done with here so I can retreat to my bedroom straight after, but again, Dad's insistence will always win and I've lost the strength to argue with him. I lift my focus. 'Fine,' I reply indifferently.

There's a black BMW parked in front of Maple Cottage gate. I wasn't paying attention to anything when I ran back from the beach, I didn't even register that the car was different, I'd just presumed it had been Guy's.

A much younger man climbs out of the driving seat when he spots our approach, dressed in a smart black suit stood, he holds the door open for me, nodding his greeting. I clamber in, sliding across the seat and noting that the interior is just as swish as the Mercedes. The smell of new, unworn leather hits my nose before Dad takes his place beside me and the door is closed, trapping us together.

The journey is silent, as expected. The awkward atmosphere clouding the air makes me sad more than anything, because this is simply how things are now between a daughter and her father. Watching the world go by in a haze, my head drops back against the headrest and as we drive past the now empty beach, a single tear pools over my eyelid and down my cheek. No matter how hard I try, I can't stop my mind from wondering where he is. Where did he go? Did he and Dex fight? What if Dex ends up kicking him out? I let my eyes close as I try to swipe the thoughts of him away. He's made his own bed, now he has to live with his mistakes. Just as Lily does.

The sun is low in the sky when the driver turns into a car park off a quiet narrow lane. It's busy, but he manages to find an empty space in a corner. Dad gets out in silence whilst I remain for a moment, mentally preparing myself for the unknown. Taking a deep breath, I reach out for the handle, but the door opens for me. The driver stands tall and smiles cordially in my direction when I slide out. He has warm, kind eyes.

'Thank you,' I offer, and he nods in response.

Dad has his head down, texting on his phone and I find the strength to roll my heavy eyes. Some things will never change. He finally glances up to the driver. 'Thanks, Sam, shouldn't be more than an hour.'

'Okay, sir,' Sam replies before climbing back into the car.

'This way,' Dad says, gesturing to the path in between two hedges.

'Does Sam not want anything to eat?' I remark rather sharply. He's driven all this way from London, and if I were him I would be starving, but Dad doesn't seem at all bothered about his wellbeing.

'He's fine, he'll take himself off to get something if he wants to.'

I stride past him on a huff, my disapproval painted on my face. The restaurant from the outside appears to be a classic, countryside pub with fields surrounding, and people sat on the randomly positioned benches outside with beer and gin glasses atop. I march on ahead, keen to get this over with. An hour is a long time to be sat alone with him, especially when I have no idea what he's going to say to me.

Two older women step out from the exit and the last of the pair holds the door open for me with a smile. I mutter my thanks as I wait behind a family who are lingering by a stand as a waitress comes over to seat them. There's a light buzz, despite the restaurant looking very busy, it's not overwhelming, unlike the Italian place Jackson took me to in Rockstone. I sigh as his face yet again forms an image in my head.

The family are taken to their seats, leaving me deserted with Dad as he steps up beside me.

'I appreciate you coming here with me, Emily.'

I watch him out the corner of my eye, he's staring around the restaurant absentmindedly. I don't entertain him with a reply as I mercifully spot the waitress walking our way.

'Hello, welcome to The Golden Sands. Table for two?' she asks, grabbing a couple of menus from on top of the stand.

'There should be a booking under Lambert,' he replies kindly, my eyes narrowing inquisitively. A booking?

'Of course, sir, this way.'

She strides on ahead and I look up at Dad expectantly to follow, but he holds his hand out, signalling for me to lead. With a clench of my jaw, I do. The waitress escorts us past the bar area into an extended space at the back, which makes me think it has recently been refurbished, because whilst appearing newer than the other room, it's giving off a charismatic vintage feel, with wooden beams overhead, slate walls and an unlit log fire built into the wall at the side. It's snug and cosy, charming with a relaxed ambiance, not too posh, but nowhere near tacky either. The features come together to provide a sense of contentment, making people feel like spending their money, in what I can imagine to be a pricey restaurant, is worth it, and going off the vibrant atmosphere, it looks to be doing the trick. Seems like Dad's type of place: affluent and persuasive. We're guided over to the table in the corner nearest the fireplace, away from other guests.

'Your waiter today will be Lucas, he'll be over in a moment to take your orders,' the young waitress says merrily with her hands enclosed together in front of her.

'Thank you,' Dad replies and I force a smile onto my lips before she leaves us. He gets stuck in, immediately scanning his eyes over the wine list. I observe him across the table, his back and shoulders are straight, the expensive Rolex on his wrist very much deliberately on show.

'You reserved a table?' I ask, not bothering to look at the menu, I'm far from hungry with a nauseous feeling having been rooted nicely in my stomach since the barbeque.

'Yes, Emily,' he replies curtly without looking up.

'How did you know I would come?'

'I know how badly you want answers. Besides, even if you didn't, it's a lovely restaurant to dine in regardless.'

I watch him for a second before shifting my gaze away and shaking my head. Presumptuous arse.

'Your mother and I used to come here a lot. It's near your aunt's old place.'

My eyes shoot back to him, he's still gazing down at

the menu. How is he able to say so much but so little at the same time? His relaxed exterior is starting to irritate me, because I know his *answers* will no doubt be as bland as unsweetened tea, and I'm going to end up ripping my hair out.

The waiter comes over and takes our orders. Dad, a large glass of red and the rump steak. Me, a tap water. Lucas is quick to depart, leaving a deathly silence hanging in the air.

'How have you been? You've got a nice colour to you, you look healthy,' Dad says, bringing my focus back from its wandering to see him pointing to my lightly bronzed skin.

'Dad… just stop. You know how I've been, because not only has Guy been filling you in, but Aunt Maggie also, who I heard you had a lovely conversation with this afternoon.'

'I see.' He rests his intertwined hands on the table as he leans forward, his eyes narrowing curiously. 'What has she told you?'

'Absolutely nothing. No one has told me a thing, Dad.' My cold eyes glare at him when he doesn't respond. 'I believe this is where you come in.'

He watches me closely. 'You're right. It's time to talk.' He bobs his head but his eyes are lowered to the table.

'So start,' I say when nothing more passes his pursed lips.

He lifts his head, our eyes locking. His desolate browns surprise me, because I've rarely ever seen any emotion behind them. 'I don't know…' He falters just as Lucas comes over with his large glass of wine and my water. My focus remains on the man opposite me as he shifts uncomfortably, his stony exterior waning ever so slightly. He resumes as Lucas leaves us. 'I don't know where to, Emily, this is new territory for me.'

'How about at the beginning?' I'm just as uneasy as he apparently is, but unlike him, I'm trying my best not to let it show.

His chest expands as he takes a deep inhale followed by a gulp of wine. He places the glass back onto the table and twists it to a place he's happy with before fixing his focus back on me. 'The first thing you should know, sweetheart, is that everything I told you all those years ago about your mother, about how she died…'

My lips press together in a tight line as I centre all of my attention onto him, the lump in my throat returning.

'It wasn't the full truth.'

I'm silent as I nibble on my bottom lip. *Stay in control*.

'January 5th 2008, I remember it like it was yesterday. That morning I was preparing myself for the sentencing of my first big case. I was representing the family of a teenager who had been murdered by a man called Patrick Mason, you won't have heard of him, you were too young, but it was a big thing at the time. I was so nervous I could barely do my tie up. Mum was watching me struggle from her dresser, she finished putting on her earrings and came over, tying it perfectly. She looked so beautiful.' Dad peers off pensively. 'That was the last time I told her that.'

Brewing tears blur my vision, but I do my best to keep them from falling, instead concentrating on every single word.

'Patrick Mason was sent down for life and we were all ecstatic, not only because my first big case was a success, but because other than the day you were born, I'd never felt so fulfilled; I was able to get justice for the poor boy's family. It was meant to be the start of everything. My career was being set, I had my little family, and we were even thinking of expanding.'

My lips part as my breath hitches. 'You were going to have another baby?'

He nods, averting his gaze with a guzzle of wine. 'That evening we went out to celebrate, nothing extravagant, just a couple of family members and friends of Maxwell's family. We went to a bar in central London to commemorate, and the atmosphere was just wholesome. Towards the end your mum was getting tired, so she left to go back home to you, and that's when the trouble started. I'd stayed behind with the family and it was my round, so I was stood at the bar... I didn't see them come in, didn't even notice they were there, that is until he came right up to the bar and stood next to me.'

'Who?'

'Patrick Mason's younger brother, Carl. Him and his *gang*,' he spits. 'He had a few words to say, and I wasn't happy about him being there, so I politely asked him to leave. You can imagine it didn't go down well. There was some commotion and in the end the security threw them out, after that I decided it was best to go home, so I got a taxi. I didn't even notice they'd been following until it was too late. I arrived home, walked up the driveway, and that's when I heard them behind me. I shouted at them; told them I was ringing the police if they didn't leave, but it was pointless. They forced themselves into the house. There were five of them. The lights were off, so I assumed you and your mum had gone to bed, I tried to text her to stay quiet, but they ripped my phone away and smashed it before I had the chance to. That's when she came out of your bedroom hearing the noise, Carl saw her and ran up the stairs. I followed, watching as she stood in his way. She wasn't scared like you would think, she looked...'

'What?' I ask barely above a whisper.

'Like a furious lioness who was protecting her cub. And she was furious. But it was like he fed on her anger, because he started to grow cocky. He'd clearly had more than a few to drink, he told her he wanted to see you, he tried to push past her and that's where I stepped in. He began mouthing off, shouting insults in my face and defending his brother, he told me I'd persecuted an innocent man. I said the judge and the rest of the courtroom didn't seem to think so. I told him his brother was a murderer and he'd gotten what he deserved, which was the most stupid decision I've ever made. He got angry, he kept saying he wanted to go into your bedroom to teach me a lesson about punishing the innocent. He kept trying and trying, but your mum and I put up a fight…' he pauses as my emotions catch up to my brain, unscrewing the taps as tears splash onto my clenched hands. 'I told you she tripped over a loose flap in the carpet, she didn't, she was pushed… *he* pushed her. I remember the sound of her piercing scream, the thumping of her head against every stair before the silence. I couldn't take my eyes away from her body as the men ran away. I'll never forget the sinking feeling; it haunts me to this day. I've only ever felt that twice in my life, the other when Guy told me Carl had come back to pay you a visit.'

I'm utterly speechless, my words entirely lost no matter how hard I search for them. I'm not sure what I was expecting, but that definitely wasn't it.

'Afterwards, my closest colleague worked with me for months to get him and the rest of the group sent down. Carl was sentenced thirteen years, the others shorter and varied going off some of their criminal history. My colleague got me through it, he did his best to get them the longest possible imprisonment, he was and still is a dear friend.'

His lips thin into a line as he contemplates his next words carefully. I feel breathless and faint, Dad is barely visible through my blurry vision.

'And that's another thing you should know, Emily. His name is Joel Garcia, William's father.'

I swallow the knot in my throat, feeling the heaviness as it unravels and smothers my gut.

'When you turned sixteen, I knew Carl had less than a year left in prison and owing to my own mistakes, my relationship with you had simmered down to basically nothing, but I still needed to keep you safe. Knowing he was a good kid, raised by a good man, I brought William to you. I told him I'd employ him with an appreciable wage, but in return, he was to connect with you and keep you safe without telling you a thing.'

My whole body feels numb, like I've been winded and had every part of me sucked away, leaving nothing but a black void of hollowness behind. 'You hired him to become my boyfriend?' I ask on a tremble, my strong and composed exterior deteriorating on every word.

'You didn't think under normal circumstances I would be happy for my seventeen-year-old daughter to date a twenty-two-year-old, did you?'

I gather my words. 'Normal circumstance is a bit of a joke when it comes to me and you, Dad. I never thought you cared enough to notice.'

'It wasn't my proudest moment, but I felt responsible, and it was necessary at the time. I knew once this man was out, there was a strong possibility he'd be coming for me, and therefore there was a risk to you. We had a system and every so often I'd ask William to update me on how you were doing, how safe you were. It only increased when I knew Carl had been released. I gave him strict instructions to be on hyper alert. On the night he came for you, William was sorting out a minor case for me, but for some reason I couldn't get hold of him for the usual check-in call, so I thought it best to send Guy and Norman to make sure everything was okay at the house, and thank God I did.'

I finally flick my teary gaze away as I try to come to terms with everything I've just been told. I'm hurt, shocked, horrorstruck, but above all angry. Hurt, because of the dishonest, shamefaced man sat opposite me; shocked and horrorstruck at how Mum was truly taken away from us and how the awful incident was kept from me; but the anger is at myself, for seeing deep down that this was all it ever was with William, not knowing that he was nothing but a gluttonous, deceitful arsehole, yet somehow seeing through the cracks of his inconsiderate choices and actions. My sudden disgusted hate for the man pushes away every ounce of compassion I was showing him before now.

'You think William was on a case that night?' I turn back to Dad emptily.

'Yes, he was speaking to one of my clients about an upcoming trial.'

'Aunt Maggie didn't tell you?'

'Tell me what?'

'What your little lapdog was really up to.' His face

darkens as I let the words flow mercilessly. 'He was at a strip club.'

Dad clenches his wine glass, his knuckles turning white. 'I'll deal with him, Emily.'

I catch his mournful expression. My exhale is shaky, but I have to jerk my face down and quickly wipe away the wetness from my face when Lucas arrives with Dad's food. Dad gives him his thanks, however something he says after captures my notice. He tells the waiter to put a gentleman's bill onto ours and when I glance around, I see who he's referring to. Sam is sat at a table across the room reading a newspaper and sipping at a coffee mug. My tired eyes narrow as Lucas agrees and leaves us, they flicker down in thought as a different version of my father is presented to me. At least he treats his staff with respect.

'Say something, sweetheart,' he eventually says in the softest way I've heard him speak to me since the day he told me Mum had gone.

'Does Aunt Maggie know everything?' I ask, somehow managing to regain composure enough to speak without faltering. 'How her sister really died? Is that what you told her on the phone?'

He stares at me carefully; too carefully.

'Em, Aunt Maggie was there.'

I recoil, my face contorting. 'What?'

'She was with you in your bedroom.'

My eyes close as I grit my teeth. 'Wait a second, I heard her on the phone,' I repeat with urgency, vocalising my thoughts more so to help me better understand. 'She said that you'd been lying to me *and* her, but if she was there then she knows the truth about what happened to Mum, she knows about the people who did it, she knows who came for me that night. She always did, since the moment I arrived. She knew everything.' I catch my breath as I let this newly found knowledge sink in. 'So what did you lie to *her* about?'

'To stop her panicking and accidentally letting it slip to you, I told her that Carl was issued an extended sentence for a further four years for misconduct, I didn't tell her he was already out on the streets. That is, until he came for you and I had to admit the truth. She didn't take it well, obviously.'

I stare at him dumbfounded, bile rising up my throat. 'Everyone's been lying to me,' I whisper in disbelief. Jackson, William, Dad, even the person I thought would never let me down; Aunt Maggie.

He leans forward. 'In my sick head I thought it was the right thing to do. I didn't want the same thing that happened to your mother to happen to you, but I've put you in more danger by not telling you the truth. Whenever I looked at you, I saw her, and the guilt consumed me. I couldn't lose both of you and I certainly couldn't face being the person you looked up to when it was all my fault. I thought I was protecting you by keeping my distance, but if anything, it pushed you away and made you all the more exposed. I was young and stupid, and unfortunately, it's shaped the man I have become today.'

My body collapses back into my chair as all the energy evaporates from within me. 'All I've ever wanted is a normal life with you, Dad. I think that's what Mum would've wanted us to have too.' His face drops at the mention of her, his eyes drifting away sadly. 'Why now?'

He looks up, studying me for a moment. 'After what happened to you, after what you said about me never being a father to you and when I saw you walk out of my office that night, something hit me, like a bloody bus. Your aunt gave me that final push today, I knew she would, that's why I called her, because deep down I knew I needed stern words to give me the courage. I can't bear it any longer. You may not want to speak to me ever again after all this, but I need you to hear it. I love you, sweetheart, and I want to do better. You're more important to me than anything in this world. I'm so sorry it's taken me so long to realise my mistakes.'

If I didn't feel so humiliated and let down, I would relish in the fact that maybe he is capable of real human emotion. He's saying exactly what I've wished to hear for so long, but it's too little too late. 'I've wanted this more than anything, for you to open up to me and talk to me, to actually want to spend time with me, but I can't pretend like it's all okay now. My whole life has been a lie, you've made it nothing but a big lie.'

'I know, Emily. Trust me, I know.' His body has deflated, his usual straightened posture is now slumped, as though someone has stuck a pin in him, emptying him of his need to appear important and authoritative, but filling him with something else, something which is evident in his face and aura. Relief.

I draw in a breath as a thought is pulled forward. 'Is Carl still free? Have you caught him yet?'

He gulps and looks away, giving me my answer. 'We are trying.'

I'm not surprised. 'How did he even know where I lived? How did he know I wasn't still living with you?'

'I don't know, but something's off. Almost as though someone's been keeping him in the loop from the minute he got out of jail. He's deranged and will stop at nothing until he's gotten his revenge on me.'

'You're a lawyer, can't you get a restraining order or something?'

'Oh, we have, but do you think that's going to stop him? This crook would put his whole life on the line if it meant ending mine.'

I sigh as my head falls into my hands before my fingers run through my hair, down my cheeks, coming to a stop over my mouth. All the information and emotion which has been thrown at me tonight has drained me. My head is airy, my chest heavy as I flick my spent, misty eyes to his worried face. 'I can't do this, I'm sorry.'

And with all the strength I can muster, I haul my lifeless body up from my chair and pace away without another glance. I allow the tears to fall, not caring who sees me.

Aunt Maggie was wrong. Bravery hasn't given me strength. I'm weaker than I've ever been, because now I know this viscous ache in my chest will never be relieved.

Now I know the truth. And it hurts more than I ever thought possible.

# THIRTY-FOUR

I'm vaguely aware that I'm walking. Slowly. I don't know where I am, I don't know where I'm going, but I carry on.

Mum died because she was protecting me. Aunt Maggie knew all along. My entire relationship with William was built on nothing but a contract. And the man I thought I could trust isn't who I was starting to believe he was. Yet again I've been made a pawn in life's toxic game.

Head lights set fire to the path ahead of me and I hear an engine coming up from behind, but I don't turn around, I just shift a little closer to the hedges on the side. So it surprises me when that engine slows to a crawl. The window is wound down and I catch a glimpse of the figure inside as my feet continue to move onwards.

'Why don't you get in, Miss Lambert?' Sam says as he creeps along beside me.

'Is he in there?' I ask, gesturing to the tinted back windows, but he shakes his head curtly.

'No, he thought it best to remain at the restaurant. He wanted me to take you back to the cottage.'

'I can't go back there, not yet.' I can't face Aunt Maggie. I know I'll only fly off the handle and I'm really in no mood to speak to anyone.

'Then why don't you get in and I'll take you anywhere you want to go?' I don't reply. I don't know where to go, I don't know what to do. 'Come on, Miss Lambert, it's getting dark and we're in the middle of nowhere.'

My feet pause. It's dusk now and soon there will be no light at all, at least in the car I can think and focus my mind – or at least attempt to. I sigh, before opening the back door.

Sam takes me to the place I know for certain won't cure my desolate state, but it's something my body craves whenever my emotions are running amok, and with nowhere else to turn, it seems all the more welcoming.

Pulling into The Marshlyn car park, I climb out of the BMW and tell Sam that when I'm finished I'll make my own way back to the cottage. It's not entirely the truth, because I don't know if I can go back there tonight.

With Aunt Maggie it hurts the most. I never thought in a million years she could deceive me the way she has. She's so quick to scorn my father for doing the exact thing she has done, to lie to me the way she has, to leave me in the dark for so many years and then accept me into her home and act entirely oblivious. I'm so far past angry; I'm disappointed and saddened. I trusted her, I believed in her. Just like I trusted William... just like I believed Jackson to be a good person. Once again, I've been proven wrong. Now I know, the only person who I can without a doubt rely on is me. All I need is the belief in myself, everyone else is a figure passing in the night; fleeting and insignificant. I need to focus on my life. I need to focus on me.

And right now, what me needs, is a large glass of Billy's sweet mixed berry white wine and stacks of shots.

The chipped brown door swings open, but I catch my breath, unmoving in the entrance. Frozen in disbelief.

'Hey, baby.' He swivels around on the stool at the bar, a beer glass half full in his hand. He's smiling, a genuine cheerful smile. It makes my stomach turn. I grit my teeth, grinding them together as my fists ball at my sides. My fury drives me forward. I'm marching towards him with a face like thunder. With all my might, I pull every scrap of built-up tension and anger together and focus it all into my swing. My fist connects with his face, forcing him backwards and making him stumble off his stool.

I've never punched anyone before, but I always thought it must feel amazing. I can safely say it does. There's no pain and I put it down to adrenaline. The way I'm feeling in this moment, I'm ready to take on the Hulk.

William groans, cradling the side of his face as my eyes narrow in on him. I can feel looks being thrown in our direction, but I couldn't give a damn. 'There's plenty more where that came from, *baby*,' I spit. His eyes are wide in surprise as mine glare back in revulsion before I turn on my heel and storm away.

'Emily, wait–

'That's for two years of my life I'll never get back!' I stride down the steps and away from him as he scurries out behind me.

'I deserved that.'

'More than you know,' I retort, keeping my legs moving.

'I'm sorry about the strip club. If I could go back–

I whirl around hastily, noting the red mark on his cheek and how his white dress shirt is opened by a couple of buttons at the top but is still neatly tucked into his black suit trousers. Just the sight of him is turning my stomach. 'I know!'

'What?' He stops abruptly, his forehead contorting.

'I know everything.' I scoff as the realisation fully dawns on me. 'It was all a lie.'

He gulps, his lips pressing together in a thin line. 'He told you?'

'You should know he's here and I happened to mention your little escapade. Big boss man is not happy, so consider this an undeserved warning, William… go home. Get as far away from here as possible.'

His lips part as he rubs the back of his neck before flicking his eyes away on a sigh. Not being able to bear him any longer, my feet turn, but before I can make any kind of distance a hand is tugging me back.

'That's the reason I came. I came to get you. I want to take you away from here, away from everything. Your aunt told me you were out, so I waited.' He pauses, watching me closely as my face scrunches in disbelief. 'Let's go together. We can go abroad and travel. It's what you've always wanted to do.'

My head shifts away, shaking from side to side, wondering how Aunt Maggie left him alive. 'Who are you, William? Because I honestly don't know. I don't think I ever have known.'

'I'm the same guy you fell in love with.'

'Did you follow Dad down here?' I ask, purposely dodging the mention of love.

'What?'

'Did you hope to get to me before he could tell me about your contract? Say some sweet things and then whisk me away so I'd never find out? I've been nothing but a business transaction to you.'

He steps up to me but hesitates when I shift away. 'No, that's not true. I didn't know your father would be here, I wanted to see you and apologise in person. I love you, Emily... truly.'

'Right, of course you do,' I reply on a mocking snort. 'When was the last time you took an interest in my life? Asked me how I was? How my day went? If you *truly* love me, why did you never tell me what was going on?'

'Your dad–

'My dad.' I laugh lightly. 'The truth is, William, you're a lapdog. You never really cared, did you? Dad made you pursue me, offered you the world, you went along with it, easy deal. But that's fine, because now I know the truth. I don't love you, William. And you don't love me. Don't you see? You got your money, your new cars, I got to escape my life with Dad.'

He attempts to reach for my hand, but again, I pull back. 'No,' he says strongly. 'That was true at the beginning, your dad offered me a good deal; money, an amazing job, everything. And, yeah, you were kind and pretty. But time went on and we got to know each other, and I fell for you, I really did.'

'Then why have you been acting like a complete dick for the past few months?'

He runs a hand through his immaculate hair, tugging on the ends. 'Your dad has been working me to the bone! As well as being completely wired on these people that are after you, I had my own job to do at the firm. I mean, fuck, I hardly had time to piss. I'm twenty-three and I'm getting grey hairs.'

'If it was so difficult for you, William, why didn't you just leave? I'm sure your father would've seen you fit.'

'Because...' he retorts slowly, 'believe it or not, I care about you. I couldn't leave *you*.' He takes a step forward. This time I don't flinch away. His eyes are locked on mine: a picture of sorrow and guilt. His long fingers brush against my wrist and for a fleeting moment a part of me is entranced, his perfect face keeping me in place. But that's all it is – a fleeting moment. I blink as my blank expression turns sour.

'You're so full of shit. You're only saying this because you're scared you'll lose your job. If you ever cared, you would've told me the truth,' I murmur, my neck craned as I glower up at him.

He nods gently, his voice soft. 'I'm sorry. I am truly. But we love each other, I know we do. We can make this work.'

I finally come to my senses, realising how close to me he's gotten in his deluded state. I groan, throwing my head back in frustration and pacing away. 'No! You're not getting it! I was in love with the idea,' I shout, stepping into him and prodding my finger against his chest, 'the idea that you were my escape, my way out.' He stands unmoving, gazing back at me with an anxious glint. 'Well, thank you, William, because you've lived up to your purpose and I'm free. I don't *need* you anymore. Now fuck off back to your strippers, because I've got a life to live that doesn't involve you. You've made your bed, and I never want to see you again.'

His mouth parts as his brown eyes change in a flash from holding remorse to showing nothing but determination. 'No, Em, come on. You love me. You do. This is just a minor glitch, something we've got to work through.' He grabs my hands with his. 'Baby, we need to be together.' His tone is desperate… pleading.

'To keep you in a job?'

'No.'

He's still in denial, and I'm finally giving up. Whatever energy I have left is not worth using on him. 'Goodbye, William,' I snap, ripping my hands free and turning on my heel.

He yells my name, letting out a loud cry of frustration when I ignore him. My adrenaline is acting as a stimulant in replace of the alcohol, and it's leading the way, my legs simply following their orders.

The door is slammed behind me.

Racing up the stairs, I grab my suitcase before drawing all my clothes out of the wardrobe and tossing them inside.

'What on earth is going on?' Aunt Maggie asks as she rushes into the bedroom.

'I'm leaving,' I state sharply, fighting the urge to look behind as I bend down and concentrate on folding the items.

'Whatever your father has said to you, Emily–

'You knew!' I cry, pivoting on the balls of my feet to meet her wide greys. 'You knew all along what happened to Mum, and you said nothing to me. My life has been this one long road of secrecy and loneliness, and you thought it best not to tell me anything?'

'Emily, I'm so sorr–'

'*Sorry, sorry*, everyone's *so* sorry!'

'We are–

'I had a right to know!' I scream, casting a top to the side as I stand and face her. 'I expected it from Dad, but you?'

She swallows, staring at me like a deer in headlights when I throw my finger in her direction. My heart pounds in my chest and my hands begin to tremble.

'Even William knew. My own mother was killed because she was protecting her daughter and I had no clue. I mean, bloody hell, the same thing almost happened to me. So at what point did you think it was a good idea to keep me in the dark?'

'We thought we were protecting you.'

'Thirteen years! Thirteen years, Aunty,' I breathe in disbelief meeting her aghast big eyes.

'Hey, hey, what's going on?' Guy enters the room, stopping beside Aunt Maggie.

'I bet you knew too.' I point at him. He pauses, his eyeline wavering guiltily. I sigh, I feel like I'm being swallowed up, like there's nothing left for the world to take from me. 'I always thought *I* was the problem, that there was something wrong with me, that I wasn't good enough. All my life I've just been there, as if I was this burden. Even my goddamned boyfriend was a lie. But it turns out, it's not me, it's everyone else around me and I've been stuck in this hole. Well, not anymore.' I'm fighting back. I'm sealing the cracks and protecting myself. Nothing else will be taken.

'Miss Lambert, I think we need to calm down for a moment,' Guy tries, taking a step into the room. I shake my head in protest. As if he has the nerve to tell me what to do.

'I don't want to calm down. I want you to take me and Buddy away from here.'

'Pidge, if you would let me explain.' Aunt Maggie reaches for me, but I shrug her off.

'Don't,' I protest. 'Just leave me alone.' My eyes narrow at her shrinking form. 'Should be easy enough for you, it's evidently what you're good at.'

She visibly tenses.

'Emily,' Guy warns.

'You won't take me, fine, I'll find somewhere on my own.' I barge past them both.

'Where are you going?' Aunt Maggie calls, a waver in her voice which almost makes me pull up. If I stay, I know I'll regret my impulsive remarks… I already do.

'I need to think!'


When your mind is running at a hundred miles an hour, it's very difficult for the noisiest of locations to help distract and slow down its pace, but when placed in the most serene of settings, the mind begins to settle; although those thoughts are still present, they seem to control themselves. As though the whisperings in the tranquil air are telling them to slow down and breathe.

As the waves crash onto the rocks and the cooling breeze brushes past my ears, I listen to those whisperings, and I'm allowing myself to breathe.

*In,* they say.

Bringing my legs up onto the bench, I hug them into my chest and rest my chin on my knee. The endless darkening ocean is before me, its still vastness helping me to draw in a deep breath.

*Out,* they continue.

The air filling my lungs is released.

*Now think, what needs to happen next?*

I close my eyes as I tell myself adamantly, I need to do what's right for me.

But as my eyes open, I'm reminded that I can't, because that man is still out there and until he's caught, I'll be constantly looking over one shoulder. Dad said someone may have been keeping an eye on me, told Carl where I live, what I'm up to. Even if I defy my father and head straight to Sunderland, there's always a possibility he'll find me there.

*Jackson,* the whisperings say.

My distraction. Who allowed me to forget with a glimpse into his sparkling emeralds. The man I thought was special but turned out to be just like the rest. What I would give to be wrapped in his strong arms, to have his warm skin against mine, to feel the safest I've ever felt with him by my side. What I would give for things to be different.

I need to leave this town. I don't know where I'll go, but I figure anywhere is better than staying in a place which is just a reminder of what could have been, of what once was before all the deceit, and before I learned the truth that to lie is human; something which is woven into our very fabric.

A tear overspills and splashes on my knuckle, but I

haven't the energy to wipe it off as my head collapses back, my eyes gazing up at the dimming sky.

*Help me, Mum. Tell me what to do. Give me a sign that everything will be okay.*

Another exhale leaves me as a few more tears tumble.

'Emily?'

My head lifts, but I don't look at him. I can't.

'Let me guess, Maggie sent you,' I say coldly. Numbly.

'She's worried. And so am I.' Jackson ambles up to the bench as though he's proceeding with caution.

'You're worried? Somehow, I find that hard to believe. It's not like we're together or anything. Isn't that what you said?' I direct my eyeline over to him briefly before turning away again, too painful to remain. I note that he must've gone back to the annex because he's changed into his black jeans. Dex actually allowed him back there?

'I was way out of line.' I feel him lower to the bench. 'Emily, what happened with me and Lily, it started way before you even came to this town, and it stopped that night at Leo's party. I'm sorry I didn't tell you, I know I should have, I just didn't think it mattered, because nothing was or is going on anymore. I didn't want to hurt anybody unnecessarily.' His voice is strong, unwavering; honest. 'Emily, look at me.'

'Okay.' I glance across at his narrowed expression.

'Okay?' he asks.

'Okay, I believe you.' My focus shifts back to the ocean as I rest my chin on my knee. 'But that doesn't matter now. Nothing does.' I'm giving him the benefit of the doubt, however that doesn't alter my desolate state. It doesn't change the fact he failed to tell me about how he treated Olivia, what he had done with Lily in the first place, even when I asked him if there was anyone else. The trust has dwindled.

He doesn't respond for a moment before I feel him lean closer. 'Emily, what's going on? Mags called me in a state and said you were upset, she said you'd stormed out after packing your things. I know that's not just because of the whole thing at the barbeque.'

'What makes you so sure?'

'Because I can read you like a book, angel. Tell me,' he encourages softly, and it amazes me when my body doesn't melt from his soothing tone. For the first time whilst being in his presence, I am completely emotionless. Maybe it's because I know what I'm about to do. If I allow myself to feel, then it will be impossible.

'*This* is the book, Jackson. It's a fairytale.'

'What is?'

'Us, this place, it's not real. My life back in London, that's my reality. You were right, I was stringing you along, you were my little distraction, my holiday. But that holiday's over now. It's time to go back to the real world.'

'Says who?'

'Me.'

'That's what you want, is it?'

I don't reply, swallowing back my words. Of course, it isn't!

He shakes his head on a sigh, rubbing his temple and focusing his attention on the dark abyss of the ocean in front of us. 'I'm sorry for what I said,' he murmurs. 'You explained your feelings about our situation, and I agreed, but my emotions were heightened earlier, and it wasn't very nice.'

It may not have been nice, but it was the truth. As harsh as his words were, I know I've been selfishly stringing him along for a joy ride, expecting him to be true to me, even if I thought I was doing it for good reasons. Despite the initial benevolence behind our actions, we've both acted unfairly and when I peer across at his regretful face, I know he knows it too.

'Before you arrived, I had never opened up to anyone the way I have with you. I'd never wanted to.' His tone is quiet, low and gentle, my expression glum as I watch him cagily. 'But something happened to me when we met. I can't stop thinking about you. Every day, every hour, every fucking minute you're in my head and it's driving me crazy... I...' His eyes flicker over to meet my wide and warning blues. 'I want to be with you, Emily. You make everything better.'

'Stop.' I try, shaking my head. He doesn't listen, instead shifting closer, gaining confidence.

'For most of my life all I've wanted is to escape the demons in my head. I found myself here, and for a while it was good. I thought I'd found a home which would drive them away, but they were still there, no matter how hard I tried. You told me you want to be free, Emily, that's everything I've always dreamed about. I thought it was a place I was searching for, but now I realise, it's not. It's you. You're my freedom. Whenever I'm with you the demons leave me in peace.'

His words warm my skin. He's saying everything I've been unknowingly yearning for him to say. But he can't, not now. 'Jackson, stop.'

'Why are you pulling away? You never wanted anyone to know about us, you told me you didn't want anything more.'

'I don't,' I reply, the human side coming out as I lie through my teeth.

'There's a difference between not wanting something, and wanting something but not being able to have it for reasons I'm unknown to, because I know it's not just you having to go to university, or back to London. Am I too damaged for you, is that it?'

'Jesus, no, of course not.'

'Then, what? What is it?'

My mouth opens as I let out an irritated exhale. 'I told you, this isn't real!' I can't allow his words to break my barriers.

'What's not real about it?' he pushes, his voice becoming firmer and more rattled. 'When I kissed you for the first time in this exact spot after I'd opened up about my father, about things that have weighed me down for so long. When we slept together. When we talked. When I helped you when you were down, when you helped me. Was all of that not real?'

'Jackson…' I beg through my tone.

'Because it felt pretty fucking real to me.'

'Jackson, please. I'm not it, there's other girls out there who can offer you better… I'm happy to be on your list, just to have been able to meet you is enough for me.' I'm not happy, I want him all to myself. I want him!

'No, shut up. This wasn't some quick summer fling, not for me. And do you want to know how I know? Because every time I think about you my heart beats out of my fucking chest, whenever you look at me with those big blue eyes and when I see you smile, I feel this fullness inside that I've never felt before. The thought of you sends me wild, and yet whenever I'm with you every cell in my body relaxes. When I look into your eyes, when I touch you, when I hold you close and your perfume stays on my clothes for hours afterwards, I forget the parts of me which I loathe and it's just you and me. I don't know what this is or what we are, but I do know one thing, I'm looking at you now and I never want to let you go. I'm scared to let you go. Because I really don't know what I'll go back to being if you're not in my life.'

I feel my heart shatter with every word he speaks. My eyes swelling with every second they remain on his face. He's been my saving grace these past few weeks, he's opened up parts of me which I never knew I even had, and he's been there to hold my hand whenever I've needed him. But no matter how hard the weaker side of my heart tries, I cannot let the words roll from my tongue. The words which say, *I never want to let you go either*. But I must, because it's what's best for me, and with everything I now know, what's best for him. No matter how painful or difficult, I have to leave. I have to let him go. I can't allow anything else to be taken from me!

Jackson's hand inches towards my own which are wrapped loosely around my legs, but before he gets there, my back pocket buzzes. A shaky breath escapes me as I fumble around, awkwardly jerking the phone from my shorts. My eyes roll as I decline the incoming call.

'Who was that?' Jackson asks just as the screen flashes and the vibrations hum in my hand once again.

'What, Dad?' I grumble, sniffing back the tears. 'I need time to pro–

A muffled noise cuts me off. His speech is inaudible over the crackling line.

'I can't hear you.'

A feeble low voice comes through, but I still can't make out a single word and I'm growing agitated.

'I can't hear you,' I repeat more harshly.

'Em..ly, yo… nee… t…they... yo.. go,' the voice crackles.

'This is ridiculous, I'm hanging up,' I sigh as I cut the call off.

'What's the matter?'

I shove the phone back into my pocket, my head shaking. If only he knew.

He shuffles closer. 'Emily–

'I can't bear any more pain, Jackson,' I cry, lowering my legs to the ground. I pace a few steps away before running my hands over my face. 'I have to go.' I say the words to convince myself. I turn to him as he watches me closely from the bench.

'Go where? Back to London?'

'I don't know.'

He pauses, his forehead contorting. 'What do you mean *pain*? I've apologised for what happened with the girls, and if you're thinking back to that scumbag cheating, just know I would never–

'No, it's not that,' I say, waving my hand in the air and feeling the cold gust from the ocean hit me as I turn back. I'd rather face that than him. Maybe if he knew the truth, he'd realise that just being around me is one big risk. That I'm one big curse. 'There's something else going on, Jackson.' My eyes close as I take a deep breath. 'I have to tell you something about me. About why I'm here.'

'Okay, I'm listening.'

'That story I told you about how my mum died...' My eyes open as the lump digs deep into my throat.

'Yeah?'

'It turns out it's not...' My brow furrows as my words taper off, something catching my eye in the distance.

'Not what?'

I vaguely hear his voice as I tread forwards, my brow furrowing.

'Em?'

'Shh, look.'

'What–

'Jackson, look,' I repeat, almost like I want him to confirm that he's seeing this too and I'm not going crazy. The cloud of smoke grasps our attentions, making my heart quicken and my mouth dry.

'Shit!' he exclaims, and he's at my side in a flash. 'It's coming from The Marshlyn.' He takes off back down the hilltop. My head whips in his direction.

'Jackson?' I call and he halts in his tracks, spinning around. His face is a mixture of worry and impatience. 'Did you really mean what you said? That it was all real to you?'

His expression drops into that of sincerity, his lips pressed together. 'In every way,' he answers with a softness that somehow shatters my heart yet pieces it back together at the same time. The urgency is quick to return. 'Let's go!'

And with a skip of my heart, I follow right behind him.

# THIRTY-FIVE

We arrive to flashing lights.

Two ambulances and a fire engine are already outside; the latter parked as close to the entrance as possible. There's a crowd gathered in the car park with all eyes on the building in front of them. A few are wrapped in foil blankets, others being tended to by paramedics in and around the ambulances.

From the amount of smoke we saw on the clifftop, I'm amazed the whole building isn't ablaze, however the thick black cloud seems to be rising from the far end of the pub, near to where the kitchens are. I observe how the fire fighters race around, pulling equipment from the back of the truck and dashing in and out of the smoky building.

'Jesus,' I murmur under my breath just as my eyes lock onto an anxious looking Billy being comforted by a woman I've never seen before. I nudge Jackson's arm and gesture to him. He nods in understanding before I follow his lead and we make our way through the engrossed crowd.

'What the hell happened, Billy?' Jackson asks, his tone carrying intrigue, yet it's indubitably full of compassion.

'It started in the kitchens. I don't know what happened, all of a sudden the alarms were bleeping and smoke was pouring out the doors. They've said it's under control, but nevertheless, a fire is a fire, it's not going to be good.'

I try my best to concentrate on his relaying, but my eyes find a nauseating face in the distance. William's leaning against his Jag, gripping his blazer by his side, his tightened eyes are zoned in on me across the car park. I hastily shift my focus on a gulp, catching Jackson's reply.

'Do we know the damage?'

Billy shakes his head as his eyes watch the smoking building restlessly. 'No idea. I knew getting new kitchen staff in for the busy season was a bad idea.'

'What are you talking about?' Jackson asks.

'The head chef called in sick this afternoon, Tom's gone away with his wife, so I had no choice but to trust the new guys to go it alone for the night. It was all going well and then boom, they ran out yelling '*Fire, fire!*' What if we can't afford the damage? The insurance is going to increase tenfold,' Billy says, his head falling into his hands.

'It will be okay,' Jackson affirms, placing a comforting hand on Billy's shoulder.

'He's right, Billy,' the blonde lady who is side hugging him says. 'Let's be positive.'

'Alright, I'm positive it'll cost me an arm and a leg.'

Poor Billy. I watch the firefighters darting in and out and around the engine. A sudden vibration in my back pocket pulls me away from the commotion when I read the text illuminated on my screen.

*Look to your right.*

My eyes immediately scan the area, searching around the groups of people until they land on the sender. Guy is standing on the far side of the car park. Once we lock eyes, he motions for me to follow. My brow furrows as I notice the pleading and insistent look on his face. As I place my phone back into my pocket, he saunters around the corner and out of sight.

Apprehensively, I flicker my eyes back to Jackson comforting Billy. His back is to me, so I take my chance, gradually stepping backwards a few gaits at a time. Once far enough away, I spin, striding with swiftness over to where I saw Guy disappear. I reach the corner, gasping when I'm yanked into the wall.

'I need to get you out of here,' Guy urges, his head darting left, right and centre, even though we're now completely out of sight.

His large hand is wrapped firmly around my wrist and I don't think he realises his own strength, because it's uncomfortably tight. I can't draw my narrowed eyes away from his twitchy form. 'Why? Because of the fire? They said it's under control,' I respond, completely puzzled as to why this is an issue.

'How do you think it started?' he asks. It's rhetorical, but it spurs my thoughts. Freeing my wrist, he rubs his forehead. 'I've been so blind.'

'What do you mean, Guy?' My heart begins to thump in my chest as I study the unusually anxious man in front of me. 'You're scaring me,' I admit.

'They've been here the whole time, Emily.' My eyes flicker down as my mind races, worry setting in my stomach. 'I missed it completely,' he says bleakly under his breath, scolding himself.

'How?' I ask, now understanding exactly what, or rather, who he's referring to.

'Someone must've given them an idea of your whereabouts, they've been one step ahead of us the entire time.'

I feel my face contort in perplexity. This doesn't make any sense. 'How come they haven't tried to kill me? It's not as if I've been kept under lock and key.'

'I think they've been watching you, who you've been getting close to, possibly deciding when to make their move. Who knows what goes on inside their sick heads.' His tone is desperate. The fearless man who I've come to know is presenting nerves, yet what he's saying is sounding utterly bizarre given the only evidence he's exercising is the situation occurring right this second.

'Don't you suppose you're overthinking this a little? Billy said it started in the kitchens, it was an accident.'

'Or made to look like one,' he insists without indecision. And that's when I shudder. 'I came in for a drink the other evening and the owner said himself he's recently hired new staff. They're sick men, Emily. They're drawing you in, playing a game, and the next attack might just be Ms Taylor's shop or even the cottage.'

I take a moment to try and arrange my scrambled thoughts. 'You're trying to tell me that Carl is here?'

'Possibly.' He nods. 'And let's not forget the others who were sent down along with him.'

I take a breath as I bite down on my lip in anxious thought. I've never seen these *other men*, I only know what Dad has told me; that there were five of them. But my nightmares are haunted by one man alone and I don't have any doubt that I could spot him a mile away, especially in such a small town. 'Okay, say you're right, say they're here, where are they?' I may have no idea what they look like, but I know that's not the case for Guy. Dad would have given him a full debrief when he started working for him, and he hasn't mentioned seeing their faces.

'I don't know, and I don't like not knowing. I need to get you away as a precaution.'

'Does Dad know? Have you told him?'

'Not yet, I've only just worked it out.' He ponders, searching around in thought before locking my arms at my side and leaning in. 'Okay, here's what's going to happen,' his voice lowers, 'I'm going to contact your father, but my main concern is your safety, so I'm taking you somewhere away from here.'

My lips part as I shake my head in response. 'I can't just up and leave right this second. If you're right, and they are capable of arson, then like you said, what if they move on to the shop or the cottage? What about Aunt Maggie and my friends?'

'They'll be safe,' he stresses.

'You can promise me that, can you?' I press. Guy has been trained to protect, so although he may be a good person, I can guarantee the art of misleading has been drilled into his very core to be used to get subjects away in high-risk situations.

'As far as I'm aware, for the moment their main interest is you, but as soon as I get through to the Lambert Law and your father, I'll have a discreet protection team sent down to keep an eye on them. But you can't stay at Ms Taylor's anymore, it's lucky they've waited until now. I need to scope out a safe place to take you. In the meantime, is there anywhere you can go, just for half an hour or so while I sort things out?'

I draw a blank, running my fingers through my hair as I try to think under pressure, there's nowher–

'She can come with me.' The voice causes both of our heads to promptly search for the source. Jackson is standing yards away, watching me with curious eyes. How much did he hear? 'I don't know what the hell is going on, but if you need somewhere, I'm off the beaten track.' His focus drifts as he solely addresses Guy who still has a grip around my arm. 'She can stay with me.'

I look to Guy, his upper body is tense and his lips are drawn into a tight line. He's considering, using his experienced judgement to assess whether this is the right thing to do; to let me go with the man with the troubled past, the man he's so wary of. Much to my surprise, Guy peers down, searching my face for the answer. The short jerk of my head gives him his response. 'Thank you, Mr Turner,' he retorts and Jackson, although gathering himself quickly, seems taken aback by Guy's term of address for him. Guy spins back to me. 'I'll talk to your aunt about packing the rest of your things, go with Mr Turner and I'll come and get you in a short while. Promise me you won't leave unless it's with me.'

*Leave.*

My eyes flicker over Guy's shoulder, and with a twang in my heart, I meet his lingering gaze. Even if Guy is majorly overthinking this and fuelling his fears, he's now giving me an excuse to go, I've got to take it.

Except, there's now a reluctance inside of me, because I don't want to leave *him.*

I swallow back my apprehension as best I can. It's for my own good. My focus lands back on the resolute stare of my protector. 'I promise, Guy.'

'Good, now go.'

'I'm parked over here,' Jackson says as Guy flashes me a look of reassurance. I jog over to Jackson and we begin our hasty strides over to the Jeep in the car park. 'Are you going to explain what the fuck's going on?' he murmurs when he knows we're out of earshot.

'Let's just get out of here first,' I reply, eager to escape the open space. Although I'm not convinced Carl and his minions are actually here and are the cause of the fire, Guy has installed a fear inside of me and now I'm very much on edge.

We clamber into the car, but as Jackson pulls away, I don't miss William climbing into his own on the far side. My head drops into my hand resting on the ledge.

Jackson takes the familiar route. I want to ask him what happened earlier, whether he and Dex had words, what Lily had to say. There's an awkwardness in the air and I'm afraid that if I do ask, it'll lead to an argument, which I could really do without right now.

'What's this jerk doing?' Jackson gripes and I glance over to see what he's referring to. He keeps flicking his eyes to the rear-view mirror and I cringe, instantly knowing who he's frowning at. Nevertheless, I twist in my seat to get a glimpse through the back window. Bright headlights are flashing, and the car is driving dangerously close to our rear.

I sigh, slumping into my seat. 'That's William,' I breathe flatly as I stare vacantly out the windscreen.

Jackson's wide eyes fly across, shooting me a surprised look. '*William*, William?'

'Yep.'

He draws his emeralds back up to the rear-view for a final glance, before puffing his cheeks out and focusing back on the road ahead. 'This should be fun.'

Soon enough we're pulling onto his driveway, and so is my ex-boyfriend.

My feet only just meet the ground before he's out of his black Jaguar and marching over. I pay him no mind as Jackson unlocks the garage door. He wrenches it open, and I carry on inside. William's eyes are like thunder, trained on me as Jackson remains composed in the entrance, arms folded and blocking his path.

'Whoa, there! Where do you think you're going?' Jackson says, forcing out his hand which presses into William's chest, stopping him dead in his tracks. William looks taken aback, as though he hadn't even registered Jackson standing there at all. His riled eyes fly down to the hand which drives him backwards.

'Get out of my way!' William spits, his shoulders seeming to broaden, his chest swelling. If I wasn't overcome with exhaustion and fear I would be smiling, because even when William attempts to play the alpha male, Jackson still appears so much bigger and stronger and is entirely unperturbed.

'This is my house. You take one step inside, you're breaking the law, and I won't hesitate to call the police. You're technically trespassing just by being on my driveway uninvited, but we'll let that one go if you get the fuck off it right now.' Jackson's tone is calm, if not slightly sarcastic which seems to irritate William with his fists balling by his sides.

'Emily, I need to talk to you,' he says through gritted teeth, ignoring Jackson entirely and craning his neck to address me directly.

'William, just leave,' I moan, tired of his nonsense.

'So you're the infamous William,' Jackson teases to which I hold my breath. Don't try and get under his skin for the love of God, the last thing I need is for a fight to break out.

'Who the fuck are you?' William presses stepping towards him, but Jackson refuses to back down.

'Who I am is none of your business.'

'You are if you're involved with my girl,' William snipes before his eyes drift to the surfboard settled against the fence. 'You're a lifeguard?'

'Excuse me?'

'The surfboard and the hoodie,' William says, motioning to Jackson's grey sweatshirt where *Marshlyn Bay Lifeguard* is printed on the back and where I know to be written in the corner of his chest. 'Not being funny, pal, but it's not much of a career, is it? Now if you don't mind, I'd like a word with my girlfriend.'

Jackson steps into him, vexed by William's snarky comment. 'Why don't you shut the fuck up before I shut you up permanently!'

'I'd love to see you try.'

'For heaven's sake, both of you stop it!' I yell. Neither look, both too busy glaring at each other with clenched jaws. The testosterone is swamping the air. 'William, I'm not having another argument with you, can you please just go?'

William's tightened eyes travel up and down Jackson's form before they flicker over to me, his lip curling up in revulsion. 'Are you two sleeping together?'

'Am I not speaking English?'

'Is he the reason you won't come with me?' he asks, his rigid finger pointing at Jackson whilst his focus remains on me.

'*He* has a name, mate,' Jackson hisses.

'I'm not your mate,' William says, swinging his incensed scowl back to Jackson.

'No, and you're not her boyfriend either because you fuckcd that up, so I suggest you do as she says and get the hell away from her.'

'You know nothing about me or our relationship.'

'I know you treated her like crap,' Jackson counters.

'And you're so perfect.'

'I never claimed to be perfect, but at least I'm not a pathetic scumbag.'

'Say that again, pretty boy, I dare you!'

'Guys, *please!* I can't deal with this now.' My arms are thrown out in the air as I take myself away from them and drop down onto the sofa, my throbbing head lolling into my hands.

I hear a soft sigh before Jackson's gentle tone. 'Em–

He's cut off by the sound of chatter. My head lifts half-heartedly to see James and Vicki approaching the annex. Their eyes glance over at William and I notice how Vicki's narrow before they step inside.

'Where are the others?' I ask, still wondering what the hell happened after I fled the beach.

'Olivia took Leo away to calm down, and Lily's with Dex over at hers, they're having a talk. You didn't answer our calls, so we went to see if you were okay, Em, but you weren't there,' Vicki says before flicking a look over to William whose focus is on me once again. 'Who's this?'

I don't give him the satisfaction as I keep my eyeline away from him. 'This is William, my–

'*Boyfriend*–

'*Ex*,' we say in unison which conjures an instant glare from me. 'He was just leaving.'

Her mouth opens and closes as her eyes waver from me over to Jackson and William. 'Oh, have you two made up or are we interrupting something?' she asks, motioning between Jackson and I, who up until this question had continued to stare William down.

His hardened glower immediately softens when it meets mine. It's like we're looking to the other for confirmation on the situation, but his expression holds the same answer as I know mine does; we have no idea.

'It's complicated. Something's happening, or rather, something happened that I need to explain,' I reply tiredly. Where on earth do I begin?

'That's what I have to talk to you about. I saw Guy in the car park, I saw his face. I know they're here. This is exactly what I need to protect you from,' William says and I'm rising to my feet.

'Please, you're not bound by any fucking contract now so save me the headache of your grovelling bullshit. I hope you realise this is because of you, the reason these people are in danger is because of your messed up decisions.'

'You can't pin this on me, this is all your father.'

'I could've *died*, William! So don't give me any of your crap.'

'I didn't ask for this, Emily. Even if I was there that night, that prick still would've shown up and what's to say he wouldn't have killed me as well?'

'He would've done us all a favour.' I scoff, turning my back on him as I feel tears sting my eyes.

'You don't mean that.'

I don't, but I'm incredibly sensitive right now and if he doesn't leave soon, he's going to get another smack in the face. I thought he'd come down here because he was scared of me finding out about his contract with Dad, then I thought he was attempting to win me back to keep me sweet and keep his job, but now I'm wondering if there's something else. He's on edge, he's been on edge for a while, and when people are on edge, they can do things out of their nature.

'Did you do it?' I sniff, turning my head over my shoulder.

'Do what?' William replies, appearing perplexed like everyone else around me.

I face him directly. 'Did you tell them where I've been staying?' I ask, not entirely convinced he's capable of such a thing, but as I've come to learn, people can surprise you. It seems to have irked him nonetheless, which is giving me some satisfaction at least.

He recoils. 'What the fuck! *No!* Why would I?'

'I don't know.' I shrug. 'Bit of a coincidence you arriving just as the fire started, maybe it's a part of your messed-up plan, come in and save the day, I'll fall at your feet and you've got me back. Your job's saved.'

'You don't know what you're saying.'

'Or maybe they bribed you. How much did they pay you to give me up? I know how you like a bribe.' I'm pushing him and he's not liking it, but I don't care.

'Babe,' he tries, taking a stride forward but Jackson is quick to step in front, ensuring he doesn't take another.

'I think I'll go with the second option, you're too much of a coward to even think about saving me.'

'Will someone please explain what is going on?'

James calls, flashing glances between William, Jackson and me.

'William?' I ask, transfixing my focus on my tense looking ex. 'Why don't you enlighten everyone?'

'Emily,' he warns.

'Go on, tell them. Tell them how our relationship was nothing more than a contract created by my dad. Tell them what was going on the night you were at that filthy strip club.'

'How many more times do I need to apologise? I'm so sorry for what I did, I'm sorry for what you went through, and I'm sorry I wasn't there!'

I laugh lightly, rubbing my forehead despairingly. 'Hannah was right about you, you're nothing but an arse.' Dragging my feet back over to the sofa, I flop down as I let my emotions take control of my exhausted, weakened body. A flurry of tears tumble down my cheeks before deep sobs are shaking my whole body, my head in my hands. I'm so tired of everything. I feel someone kneel in front of me as a large hand is placed on my thigh.

'Hey,' Jackson coos. 'Emily, look at me.' When I fail to move, his hand leaves my leg to wrap loosely around my wrist, encouraging me to face him. Reluctantly and with a couple of sniffles, my eyes meet his warm but concerned emeralds. 'Whatever's happening, I'll help you. We all will. But you've got to give us some insight here.' He leans in closer. 'Please, angel,' he whispers so only I can hear. His thumb is brushing light circles over my skin and it's like the tiniest piece of my broken heart is being fixed back into place.

I release a shaky breath. 'It's them.'

'Who?' he asks, his eyes narrowing in confusion.

'The reason I'm here.'

'You told me it was because your dad messed up?'

'The n... the night it happened,' I stutter my way through, the weight on my shoulders becoming too much to bear.

'When what happened?'

'Emily,' William warns again.

'Jesus Christ,' Jackson groans. '*Shut up!*' he spits, throwing William a warning glare.

'Don't tell me what to do.'

'I'll do whatever the hell I want, let her speak!'

'That's rich, William,' I say, my eyes remaining on Jackson who glances back to me.

'Seeing as you've been Dad's bitch ever since you started working for him, coming to his every beck and call, his every need.' I shift my scowl over to my ex whose jaw is now clenched tight. 'Except that one night when *I* needed you, you weren't there.'

'What night?' Vicki asks.

'When he was at a strip club, running away from his problems like a coward, his house was broken into with me inside. The man had a gun on him and if it wasn't for Buddy, I would probably be dead.' It's like the air has evaporated from the room, taking the sound with it. Jackson's grip on my leg tightens, his knuckles turning white. 'That's why my dad sent me to stay with Aunt Maggie,' I continue, speaking solely to the stunned, lifeguard in front of me. 'The same man killed my mum. My dad's a lawyer, he got him locked up years ago and now he's been released, he wants to make my father suffer by getting to me. I've been hiding, but him and his gang have found me.'

Jackson is frozen, his expression unreadable but his eyes remain on me. I should be feeling relief as a section of the weight crushing me has been lifted, but the sickness in my stomach is overriding everything.

'That's why I've come to take you away,' William announces, and it's now I notice he's stepped over the threshold and into the living room, his daggers zoned in on Jackson's back.

'Take me away?' I snort, laughing incredulously. 'You know when I walked into Dad's office that night you were as white as a sheet, obviously I thought it was because you were worried about me, but it wasn't, was it? It was because you were worried that Dad would find out what you had been up to. You were worried you'd lose your job, your money, your reputation. Not one ounce of you was worried about me!' I cry through my tears.

'That's not true,' William murmurs. 'I care about you.'

'You only care about yourself, and it's taken me two years to realise it.' I turn my head away, unable to stand the sight of him any longer.

'Emily, please,' he tries.

'I think it's time you left.' Vicki's tone is chilling, unsympathetic, her arms folded with James's dotingly around her waist.

'Not without Emily.'

'I'm not coming with you. I never want to see you again.'

'Bab-

'You heard her.' Jackson breaks his silence. His eyes are set, exuding a deep hatred. He rises slowly, facing William.

'What are you going to do?' William remarks, his arms opening up confidently either side of him. 'I've been by her side for two years. I know her, and I know what's right for her, and that's for me to take her far away from here.'

'What, so you can hurt her again? So you can leave her for dead to stick your tongue down a strippers throat?' Jackson barks back.

'You don't know what's going on, you have no idea what's best for her.'

'And you do?'

'Yes. I have money, I have contacts and clients who

can help us build a life elsewhere,' William snickers. 'What have you got? A shitty so-called job in a shitty town. You're not what she needs. She needs a man who can look after her, not some pathetic, penniless lifeguard with nothing but a tragic garage and fucking toffee-nosed friends.'

It happens too quickly for anyone to react. Jackson lurches forward, grabbing William by the collar of his shirt and shoving him hard against the back wall. James responds first, racing over in attempt to haul Jackson away, but he's too strong and determined.

'Jackson!' I cry, standing from the sofa.

'Do it, hit me!' William taunts as Jackson raises his fist.

Vicki is looking on with her hand over her mouth, but I'm not surprised. After what happened on the beach I now know how Jackson is capable of lashing out when he gets worked up, and I'm in no way arguing that William deserves another punch to the face, but this will cause more problems than he's worth.

'Jackson, stop!' I exclaim, however as I'm about to sprint over to help James, another body is ripping Jackson away.

'What the hell have I missed?' Dex pants with his hands clamped around Jackson's arms.

William fixes his shirt whilst continuing to eyeball Jackson. He pushes himself off the wall and turns his darkened expression onto me. 'This is the person you want to stay with?' he laughs disbelievingly.

I follow his outstretched arm which leads me to Jackson. He's scowling at William. His wavy hair is ruffled and his breathing rugged as his chest heaves up and down, but he still looks so perfect. My eyes flicker to the floor before they meet William's dark, narrowed, expectant stare. 'Yes,' I declare.

Jackson's head shoots over to me, but I don't look back, instead making my resolute decision known to William with a strong, unwavering glare.

'You're making a huge mistake, Emily.'

I shake my head slowly from side to side. 'My mistake was ever trusting you.'

He appears taken aback for a moment, wounded by my comment, but he's quick to gather himself. His head bobs up and down, sniffing harshly before sauntering over to me, Dex the only barrier keeping Jackson from tearing William's head off. He peers down at me as my neck cranes to maintain our eye contact, my jaw clenched as I refrain from slapping him. 'You'll realise soon enough,' he murmurs, 'and I'll be waiting when he breaks your heart.' Flashing one last look of disdain over to Jackson, William marches away before climbing back into his Jag and zooming off the driveway.

The tense atmosphere consumes the room with no indication of it waning anytime soon.

'He seems lovely,' Dex says as he releases his grip on Jackson. 'Are you okay, Em?'

My eyes sink. 'Yeah,' I reply, my chest finally breathing as the weight from the intense atmosphere is lifted.

'I thought you were with Lily?' Vicki asks.

'I was,' Dex replies.

'Look, mate–

My gaze lifts.

'It's okay, Jackson,' Dex says. 'She explained and I believe you, I just wish you would have told me.'

Jackson avoids his stare, flicking his eyes around the room as he nods regretfully. 'I'm sorry. I didn't want to spoil what you had going on... what you *have* going on.'

'I know, I get it. We're good, brother, trust me,' Dex retorts, patting him reassuringly on the back. 'But go near her again and I'll kill you,' he adds on a chuckle.

'That's fair.' Jackson breathes a sigh of relief, squeezing Dex's shoulder.

Somehow, I manage to raise a small smile as I watch the pair make up, but Dex's next question causes it to drop instantly.

'Now, would someone care to explain what the hell all that was about?' he asks, peering around the room in confusion.

'From what I gathered, someone is after Emily and shit hit the fan because the prick of an ex found out about her and Jackson,' James explains when nobody responds.

My bottom lip is brought in between my teeth as I

chew on it anxiously. 'Where is Lily?' I manage to ask, shifting the subject, my blood mercifully beginning to cool.

'She was getting changed and coming over, I told her I had to speak to Jackson so left her to it.'

Jackson moves cautiously to my side. 'Can we talk?' he asks softly.

I gaze up at him sadly, but the buzzing of my phone prevents my reply. The name lights up on my screen. I bring it to my ear on narrowed eyes. 'Lily?'

Every head, every pair of eyes and every body in the room turns to me.

Heavy pants travel down the line, but it's the helpless sob which causes my heart to plummet into my stomach.

'Not quite,' the gruff, unfamiliar voice replies, 'but she is here.'

'Who is this?' I breathe, swallowing down the lump in my throat, turning my back on everyone and treading a few paces away. The cloying feeling in my gut tells me I already know.

'You know what we want, Emily. We're on the beach bank waiting for you.'

I pause, clamping my eyes shut. 'And if I don't come?' Stupid, *stupid* question!

'Oh, I think you're aware of what we're capable of. If you phone the police or bring anyone along we'll know, and we'll be forced to do something to your little friend which by all means can be avoided. Come alone and she'll be safe. You have ten minutes.'

The line goes dead. The phone, heavy in my hand, slips from my grip, crashing onto the floor as my heart sinks.

*Fuck!*

# THIRTY-SIX

'No. No way am I letting you go!' Jackson argues sternly, now at my side.

'Surely there's another way,' Vicki adds, her fingers rubbing her forehead anxiously.

When I let the words pass my lips, *'They've taken Lily'*, panic set in, bouncing off all five bodies in the room and suffocating us.

'Let me get this straight, these are the men who killed your mum?' Dex asks, his hands clamped together in a prayer position.

'They were there when it happened, yes,' I reply, my breathing rugged.

'And if you don't go, they'll hurt Lily?' he continues, his words trying to comprehend, but his voice trembling.

'Or worse.'

'Shit,' he curses, his fingers running over his spiky hair.

'You're not going,' Jackson says resolutely.

'What about Lily? I'm not going to leave her!'

'We'll all go, how many of them are there?' James asks, stepping forward.

'I don't know, Dad told me the night it happened

there were five of them, but that was over thirteen years ago. I'm walking into the unknown.'

'Five of them, five of us. Like James said, we'll all go,' Dex says, his body bold and confident, but his eyes and tone are patently laced with worry.

'No.' I shake my head. 'I can't risk your lives as well as Lily's, I have to go alone.'

'What about your life, doesn't that matter?' Jackson argues and I avert my gaze. 'Emily, this is fucking ridiculous, you're unprotected!'

'I know!' I shout, my body is getting worked up as my mind shuts down, overcome with anxiety and fear. That is, until a single spark triggers in my mind as I remember.

'There must be something we can do,' Vicki says.

'There is.' All eyes fix on me. 'I have to do this on my own, there's no getting away from that, but I won't be completely unprotected.' Every face contorts in confusion as I swallow and glance up, peering into Jackson's apprehensive emeralds. 'I have a gun,' I murmur.

'Say that again?' James says as Jackson's eyebrows screw.

'It's not mine, it's his; the man who attacked me,' I explain, facing James. 'I snatched it the night he came for me.'

'Where is it?' Dex asks, Jackson still quiet. My skin is on fire, his hardened stare remaining set on me.

'Under my bed at the cottage. I can get it, but I have

to be quick. They gave me ten minutes.'

'I'll drive,' Jackson says faintly but adamantly as he stalks out to the Jeep before I can argue.

I turn to the others. 'Please stay here, I don't want anyone else getting hurt.'

'Em, she's my girlfriend, I can't–

'She'll be fine, Dex. As long as they see me, she'll be safe.'

He strides over, pulling me into a strong embrace. 'I need you to be safe too, you and Jackson.'

'We'll be okay,' I say, struggling to sound as confident as I can whilst crumbling on the inside. He's very much aware of this because he squeezes me incredibly tight, placing a gentle kiss on my cheek.

He breaks away just as Vicki draws me into her. 'Be safe, but remember you're more confident than you believe,' she whispers into my ear as James rubs my arm and tries to show as much of a reassuring smile as he can manage to which I reciprocate, but as soon as my back is turned, my heart breaks as my hands begin to quiver and my legs turn to jelly.

My bum hits the seat and Jackson speeds away.

'Why didn't you tell me?' he mutters on a low tone. There's no anger in his question just disappointment, which is the worst of all.

'Where would I have started, Jackson?'

My fidgeting fingers meet my lips as I stare into the pitch-black world beyond the Jeep's headlights. He sighs, his hand coming to rest on my naked thigh, squeezing softly. My eyes flicker down at our connection before locking with his gaze momentarily, our somber expressions matching. No words spoken. No words need to be spoken so long as he's next to me and I am him. He focuses his attention back onto the road, but mine remains on him. I know what he'll say – what he'll keep saying. But I can't let that happen. I have to keep him safe. I have to go alone.

Seconds after we arrive outside, we're racing into the cottage and up the stairs. I dash over to my bedside table. Flicking the lamp on, I discreetly slide the silver key from on top of the table into my palm before heading over to the other side of the bed and drawing out the material from my backpack. I feel Jackson's watchful daggers flicking between me and the hoodie as I carefully unfold it. My heart quickens as the menacing looking black object is revealed to us.

'You weren't kidding,' he says on a nervous scoff.

I place the gun onto the bed before pulling the thick material over my head. With bated breath, I wrap my clammy fingers around the handle, gingerly manoeuvring it behind my shorts and fixing it on my waist. The cold metal against my skin makes me shiver as I pull my hoodie down to conceal the gun.

'Do you know how to use that thing?' Jackson asks, gesturing to my hip.

'Guess I'll find out.' I shrug, my voice wavering as I try desperately to keep the tears at bay. Jackson gazes back at me helplessly and it's as though someone's jabbing several knives into my heart at once. 'I'm sorry I've gotten you involved in this mess,' I say solemnly, the quiver in my voice undeniable. 'Do you see now why I tried to tell you we shouldn't become too involved? Not just because I'm leaving, but...' I hinder the growing lump in my throat with a swallow and a sigh. 'I wasn't only protecting my own heart; I was protecting you from me. Jackson, everything I touch goes wrong. Dad, William, Mum, Aunt Maggie... I didn't want *you* to go wrong. I didn't want anyone else affected because of me, and now Lily's in danger...'

His jaw clenches and his chest expands when I fail to finish. He strides over, tugging me into his body and wrapping his arms tightly around my small frame.

'Lily is going to be okay, and so are you.'

'All of this is not what you need, Jackson.'

I hear him sigh as his chin rests in my hair. 'What I need is *you*,' he murmurs softly.

I gulp, glancing up at him. His eyes would be keeping me in place even if his arms were not. His thumb traces over my cheek. How has my life gotten to this point? All this pain and fear, and yet just having him here, feeling his touch on my skin, his eyes on mine, it's providing the comfort I need to keep my legs from crumpling under this pressure. It would be too much to handle if anything happened to him, especially as it would be my fault.

'No one is getting hurt, not today,' he affirms, like he can read my mind. 'Let me come, we can work out a plan.'

'I don't want to risk it.'

'But you'll risk your own life?'

'For the sake of my friend, yes.'

His eyes run over my face, before he sucks in a breath and unites them with mine again. 'You're the bravest person I know, angel.'

'You might want to rethink that statement, because right now I'm shitting my pants,' I say, my eyes now glassy.

'Whilst we're in the moment, are there any other surprises you want to spring on me?' He's trying to ease the situation, but it doesn't help to calm me, because I know what I'm about to do and he isn't going to like it.

'Just one.' I lean up on my tiptoes and connect my lips with his. It's passionate, intense and desperate. Neither one of us wanting to be the first to retract, knowing that when we do, it will be time to face what's waiting in the darkness. Gripping his hoodie tight, with an irrepressible sob, I reluctantly pull back. Our lips are still so close, lightly brushing before he leans down, resting his forehead on mine. I close my eyes, savouring his touch, his smell, his presence; they should make me stronger, but in this instance, they're my weakness.

I force myself to block them out, enabling me to build

up my courage. 'I'm sorry,' I whisper before rushing past him and yanking the door shut. He calls out my name over and over, banging on the wood. The handle jolts up and down frantically as he tries to get out. It's too late, he's locked in.

I try to ignore the pain in my chest which pangs with every cry from my bedroom and every step I take away from him.

Aunt Maggie and Buddy are waiting for me in the hallway. 'Let him out in about half an hour,' I say, tossing her the key. That should be enough time… for what I'm not so sure on. She catches it effortlessly, but her eyes are narrowed as she stares at the object in her palm.

'What's going on?'

'Where's Guy?' I ask, ignoring the question, instead searching behind her, hoping he'll appear from the living room ready with a plan to get us out of this disarray. But he doesn't.

'I don't know, he went to the restaurant because we saw the smoke. I haven't seen him since.'

My sigh is shaky as I run my hands nervously through my hair before scraping it all up into a ponytail.

'It's them, isn't it? They're here,' she says whilst I try my best not to look at her directly; still mad at her, but also feeling guilty for being so.

'Just promise me you won't follow, or call the police, or do anything.'

'Emily…'

'Promise me, Aunty! Please,' I beg, my voice quivering and my throat burning as I desperately try to keep myself together. 'I'll be okay.'

She hugs me tight. 'I love you. Remember that.'

I nod, still avoiding eye contact as we pull away. I don't want her to see me breakdown. Kneeling on the floor, I bury my head in Buddy's fur, his comforting smell sending me over the edge. My face scrunches up and the tears fall. 'No saving me this time, Bud.' He conceals his head in my lap, like he knows something's wrong, because this is his way of soothing both himself and me. With a deep and shaky breath, I straighten before spinning on my heels, letting Jackson's distant yells and bangs wash over me.

My footsteps smack onto the tarmac, carrying me down the hill. It seems to take forever and my nerves increase with every footfall. I don't know what to expect. I don't know what state Lily will be in. I don't know how many of them there will be. But what I do know is, no matter how terrified I am, I'm putting up a fight to save my friend; just like Mum did. I'm staying strong like I know she would. How I know she did.

Passing The Marshlyn, I see the blue lights have vanished and from what I can tell, the car park is empty, which only frightens me more. I was secretly hoping people would still be around, because then there might have been a chance someone would see or hear something and come to help. But now there really is only me.

My chest heaves as I slow to a cautious walk, the murky car park nearing. My eyes are vigilant, darting every which way, but it's so dark I can hardly make out a thing.

As I approach, I halt, knowing that out the corner of my eye I've spotted a parked car overlooking the bank. After a few tense moments of nothing but the sound of my heavy pants and the sea crashing onto the shore, I hear Lily. Her sobs carry through the air, touching my skin as they crawl down my spine causing a chilling shiver.

*Big girl pants. Big girl pants. Put them on for Lily!*

My feet move once again, but not as expected as the air is knocked from my lungs. I land on my knees with a thud, cursing as the gravel digs and cuts into the skin on my legs and palms, only the pain is quickly suppressed. I recoil on a gasp, eyes wide as they gape over Guy's unconscious form lying face down on the gravel.

'Glad you could make it, Emily,' a gruff voice calls, making me wince. My head shifts to where it came from and my heartbeat doubles when I see the outlines of three figures across the car park. They're not clear but it's still fairly obvious as to what's happening, which only adds to the nauseous feeling in my stomach.

'What did you do to him?' I ask, scolding myself for my obvious timid tone. Although I feel like they're going to collapse, I force my legs to straighten and take a few small and steady steps towards the dark figures.

'Oh, he's okay. He'll have a nasty headache when he wakes up. Apparently not as tough as he looks.'

I pause as the shapes begin to move towards me and I wait with bated breath as their faces become clearer. Two men; one tall, one much shorter, both beckoning bile in my throat as the taller man drags Lily along beside him. Her weak and shaky knees only being supported and encouraged to hold out by the knife held across her throat. Her cheeks are tear stained, her red hair messy, but what sickens me the most is the thick inflamed mark below her mouth.

'Let her go,' I say, mustering as much confidence as possible to not sound like a pathetic, nervous mess.

'E–Emily, what's go...ing on?' she whimpers, breaking my heart in two. Her eyes are filled with alarm, but I attempt to make mine appear as assuring as I can.

'Lily, it's okay.' My hardened stare slithers between the two men dressed in baggy black and white chef trousers and dark jackets. 'You have me now, I'm here. Let her go,' I beg, the pain evident in my voice as it shakes on every word.

The lanky man doesn't listen, he watches me before glancing smugly across to his hand gripping the knife against my friend's throat. 'Carl Mason sends his regards, he's sorry he couldn't be here personally.'

'Did he get a better offer?' I inwardly wince at my bite back, but the name, along with what I'm currently witnessing, induces a fire inside which I can't control.

'He has other urgent matters to deal with,' the shorter man speaks for the first time.

'Being a bastard criminal must be hard work, such a busy schedule it seems,' I retort, channelling my angst through my fingertips as I dig my nails into my palms. My stomach is in my throat, but I mustn't let it show.

'Oh, he's not the criminal, Emily,' tall guy counteracts, a subtle lightness to his tone as though he's laughing at me.

'Yes, he is! Look at what he's done. Look at what *you're* doing!' I seethe through gritted teeth, throwing my hand up angrily to gesture towards Lily who is trembling with streams of tears sticking to her face.

'We like to call it restoration of balance,' the shorter man with darker features says on a lick of his teeth. I notice how he's shuffled forward, inching closer to me.

'What are you talking about?' I ask, naturally edging back with microscopic steps.

'We didn't call you here for a chinwag,' lanky man grumbles. He jerks Lily closer to him which makes her cry out, and my hand instinctively hovers over the gun on my hip. 'You see, we want your father to pay for what he did to us, especially Carl,' he expresses with a calmness that is dangerously menacing, his mouth brushing Lily's ear. 'He thinks by killing you it'll break your dad completely, ideally he wanted to be the one to do it, but he told us if an accident was to occur and you just so happened to be caught in the midst, that would be absolutely fine. A dead daughter is a dead daughter after all. And those cliffs,' he whistles, 'they are perilous. Would be terrible if someone were to get a little too close to the edge.'

'You think you'll get away with this? You're willing to risk a life sentence in jail for the sake of revenge? Revenge that doesn't even make sense. My dad sent you all away for crimes that were completely justified.'

'That's what he told you, is it?' He laughs lightly. 'Oh, naïve little Emily, you have a lot to learn about the world, and your father it seems. It's a shame you'll never get the chance.' I swallow at his words as the shorter man smirks. 'Why don't we have a wander up to the clifftops?'

'Let her go first.'

His eyes narrow before he frees the knife from Lily's neck. With it still in his grip he motions to the shorter man, silently telling him to make a move on me before returning the blade to Lily's skin. Instinctively I begin to lift the bottom of my hoodie, but as he starts towards me, headlights illuminate the car park, and my head is snapping around. Stones crunch underneath the wheels, my eyes squinting as the fluorescent lights blind me.

'Who the hell is this?' I hear the shorter man's voice carry from behind.

The lights flick off, as does the engine, and four figures climb out of the car – James's car.

*No! Get back inside. Turn around. Drive away!*

'*Emily!*' the voices call.

'*Lily!*' more voices yell over the top.

'Emily,' tall man cautions as my disconcerted focus remains on the four people running towards us, 'think about your friend. We won't hesitate,' he forewarns.

I act on reflex; my hand leaves my waist as I throw both of them out in front. 'Stop!' I call. They all halt. Except Jackson. 'Jackson!' He pauses at my despairing scream, his face etched with fear, anger, concern... pain.

'We told you to come alone,' the rough voice from behind gripes sharply.

My chest heaves as my eyes remain locked on my floppy haired lifeguard, mentally padlocking him to the floor. I'm scared that if I shift, he'll move from his fixed stance and let his anger take over, something which I'm not prepared to watch the consequences of.

'I told them not to follow,' I reply shakily, aiming it more so at Jackson whose concerned expression only grows.

'Let's cut the crap, shall we?'

I slowly turn myself around.

'Up,' tall guy asserts, gesturing to the steps leading to the clifftop. My eyes lower as my mind races, trying to find a way to get out of this. 'Now!' he yells. I flinch. He lifts the knife to point at the others behind me. 'If you try anything stupid, your friends are dead.'

My eyes flutter closed. 'Were you responsible for the

fire at the restaurant?' I dare, opening up my eye lids to glare at the two men.

The shorter guy throws his head back, laughter echoing around us. 'What do you think?'

'Why?'

'For fun,' he spits, and Billy's distressed face forms an image in my mind, merging with the sound of Lily's sobs. 'Now, shall get this fucking show over with?'

I find the strength. 'Yes.' In a flash I'm drawing the gun. Both men recoil.

'Put that down, girl. Don't mess with what you don't understand,' shorter guy warns, his lip curling into a snarl as my fingers tremble over the trigger and I aim the barrel at him.

'Never underestimate a girl in desperation,' I murmur. With a quivering grip, a pounding heart and gritted teeth, my breathing is ceased… *Click!*

Nothing.

No bang.

No crumpling of a body.

'Fuck,' I rasp, gaping at the useless object in my hands.

'Jesus Christ, I'm done with this shit! Just grab her, Mitch!'

My eyes widen as my focus darts up. Mitch releases a grunt and snarl as he closes the space between us.

I'm frozen in place... until I see a figure lurking behind Lily.

'Emily, move!' Jackson's call resonates through my whole body, seeping into my legs which waste no time in shifting. I put my training to good use, sprinting as fast as I can across the car park as I catch Guy ripping the man away from Lily. The hammering of footsteps behind spurs me on, adrenaline acting as my fuel and accelerating my pace. I reach the bank, quick little steps carrying me down – until they don't.

I'm grasped.

My feet falter and the force from the man attached to my arm pulls us both to the ground. Round and round, unable to stop the momentum as my head hits the sand, an amalgam of limbs flailing everywhere as we tumble down the never-ending bank.

My body crashes to the bottom and both of our groans of pain and discomfort fill the air. Whilst he remains on the floor, I frantically take the chance to struggle to my feet. '*Shit!*' I hiss when my foot meets the ground, a shooting sensation springing from my ankle, bouncing up my leg as I put one foot in front of the other. My attempt of pushing through the pain ends abruptly when he lets out a guttural cry, seizing my body. The gun is thrown from my hand as I grapple with him, pushing, hitting, shoving. His strength is too much for me, until I throw my working foot in the air and connect with his groin.

'*Arrgghhh!* Little bitch!' He crumples to the floor as I free myself and hobble over to where I hope the gun had been tossed. It's so dark I can't see anything. My eyes are drawn into slits trying to locate it.

My gasps are heavy as my leg is snatched from under me. My body plummets to the floor, but as I land, the once threatening object now fills me with courage as it reveals itself to me.

Despite Mitch clawing at my ankles, I grunt and groan, throwing all my energy into crawling along the sand to reach it. It's in vain. His heavy body skulks on top of me and wrenches me onto my back. I don't have time to think or put up a fight as his big, resilient hands wrap around my neck in a death grip. My legs flail and my fingernails claw and dig into his wrists, but nothing helps. All I can do is stare up into his determined, dark eyes as the smirk on his evil face grows with every second I spend unable to breathe. I can feel my lungs aching as I let out a strangled scream and squirm underneath him. This only causes him to push down harder, the edge of my vision darkening. My hand smacks down onto the sand as I make a last attempt at searching for the gun, desperately and blindly hunting the area in reaching distance before I lose consciousness altogether. Every part of me starts to slow; my heart, my energy, my mind.

Every part of me, except my hope.

My fingers, still in search, knock against something solid and it's like everything in me restores as I grip the object and hurl my arm through the air until it connects with the side of his head. His hands loosen enough for me to draw in air. I hit him again, this time he collapses off me and I'm able to escape from under him, rolling to the side. I splutter and wheeze, every intake of oxygen like a morphine shot to my lungs.

Forcing my legs up, the gun is held in my outstretched hand as I stand gasping over his weakened body.

'Do it. Go on,' he spits feebly, the blood trickling down the side of his face in a slow pool.

My throat hurts, burning every time I swallow or inhale. My head is woozy. I can feel myself swaying on the spot as my body works to recover from the dizziness. But through my pain and weakness, I try to appear as poised and confident as I can to show this bastard I'm stronger than he expected.

'*Emily!*'

'Pull the trigger,' he dares.

I glance to the gun and notice a catch on the top.

'*Emily!*' the voice calls again. It's Jackson. I don't turn around but I can hear hustling behind me as he charges onto the beach.

Without a thought I pull the safety lock towards me and there's a click as it bolts into place. It dawns on me that I'm holding a loaded firearm which is now ready to kill. My shaking finger hovers over the trigger as I aim the barrel at the unusually composed man beneath me.

'Don't, Emily,' Jackson says, now beside me.

I don't reply or shift my gaze as I concentrate on watching the man lying on his back, too scared to look away in case he makes any sudden movements.

'The other guy pissed off,' he continues.

Mitch flashes Jackson a brief startled glance before setting his narrowed face and fixing it on me again.

'Lily's safe, they're calling the police. It's over, Emily.'

*Over?*

Mitch laughs, grating on me like nails down a blackboard. 'Just like your mother, weak and pathetic.'

'Shut up,' I warn, my breathing heavy and jagged.

'*Emily!*' More voices travel from behind, but they're distant. I'm too focused on the gun in my hand and the man it's aimed at to acknowledge who they belong to.

'Emily, listen to me, be the bigger person,' the voice beside me says.

I risk a glance. His arm is snaked across his body as it clenches his other, and that's when I see the blood between his fingers. My stare hardens as the voice from the ground has the nerve to comment again.

'It really was a shame she died, good looking woman like that.'

My teeth grind, my eyes turning to glassy slits. 'I said, shut up!'

'Emily,' Jackson tries again but it's washed-out by the ringing in my ears.

'I bet she was a damn good shag.'

The words release the trigger, my finger acting of its own accord. A harrowing cry echoes around me as my senses go completely numb. My hearing blurs and distorts along with my vision. It's like my brain has shut down my entire body, and it's a wonder how I'm still standing on my feet as everything deadens into an emotionless mist.

The blood is the first I see when my vision returns. It's oozing from his leg as he rolls around in distress. My arm is still outstretched, the gun feeling like a giant boulder in my hand.

A touch on my shoulder brings me back, I flinch and swing around, the gun still pointed. Guy has his hands up, ready to take it from me. 'It's okay, Emily. Give me the gun.'

I hesitate. My mind is frozen, cutting off the flow of all activity and instructions to the rest of me. My whole body is dazed and weak. He steps up to me carefully, shifting to the side and out the way of the barrel. Wrapping his hand over the top, I finally release and it's as though strings have been cut, my arm flopping to my side. I can only watch as Guy races into action, putting Mitch on his front, pinning him down.

Reality dawns on me and my feet stumble backwards as my legs finally give way. I drop to the floor, my eyes focused on the two men directly in front, but my mind elsewhere. Arms are around me in seconds and I let my head fall, burying it into the recognisable, soothing smell of Jackson's chest. I let the sobs escape.

'Shhh, shhh. I'm here,' he coos. 'You're safe.' His breath fans my neck as he pulls me close and his hand cradles my head. I'm drawn onto his lap as I hide myself away, concealing into his body. 'Everything's okay now.' His words should fill me with hope and comfort, but somehow, I don't believe them to be true.

My head lifts as I remember the sight of blood on his fingers as he clutched his arm. 'You're hurt,' I blubber, inspecting the cut which has pierced through the material of his hoodie.

'It's not bad, angel. Just a nick.'

The side of my head slumps back onto his chest as my hands grip him tight. The mere feel of him is a gift. I didn't think I would ever again 'I'm sorry,' I whisper desolately.

'Stop now,' he croons as I'm cuddled closer.

The sound of shuffling of feet is faint, until Vicki appears in sight and kneels down beside us. She doesn't say anything, her flustered and saddened exterior speaking for her.

Blubbering sounds touch my ears, rotating my head. Dex has Lily in a hold as she cries into him and James watches the man groaning on the floor in shock. Vicki's hand meets my back, rubbing soothing circles as I weep into Jackson's chest.

My friends are okay. They're safe. But there's a new feeling settling in my gut, because something tells me this isn't over.

# THIRTY-SEVEN

The hollowness all around seems unfamiliar, and yet at the same time, it feels like I've carried it all my life. Though right now it's so much more heightened than I've ever known.

It's still dark as I rest on Aunt Maggie's front garden bench. The seeds of morning are being sown through the marginal lightening of the black sky over the clifftops. Buddy is lying at my feet, providing the only smidgen of warmth to my body. It has been hours since my friend was taken, since I felt the darkness creeping in as I was strangled mercilessly, since I fired the gun.

The police came, as did a couple of ambulances carrying paramedics who saw to Jackson and Lily's wounds, as well as my own. We each gave a statement about what had happened, Guy made sure the police were aware that my impulsive pull of the trigger was entirely in self-defense; he took care of the rest, speaking to them for a good hour. Mitch was formally arrested and taken away in an ambulance, but no news came of the other who had driven off.

My hands haven't stopped trembling. What occurred is now a deep blur, but my body seems to remember as it betrays me, exposing my emotions. Jackson is with Guy next to the Mercedes, their backs to me. He refused to leave my side, and normally I would be relieved by that gesture; to feel safe in his arms. But my need to be alone in this moment is great, which is ironic considering it's what I've been trying to escape from practically my whole life.

I draw in a jolted, pain-filled breath – my throat and lungs still aching – and allow my eyes to close. I'm so tired, but my fear of falling asleep is worse than before, because now there are more faces to see, and a bleaker darkness waiting to suffocate me in my nightmares.

'Keep your face to the sun and you will never see the shadows,' the voice from beside the bench says softly. 'Helen Keller,' Aunt Maggie confirms as she peers down at me, her grey eyes are big and sad, but mine hold no expression as I return my gaze to the distance. 'Easier said than done though, hey?' she murmurs, gaging my current state.

Even if I was able keep my face to the sun, the shadows would find some way of creeping into sight.

'Here,' she says, breaking the silence and offering me the mug of tea she's cupping. I reach up, momentarily forgetting about my quivering hands. She notices and smiles sadly before balancing the steaming mug on top of the arm rest and sitting down beside me. She takes both of my hands from my lap and holds them in hers. 'It'll stop.'

I swallow my words. 'I doubt it.'

I can feel her eyes wandering about my face as I stare thoughtlessly at our connected hands. 'Do you see those baskets up there?' she asks, motioning to the wicker hanging baskets filled with pale pink and white flowers on either side of the porch.

'I noticed them when I first arrived,' I reply, wondering where on earth this is leading.

'What do you see in them?'

'Flowers,' I say in a perplexed tone. Is my own madness rubbing off on her?

'Not just any flowers, Pidge. Primroses,' she declares, and it's as though someone has lit a match inside my mind, like it's beginning to kickstart again. The name sounds familiar and my stomach swirls with something I can't quite determine. 'I mix them up,' she continues as her eyes dance between the baskets, 'but I try to include more of the white; they were your mum's favourite.' My eyes widen as it finally registers. Of course! I was too young to know that before she died, but Mum's grave is never without their decoration. Now I know why. 'She said they always made her feel at peace with the world, even when she felt the world was doing her no favours. All around the garden you'll see them.'

My eyes travel the entirety of the lawn, from corner to corner; white Primroses everywhere. The edges of my lips perk as my pulse beats a little quicker, but not in the way it had tonight through fear and dread, no, this is the feeling of fullness and contentment, and it's making my heart swell.

'It's as though I've still got a piece of her here, like she's alive in the flowers, like she's–

'At peace,' I finish, my eyes basking in the calming beauty of the white petals. I'd known it was a beautiful front garden before, but it's only now I'm realising just how scenic and charming it is. It adds a whole new meaning to peaceful.

'Exactly,' Aunt Maggie agrees.

'Those pretty flowers on Mum's grave are always you,' I think aloud, flickering my focus to her as she continues to gaze around the front lawn. I'm saying the words for confirmation that I don't necessarily need. I know it's her, and the fact she travels all that distance and never lets those flowers die, brings a warmth to my heart which seems to be burning away the majority of the cold plaguing my body.

She remains quiet, her chest rising and falling, as though she's contemplating her words. 'No matter how hard I try, my mind always finds ways of travelling back to that frightful night.'

My breath hitches as her glassy grey eyes meet mine.

'Your dad was right,' she says tenderly, and I brace myself for what's to come, 'I was with you when it happened. I had been looking after you whilst your parents were at the trial and your mum came home early that night. I'd just put you to bed as she was getting herself changed, and that's when she charged into your bedroom, telling me to stay with you. I didn't know what was happening, but by the look on her face it clearly wasn't pleasant. Nonetheless, I never thought it would end the way it did. I don't think anything could prepare you for something so sudden and instant.'

I swallow the lump in my throat as I remain muted, too entranced by her words; by her side of the story.

'We heard the commotion coming from downstairs, and that's when she left and closed the door behind her. It's so vivid in my mind, standing in that pitch black room, staring at the landing light shining through the gap under your bedroom door and listening to the shouting. That's when you began to stir, I told you that it was okay and to go back to sleep, and mercifully you did, heaven forbid you were to hear what I did.' She pauses, gathering her words. 'I sat on your bed, holding your hand, until the yelling stopped.' Her voice is shaky as she shifts her gaze away from mine and back to the flowers in the garden, the grip on my hands tightening. 'That was the last time I saw her alive.' A tear escapes the corner of my eye, trickling down my cheek before splashing onto the sleeve of my hoodie. 'The worry on her face will be an image etched in my mind for the rest of my days.' She sniffs, but she doesn't allow me to see the tears I know are staining her face.

'Why did you never tell me?' I rasp weakly.

Her hand loosens our hold and brushes across her face, drying her cheeks before she turns back to me on an encouraging sigh. 'I honestly thought I was protecting you. We were hoping when Carl Mason was sent away, that would be it, we wouldn't have to worry. And yet there was always that thought buried beneath the relief:

what if he came back? And that's what we needed to protect you from. We didn't want to distress you anymore than what you were already going through. You were so young, Pidge, you didn't need that burden. Now I realise, looking at you all grown up, just how wrong we were to keep it from you.'

'I'm sorry for yelling,' I say regretfully. This wasn't her fault, none of it was. The only thing she is guilty of doing is what she thought was best for me and persuading Dad to tell me the truth. How can I be mad at her for that?

'You had every right. Your anger was justified.'

'You've been so kind to me, Aunty,' I say, but her focus lowers, her smile vanishing. 'What is it?' I ask, leaning closer.

'Just something that will forever haunt me. What would have been if I had gone out and helped her?'

I shake my head firmly, earning her gaze. 'You did as she told you, you stayed with me and protected me, and for that I know she's grateful. Our past is our past, we can't change that, but our future is what we want it to be, and I can't see mine being any good if it doesn't include you.' I pause. 'I love you, Aunty,' I announce, and it feels like a whole weight lifted as I tell her for the first time in thirteen years.

'I love you too, Pidge,' she echoes, pulling me in for a tight hug. I think it's mostly to mask her watering eyes again as she holds me close, but nevertheless, I take it, sighing in comfort as her naturally relaxing lavender smell somehow makes the pain easier to bear.

'Although I'm not happy that you let Jackson out of my room,' I murmur into her shoulder. I know she would have opened that lock as soon as I left, and to be honest, despite my words, I think that's the reason I passed her the key. Deep down I knew she wouldn't leave me on my own. 'You promised.'

'No, I didn't,' she remarks, pulling back and holding me at arm's length. 'You think I was going to sit back and wait for you to maybe or maybe not walk back through that door? No way, José.' Her hands cup mine once more. The reassuring squeeze from her fingers draws my attention down and I gasp.

My hands are still; the shaking has stopped.

'Told you,' Aunt Maggie whispers on a small grin which, in what feels like a lifetime, I'm able to mirror.

Unfortunately, it's quick to pass. Guy's heavy footsteps pound on the cobblestone path as he rushes over. My heart sinks at the look on his face.

'Excuse me, Ms Taylor,' he remarks anxiously, which immediately causes my fatigued body to tense.

'Oh, formalities. It's Maggie, Guy.' She waves her hand, dismissing the comment.

'Sorry, Maggie,' he corrects, 'but I have some news.'

'News?' she asks her, crow's feet becoming more pronounced as her eyes narrow.

'Regarding your father, Emily.' Guy directs his focus onto me and a wave of dread washes over me. Judging by his demeanour it's not good news, and although I know that the majority of anything regarding my father is rarely decent news, I don't think I'll ever get used to the feeling of my heart falling into the pit of my stomach whenever he's mentioned.

'What's happened?' I feel Aunt Maggie's fingers instinctively squeeze my hands which are trembling once again. I'm not sure what I was expecting him to say, but what carries through the air next is something which was definitely not present in my thoughts.

'Mr Lambert has been taken.'

My pulse doubles.

'Taken?' Aunt Maggie asks. 'What do you mean, Guy?'

His chest expands as he sucks in a breath. 'I've just gotten off the phone to Sam; Mr Lambert's driver. He informed me it's Carl Mason… he's abducted your father.'

I'm stunned, my eyes wildly searching around as my mind battles all the swarming panic stricken thoughts.

'Do the police know?' Aunty questions when she notices my struggle to speak. Her tone is calm but I know it's forced; she's trying to keep her composure for the sake of my angst.

'Yes, Sam is at the station as we speak.'

It's all making sense now as my memory is sparked by what the two men had said in the car park, that Carl had been too busy elsewhere to show his face and finish the job he started in William's kitchen.

'What happened?' I finally ask weakly.

Guy studies me closely, his eyes turning desolate as his expression twitches into one of guilt. 'It's a little delicate.'

'Tell me, Guy,' I push.

Reluctantly his shoulders lift before the explanation passes his thin lips. 'Sam said he was returning to the car park of the restaurant Mr Lambert was dining at with you when he saw the men drag your father into the boot of a car. There was nothing he could do, he's devastated. He told me to tell you he's very sorry.'

I take a moment. But that moment doesn't give me the chance to prepare for the incredible amount of pain which floods my veins. 'He tried to phone me on the clifftop,' I explain on a quiver. My words struggle to get past the lump in my tight throat as realisation dawns on me. 'The line was fuzzy and I was angry so I hung up.' The ache of my crushing guilt swamps me like I've been submerged into a deep pool of water and I can't escape. 'Is… is this my fault?' I falter. If I hadn't stormed away, if I had stayed and left the restaurant with him instead of running off and leaving him on his own.

Aunt Maggie and Guy share a glance before both sets of eyes shift to me with a forlorn expression written on their faces. 'No, don't you dare think that,' Aunty coos, hugging my side.

'We'll get him back, Emily,' Guy declares confidently, but it's a confidence I can't quite believe. There's a hidden doubt to his tone, because no matter how he looks at it, the truth remains; we don't know if we will get him back. I know what these people are capable of and the thought of what they might do to him doesn't bear thinking about. 'I have to figure out if here is the best place for you to stay,' he says more gently, as if cautious about the words he's speaking.

I shoot him a look. 'Yes, of course it is. The police around here are aware of them.' I can't possibly leave now, not with everything that happened tonight, not now Dad's been taken.

'That doesn't take away the fact that they know where you are.'

I rip my hands from Aunt Maggie's grasp and run them into my hair as my elbows rest on my thighs. Why is this happening? I rack my jumbled brain, trying to find some sense of logic.

'I'm still meant to be moving to university in a week or so, I can go there?' I offer, but the look on Guy's face says it all.

'No, you can't.'

My brow contorts as my narrowed eyes beg for answers.

'Before he was taken, your father informed me that William found a letter addressed to you from the University of Sunderland. He deferred your place.

Apparently, he told Mr Lambert when it was too late. He said William was hell bent on keeping you with him, that it was for your safety. I was going to tell you, but when Mr Lambert arranged his visit here, I thought he would let you know himself. I'm sorry, Emily, university isn't an option anymore.'

That self-centered, narcissistic arsehole! How dare he!

I have to force myself to brush this new-found knowledge to the side, knowing if I dwell on it I'll only burn out any rational ideas and thoughts through my rage, and those are things I desperately need right now. 'I can help with the search somehow to find him. I can't sit back and do nothing.'

'That's exactly what you need to do. I'm not putting you in any more danger than you're already in,' Guy retorts and I deflate against the back of the bench.

'Guy's right, Emily. And as much as it pains me to say, you can't stay here. I don't want you to, because if anything happened to you whilst you were here, I would never forgive myself. You almost gave me a coronary tonight and I'm not risking another, I don't think my old heart would hold out.'

'So what happens now?' I sigh, all out of drive and energy.

'I believe Mr Turner would like a word,' Guy replies softly, and that's when my neck cranes around my towering security guard.

He's beside the Benz overlooking the sea. My aching body pulls itself up from the bench and I hold my eyeline on his back, finding he is acting as my final drop of energy, encouraging me to keep going until I can reach him.

'I'm sorry, angel,' he says as I come to a stop by his side, our eyes locked on the serene ocean as dawn breaks in the distance with a burst of warm multi-colour. My eyes close at the nickname, letting the solace the word brings seep into my skin. I breathe his tired and raspy voice in, knowing it's providing me with the only fragment of consolation my body is crying out for. 'I know there's nothing I can say to make it any better, but there's something I can do.' I search his drowsy eyes as they connect with mine. 'I can take you away from here.'

I blink through genuine shock, what he's offering to do is not something I thought he ever would. He loves it here. His whole life is here. 'Where?' I ask simply, because I don't have anything else to give.

'I don't know, but we'll figure it out.' He's convinced himself. There's not a drop of uncertainty to his tone.

'You know how fucked up my life is,' I remind him. I warn him.

'And you know how fucked up mine is.'

He's unaware of just how much I know, or don't. There are so many questions about him and his past, the answers all hidden deep inside, waiting to be uncovered. He holds his hand out, wiggling his fingers; his mother's silver ring adorning his pinky.

'Together?'

The initial shock of his suggestion is quick to pass as I realise I don't want to be away from him. The pull is too strong. Even though our lives are far from perfect, and there's many cracks in my heart to prove it, I know that with him I strengthen, because cracks are there for a reason; to allow the light to shine through. And his light is shining through mine. He is my sun, and when I look at him, I don't see the shadows.

So, with my decision already made, on a brave smile, I put my undying faith in him by taking his hand.

'Together,' I vow.

I'm not sure what will happen now, or where the road ahead will take us, but what I do know is, he'll be by my side.

And that is absolutely all I need.

Alexandra Bradley

# EPILOGUE

From the minute his friend left, Liam had found himself in a rut. For most of his short life he'd been in some form of trouble, but once his partner in crime had escaped the depraved ways and disappeared off into the sunset, Liam's only source of rationality had vanished, leaving him to his own devices. And he knew that was dangerous.

Soon enough, bad developed into the worst, and Liam had nowhere else to turn. He knew he had to seek the only person who understood; the only person who cared. He had to find his brother, because he'd once told Liam that he'd always be there for him, and tonight he needed him more than ever.

Searching through the pile of unpaid bills and eviction notices, Liam's unsteady hands eventually brushed over the letter he'd been desperately hunting for. His quaking fingers rid of the dirty white envelope, tossing it onto the moth eaten, grimy sofa as the single piece of paper was unfolded. From left to right, he frantically read the words before stuffing it into the pocket of his old grey and stained jogging bottoms.

Scurrying to his bedroom – the term being used lightly, for the only items in the room were a worn smelly mattress and an equally filthy blanket – he lifted his mattress and scooped up his final stash along with a £10 note and some loose silver. In a heartbeat he was dashing out of his dismal flat, hurrying away before they turned up on his doorstep ready to make him pay the consequences for his betrayal.

Huddled into the corner of a bus shelter, cold and shivering at three in the morning, he awaited the first scheduled bus to take him to the coach station. He'd have to stand outside and beg for some spare change to make up a single ticket, but eventually he knew he'd be on his way. The letter was slipped from his pocket and read more carefully this time.

*Liam,*

*Sorry it's been a while, but I've found my escape, finally. My time with the Romano's came to an end, so I travelled on, eventually finding a beautiful place by the sea. I'm living with a family who have let me stay for as long as I need. I've also got myself a job, it's only a small thing, but I like it. I think you'd like it here too.*

*I'm sorry I had to leave you, mate. I really am. But you know I can never come back. You're in my thoughts all the time and I hope you're doing okay – well, as okay as can be in that place. I meant what I said before I left, I will always be there for you even when I'm not physically by your side. I know money is tight, but I would love for you to see this place; it's honestly magical. Here's the address if you're ever up for a trip.*

*65 Hockley's Lane,*
*Marshlyn Bay, Rockstone,*
*Cornwall,*
*PL28 8PE*

*I hope things aren't too bad up there and you're taking my advice and getting out of the old ways. Looking forward to seeing you again sometime, buddy.*
*All the best,*
*Your brother, Jackson.*

*The old ways are a lot harder to get out of than we first thought, brother,* Liam thought.

He scrunched it back into his pocket before jerking the strings of his hoodie to shelter himself further, hiding away from the world which had done nothing but let him down.

*Soon things will be better,* he considered as his shivering fingers fumbled for the packet of white powder in his front pocket. The packet was pulled out, but so was

Liam's protection. He used the shiny edge to sprinkle a line before snorting the substance and gasping in pleasure. Licking his fingertips, he ran them along the knife's edge. *Because soon I'll be reunited with my brother,* he pondered, rubbing the remaining powder over his teeth and sucking his fingers in the process. *And my life is finally going to change.*

*To be continued…*

# *ACKNOWLEDGEMENTS*

First of all to everyone below who has played a big role in showering me with support and encouragement – this has been the toughest project I have ever done, so you're all to blame for the sleepless nights, tears, questioning of my worth and the occasional paper cut... you're lucky I'm so grateful!

A big thank you goes to the hard-working people at Publishing Push, without your help and guidance this book would never have been. Thank you.

To my wonderful friends: Laurie, Rachel, Charlotte, Jonathan, Grace, Jade, Daisy and Lizzie. You were there when I first began tip-tapping and you've stayed with me all the way – I have nothing but love for you all and want to give you my biggest thanks for being the best friends a girl could have.

A hearty shout out to Richard Simpson for the Italian!

To the ACS gang, you appeared at the end of this adventure but have been nothing but supportive and encouraging so thank you!

I have to give a special thank you to both of my wonderful Nans. It's been your support and love which has kept me going, and Aunt Maggie is very much based upon the two strongest women I know. Thank you for being so bloody amazing!

To Mum, Dad and Han– your patience over the past three years hasn't been taken for granted. Never once have you questioned my crazy endeavour, you've only encouraged and supported it and me – even when at times I questioned myself. Without your understanding and trust in me to finish my first novel, I probably would have crumbled after the first sentence. But guess what… we did it!

A big woofing thanks to Murphy – thank you for keeping me company and my feet warm through all the long days and sleepless nights.

Isaac – Thanks for the character notebook, it's certainly going to get scribbled to death!

To the most special and unique family in the world – now when you ask, 'How's your book going?' I can say, 'Here's a copy!' Love you all loads!

And finally – thank you to my grandads, who were so encouraging when I first told them what I wanted to do with my life after university. You were there during the first words of this book, but sadly you couldn't see the last… well, I did it. I hope I've made you proud. I'll save two copies for you both!

And, to you, my reader, welcome! Thank you for taking a chance on an unknown, and I hope to see you again in the sequel!

Printed in Great Britain
by Amazon